INCREDIBLE DOOM

[vol 1]

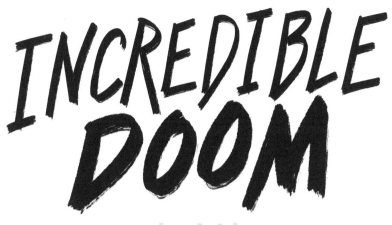

INCREDIBLE DOOM

[vol 1]

Written and illustrated by
MATTHEW BOGART

Story by
**MATTHEW BOGART &
JESSE HOLDEN**

HARPER alley
An imprint of HarperCollinsPublishers

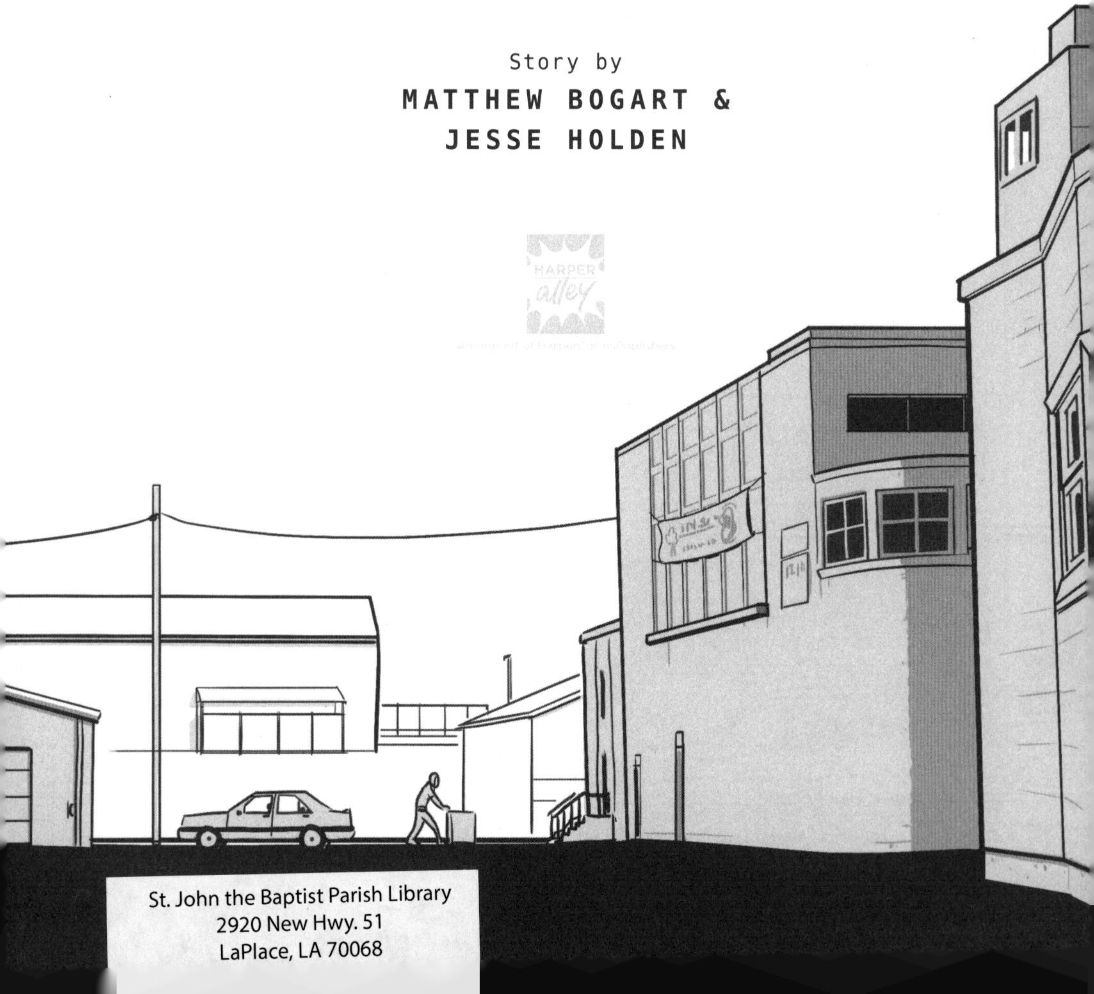

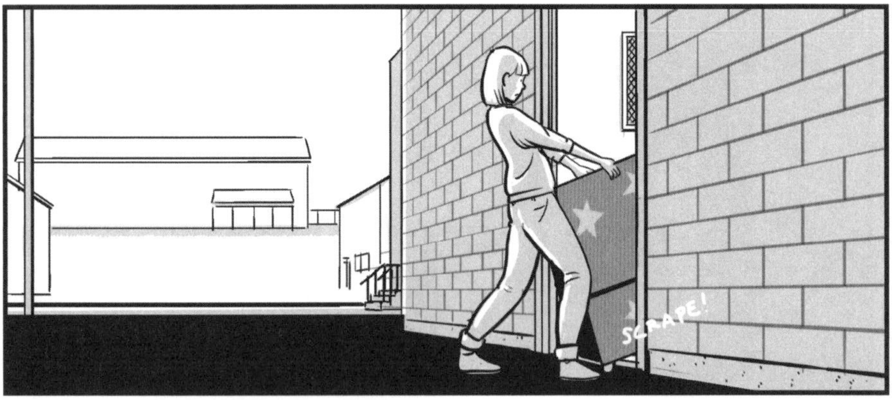
SCRAPE!

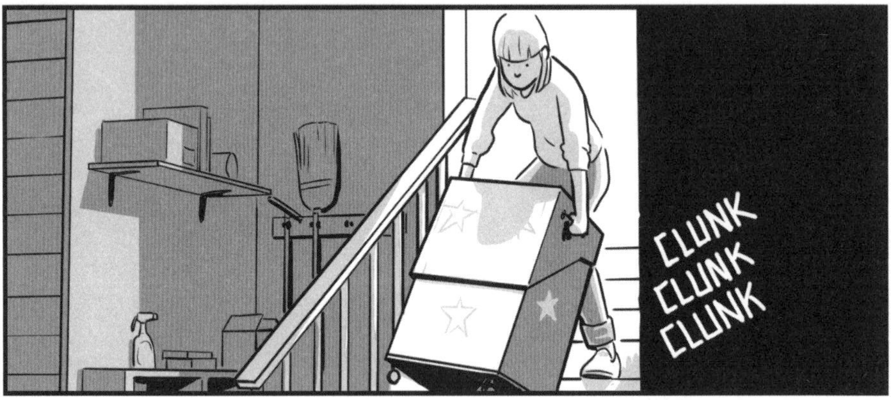
CLUNK
CLUNK
CLUNK

PROLOGUE: 1991

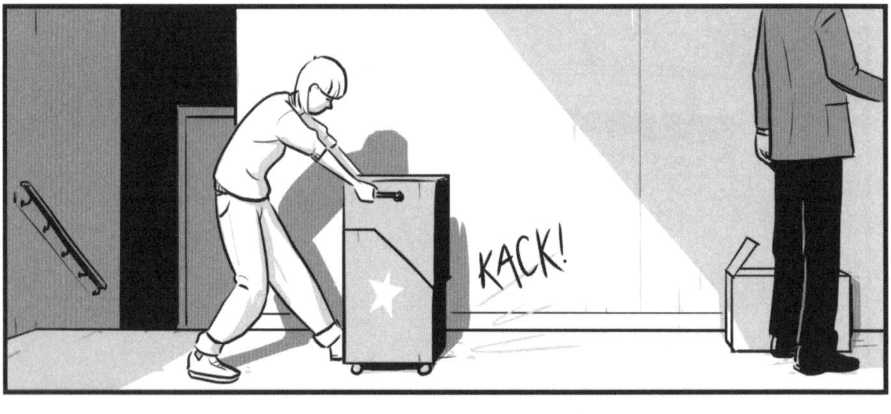
KACK!

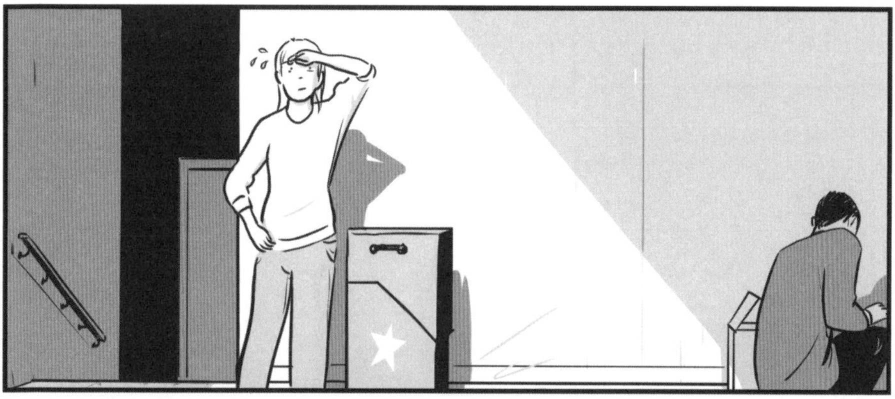

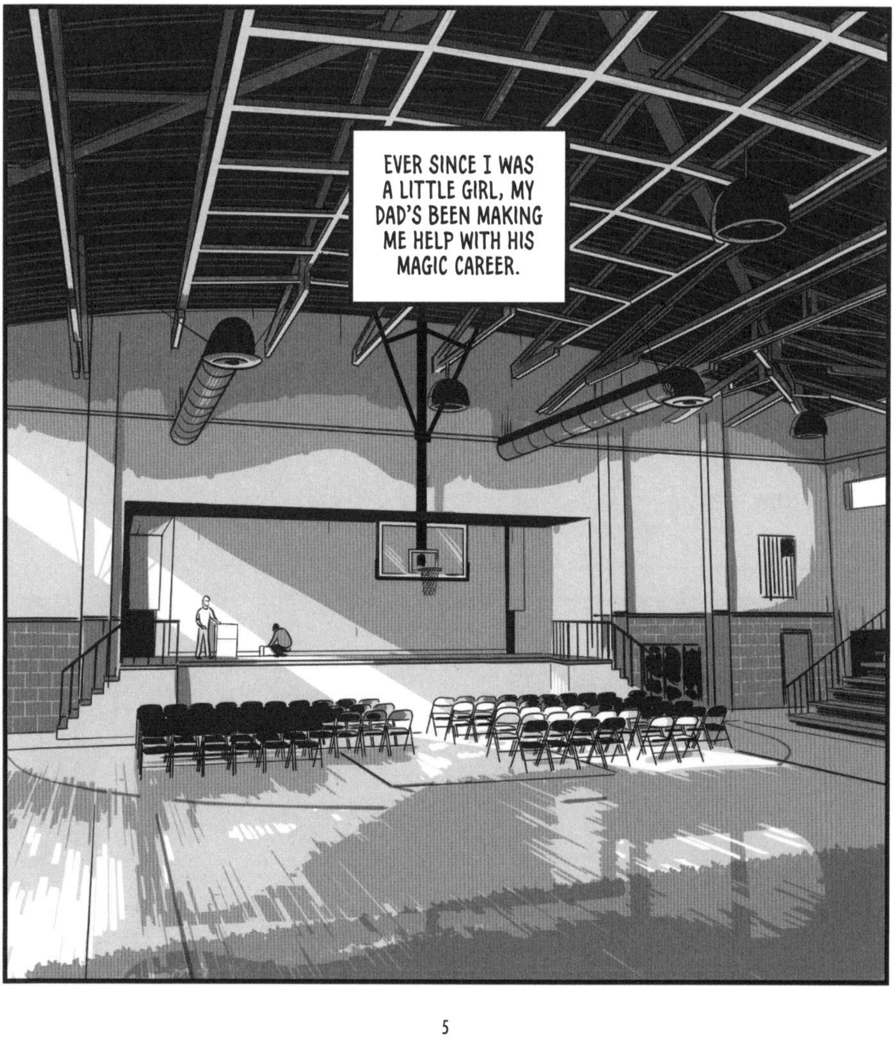
EVER SINCE I WAS A LITTLE GIRL, MY DAD'S BEEN MAKING ME HELP WITH HIS MAGIC CAREER.

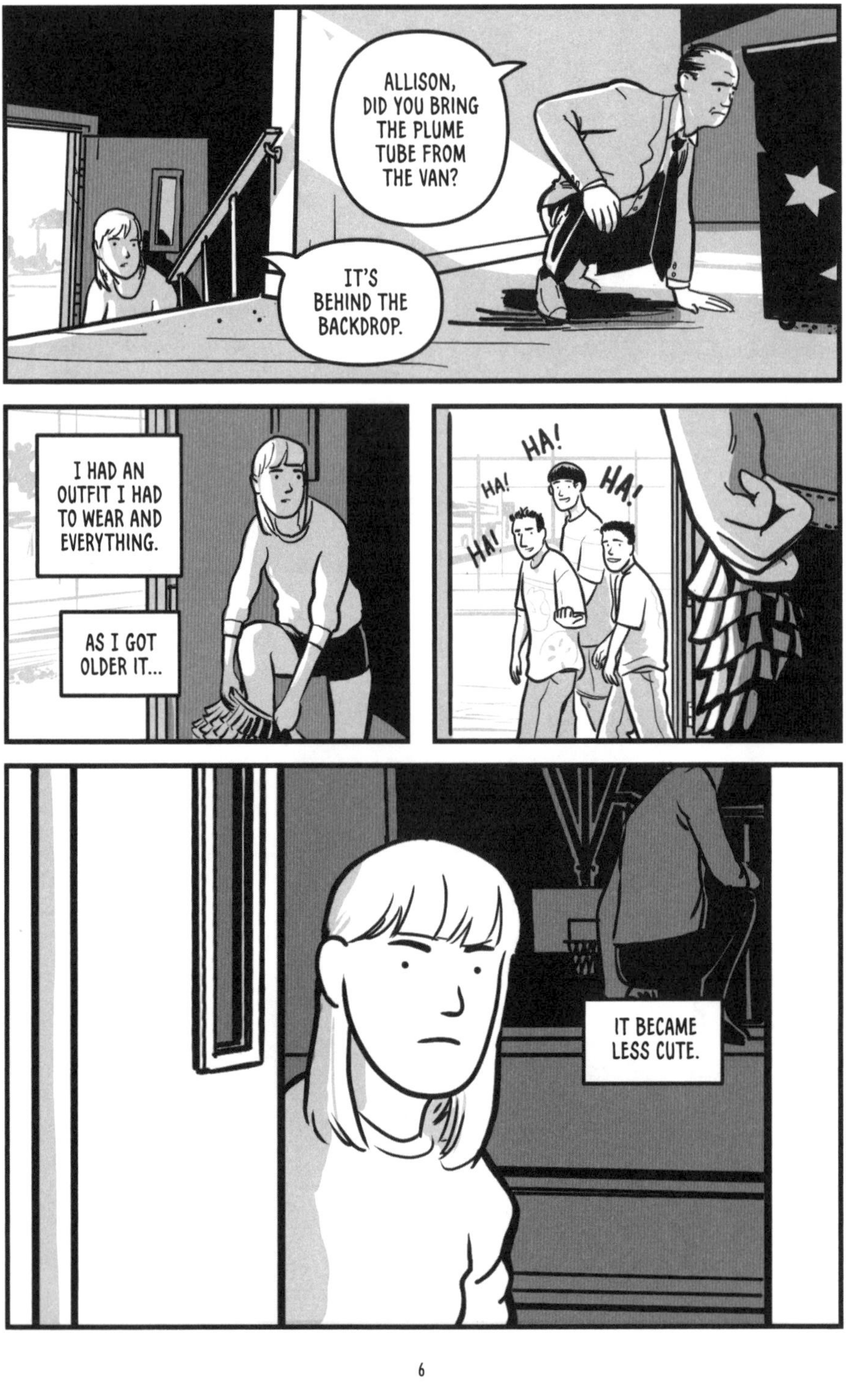
ALLISON, DID YOU BRING THE PLUME TUBE FROM THE VAN?
IT'S BEHIND THE BACKDROP.
I HAD AN OUTFIT I HAD TO WEAR AND EVERYTHING.
AS I GOT OLDER IT...
HA!
HA!
HA!
HA!
IT BECAME LESS CUTE.

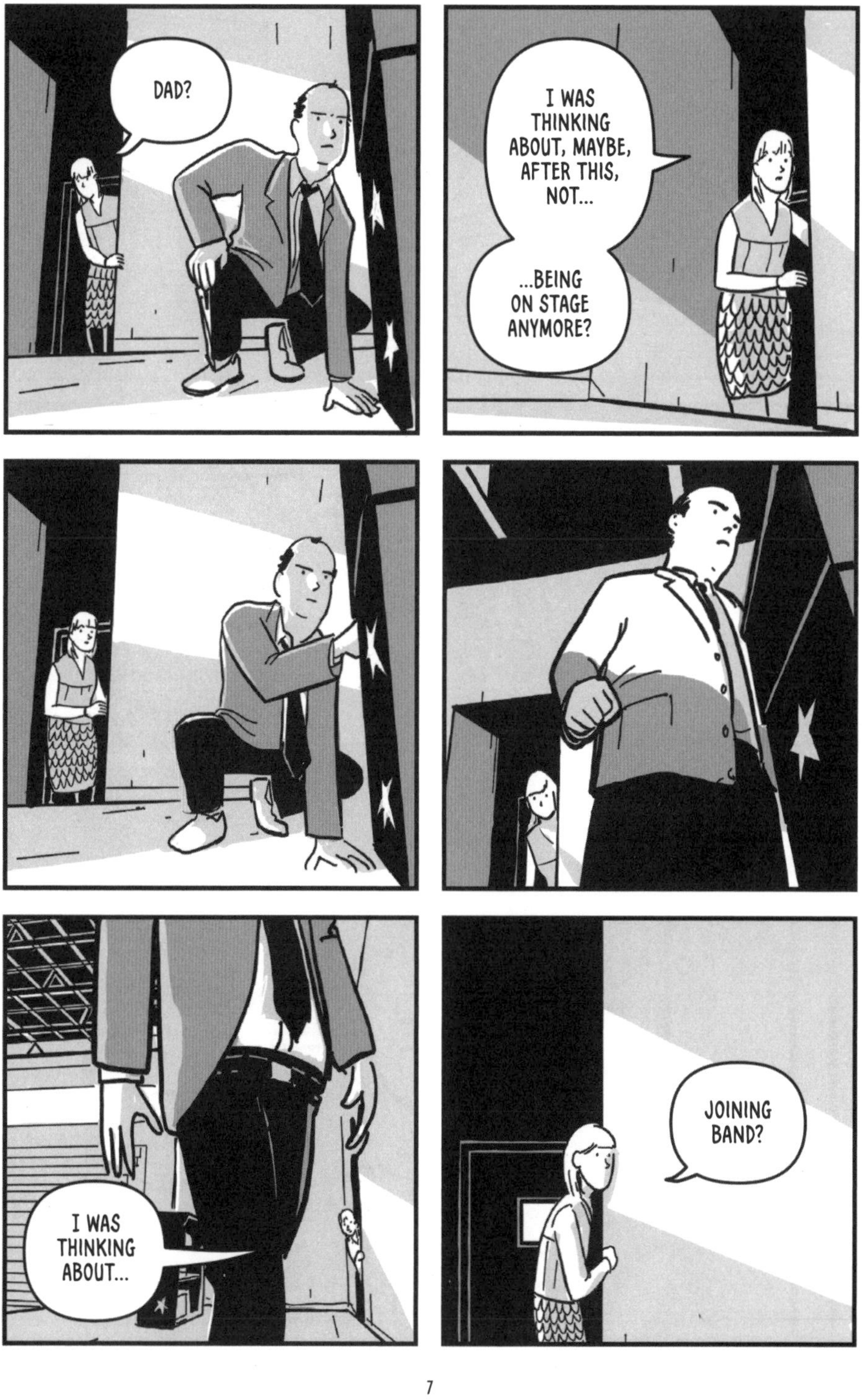
DAD?
I WAS THINKING ABOUT, MAYBE, AFTER THIS, NOT...
...BEING ON STAGE ANYMORE?
I WAS THINKING ABOUT...
JOINING BAND?

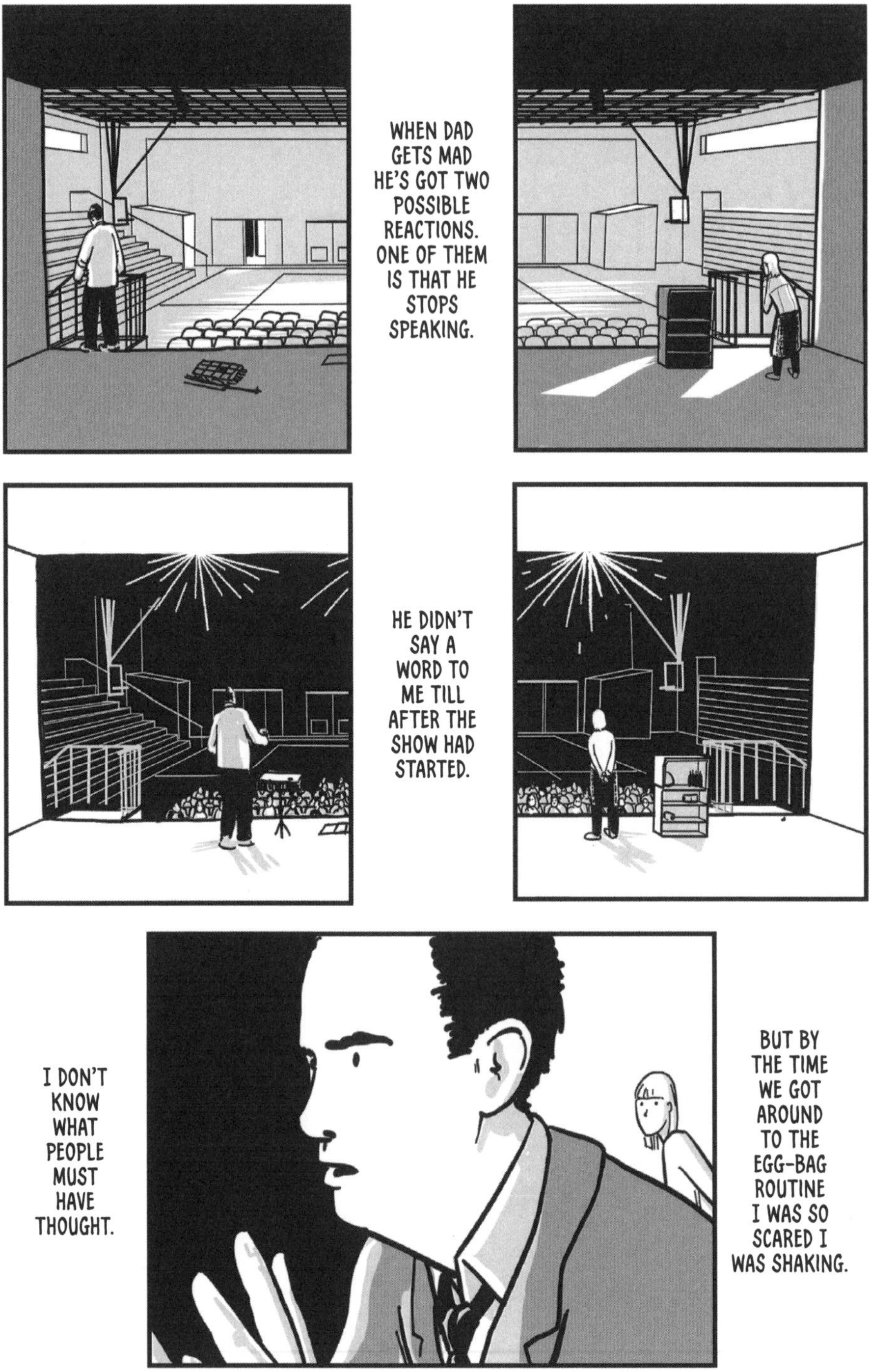
WHEN DAD GETS MAD HE'S GOT TWO POSSIBLE REACTIONS. ONE OF THEM IS THAT HE STOPS SPEAKING.
HE DIDN'T SAY A WORD TO ME TILL AFTER THE SHOW HAD STARTED.
I DON'T KNOW WHAT PEOPLE MUST HAVE THOUGHT.
BUT BY THE TIME WE GOT AROUND TO THE EGG-BAG ROUTINE I WAS SO SCARED I WAS SHAKING.

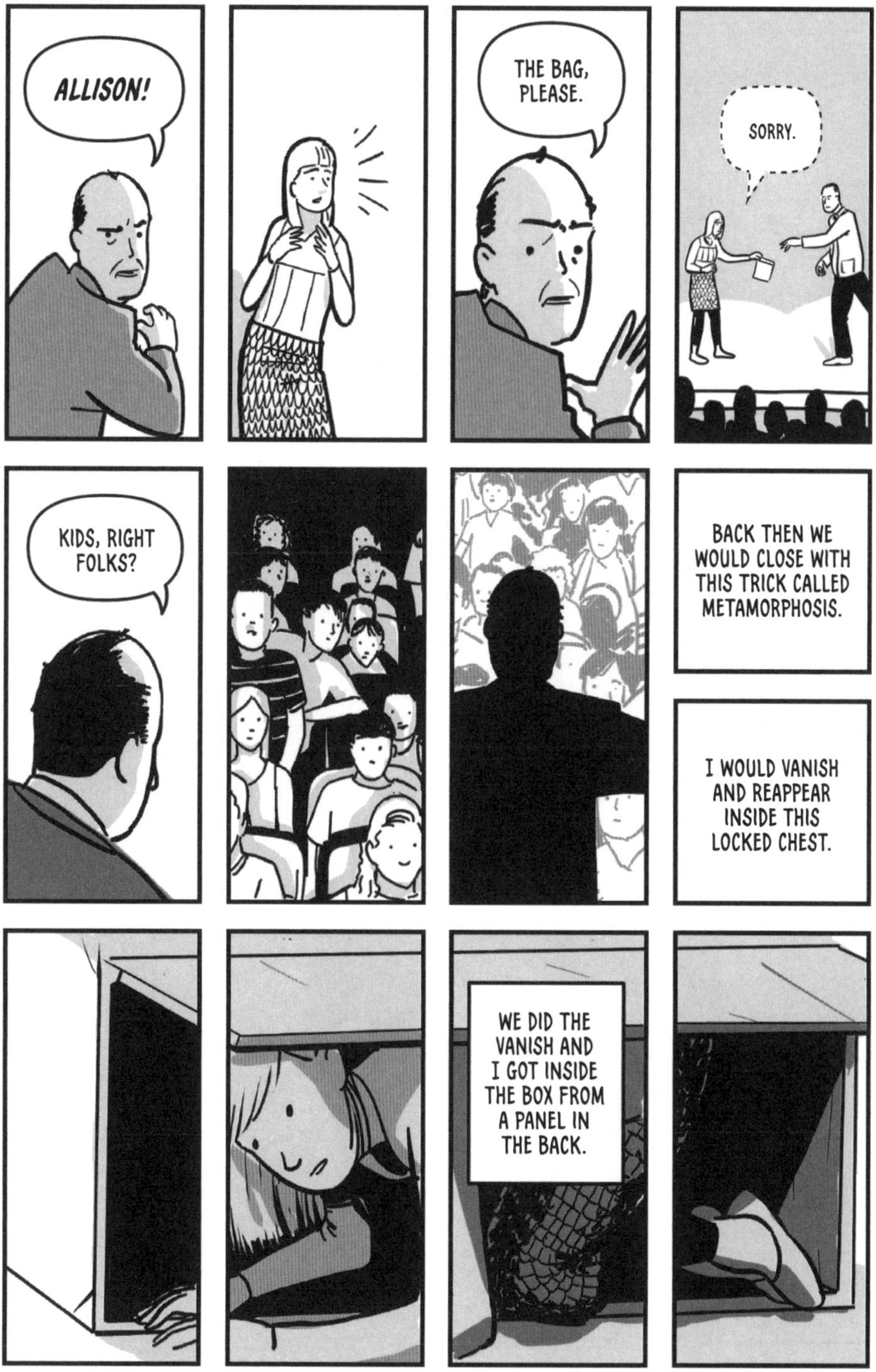
ALLISON!
THE BAG, PLEASE.
SORRY.
KIDS, RIGHT FOLKS?
BACK THEN WE WOULD CLOSE WITH THIS TRICK CALLED METAMORPHOSIS.
I WOULD VANISH AND REAPPEAR INSIDE THIS LOCKED CHEST.
WE DID THE VANISH AND I GOT INSIDE THE BOX FROM A PANEL IN THE BACK.

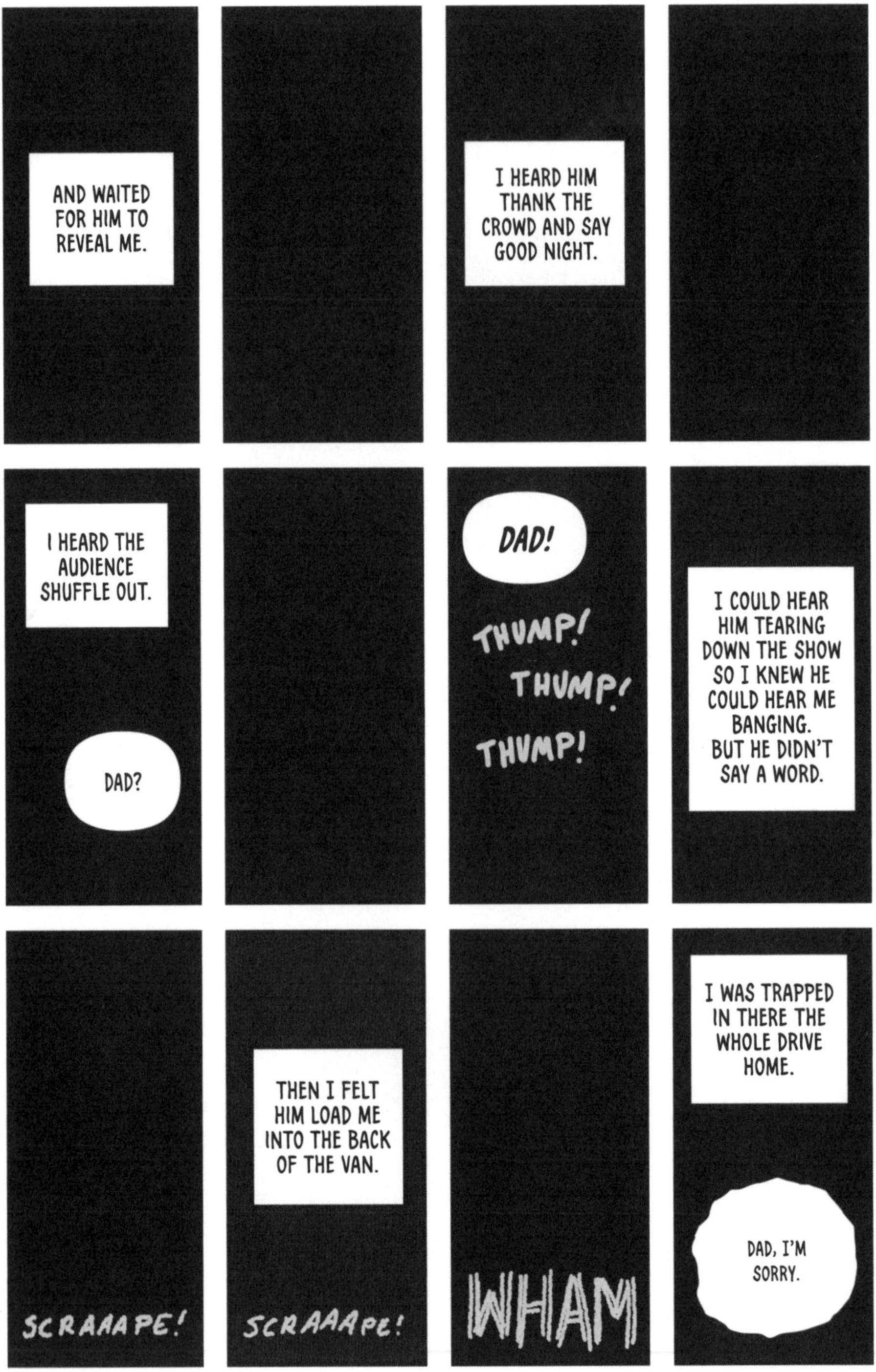
AND WAITED FOR HIM TO REVEAL ME.
I HEARD HIM THANK THE CROWD AND SAY GOOD NIGHT.
I HEARD THE AUDIENCE SHUFFLE OUT.
DAD?
DAD!
THUMP!
THUMP!
THUMP!
I COULD HEAR HIM TEARING DOWN THE SHOW SO I KNEW HE COULD HEAR ME BANGING. BUT HE DIDN'T SAY A WORD.
SCRAAAPE!
THEN I FELT HIM LOAD ME INTO THE BACK OF THE VAN.
SCRAAAPE!
WHAM
I WAS TRAPPED IN THERE THE WHOLE DRIVE HOME.
DAD, I'M SORRY.

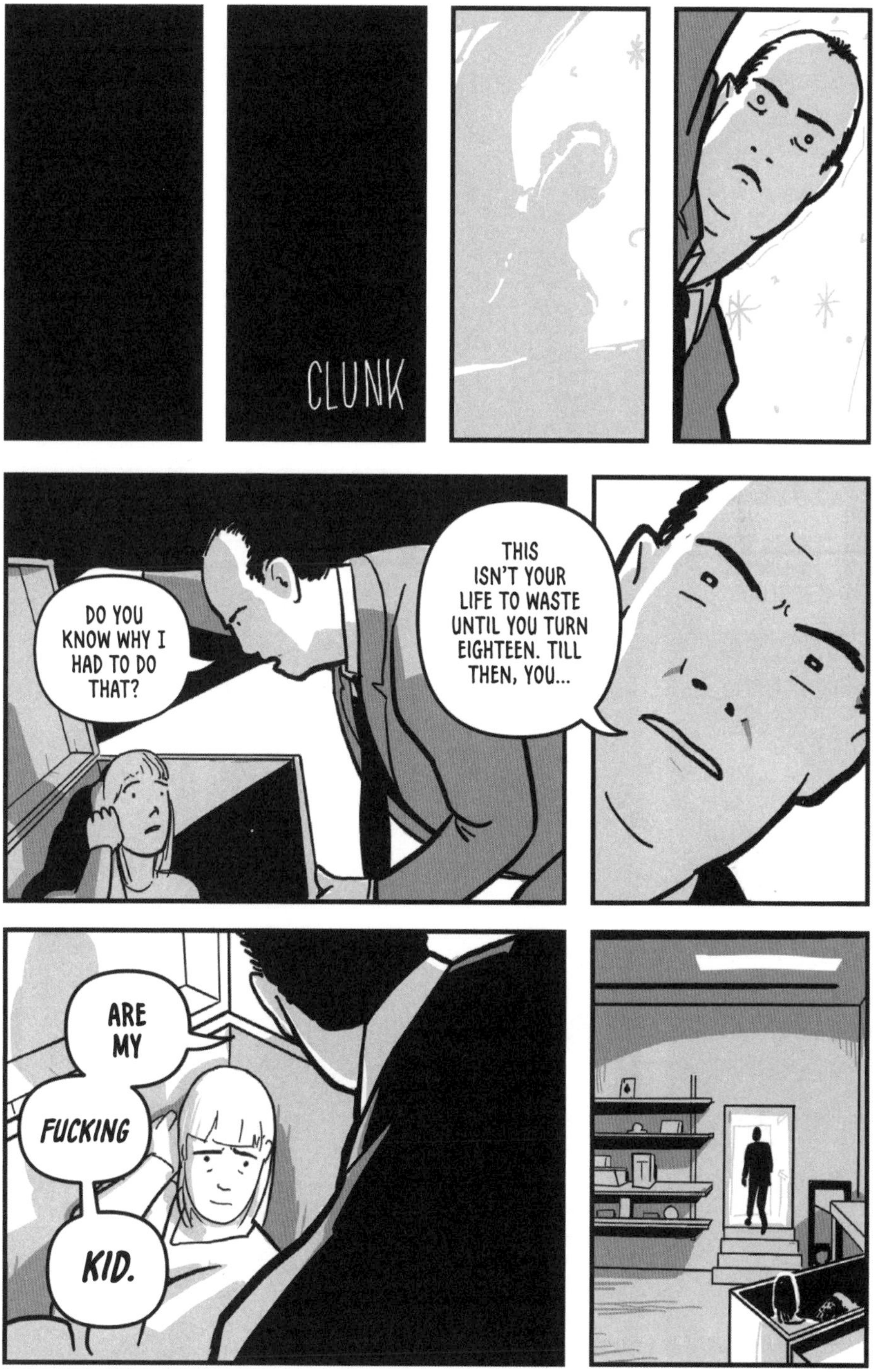
CLUNK
DO YOU KNOW WHY I HAD TO DO THAT?
THIS ISN'T YOUR LIFE TO WASTE UNTIL YOU TURN EIGHTEEN. TILL THEN, YOU...
ARE MY
FUCKING
KID.

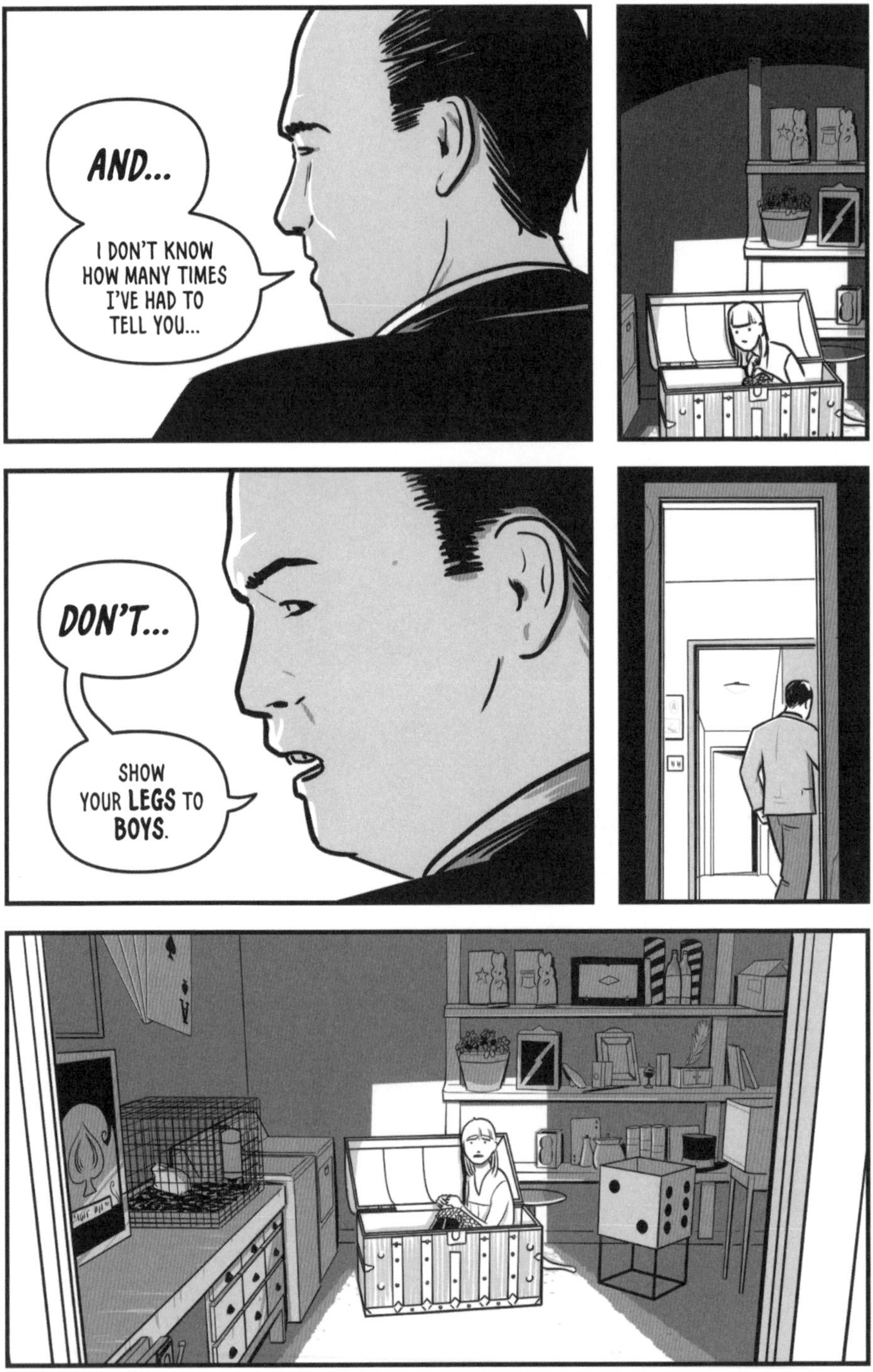
AND...
I DON'T KNOW HOW MANY TIMES I'VE HAD TO TELL YOU...
DON'T...
SHOW YOUR LEGS TO BOYS.

Chapter 1

THE WORLD OF TOMORROW

1994

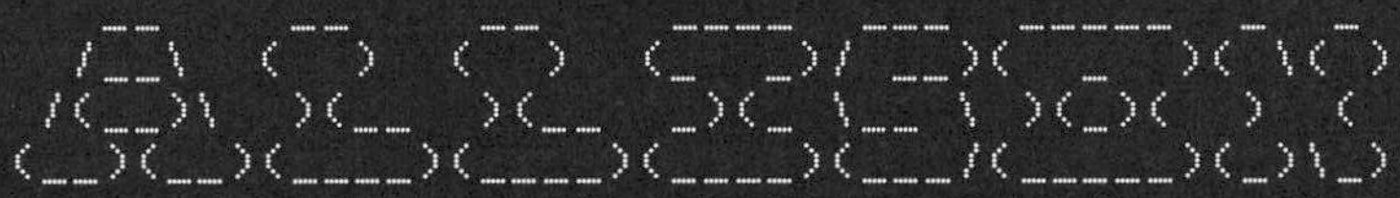

GU D-- -P+ C+L? U E M+ S-/+ N--- H-- F--(+) !G W++ T R? X?

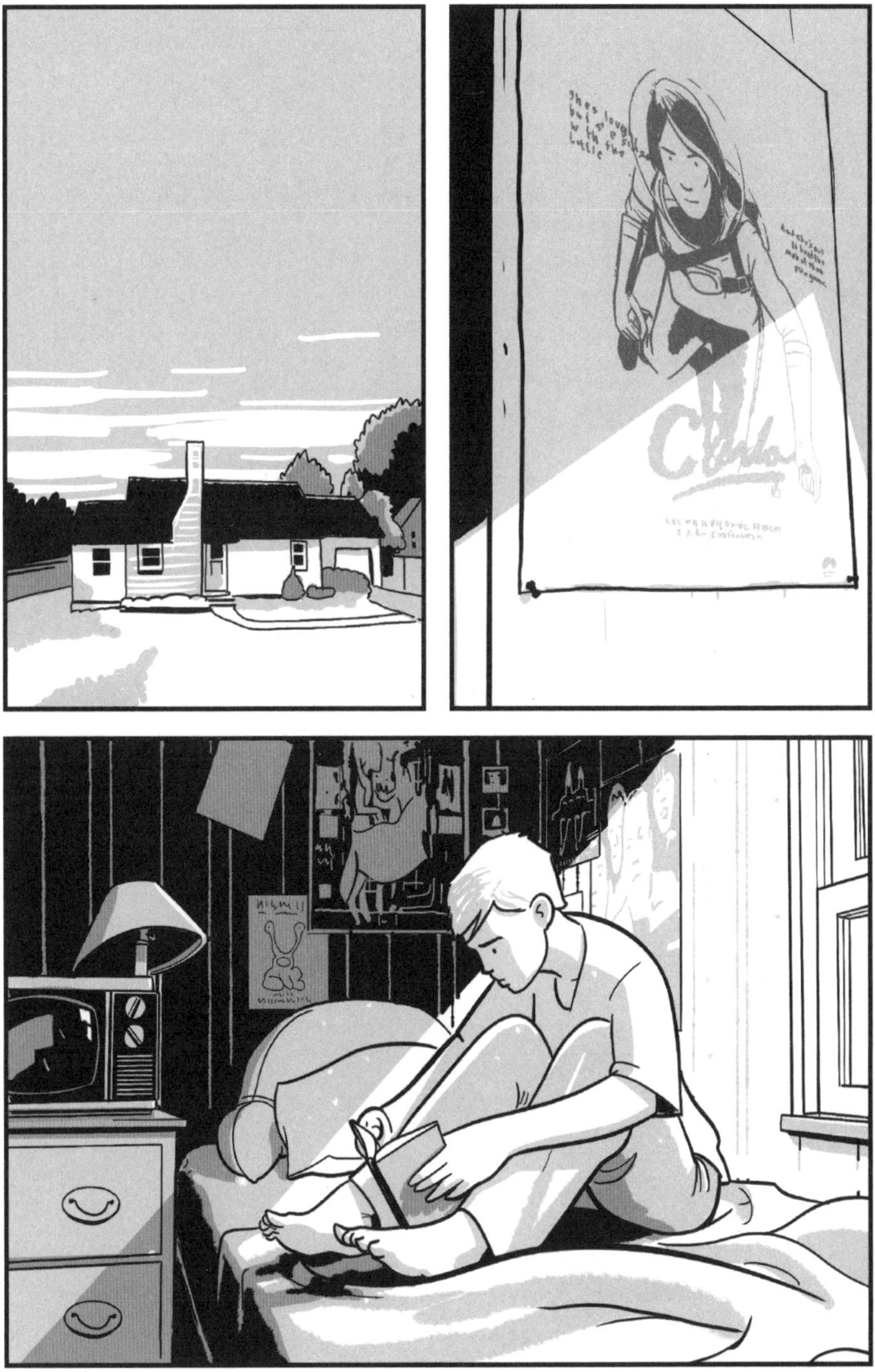

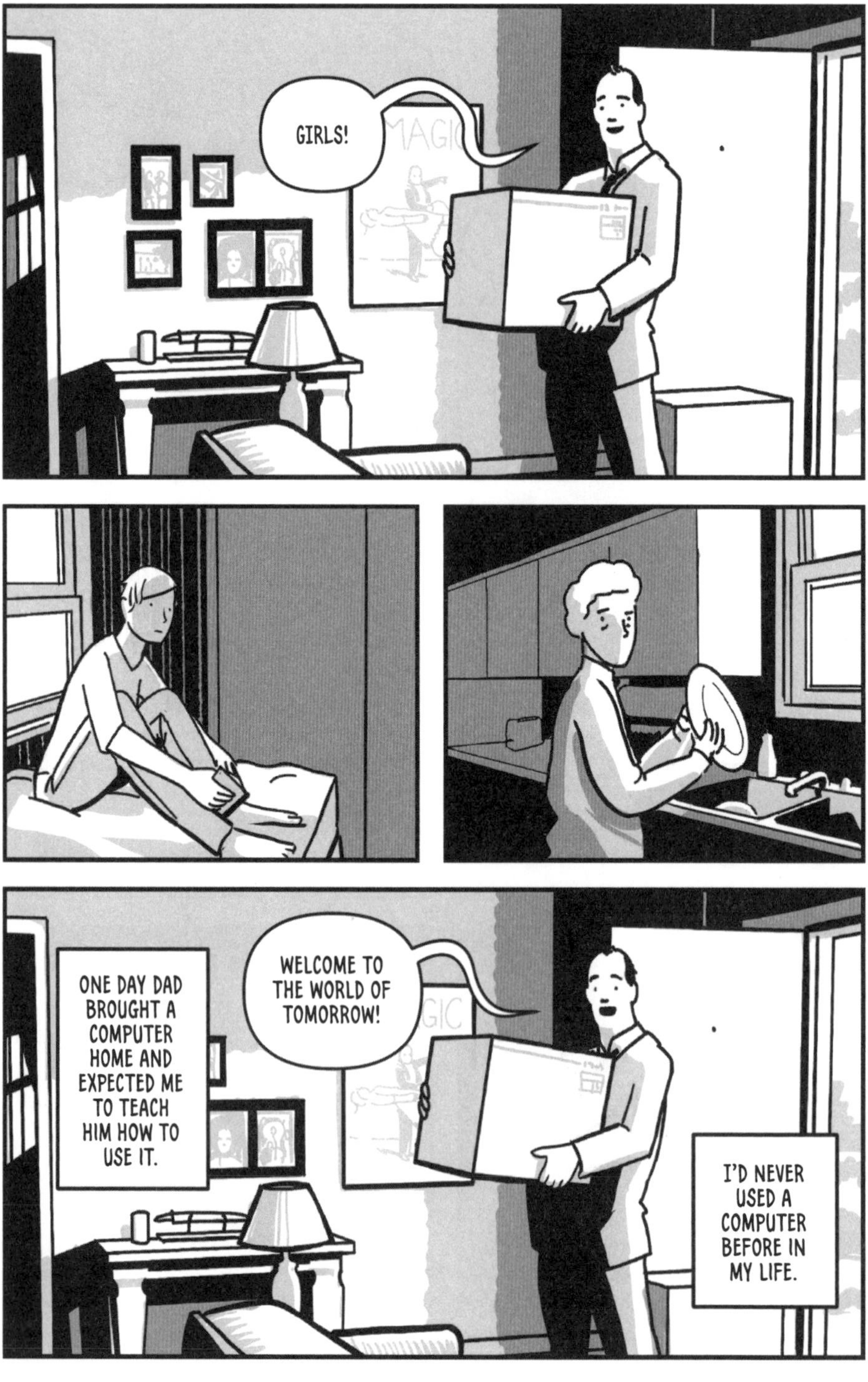
GIRLS!
ONE DAY DAD BROUGHT A COMPUTER HOME AND EXPECTED ME TO TEACH HIM HOW TO USE IT.
WELCOME TO THE WORLD OF TOMORROW!
I'D NEVER USED A COMPUTER BEFORE IN MY LIFE.

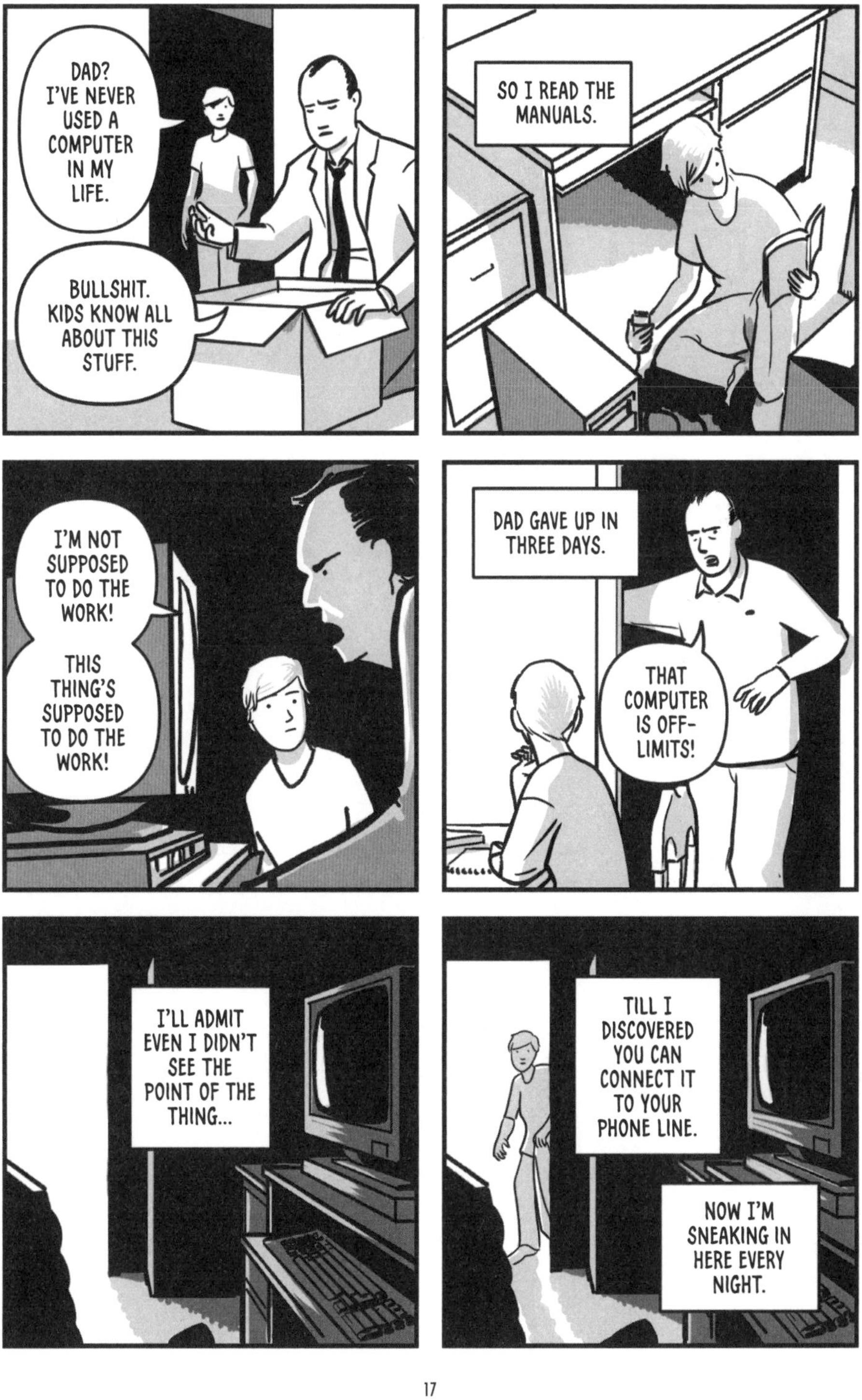
DAD? I'VE NEVER USED A COMPUTER IN MY LIFE.
BULLSHIT. KIDS KNOW ALL ABOUT THIS STUFF.
SO I READ THE MANUALS.
I'M NOT SUPPOSED TO DO THE WORK!
THIS THING'S SUPPOSED TO DO THE WORK!
DAD GAVE UP IN THREE DAYS.
THAT COMPUTER IS OFF-LIMITS!
I'LL ADMIT EVEN I DIDN'T SEE THE POINT OF THE THING...
TILL I DISCOVERED YOU CAN CONNECT IT TO YOUR PHONE LINE.
NOW I'M SNEAKING IN HERE EVERY NIGHT.

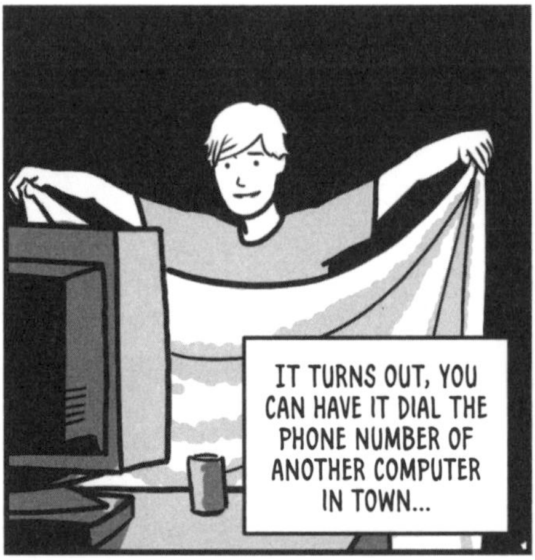
IT TURNS OUT, YOU CAN HAVE IT DIAL THE PHONE NUMBER OF ANOTHER COMPUTER IN TOWN...

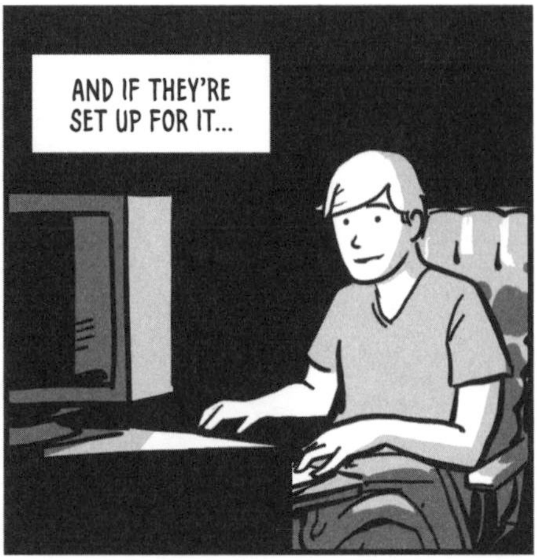
AND IF THEY'RE SET UP FOR IT...

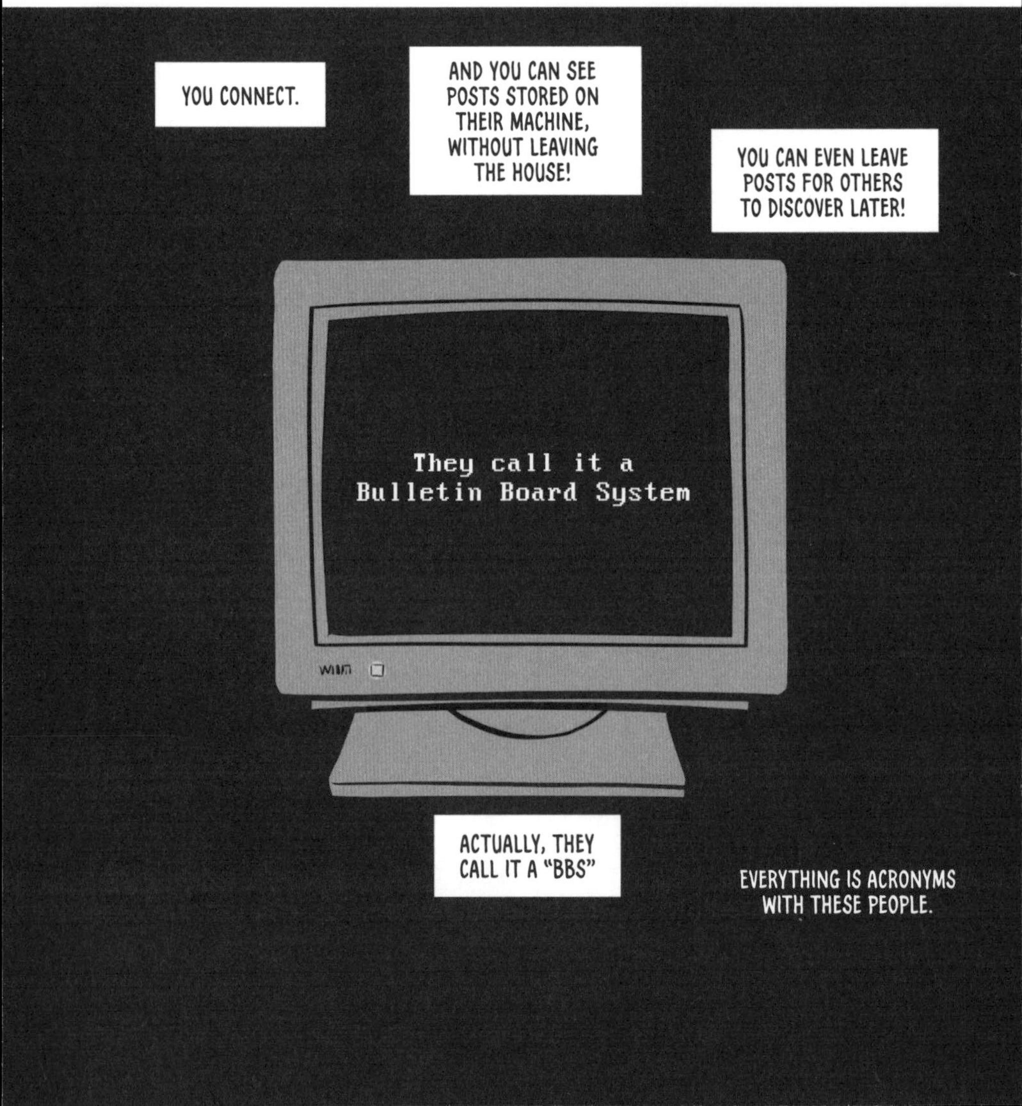
YOU CONNECT.
AND YOU CAN SEE POSTS STORED ON THEIR MACHINE, WITHOUT LEAVING THE HOUSE!
YOU CAN EVEN LEAVE POSTS FOR OTHERS TO DISCOVER LATER!
They call it a
Bulletin Board System
ACTUALLY, THEY CALL IT A "BBS"
EVERYTHING IS ACRONYMS WITH THESE PEOPLE.

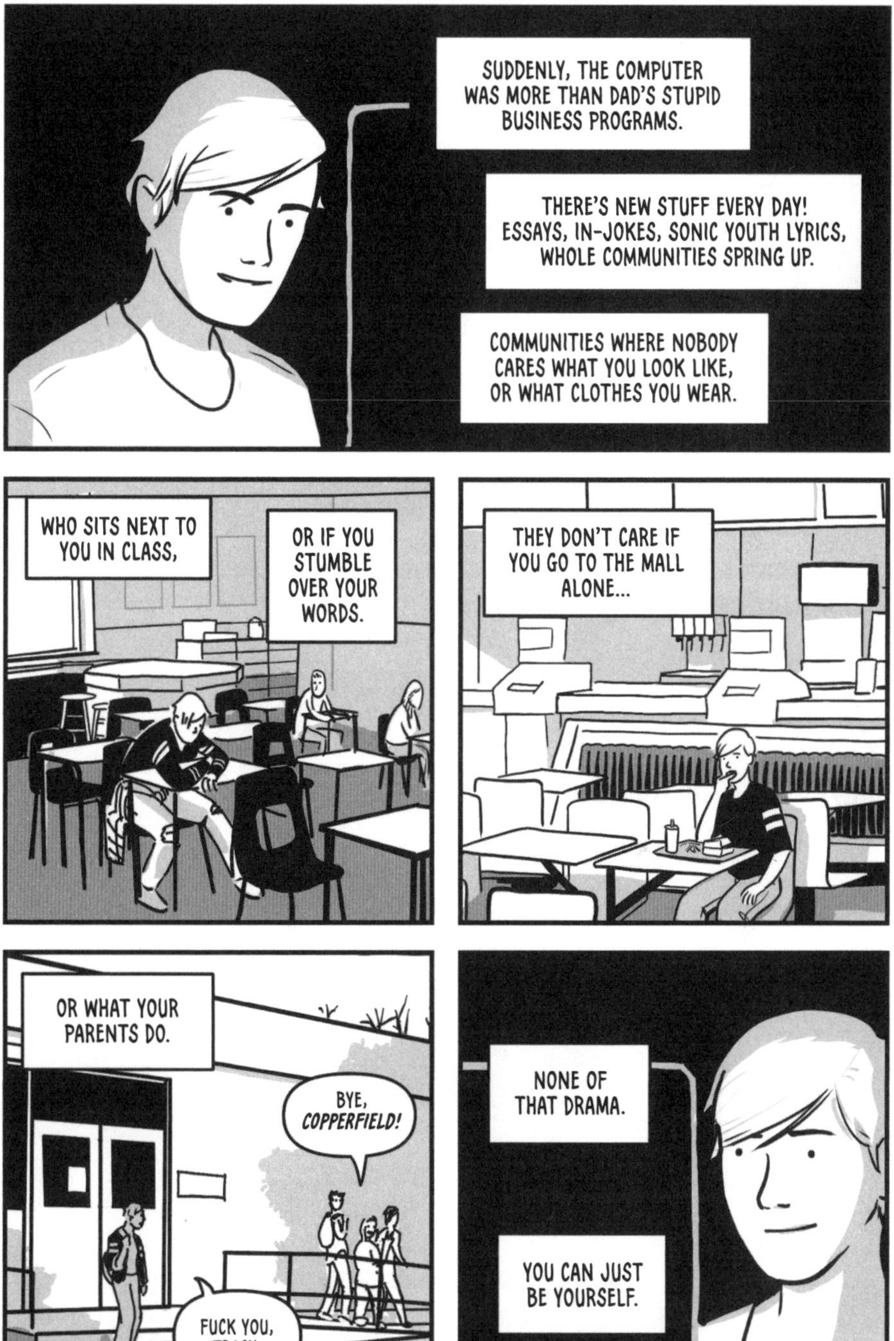
SUDDENLY, THE COMPUTER WAS MORE THAN DAD'S STUPID BUSINESS PROGRAMS.
THERE'S NEW STUFF EVERY DAY! ESSAYS, IN-JOKES, SONIC YOUTH LYRICS, WHOLE COMMUNITIES SPRING UP.
COMMUNITIES WHERE NOBODY CARES WHAT YOU LOOK LIKE, OR WHAT CLOTHES YOU WEAR.
WHO SITS NEXT TO YOU IN CLASS,
OR IF YOU STUMBLE OVER YOUR WORDS.
THEY DON'T CARE IF YOU GO TO THE MALL ALONE...
OR WHAT YOUR PARENTS DO.
BYE, *COPPERFIELD!*
FUCK YOU, TRACY.
NONE OF THAT DRAMA.
YOU CAN JUST BE YOURSELF.

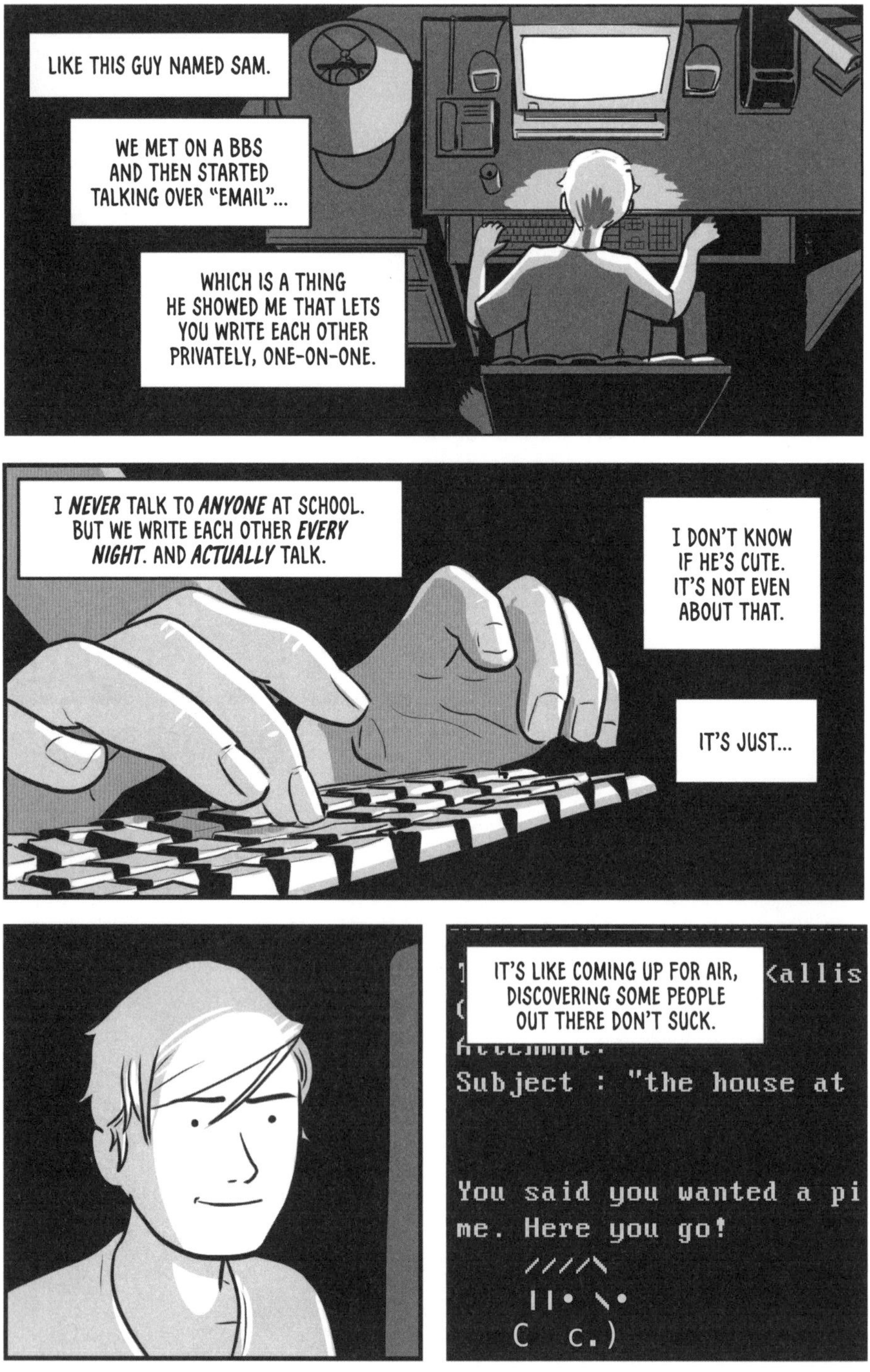
LIKE THIS GUY NAMED SAM.
WE MET ON A BBS AND THEN STARTED TALKING OVER "EMAIL"...
WHICH IS A THING HE SHOWED ME THAT LETS YOU WRITE EACH OTHER PRIVATELY, ONE-ON-ONE.
I *NEVER* TALK TO *ANYONE* AT SCHOOL. BUT WE WRITE EACH OTHER *EVERY NIGHT*. AND *ACTUALLY* TALK.
I DON'T KNOW IF HE'S CUTE. IT'S NOT EVEN ABOUT THAT.
IT'S JUST...
IT'S LIKE COMING UP FOR AIR, DISCOVERING SOME PEOPLE OUT THERE DON'T SUCK.
Subject : "the house at
You said you wanted a pi
me. Here you go!

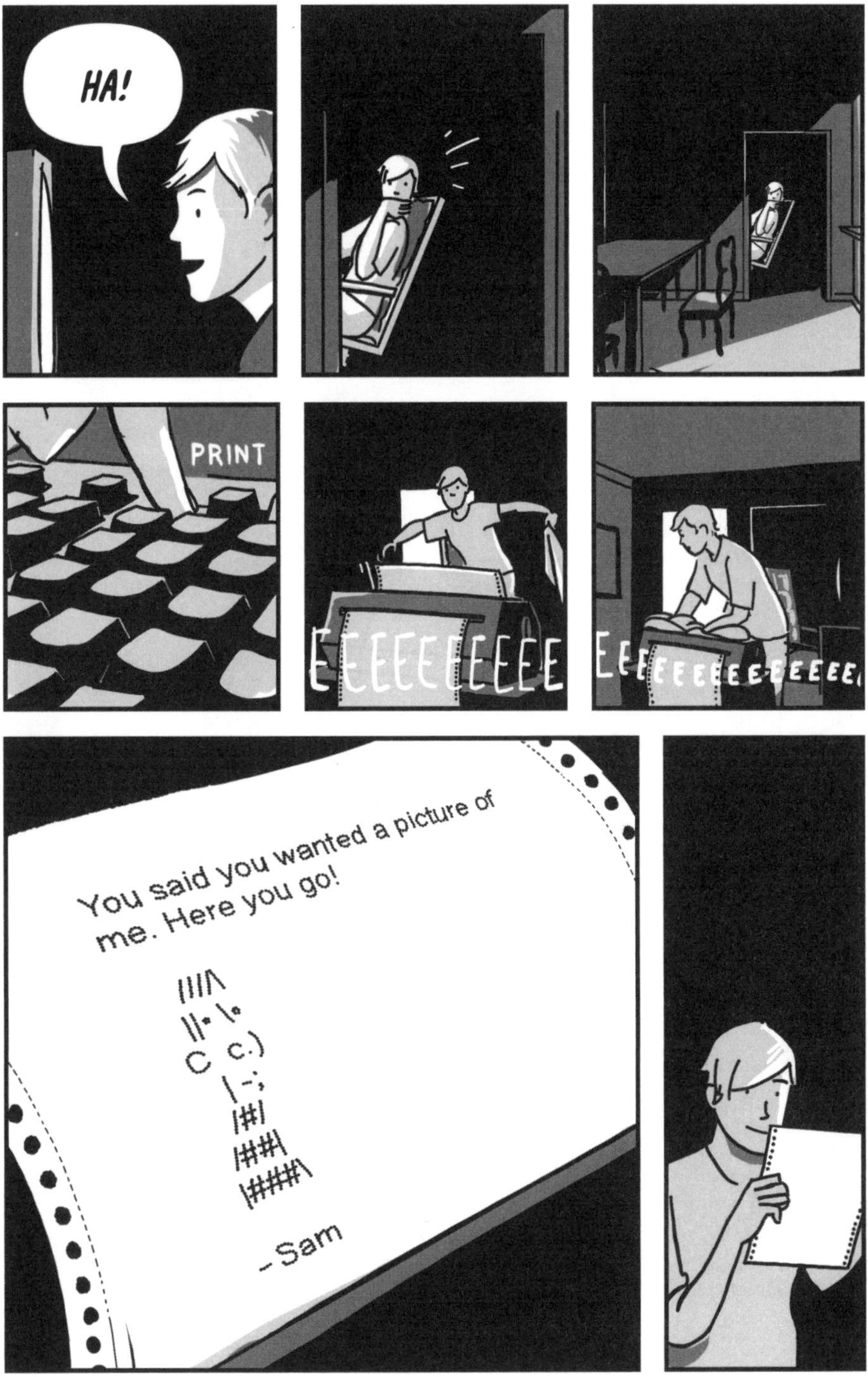
HA!
PRINT
EEEEEEEEEEE
EEEEEEEEEEEEEEEE
You said you wanted a picture of me. Here you go!
|||/\
||• \•
C c.)
\ -;
/#|
/##\
|###\
-Sam

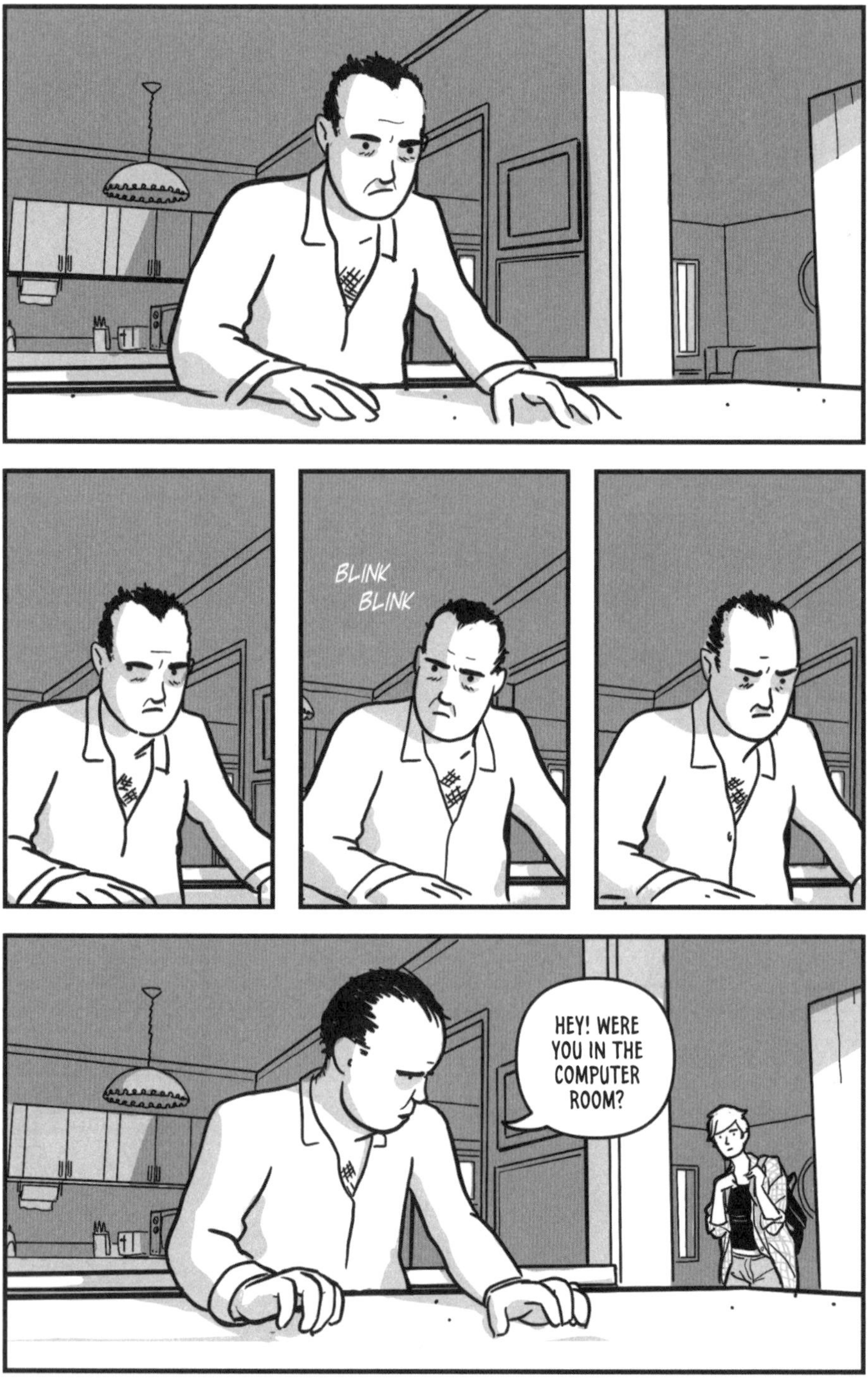
BLINK
BLINK
HEY! WERE YOU IN THE COMPUTER ROOM?

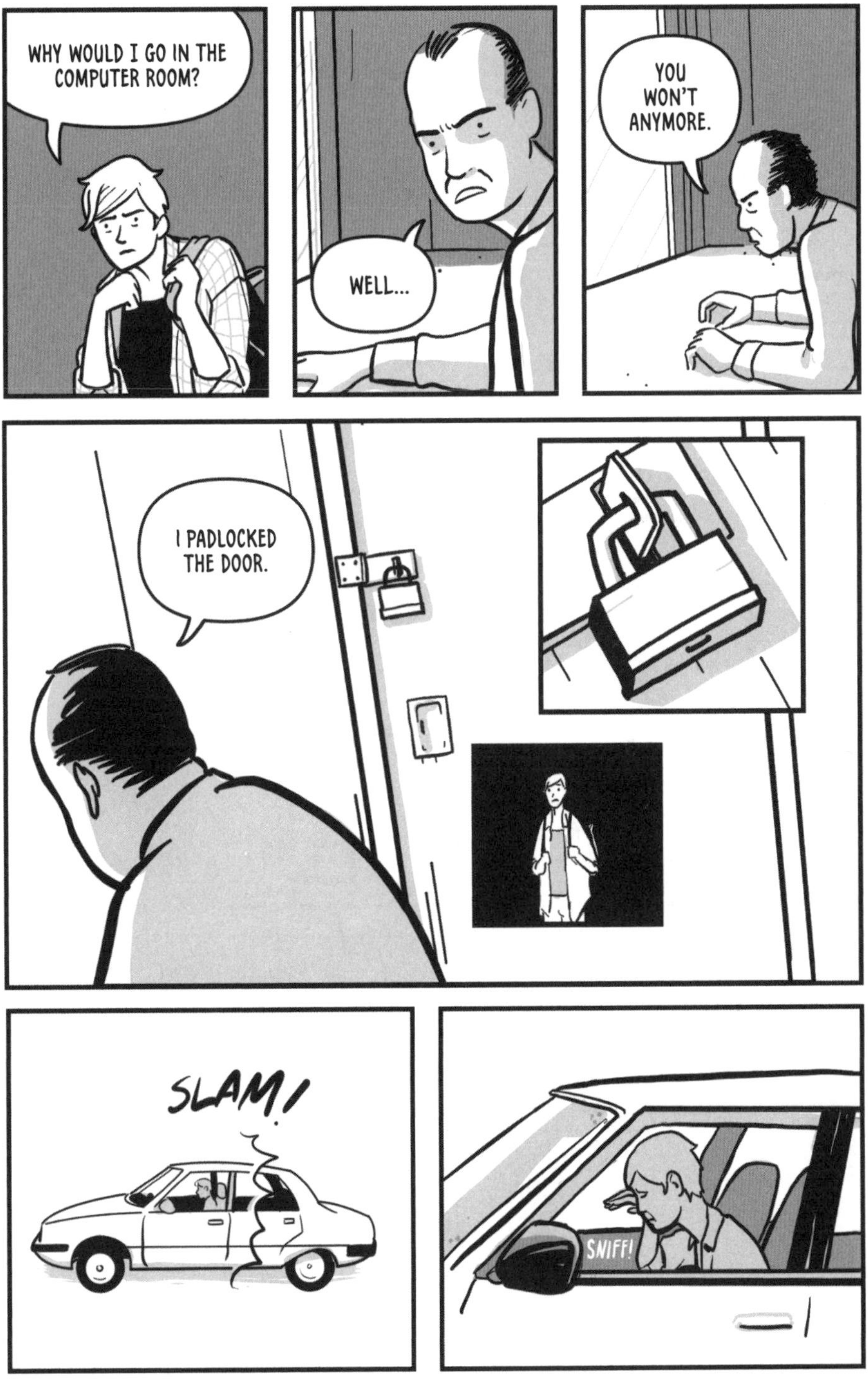
WHY WOULD I GO IN THE COMPUTER ROOM?
WELL...
YOU WON'T ANYMORE.
I PADLOCKED THE DOOR.
SLAM!
SNIFF!

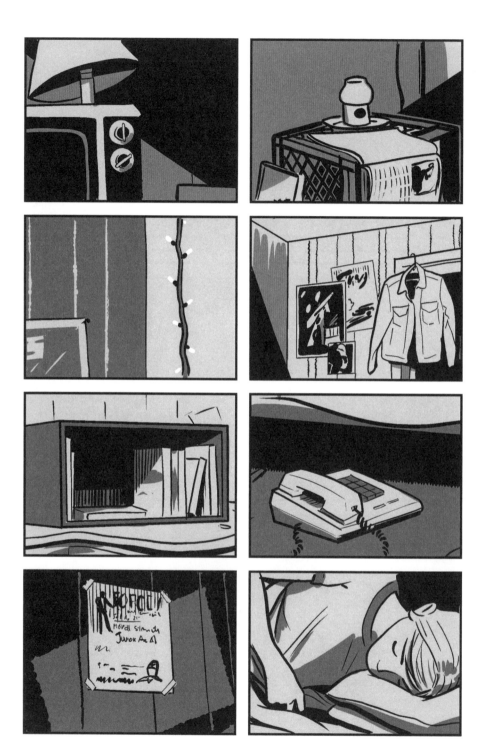

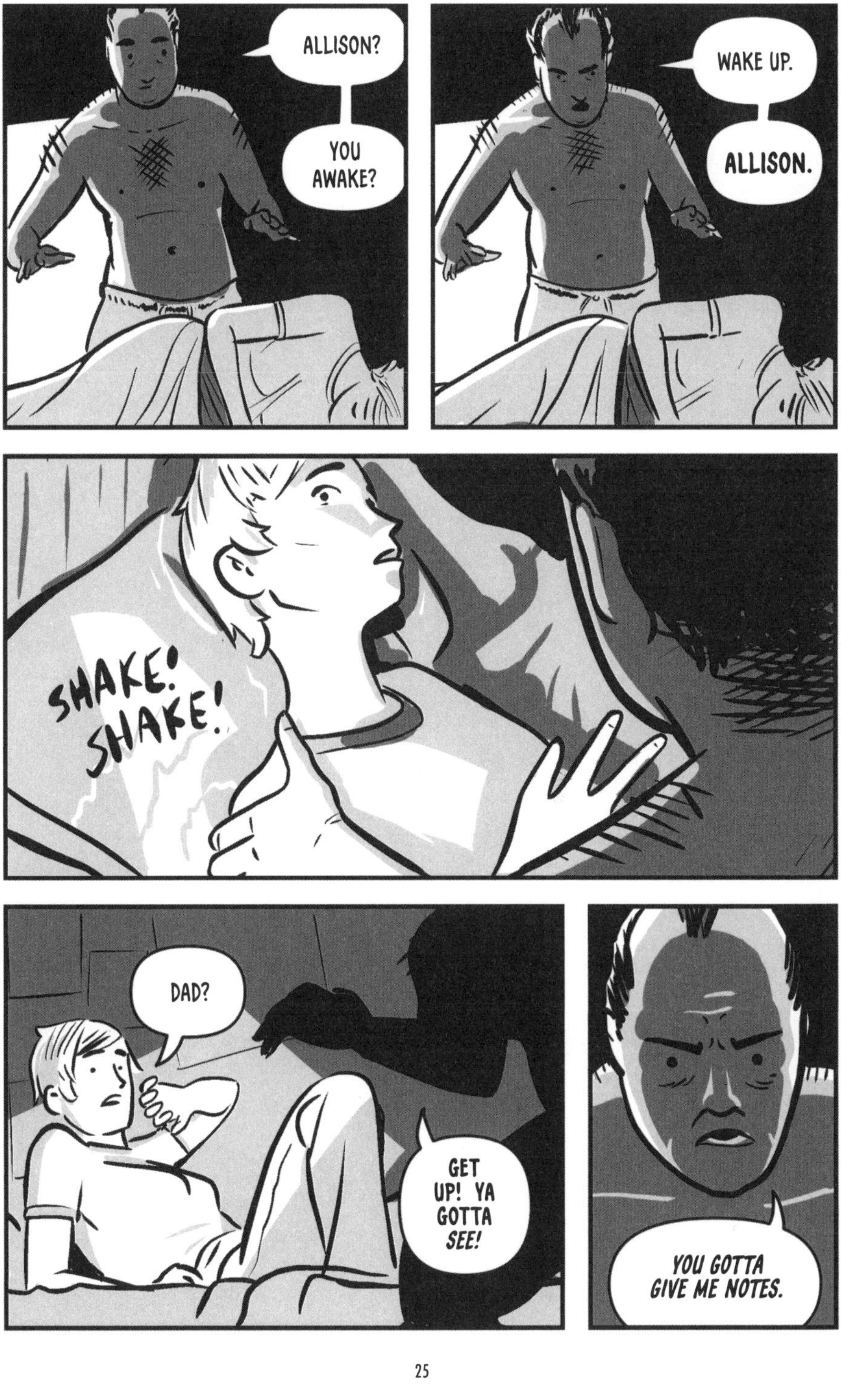
ALLISON?
YOU AWAKE?
WAKE UP.
ALLISON.
SHAKE! SHAKE!
DAD?
GET UP! YA GOTTA *SEE!*
YOU GOTTA GIVE ME NOTES.

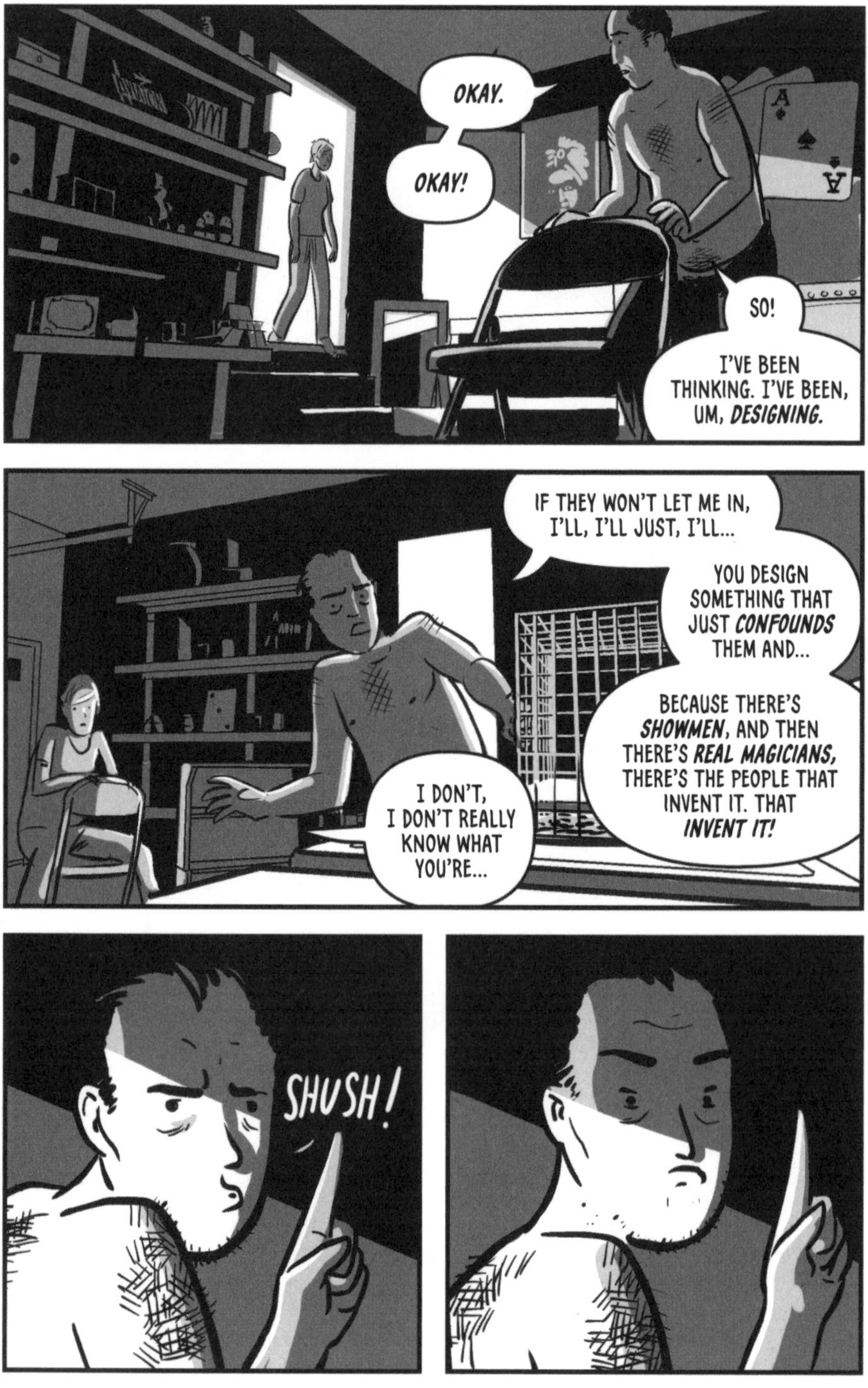
OKAY.
OKAY!
SO!
I'VE BEEN THINKING. I'VE BEEN, UM, DESIGNING.
IF THEY WON'T LET ME IN, I'LL, I'LL JUST, I'LL...
YOU DESIGN SOMETHING THAT JUST CONFOUNDS THEM AND...
BECAUSE THERE'S SHOWMEN, AND THEN THERE'S REAL MAGICIANS, THERE'S THE PEOPLE THAT INVENT IT. THAT INVENT IT!
I DON'T, I DON'T REALLY KNOW WHAT YOU'RE...
SHUSH!

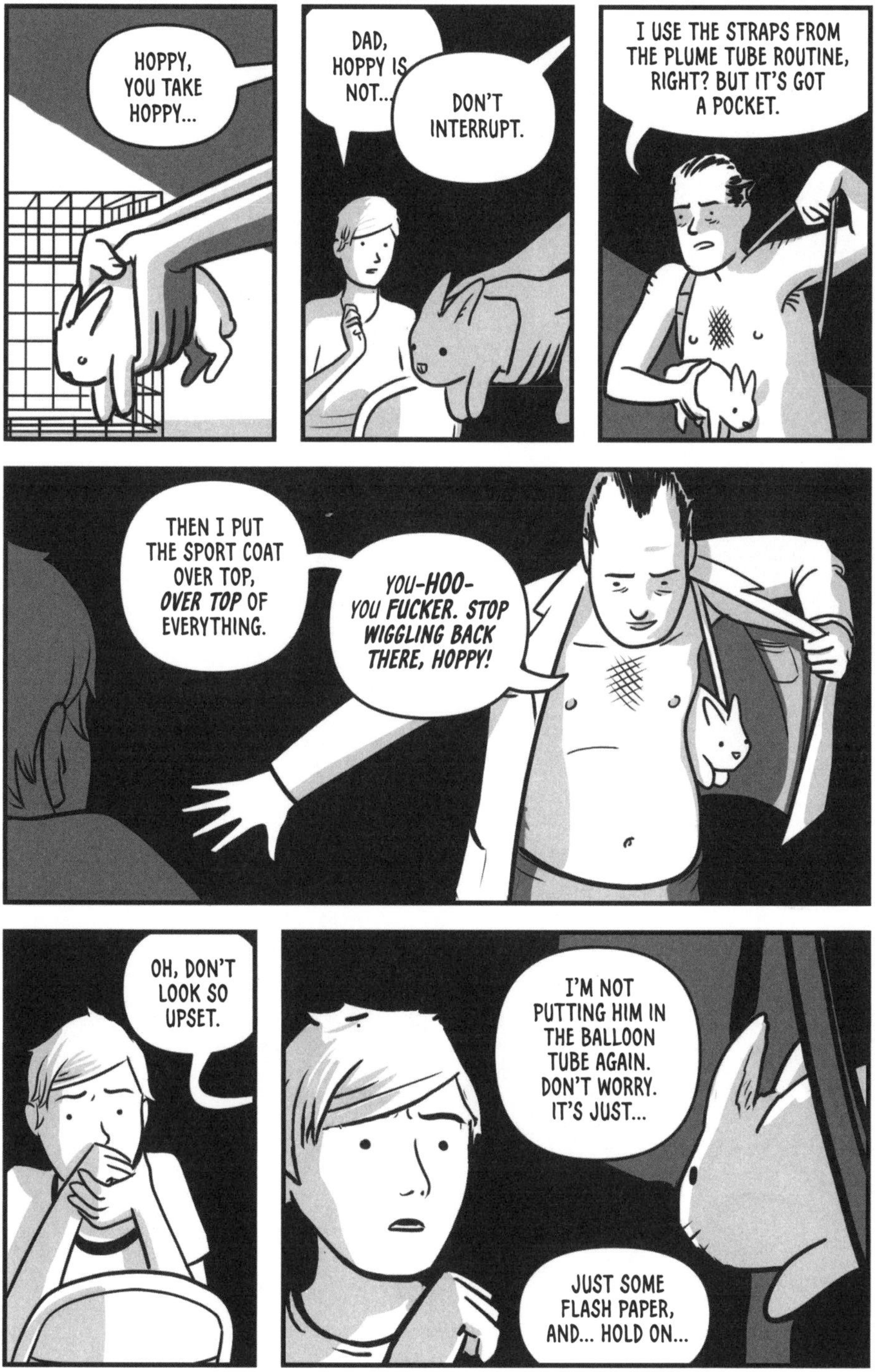
HOPPY, YOU TAKE HOPPY...
DAD, HOPPY IS NOT...
DON'T INTERRUPT.
I USE THE STRAPS FROM THE PLUME TUBE ROUTINE, RIGHT? BUT IT'S GOT A POCKET.
THEN I PUT THE SPORT COAT OVER TOP, *OVER TOP* OF EVERYTHING.
*YOU-**HOO**- YOU **FUCKER**. STOP WIGGLING BACK THERE, HOPPY!*
OH, DON'T LOOK SO UPSET.
I'M NOT PUTTING HIM IN THE BALLOON TUBE AGAIN. DON'T WORRY. IT'S JUST...
JUST SOME FLASH PAPER, AND... HOLD ON...

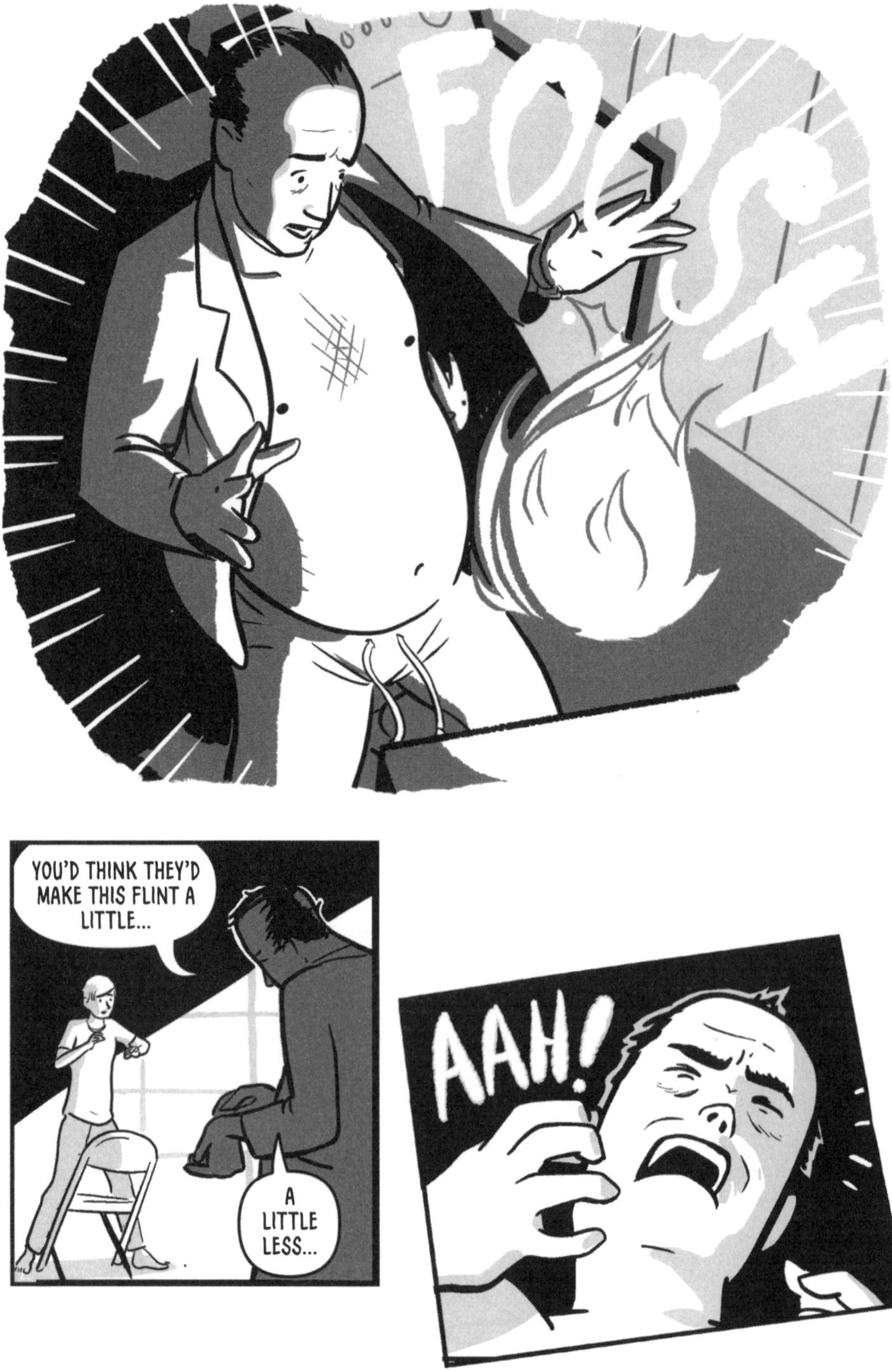
FOOSH!
YOU'D THINK THEY'D MAKE THIS FLINT A LITTLE...
A LITTLE LESS...
AAH!

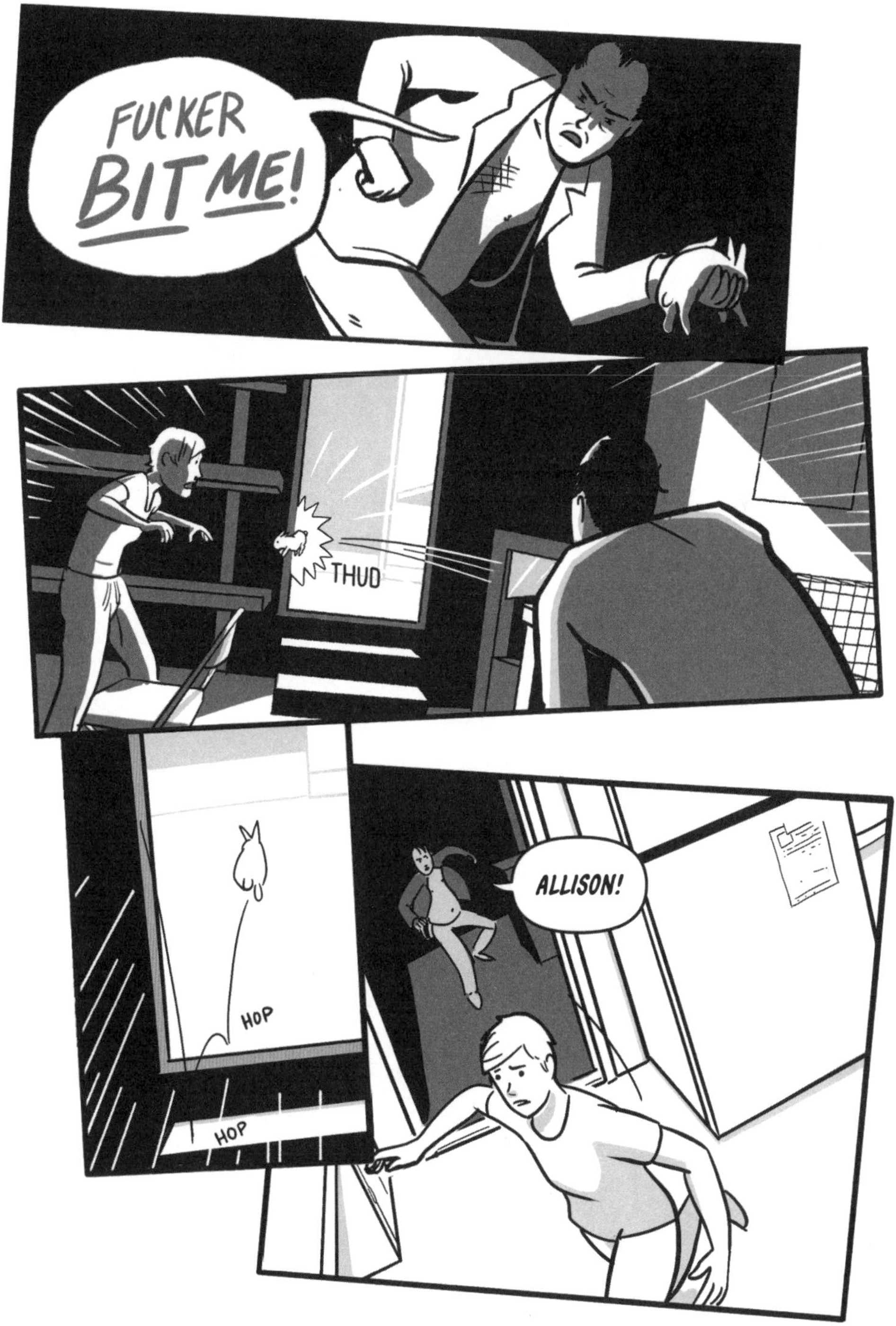
FUCKER BIT ME!
THUD
HOP
HOP
ALLISON!

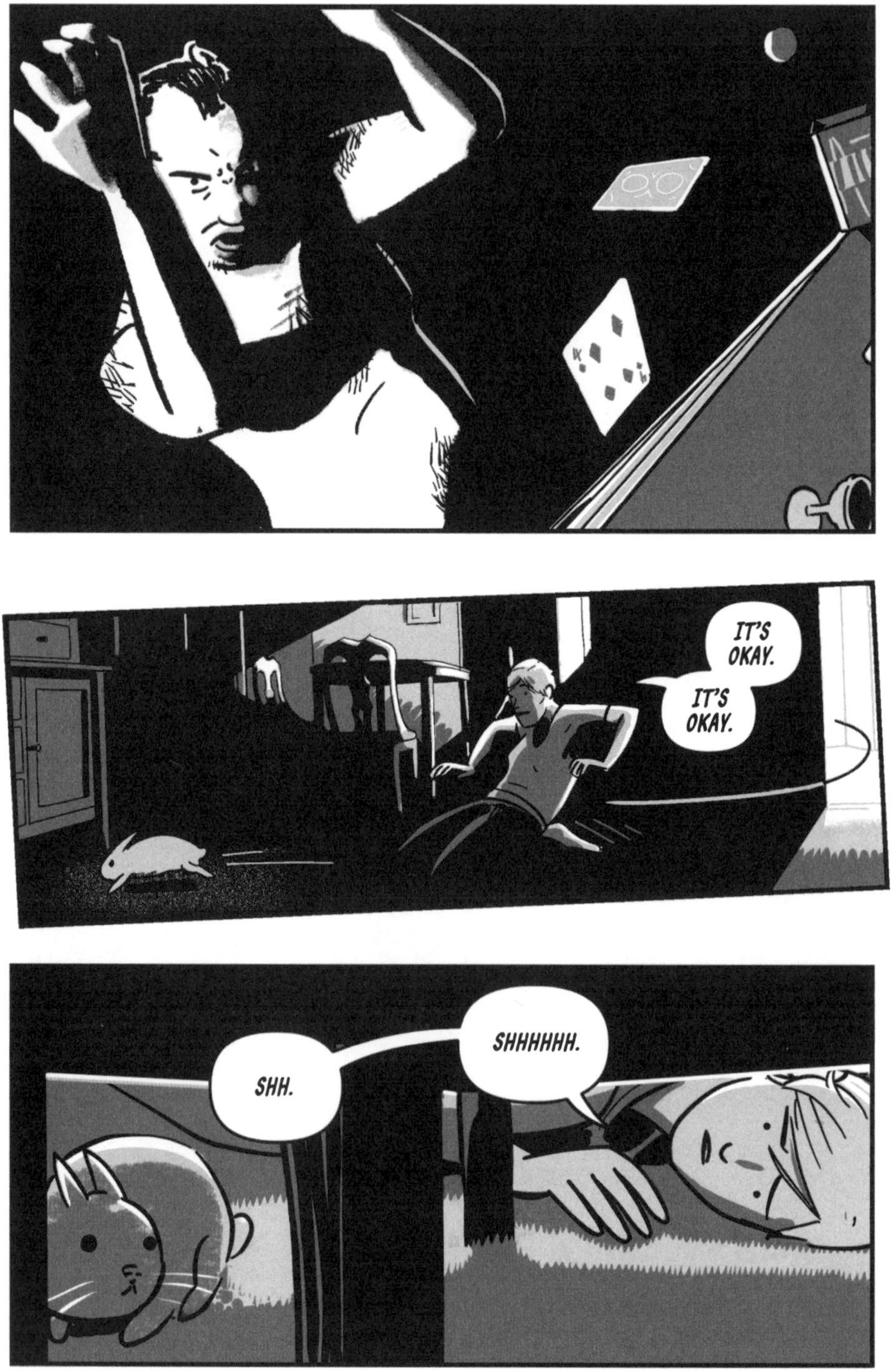
IT'S OKAY.
IT'S OKAY.
SHH.
SHHHHHH.

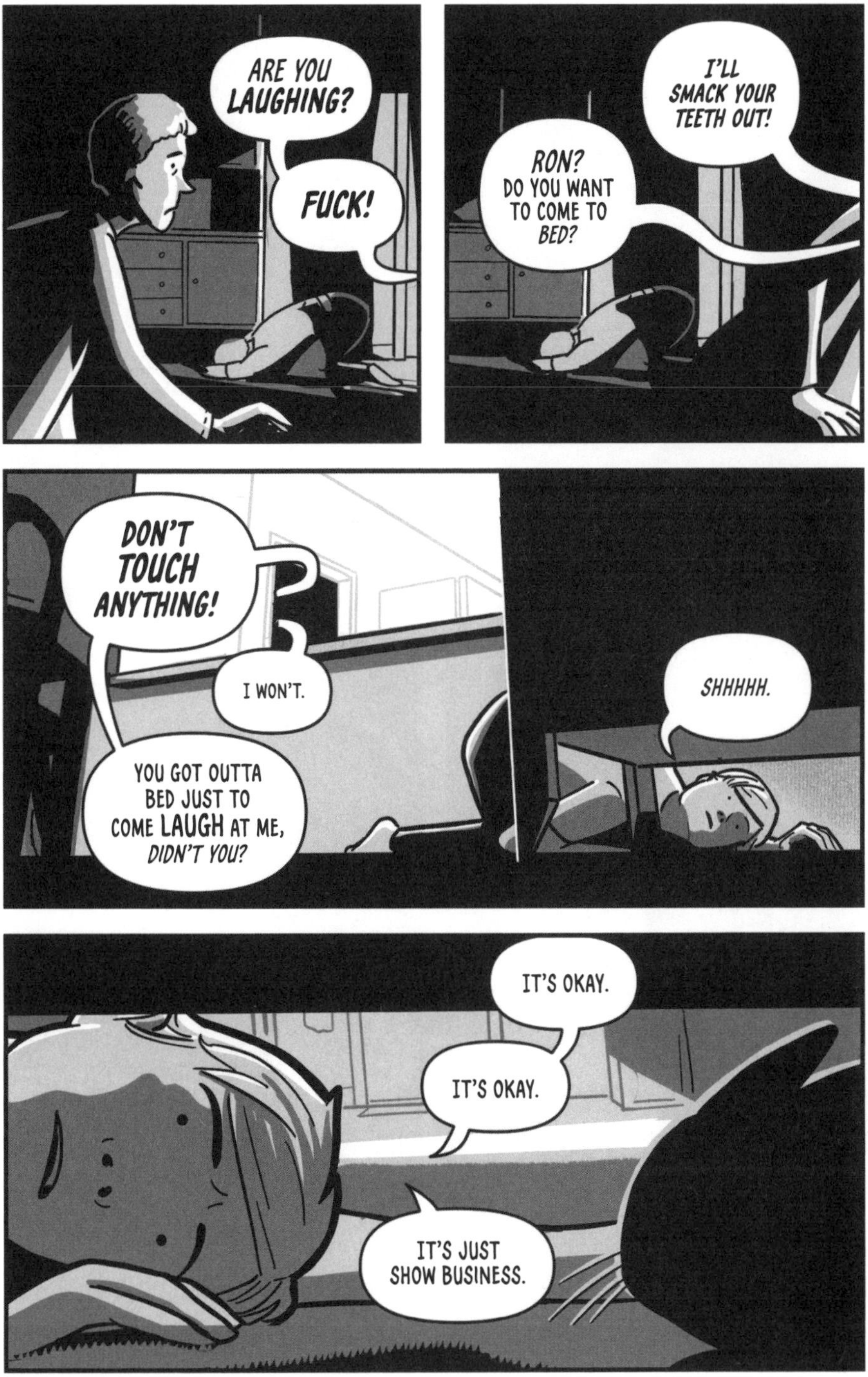
ARE YOU LAUGHING?
FUCK!
I'LL SMACK YOUR TEETH OUT!
RON? DO YOU WANT TO COME TO BED?
DON'T TOUCH ANYTHING!
I WON'T.
YOU GOT OUTTA BED JUST TO COME LAUGH AT ME, DIDN'T YOU?
SHHHHH.
IT'S OKAY.
IT'S OKAY.
IT'S JUST SHOW BUSINESS.

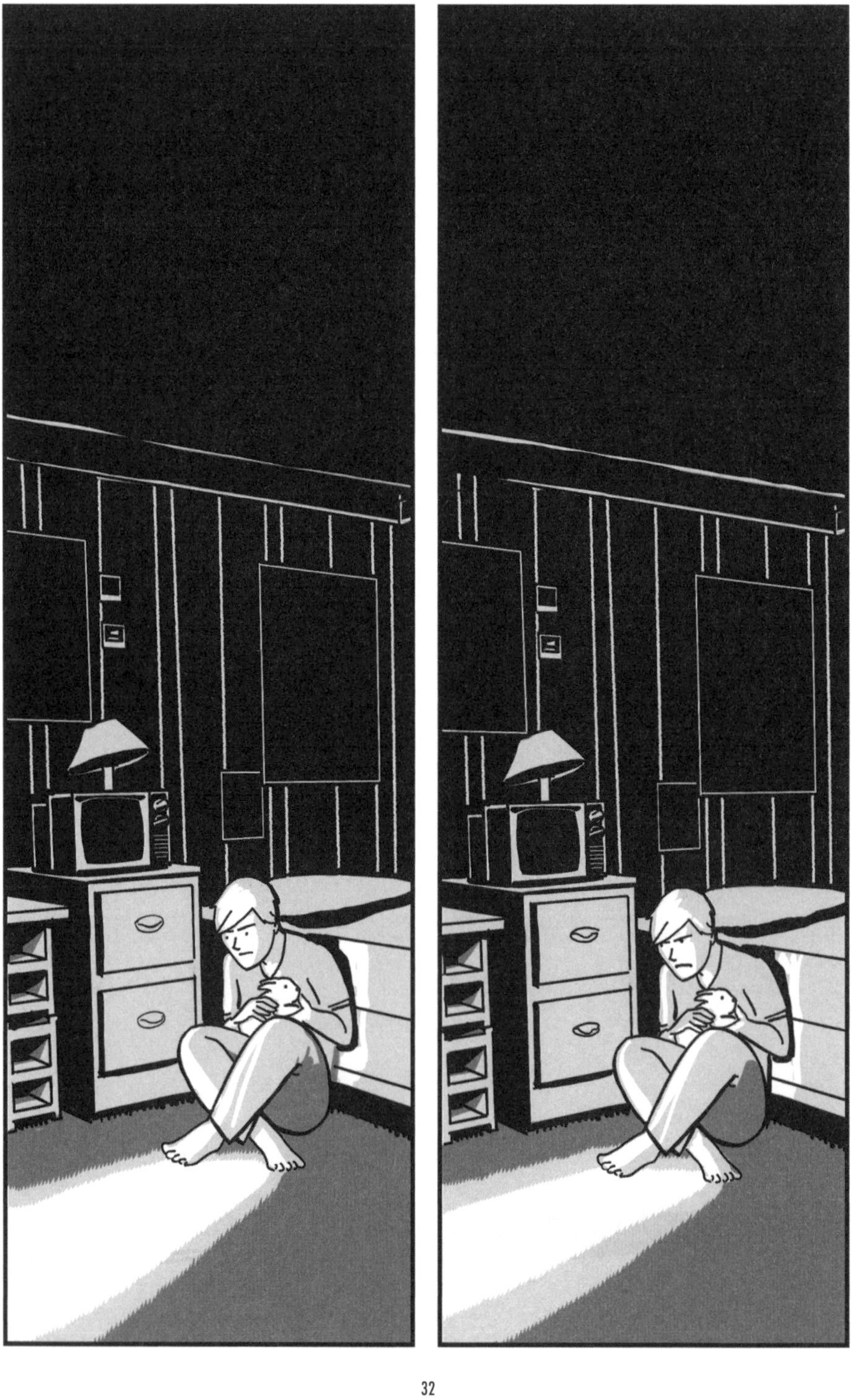

```
starting rpc daemons: portmap rpcd.
starting system logger
starting local daemons: routed sendmail biod.
preserving editor files
clearing /tmp
standard daemons: update cron.
starting network daemons: inetd printer.

Wisconsin UNIX (root console) .
4.3+NFS > V.*

login: samir
password: *******
4.3 BSD UNIX #2

-=-=-=-=-=-=-=-=-=-=-=-=-=-=-=-=-=-=-=-=-=-=-=-=-=-=-=-=-=-=-=-=-=-

                    4.3+NFS Winsconsin Unix

-=-=-=-=-=-=-=-=-=-=-=-=-=-=-=-=-=-=-=-=-=-=-=-=-=-=-=-=-=-=-=-=-=-


samir# /usr/bin/pine
```

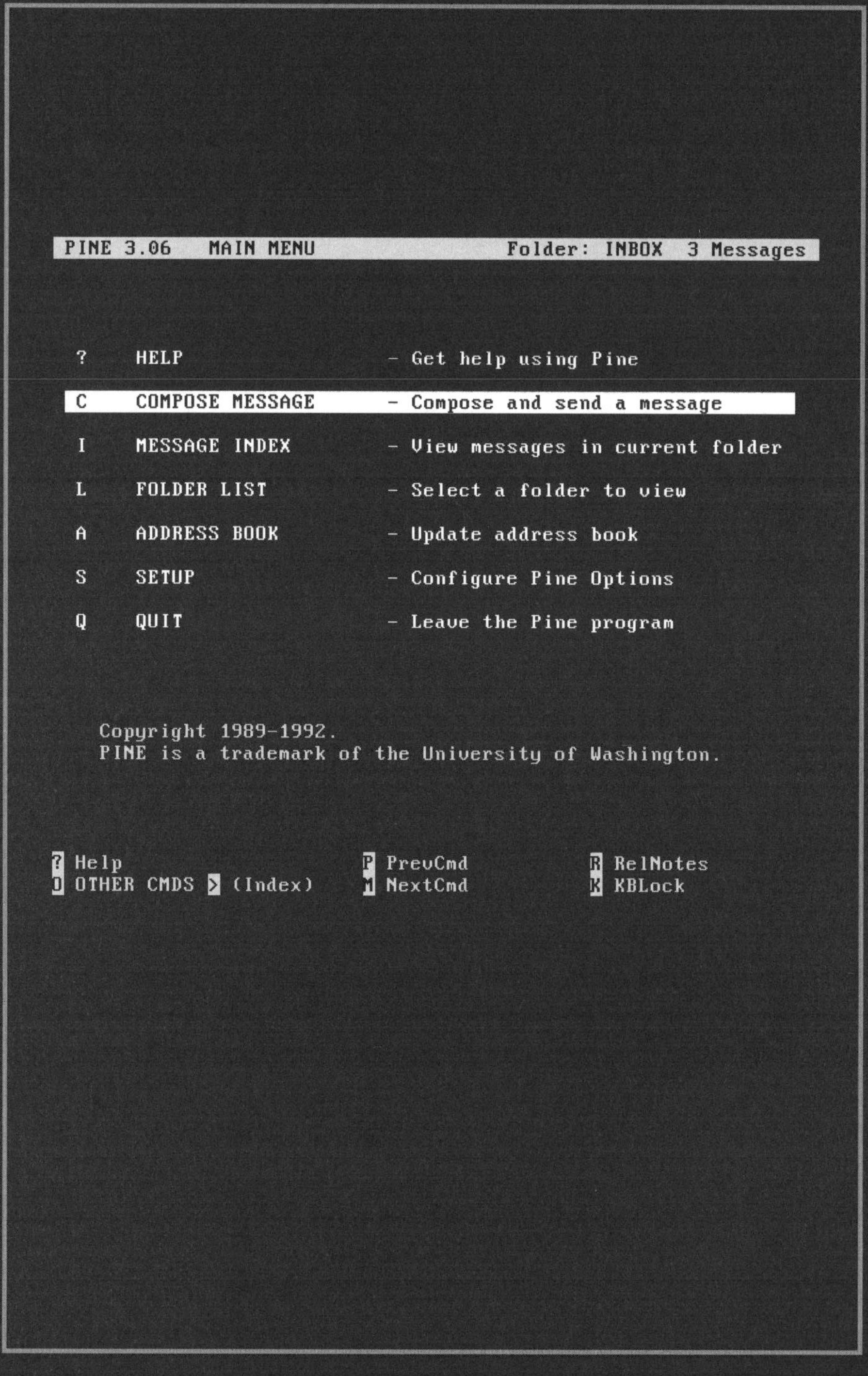
PINE 3.06 MAIN MENU Folder: INBOX 3 Messages
? HELP - Get help using Pine
C COMPOSE MESSAGE - Compose and send a message
I MESSAGE INDEX - View messages in current folder
L FOLDER LIST - Select a folder to view
A ADDRESS BOOK - Update address book
S SETUP - Configure Pine Options
Q QUIT - Leave the Pine program
Copyright 1989-1992.
PINE is a trademark of the University of Washington.
? Help
O OTHER CMDS > (Index)
P PrevCmd
N NextCmd
R RelNotes
K KBLock

PINE 3.06   COMPOSE MESSAGE REPLY   Folder: INBOX 3 Messages

To   : Allison <allison.r@zephyrtech.net>
Cc   :
Attchmnt:
Subject : "a lot more than just being bored"

----- Message Text -----

Hey Allison

I couldn't sleep. I've gotten used to e-mailing you at 1am.

Ever think about what would have happened if one of us lived in a different town? The billion dollar long distance charges to dial into a BBS in a different area code? We'd never have met.

Thanks for talking about my parents split. I think I'm kind of in the way of them saying what they need to say to each other. I just want them to be done with it. Does that make me a selfish prick?

Aaaaanyway. I got that Daniel Johnston album. I kind of love it? There's a scratch on the CD that makes the line "they were mean to him but he never burned us" repeat and sound like Big Bird when he snores. "They were me-me-me-me-me-me-me-me".

Well, enough about me. What are you doing?
-Sam

^G Get Help ^X Send ^R Read File ^K Cut Text ^O Postpone
^C Cancel ^J Justify ^W Where is ^U UnCut Text ^T To Spell

PINE 3.06 MESSAGE TEXT Folder: INBOX Message 1 of 3 ALL ANS

From: Allison <allison.r@zephyrtech.net>
To: s.omid@campuslink.net
Subject: RE: "a lot more than just being bored"

Sam! You are the farthest from selfish I've ever met!

I missed talking to you too. It's kinda ALL I think about. It's possible I'm a crazy person. You should know that about me.

Hey, there's something we need to talk about as soon as you get this.

Are you up?

Can I have your phone number?

[ALL of message]

H Help < MsgIndex P PrevMsg D Delete R Reply
O OTHER CMDS > ViewAttch N NextMsg U Undelete F Forward

Can I have your

phone number?

```
To       : Allison <allison.r@zephyrtech.net>
Cc       :
Attchmnt:
Subject  : RE(2): "a lot more than just being bored"

----- Message Text -----
```

```
To       : Allison <allison.r@zephyrtech.net>
Cc       :
Attchmnt:
Subject  : RE(2): "a lot more than just being bored"

----- Message Text -----

I don't think I sh
```

```
To       : Allison <allison.r@zephyrtech.net>
Cc       :
Attchmnt:
Subject  : RE(2): "a lot more than just being bored"

----- Message Text -----

I
```

```
To      : Allison <allison.r@zephyrtech.net>
Cc      :
Attchmnt:
Subject : RE(2): "a lot more than just being bored"
----- Message Text -----
It's 858-5322 but don't call now. It's 1am. My dad's asleep.

-Sam
```

```
From: Allison <allison.r@zephyrtech.net>
To: s.omid@campuslink.net
Subject: RE(3): "a lot more than just being bored"


Better log off. Your phone's about to ring.

- Allison
```

Your phone's about to ring.

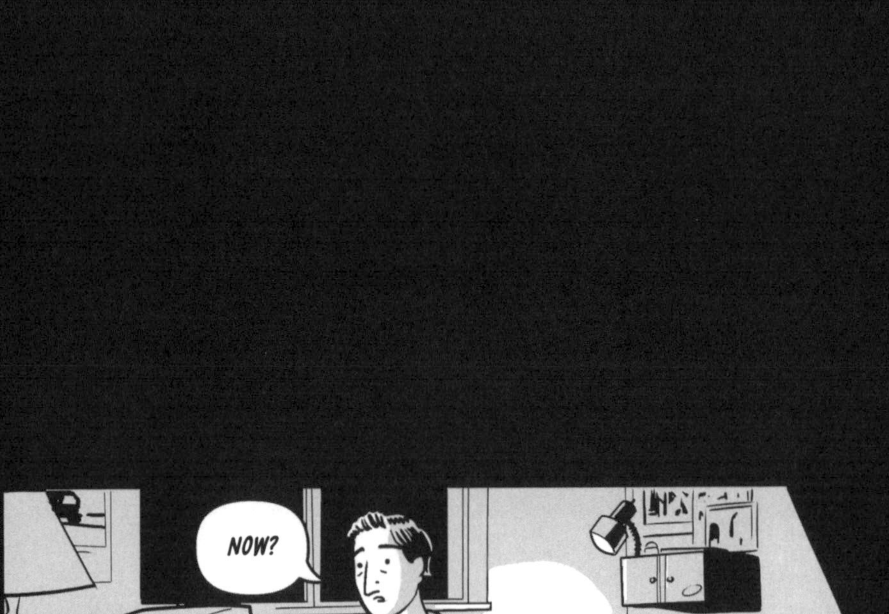
NOW?

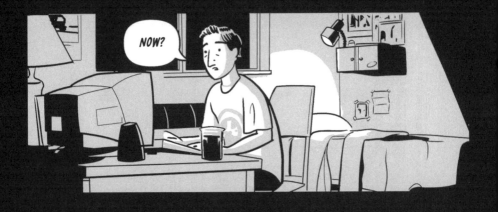

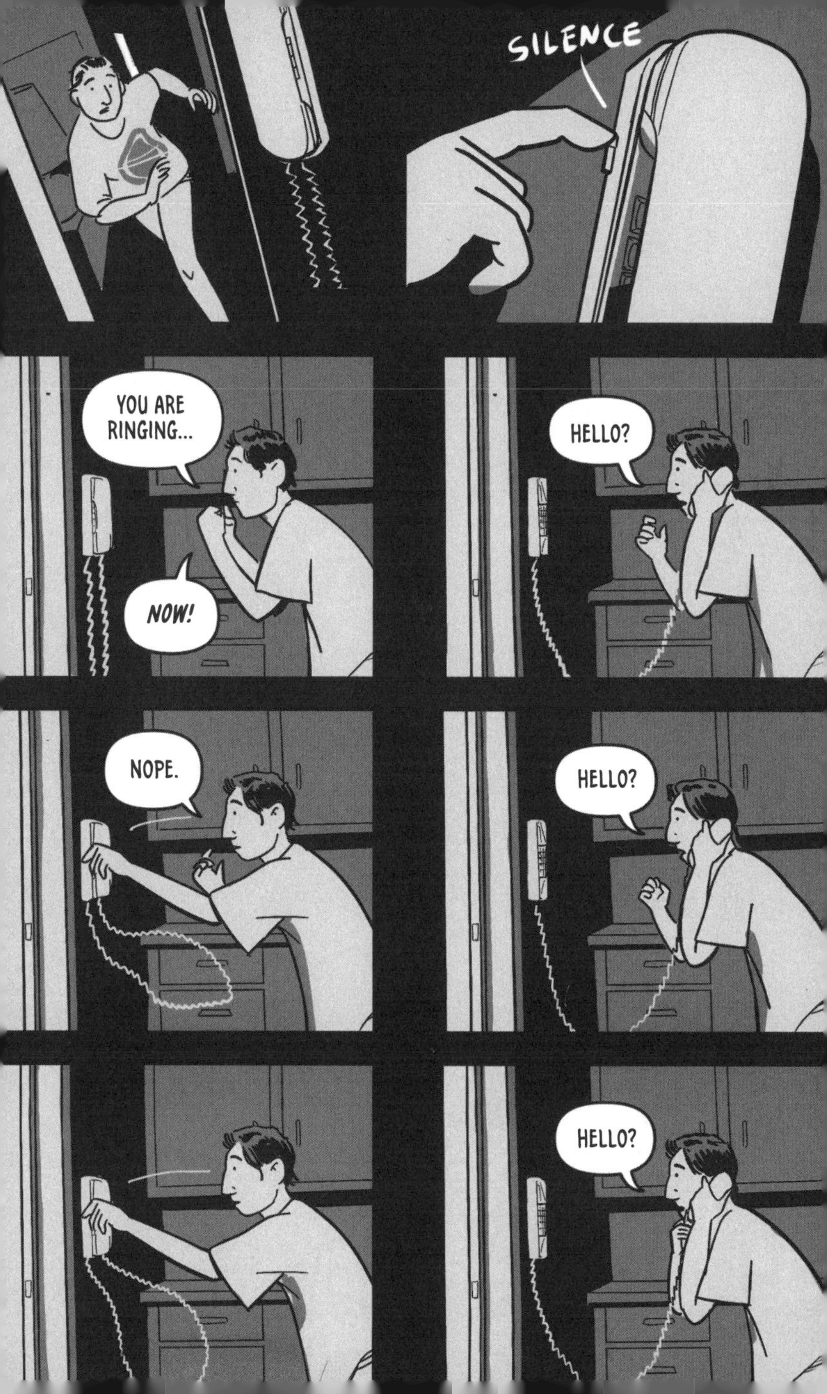
SILENCE
YOU ARE RINGING...
NOW!
HELLO?
NOPE.
HELLO?
HELLO?

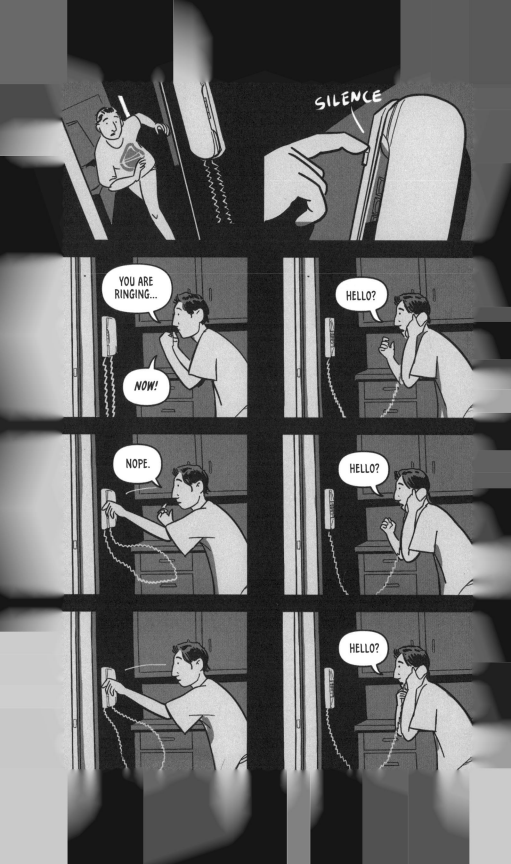

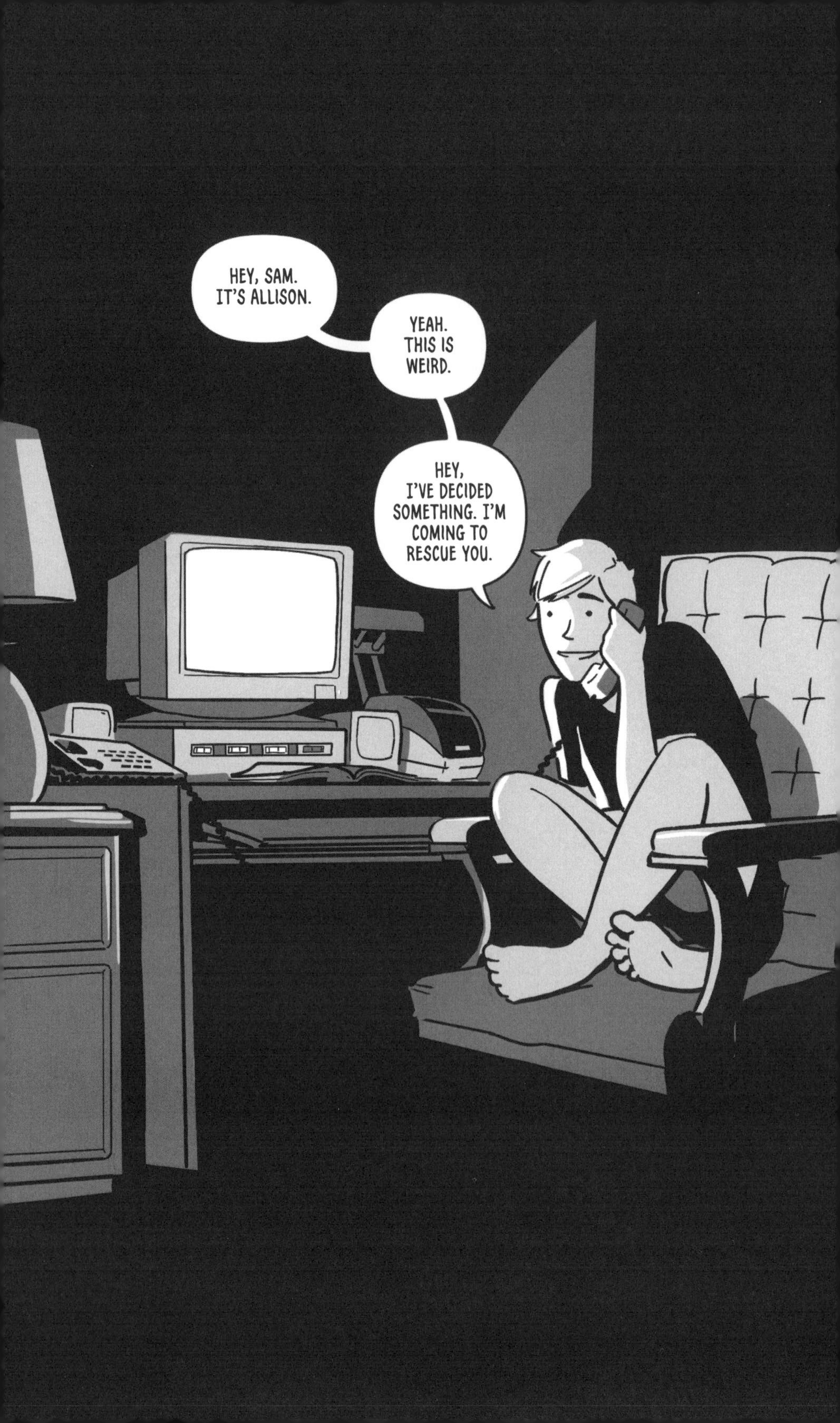
HEY, SAM.
IT'S ALLISON.
YEAH.
THIS IS
WEIRD.
HEY,
I'VE DECIDED
SOMETHING. I'M
COMING TO
RESCUE YOU.

Chapter 2

WELCOME TO MALABAR

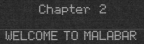

```
GAT GCS GM GS d -p+ c+++(++++) l++(+++) u+@ e×
m(+) s+/- n--- h× !f(+) g+ w++ t++(+++) r? y?
```

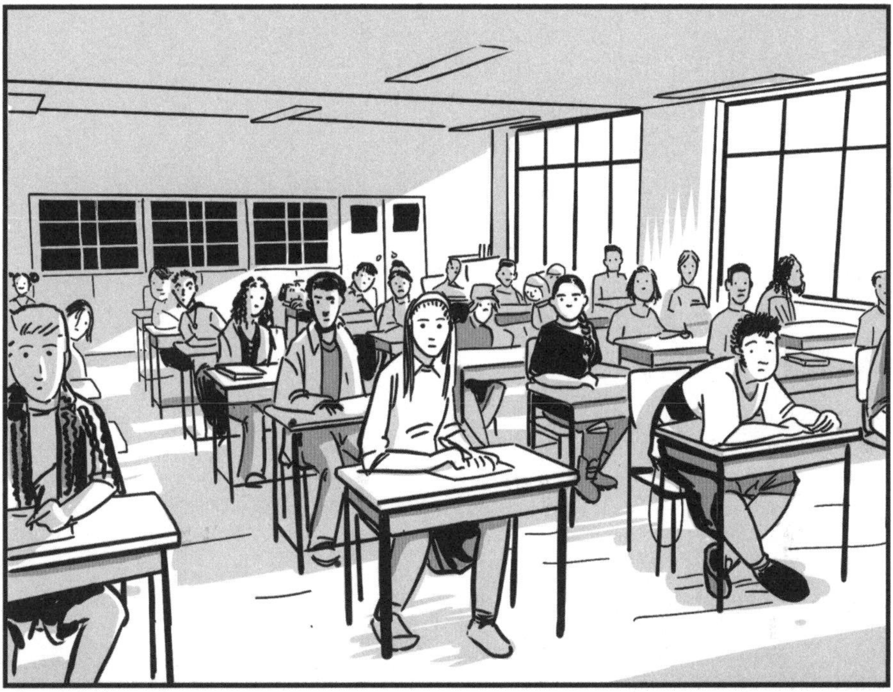

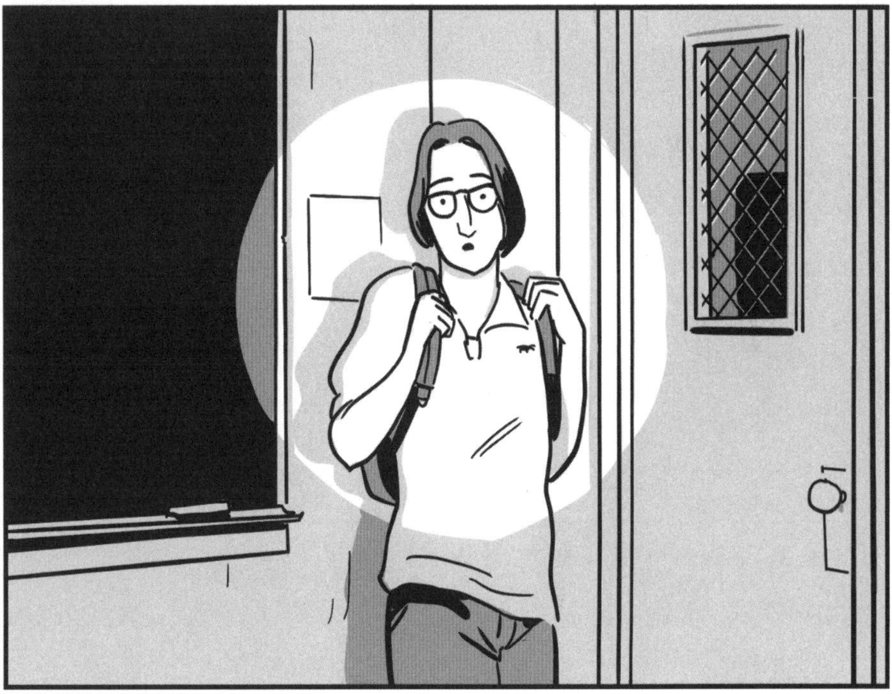

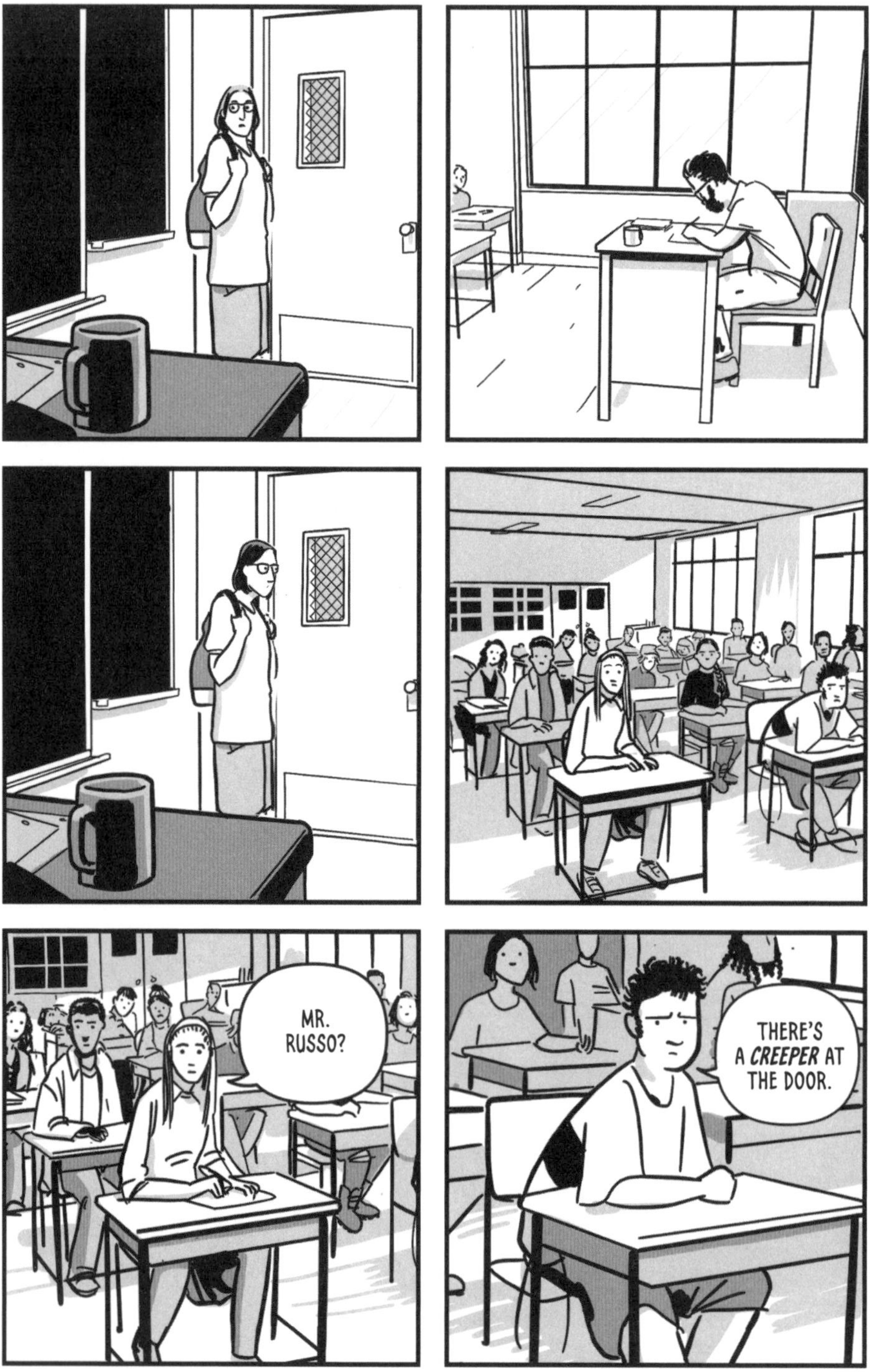
MR. RUSSO?
THERE'S A *CREEPER* AT THE DOOR.

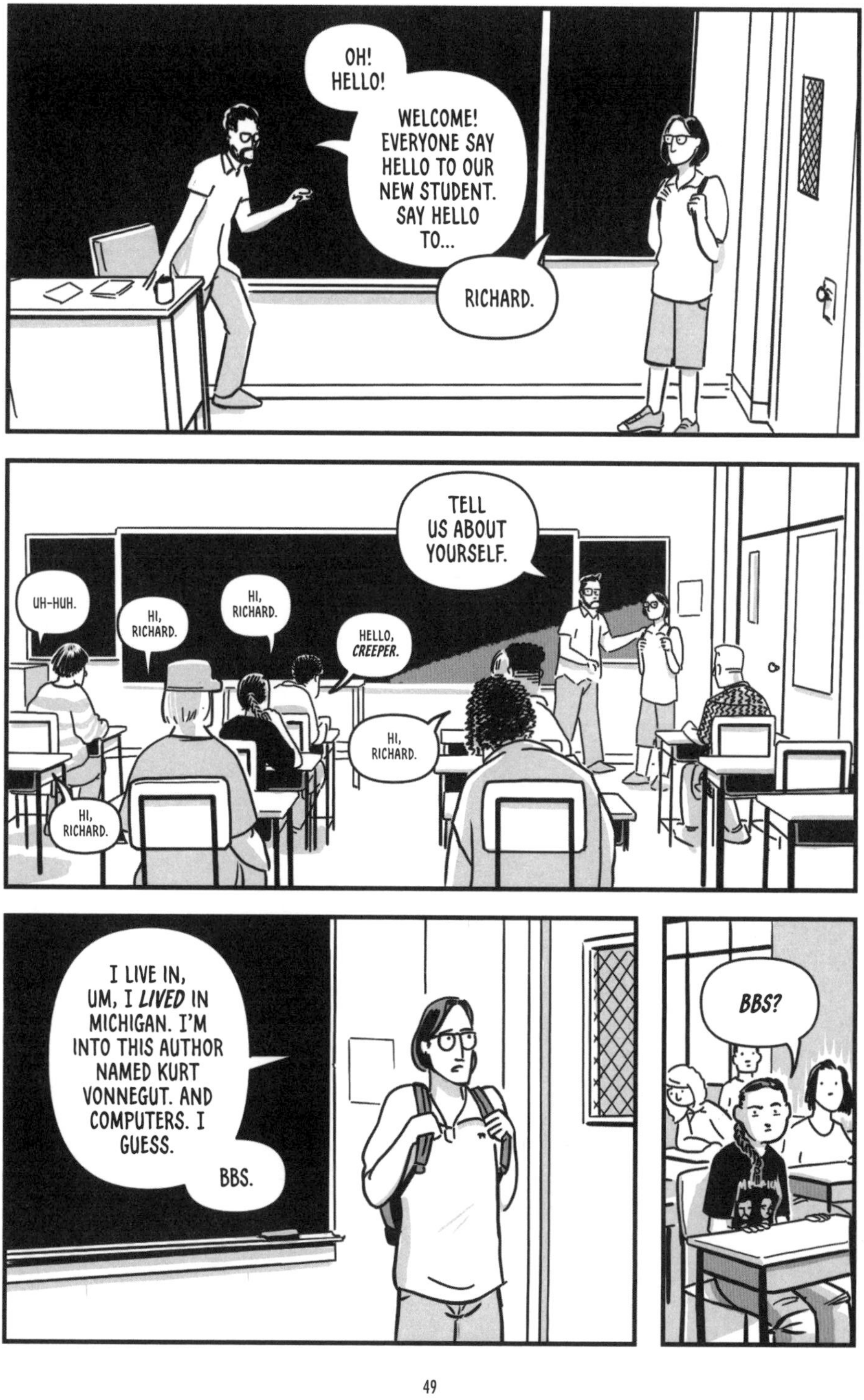
OH! HELLO!
WELCOME! EVERYONE SAY HELLO TO OUR NEW STUDENT. SAY HELLO TO...
RICHARD.
TELL US ABOUT YOURSELF.
UH-HUH.
HI, RICHARD.
HI, RICHARD.
HELLO, *CREEPER.*
HI, RICHARD.
HI, RICHARD.
I LIVE IN, UM, I *LIVED* IN MICHIGAN. I'M INTO THIS AUTHOR NAMED KURT VONNEGUT. AND COMPUTERS. I GUESS.
BBS.
BBS?

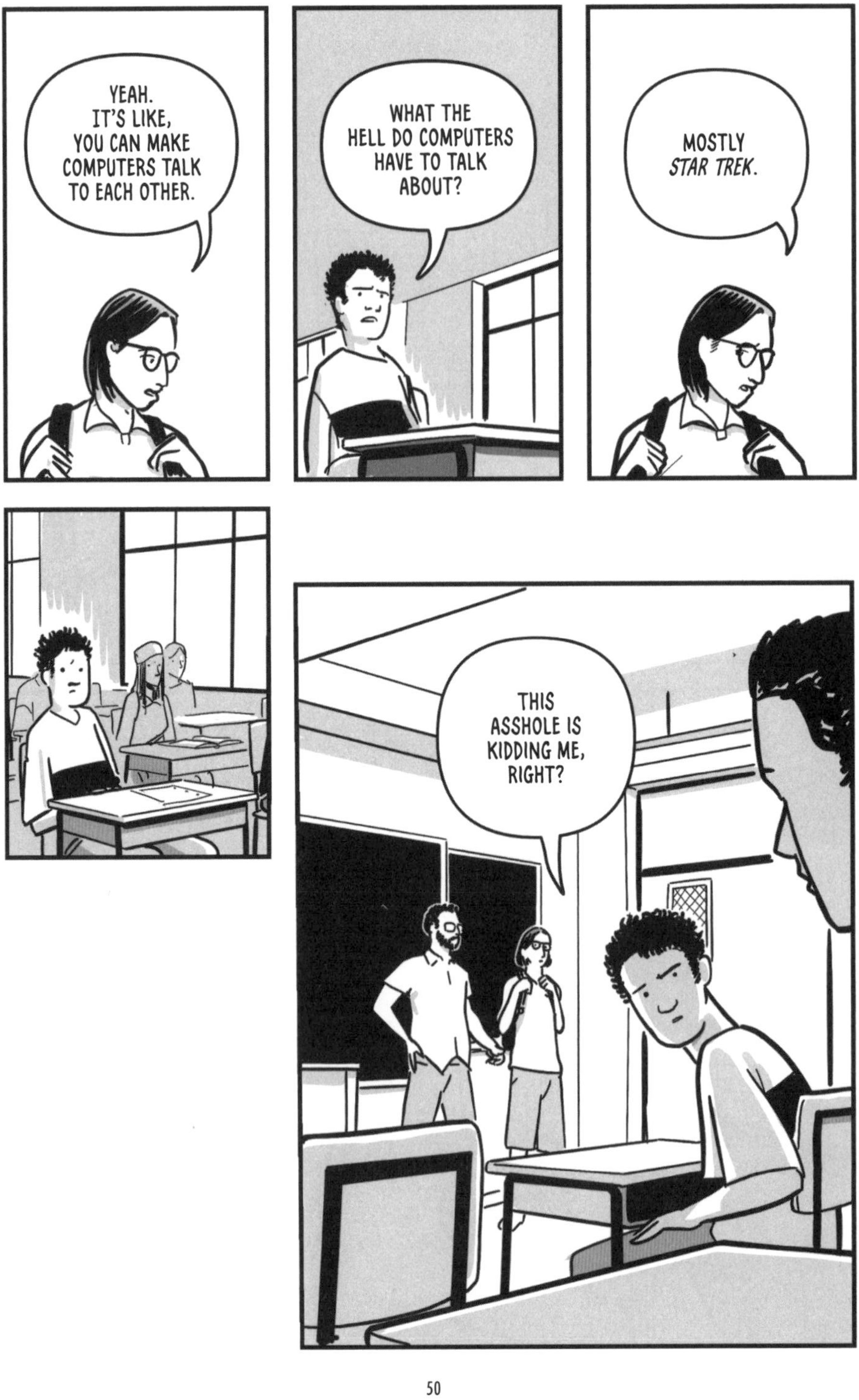
YEAH. IT'S LIKE, YOU CAN MAKE COMPUTERS TALK TO EACH OTHER.
WHAT THE HELL DO COMPUTERS HAVE TO TALK ABOUT?
MOSTLY *STAR TREK*.
THIS ASSHOLE IS KIDDING ME, RIGHT?

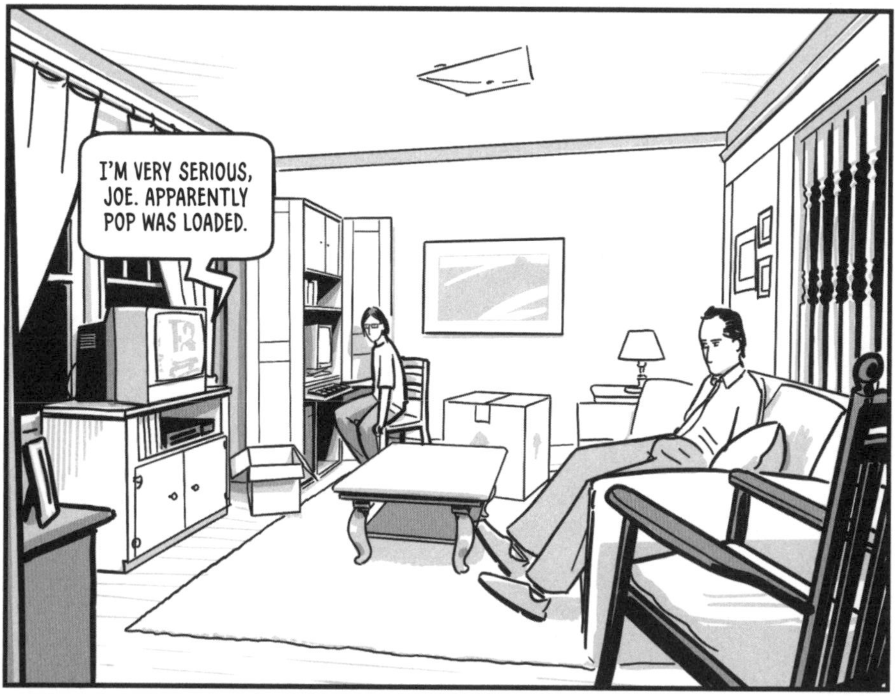
I'M VERY SERIOUS, JOE. APPARENTLY POP WAS LOADED.

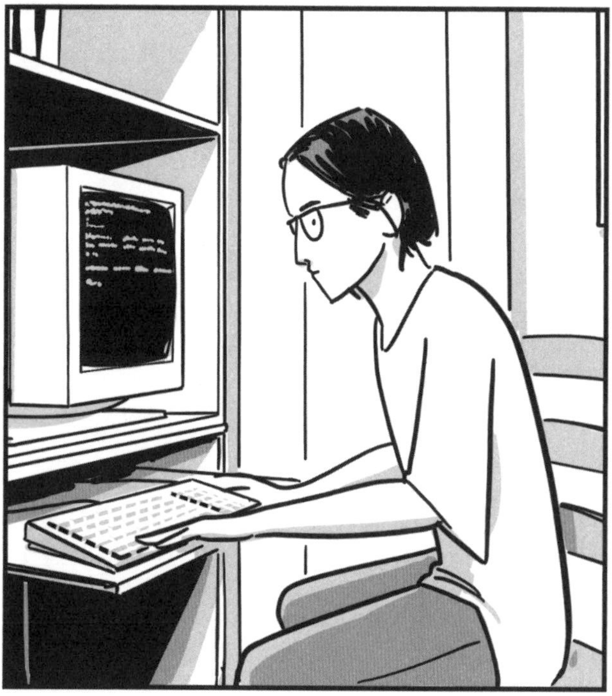

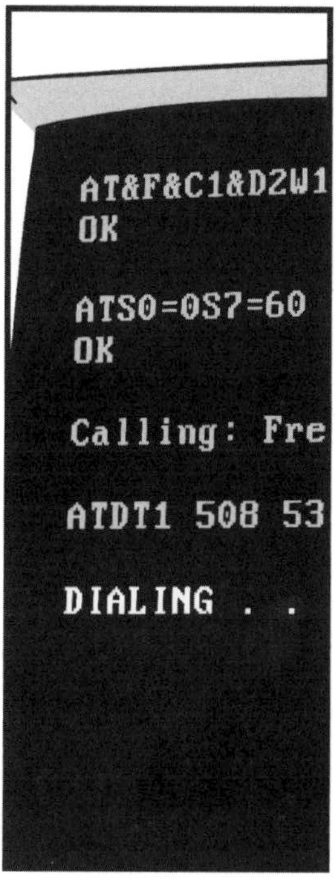
AT&F&C1&D2W1
OK
ATS0=0S7=60
OK
Calling: Fre
ATDT1 508 53
DIALING . .

```
DIALING. . . . . . . . . . . .
CONNECT 2400/ARQ/TEL

PCBOARD BBS +v1.2
```

```
 ,_____,
 | HOOT!    Welcome to FreeBBS! |
 | : Multinode 1200/2400 Baud : |
 | Closed 1-2AM for maintenance |
 '____|/_____'
  {o,o}
  |)  )
==="="==============================
Log in with "GUEST" for free access,
"NEW" for new user or Ctrl-D to exit

NAME: radrichard
PASS: //////

You've logged 0 of 60 minutes today!
Your session will expire at 10:19:03

MOTD: Don't Panic!! SYSOPS are ditto
and altair

To list available commands, type <?>
```

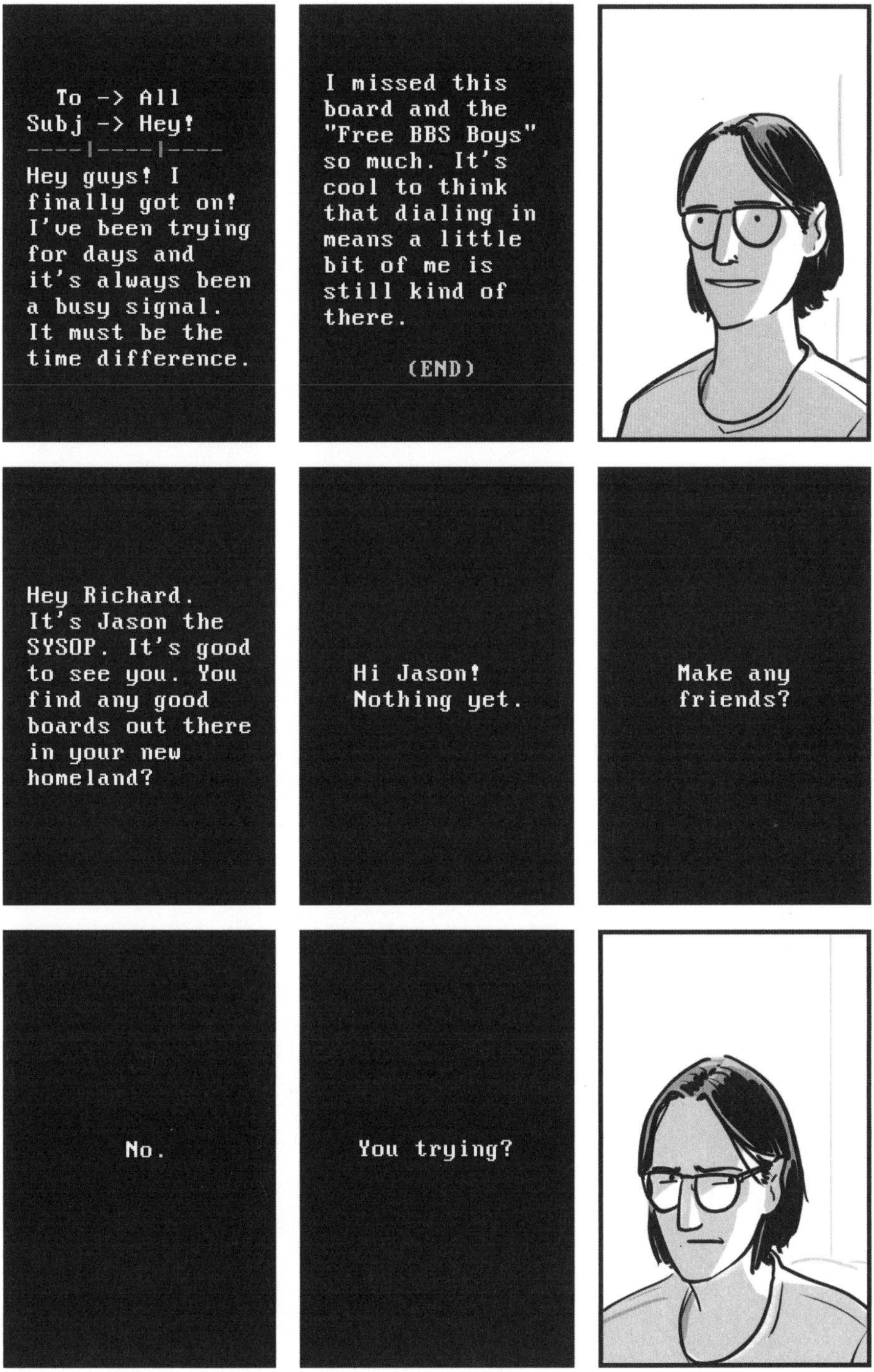
To -> All
Subj -> Hey!
----|----|----
Hey guys! I finally got on! I've been trying for days and it's always been a busy signal. It must be the time difference.
I missed this board and the "Free BBS Boys" so much. It's cool to think that dialing in means a little bit of me is still kind of there.
(END)
Hey Richard. It's Jason the SYSOP. It's good to see you. You find any good boards out there in your new homeland?
Hi Jason! Nothing yet.
Make any friends?
No.
You trying?

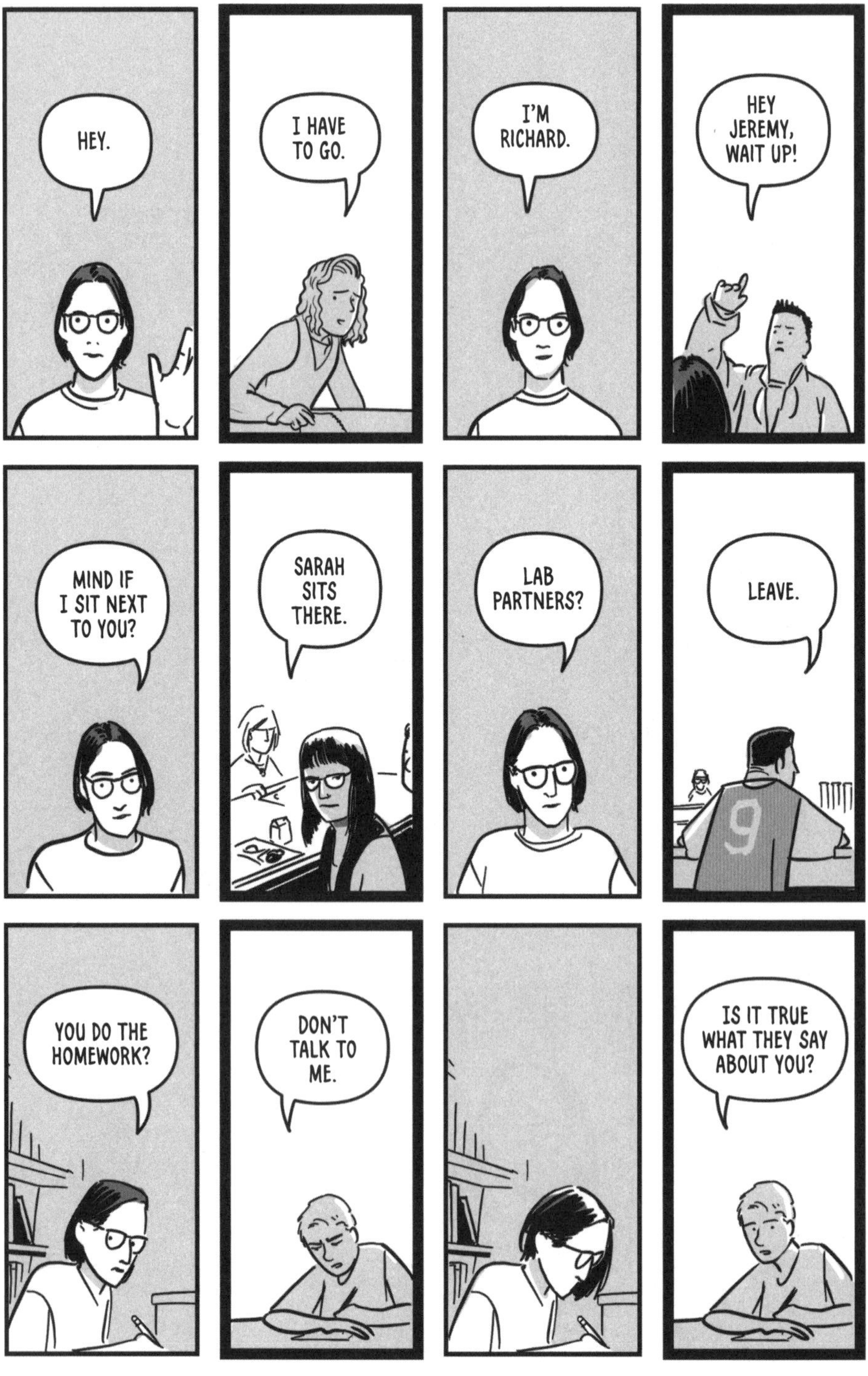
HEY.
I HAVE TO GO.
I'M RICHARD.
HEY JEREMY, WAIT UP!
MIND IF I SIT NEXT TO YOU?
SARAH SITS THERE.
LAB PARTNERS?
LEAVE.
YOU DO THE HOMEWORK?
DON'T TALK TO ME.
IS IT TRUE WHAT THEY SAY ABOUT YOU?

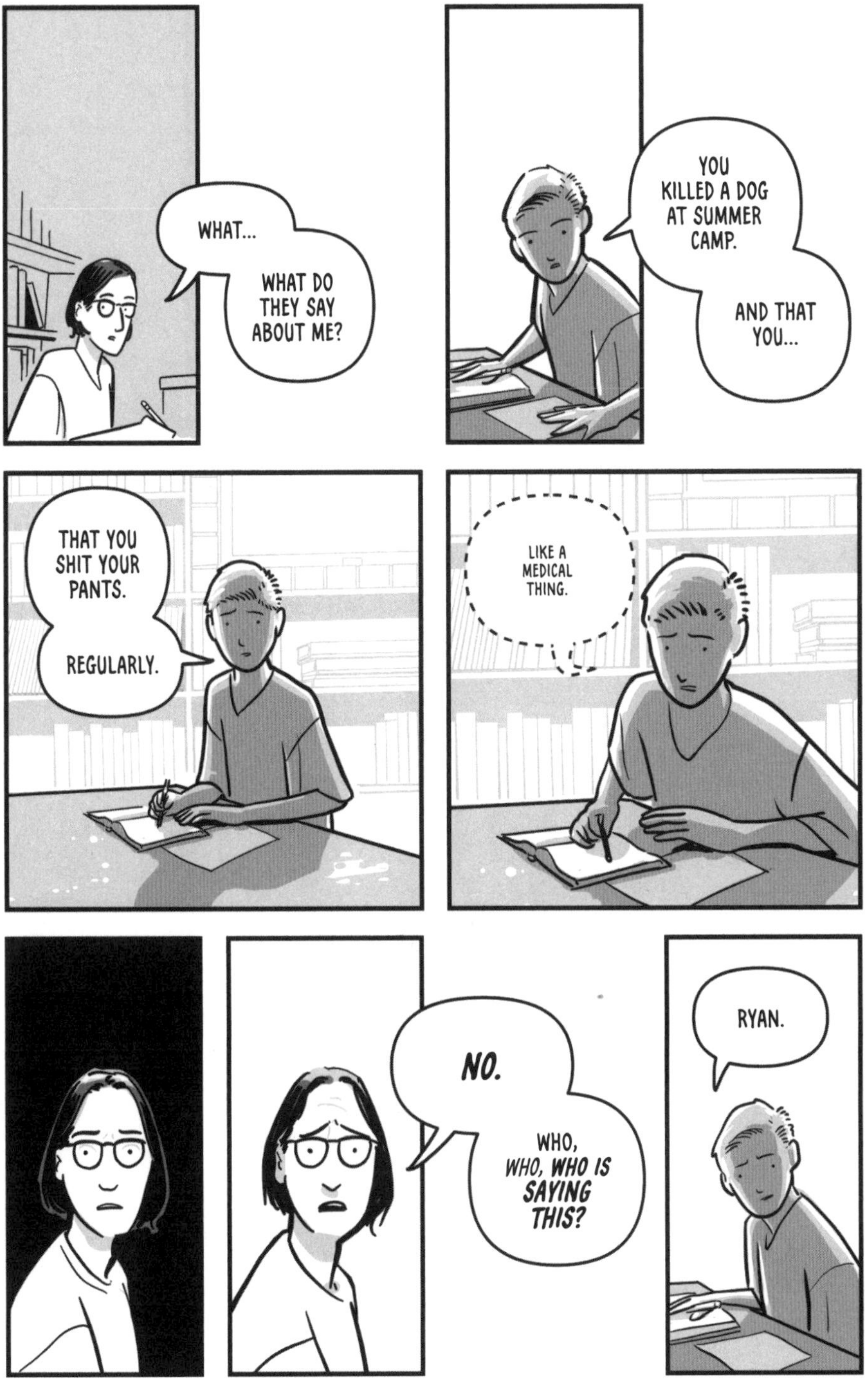
WHAT...
WHAT DO THEY SAY ABOUT ME?
YOU KILLED A DOG AT SUMMER CAMP.
AND THAT YOU...
THAT YOU SHIT YOUR PANTS.
REGULARLY.
LIKE A MEDICAL THING.
NO.
WHO, WHO, WHO IS SAYING THIS?
RYAN.

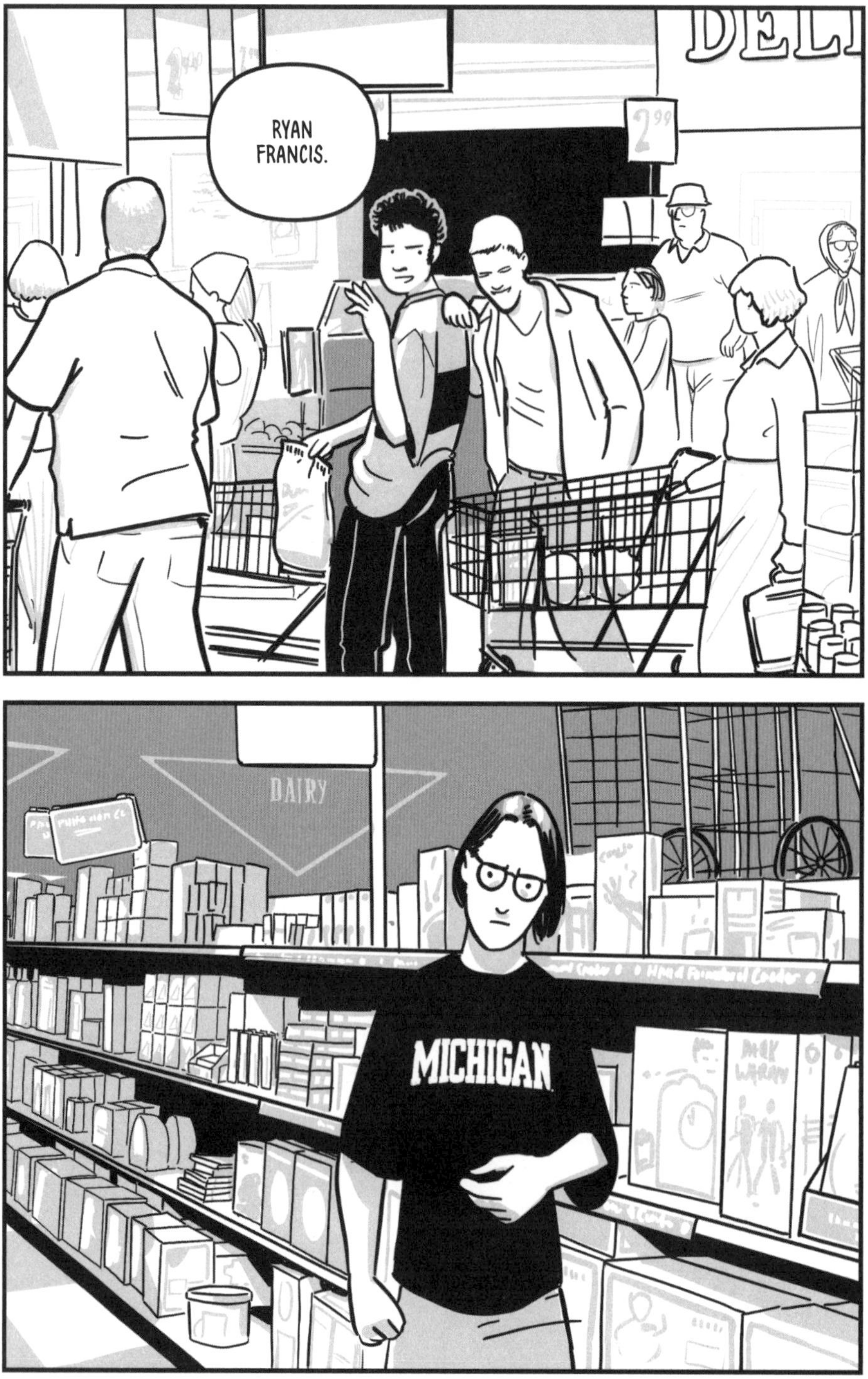
DELI
2.99
RYAN FRANCIS.
DAIRY
MICHIGAN

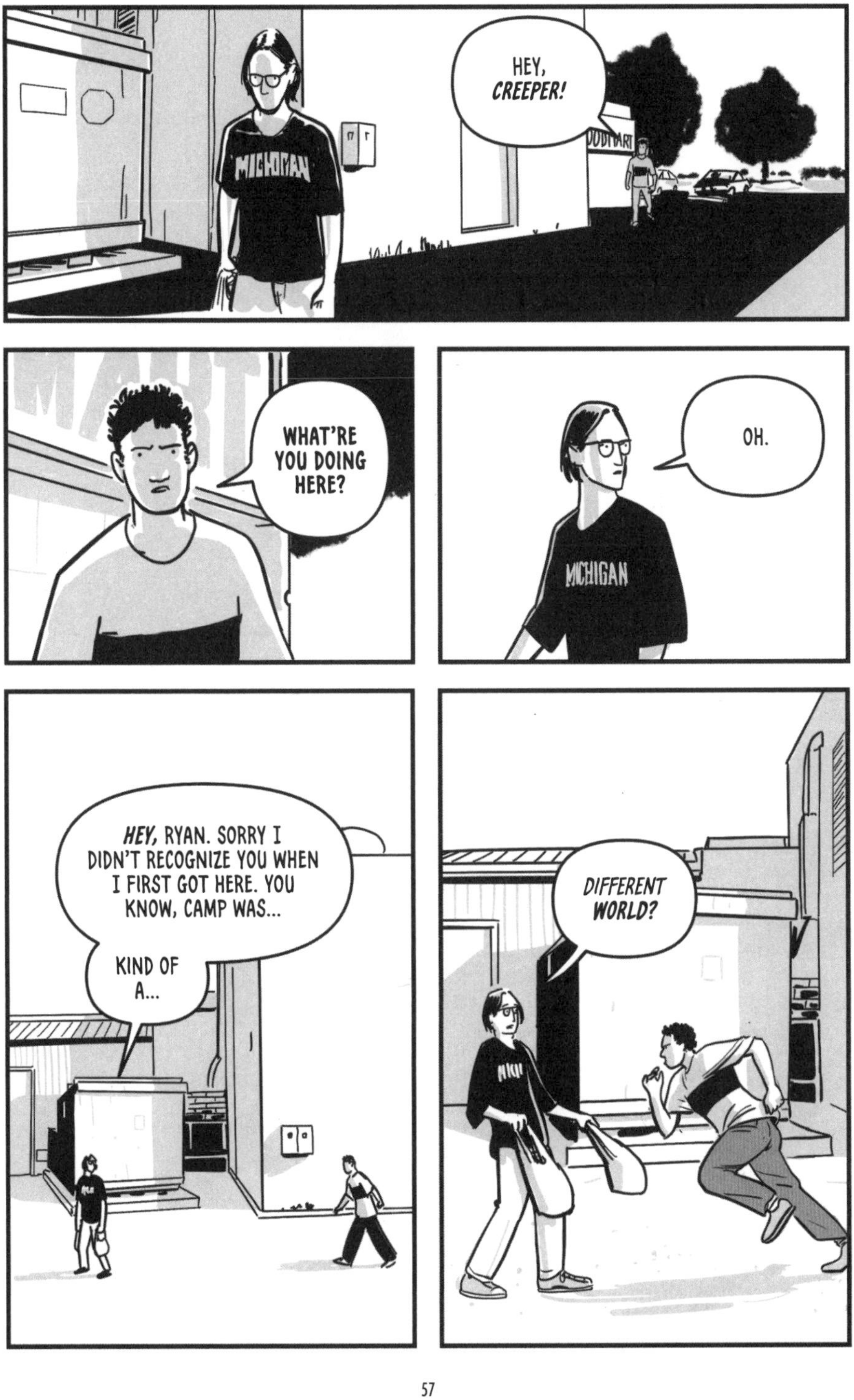
HEY, CREEPER!
MICHIGAN
WHAT'RE YOU DOING HERE?
OH.
MICHIGAN
HEY, RYAN. SORRY I DIDN'T RECOGNIZE YOU WHEN I FIRST GOT HERE. YOU KNOW, CAMP WAS...
KIND OF A...
DIFFERENT WORLD?

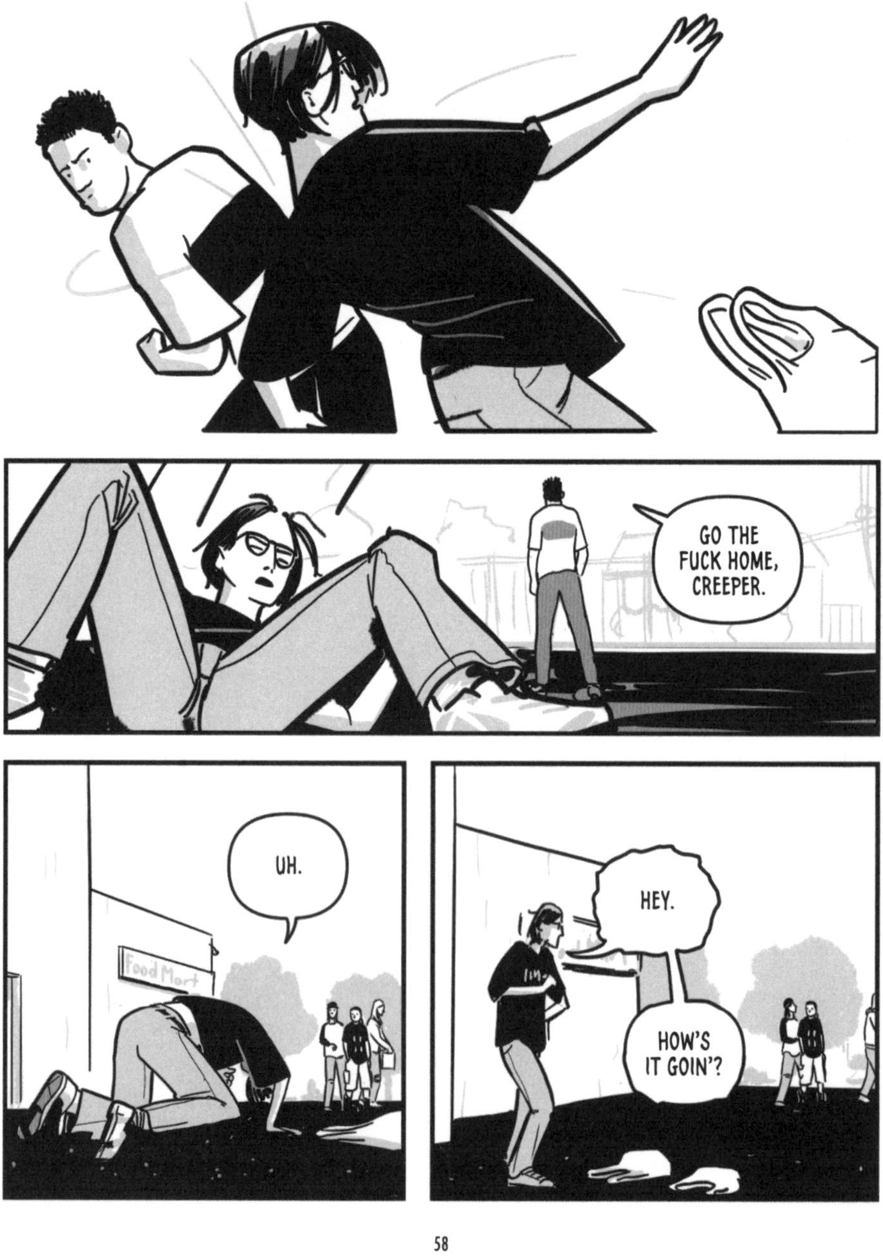
GO THE FUCK HOME, CREEPER.
UH.
Food Mart
HEY.
HOW'S IT GOIN'?

```
    In -> All
Subj -> This Town
----|----|----|----|----|----|----
So...I don't know.
Evidently I'm already screwed in
this new school. I thought I left
the sign that said "Be a dick to
me" in Ann Arbor.

I miss the Denny's on Edgewood Rd.
I miss Larsen Electronics and you
guys.

To heck with these people. I'll
always have this board. Post a
lot about what's going on okay? I'm
just going to live vicariously
through you.


-_-_-_-_-_-_-_-_-_-_-_-_-


"It is a hard daydream to let go
of - that one has friends."
- Kurt Vonnegut Jr.
```

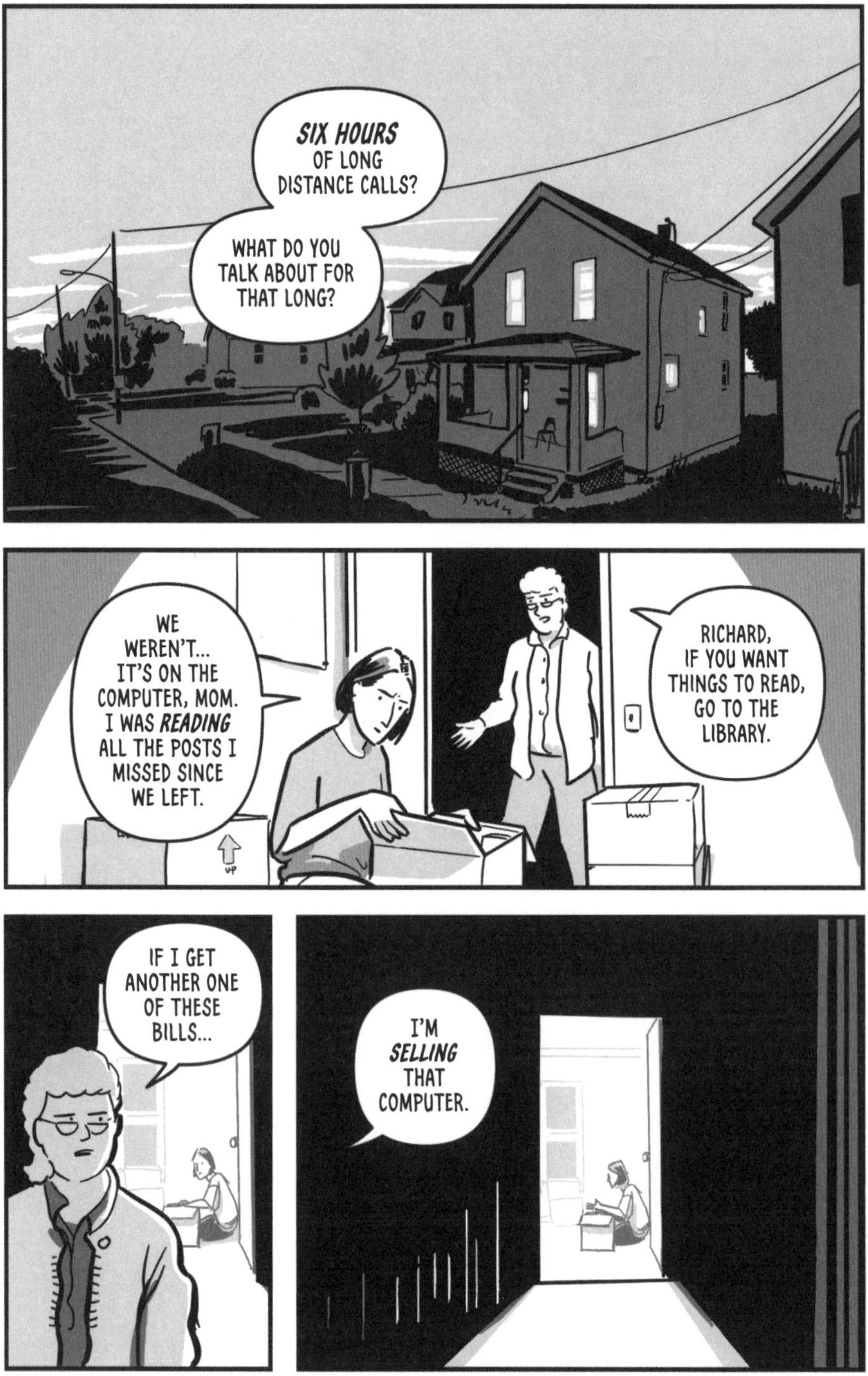
SIX HOURS OF LONG DISTANCE CALLS?
WHAT DO YOU TALK ABOUT FOR THAT LONG?
WE WEREN'T... IT'S ON THE COMPUTER, MOM. I WAS READING ALL THE POSTS I MISSED SINCE WE LEFT.
RICHARD, IF YOU WANT THINGS TO READ, GO TO THE LIBRARY.
UP
IF I GET ANOTHER ONE OF THESE BILLS...
I'M SELLING THAT COMPUTER.

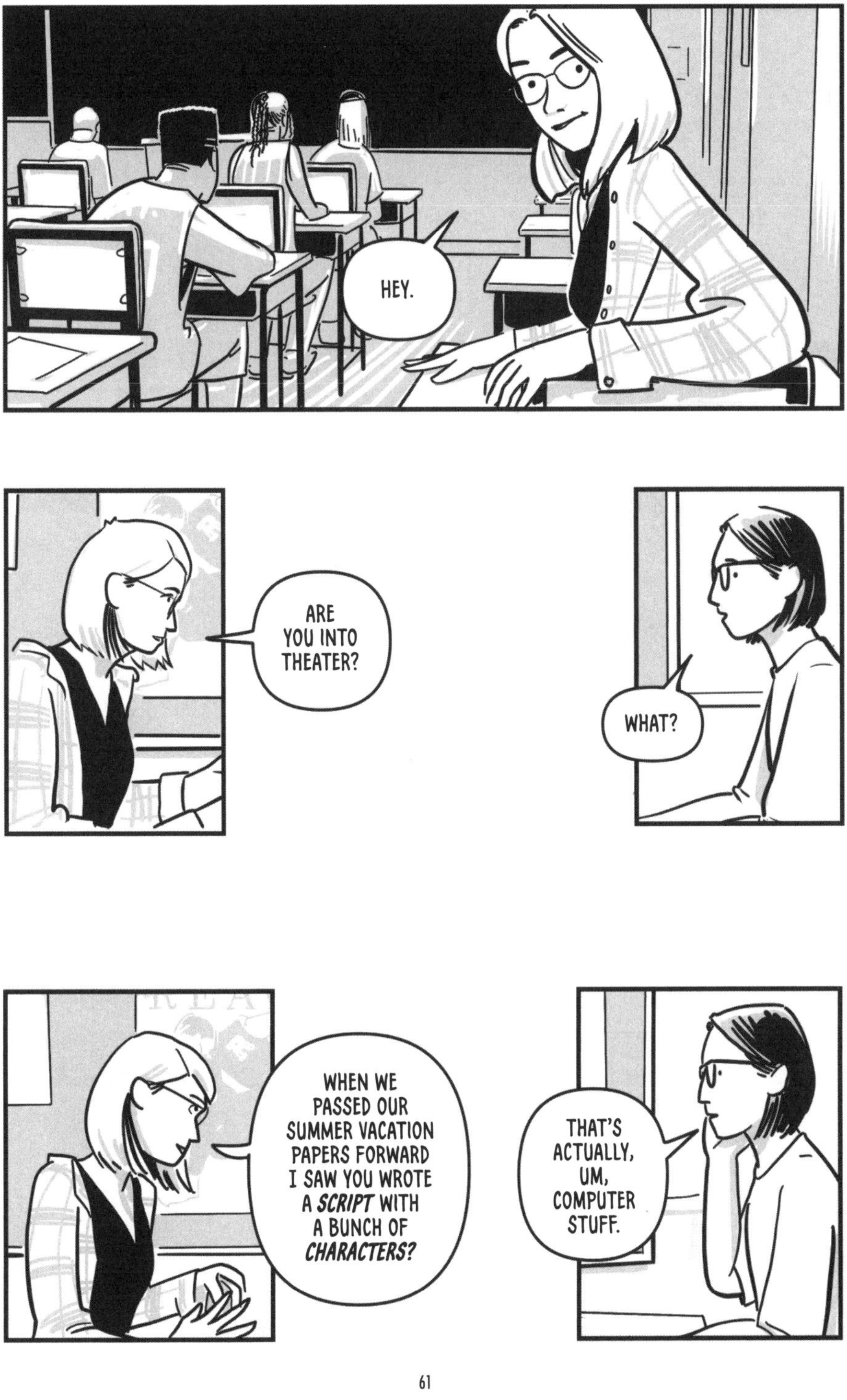
HEY.
ARE YOU INTO THEATER?
WHAT?
WHEN WE PASSED OUR SUMMER VACATION PAPERS FORWARD I SAW YOU WROTE A *SCRIPT* WITH A BUNCH OF *CHARACTERS?*
THAT'S ACTUALLY, UM, COMPUTER STUFF.

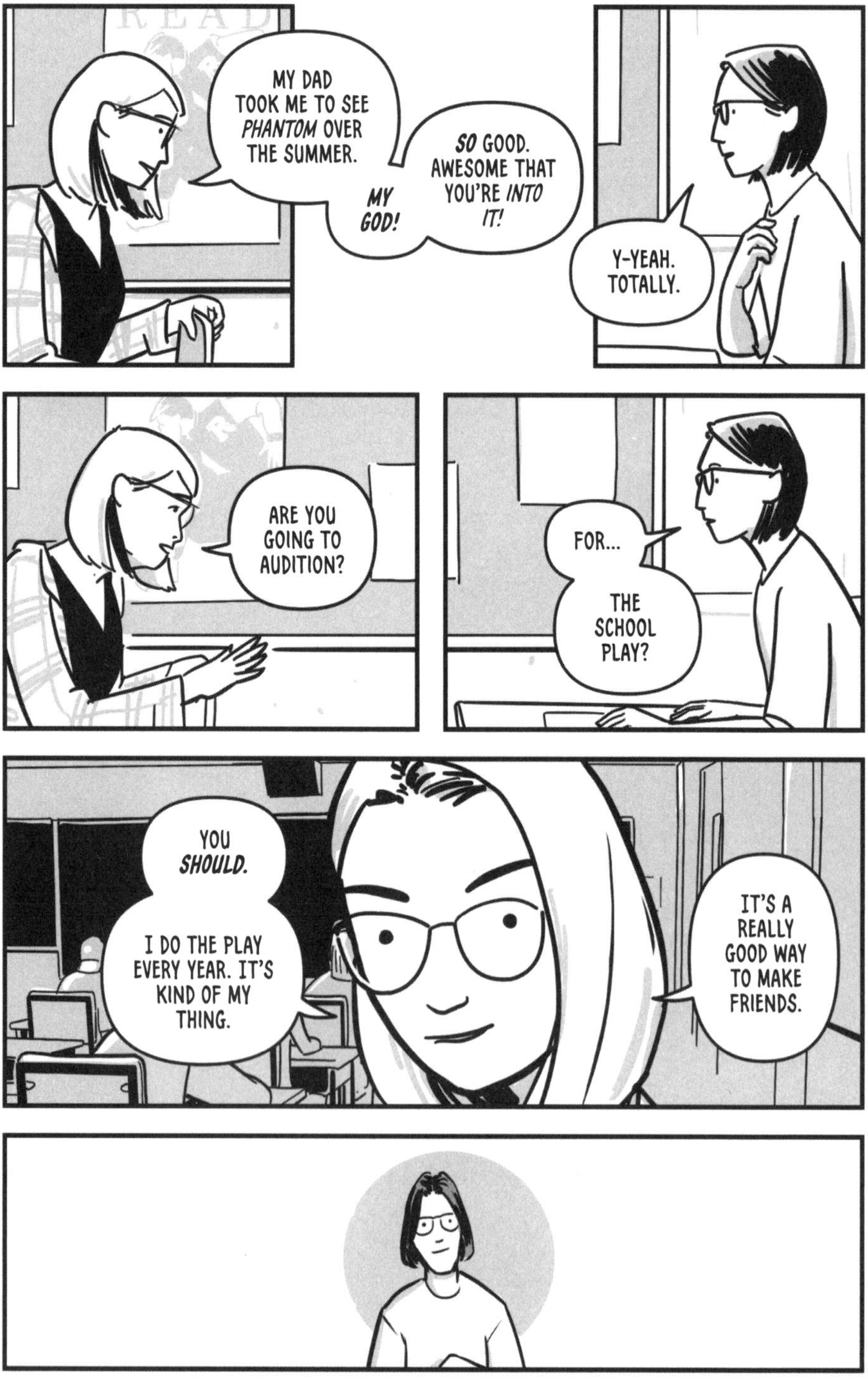
MY DAD TOOK ME TO SEE *PHANTOM* OVER THE SUMMER.
MY GOD!
SO GOOD. AWESOME THAT YOU'RE *INTO IT!*
Y-YEAH. TOTALLY.
ARE YOU GOING TO AUDITION?
FOR...
THE SCHOOL PLAY?
YOU ***SHOULD.***
I DO THE PLAY EVERY YEAR. IT'S KIND OF MY THING.
IT'S A REALLY GOOD WAY TO MAKE FRIENDS.

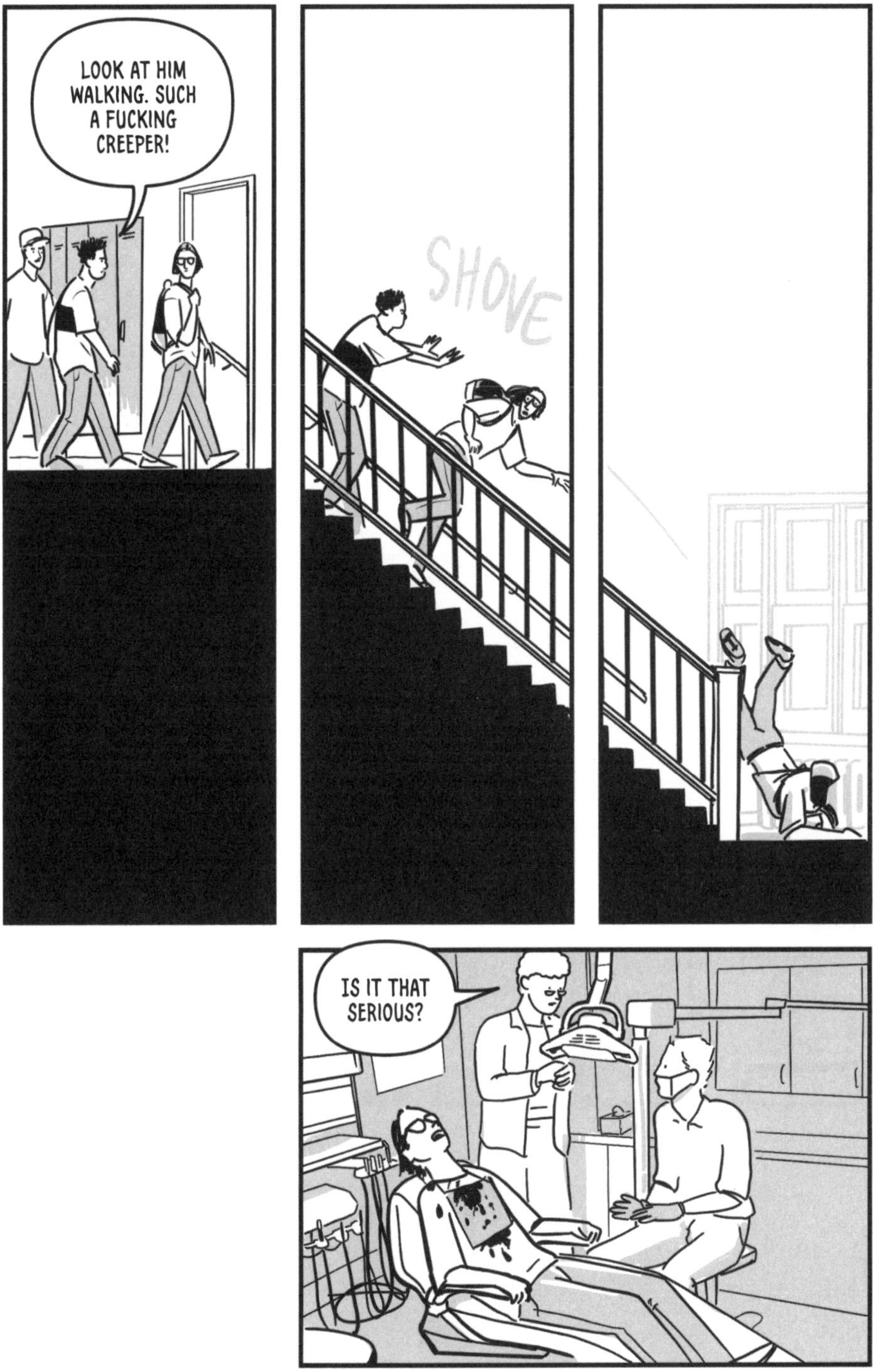

LOOK AT HIM WALKING. SUCH A FUCKING CREEPER!
SHOVE
IS IT THAT SERIOUS?

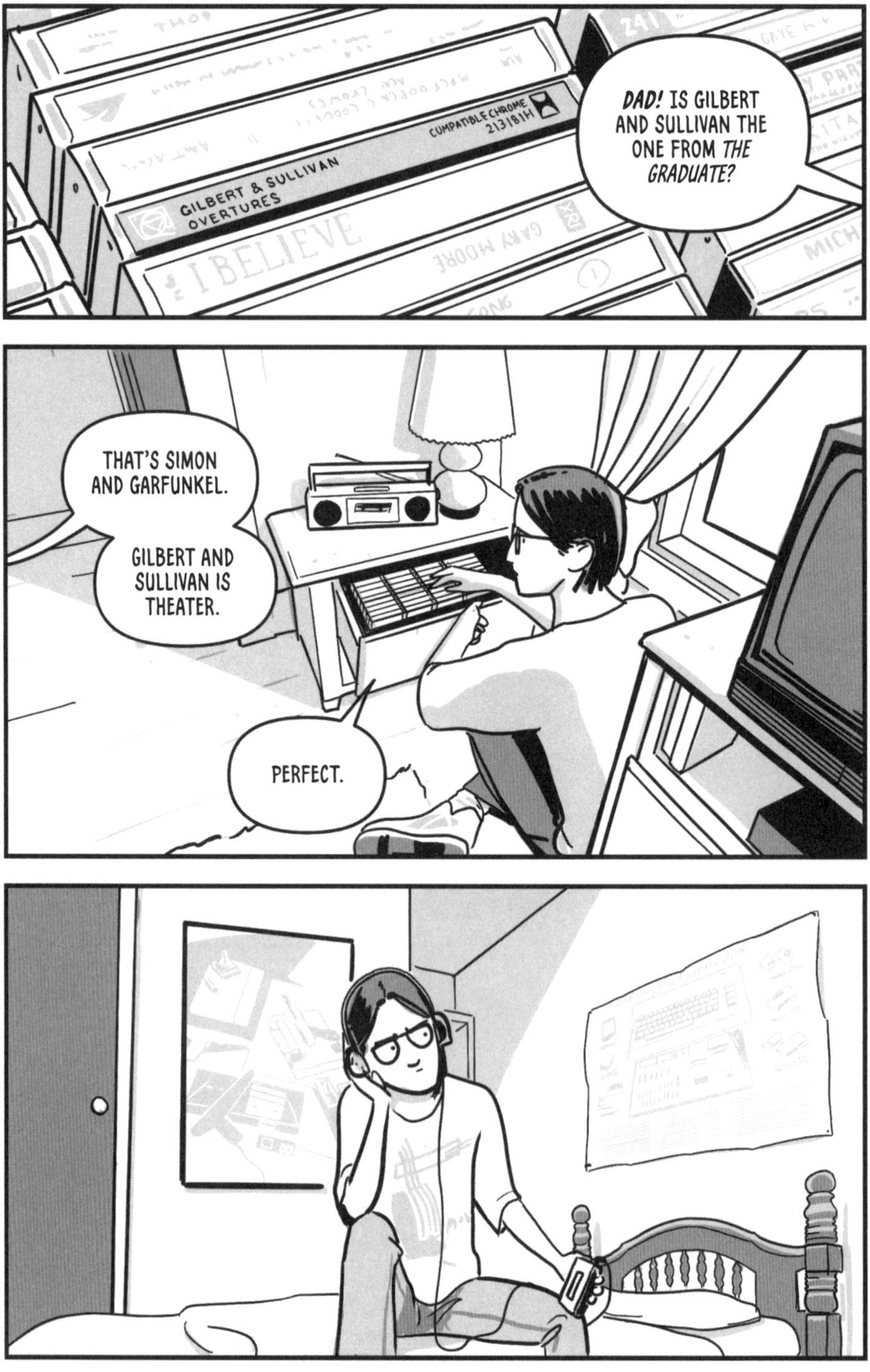
GILBERT & SULLIVAN OVERTURES
I BELIEVE
GARY MOORE
DAD! IS GILBERT AND SULLIVAN THE ONE FROM *THE GRADUATE?*
THAT'S SIMON AND GARFUNKEL.
GILBERT AND SULLIVAN IS THEATER.
PERFECT.

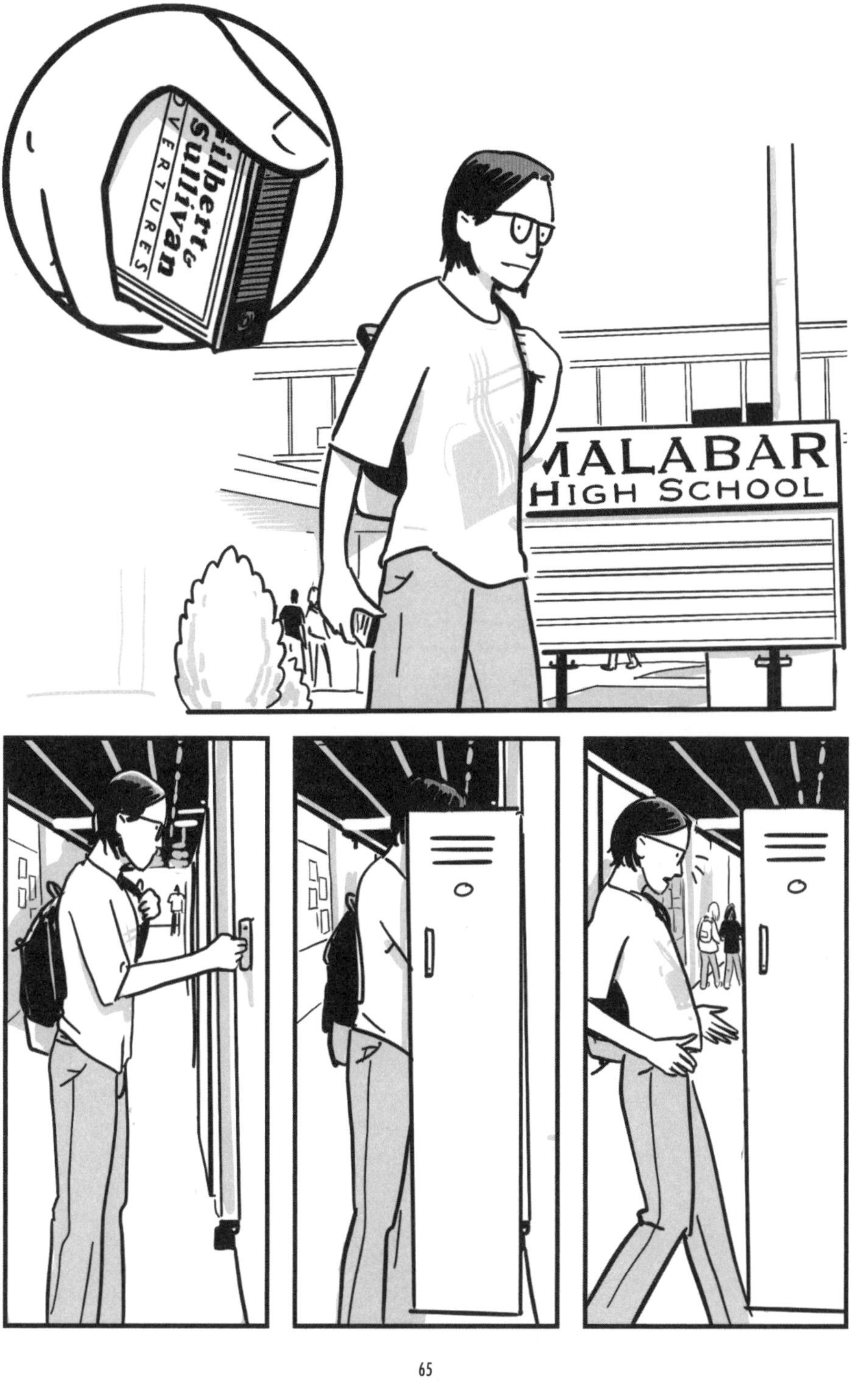
Sullivan
OVERTURES
MALABAR
HIGH SCHOOL

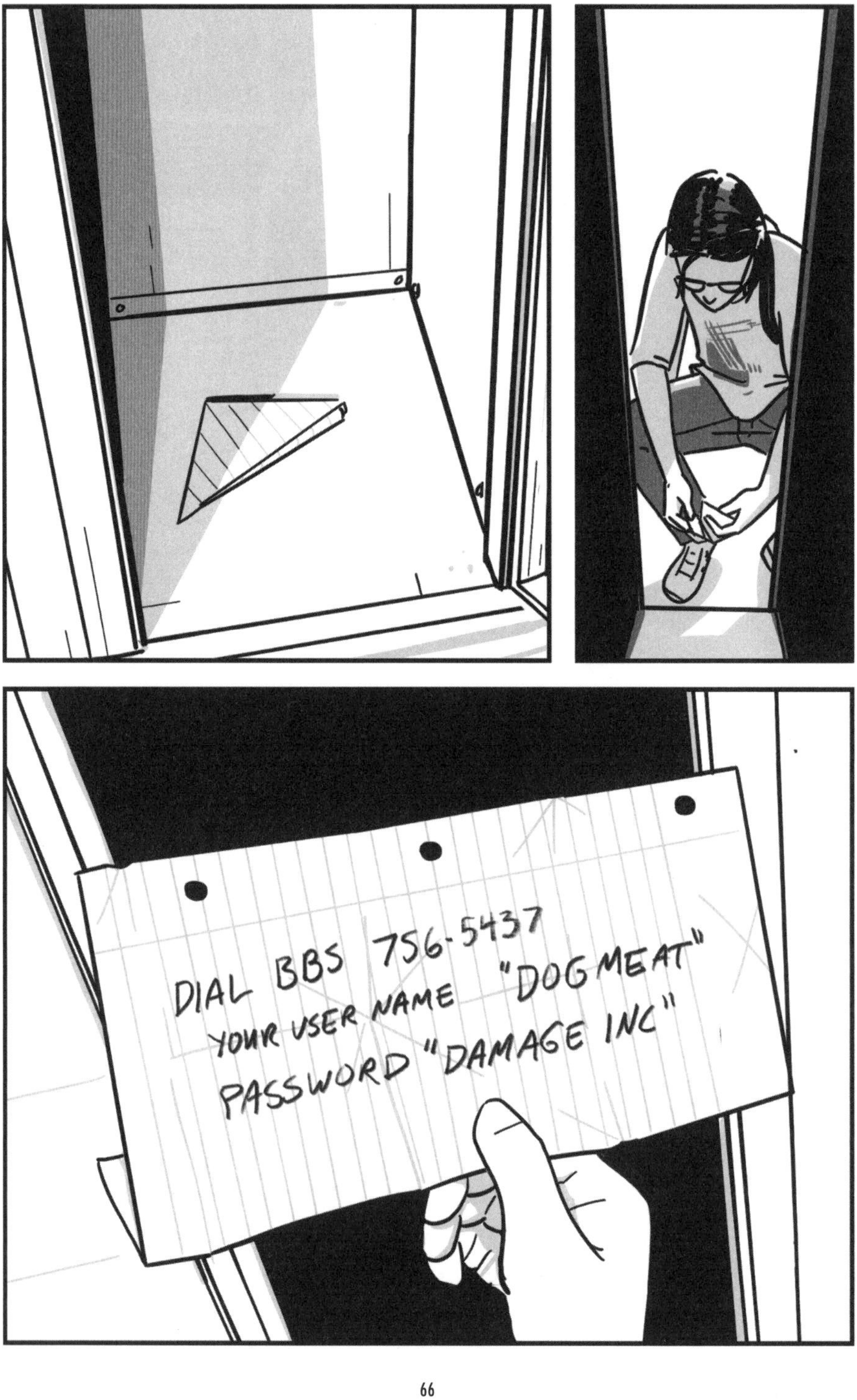
DIAL BBS 756-5437
YOUR USER NAME "DOGMEAT"
PASSWORD "DAMAGE INC"

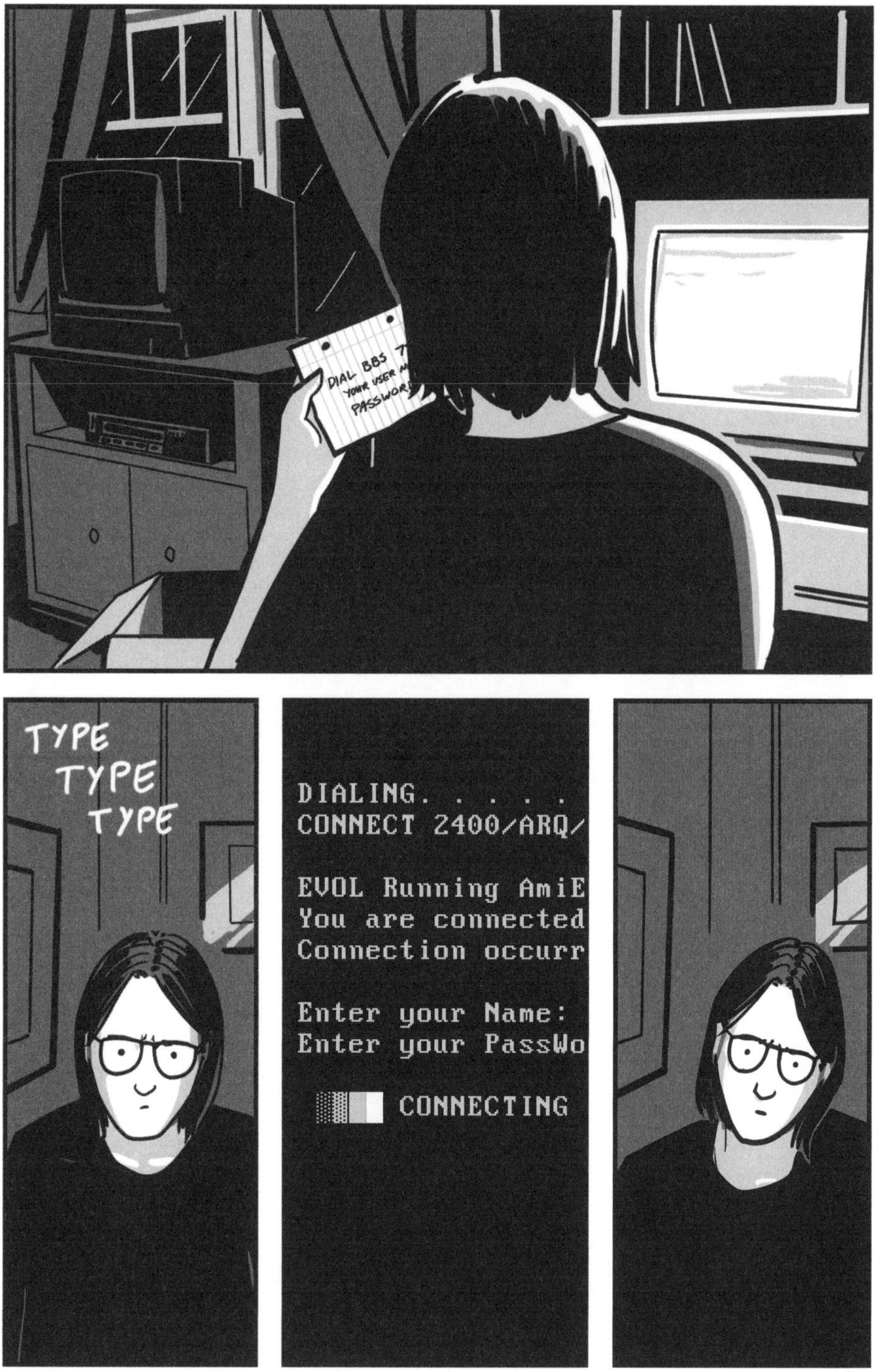
DIAL BBS
TYPE
TYPE
TYPE
DIALING. . . . .
CONNECT 2400/ARQ/
EVOL Running AmiE
You are connected
Connection occurr
Enter your Name:
Enter your PassWo
CONNECTING

```
DIALING. . . . . . . . . . .
CONNECT 2400/ARQ/TEL

EVOL Running AmiExpress 4.12 /X for life
You are connected to Node 2 at 2400 baud
Connection occurred at 11:13:21

Enter your Name: dogmeat
Enter your PassWord: damageinc

     ▓▓██  CONNECTING
```

```
▓██  CONNECTED TO EVOL BBS  ▓▓██  ▓▓
     NO GUESTS/NO LAMERS  ▓▓██  ▓▓
     NO GODS/NO MASTERS  ▓▓██  ▓▓        B B S

Welcome "dogmeat"
```

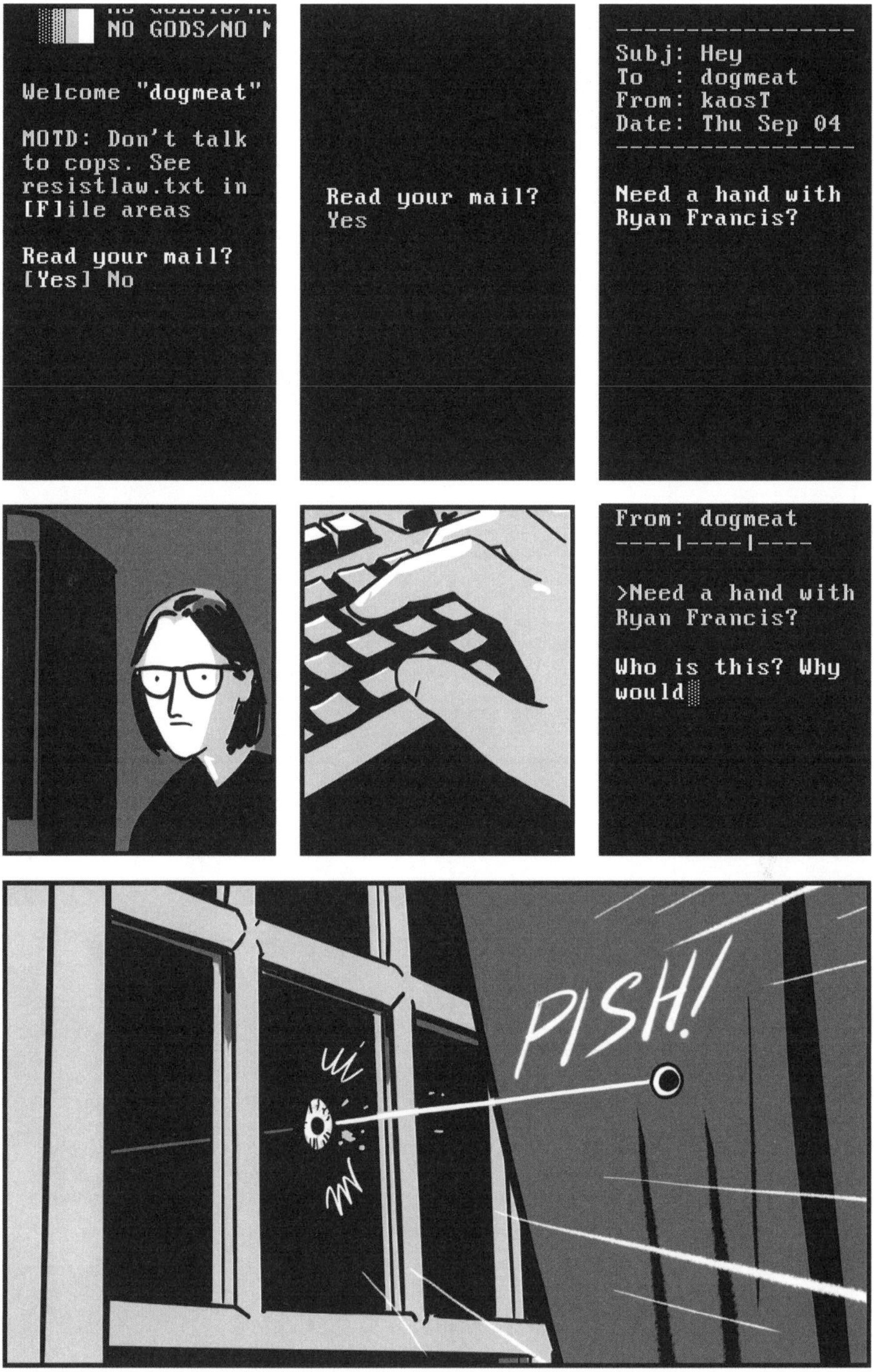
NO GODS/NO
Welcome "dogmeat"
MOTD: Don't talk to cops. See resistlaw.txt in [F]ile areas
Read your mail? [Yes] No
Read your mail? Yes
Subj: Hey
To : dogmeat
From: kaosT
Date: Thu Sep 04
Need a hand with Ryan Francis?
From: dogmeat
>Need a hand with Ryan Francis?
Who is this? Why would
PISH!

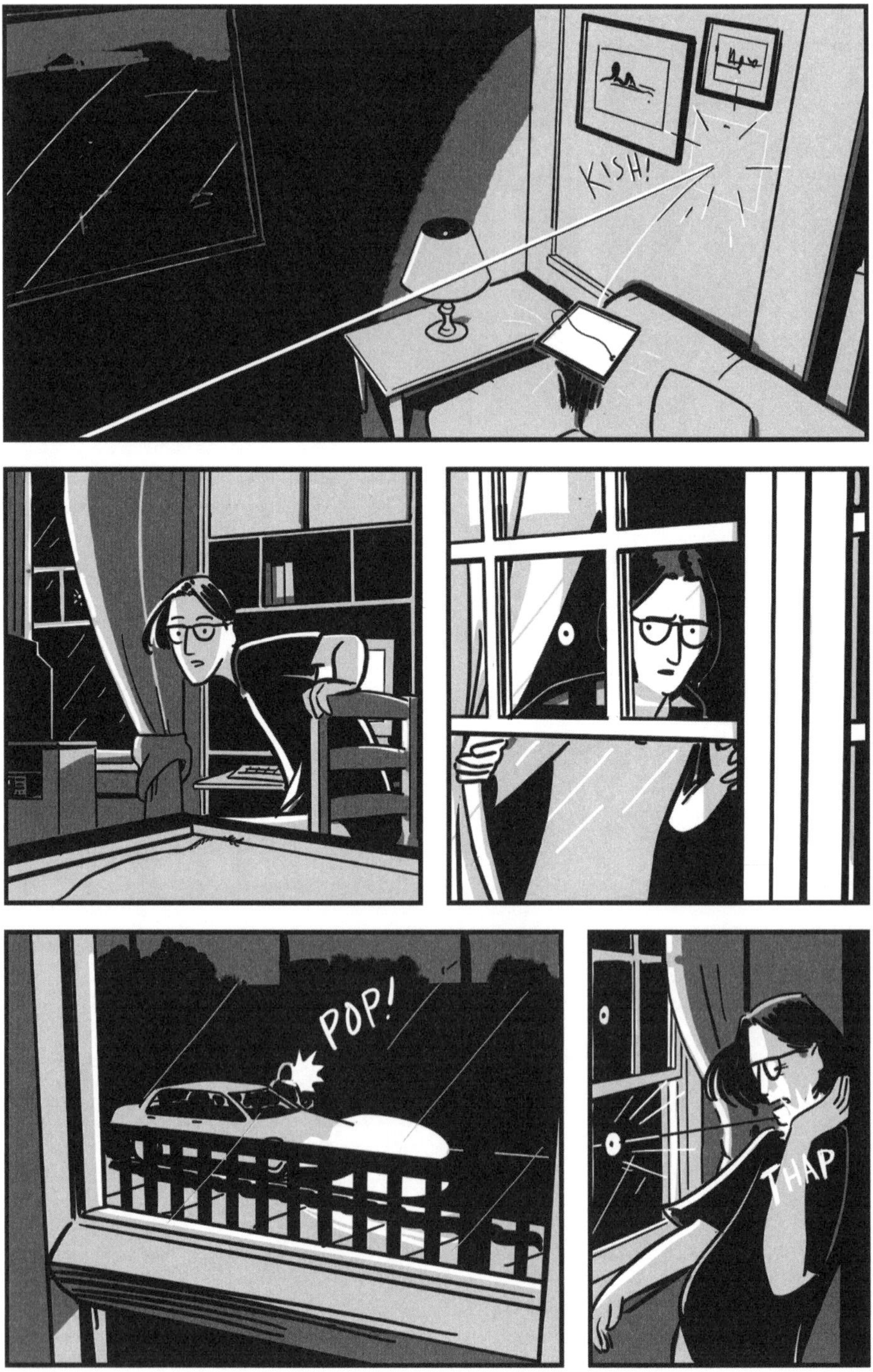
KISH!
POP!
THAP

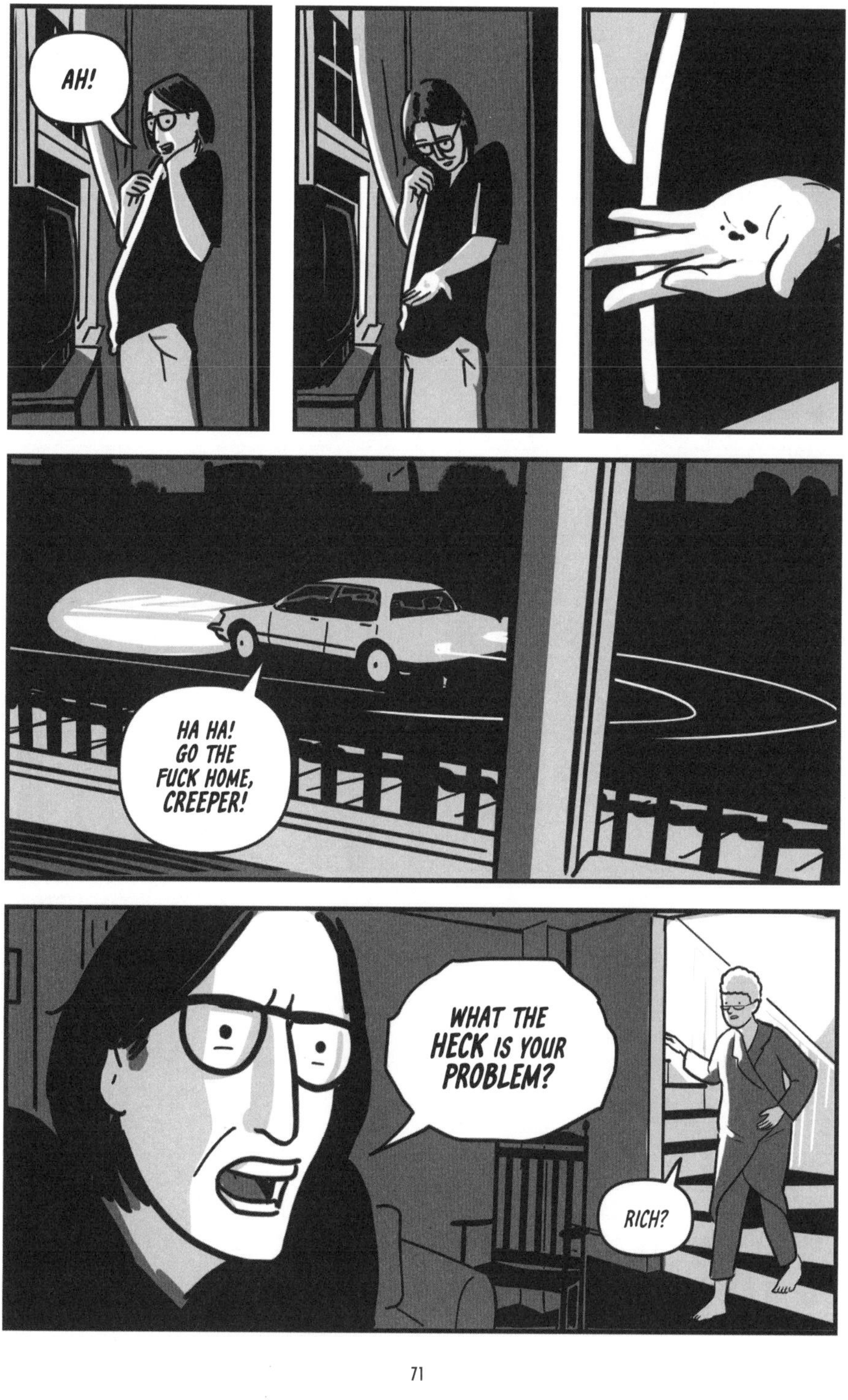
AH!
HA HA! GO THE FUCK HOME, CREEPER!
WHAT THE HECK IS YOUR PROBLEM?
RICH?

```
Subj: Re: Hey
To  : kaosT
From: dogmeat
----I----I----I----I----
>Need a hand with
Ryan Francis?

Whatever you can do.█
```

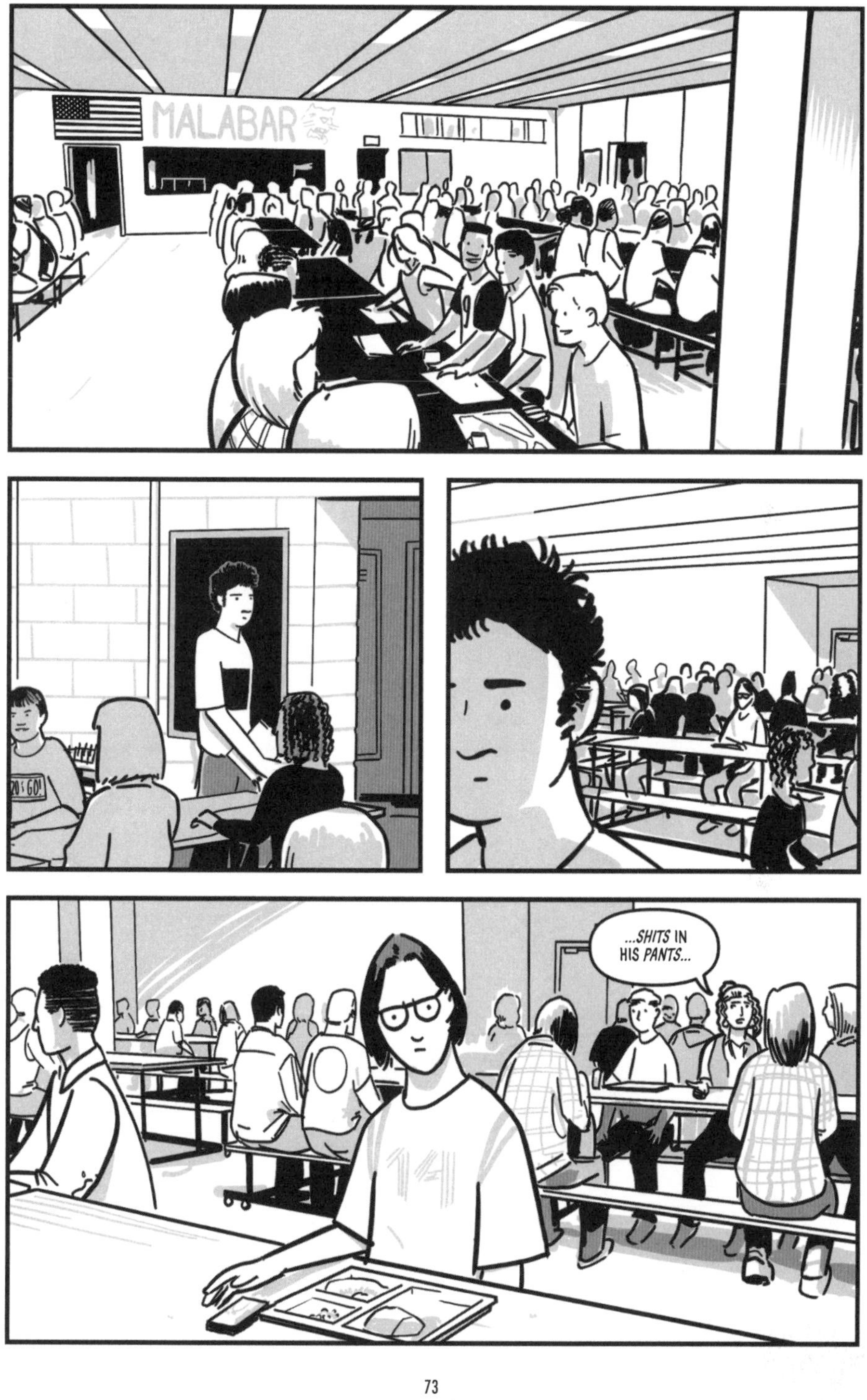
MALABAR
20's GO!
...SHITS IN HIS PANTS...

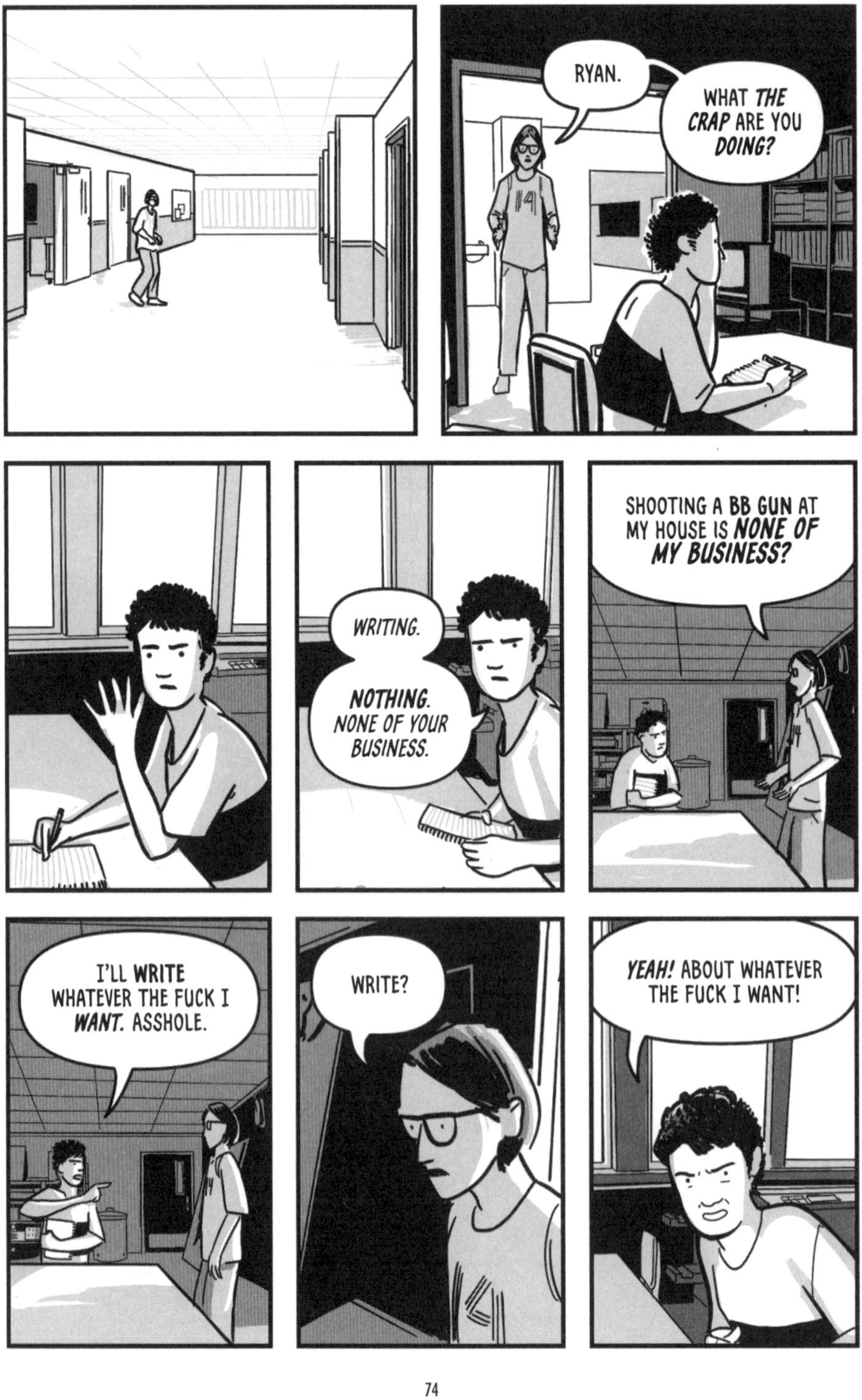
RYAN.
WHAT *THE CRAP* ARE YOU *DOING?*
WRITING.
NOTHING. *NONE OF YOUR BUSINESS.*
SHOOTING A **BB GUN** AT MY HOUSE IS ***NONE OF MY BUSINESS?***
I'LL **WRITE** WHATEVER THE FUCK I ***WANT.*** ASSHOLE.
WRITE?
YEAH! ABOUT WHATEVER THE FUCK I WANT!

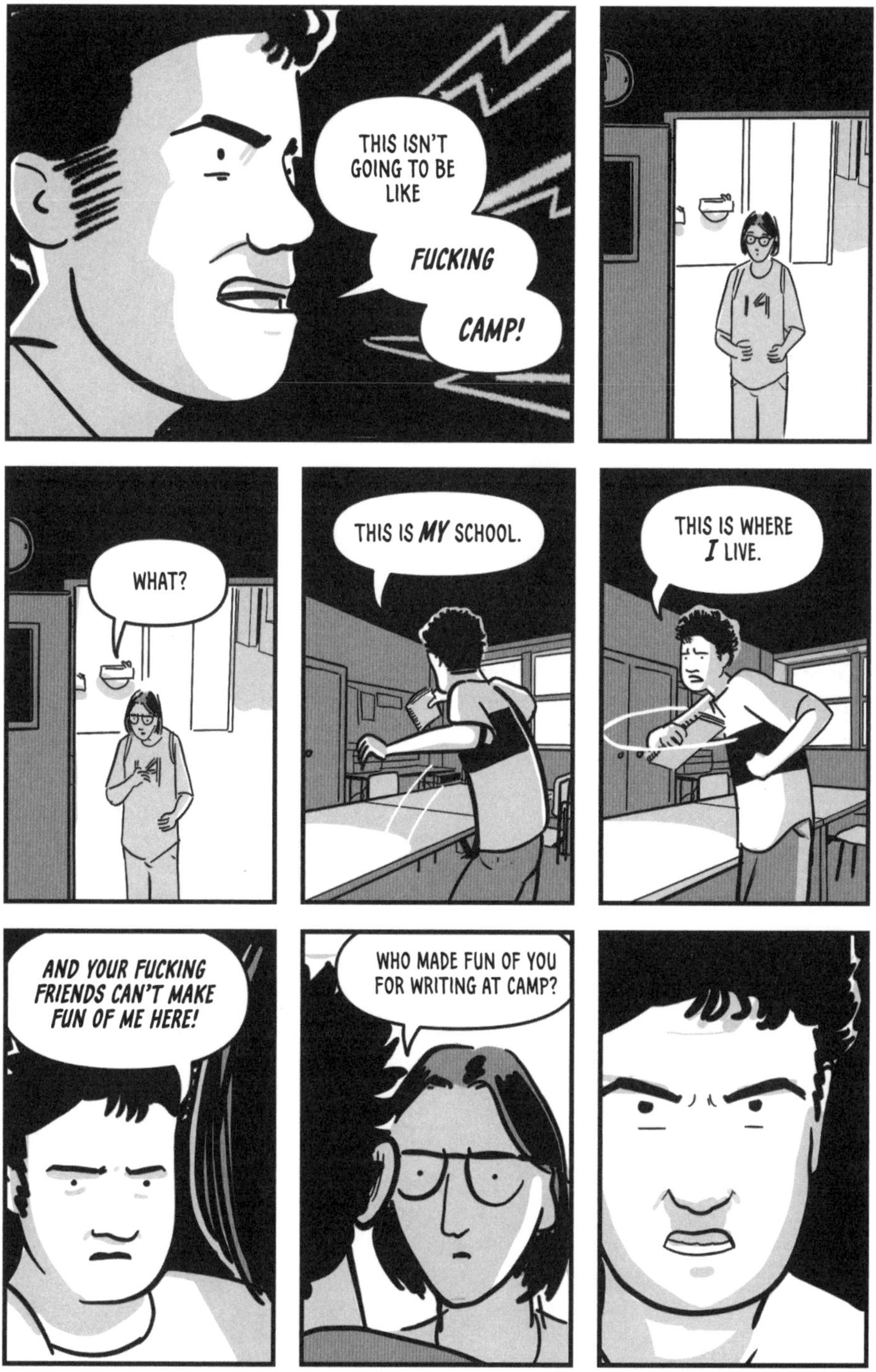
THIS ISN'T GOING TO BE LIKE
FUCKING
CAMP!
WHAT?
THIS IS MY SCHOOL.
THIS IS WHERE I LIVE.
AND YOUR FUCKING FRIENDS CAN'T MAKE FUN OF ME HERE!
WHO MADE FUN OF YOU FOR WRITING AT CAMP?

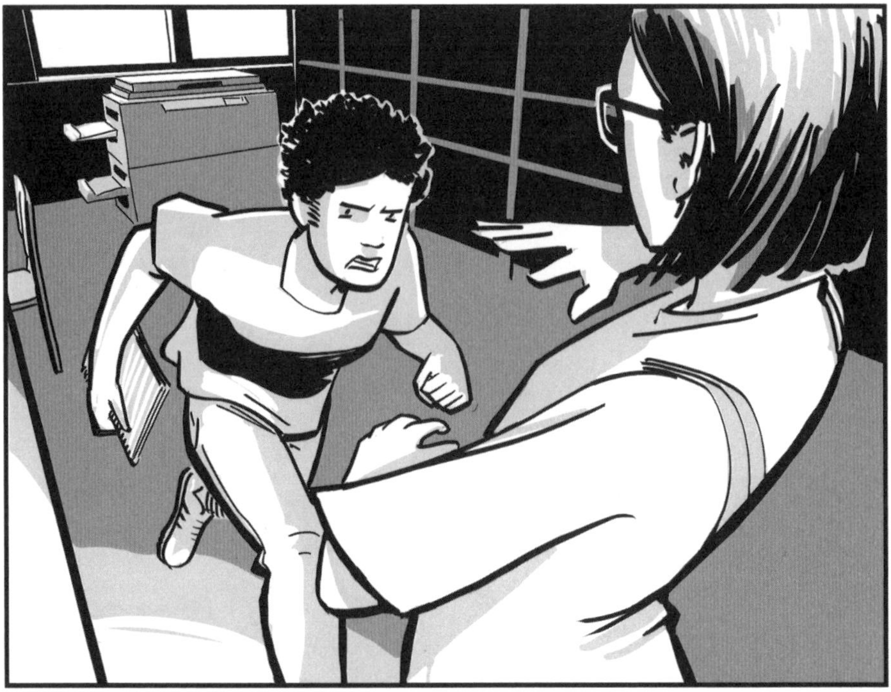

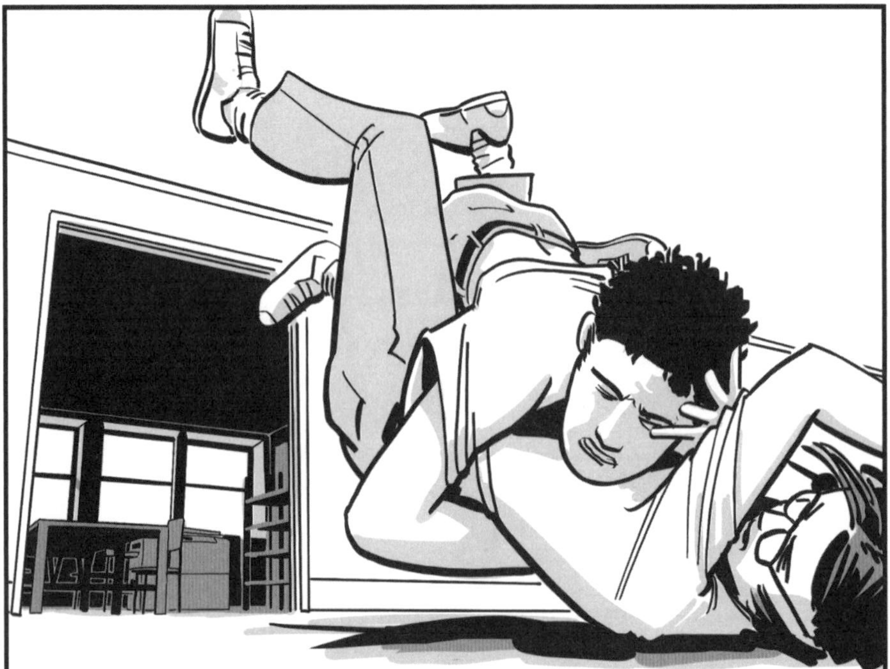

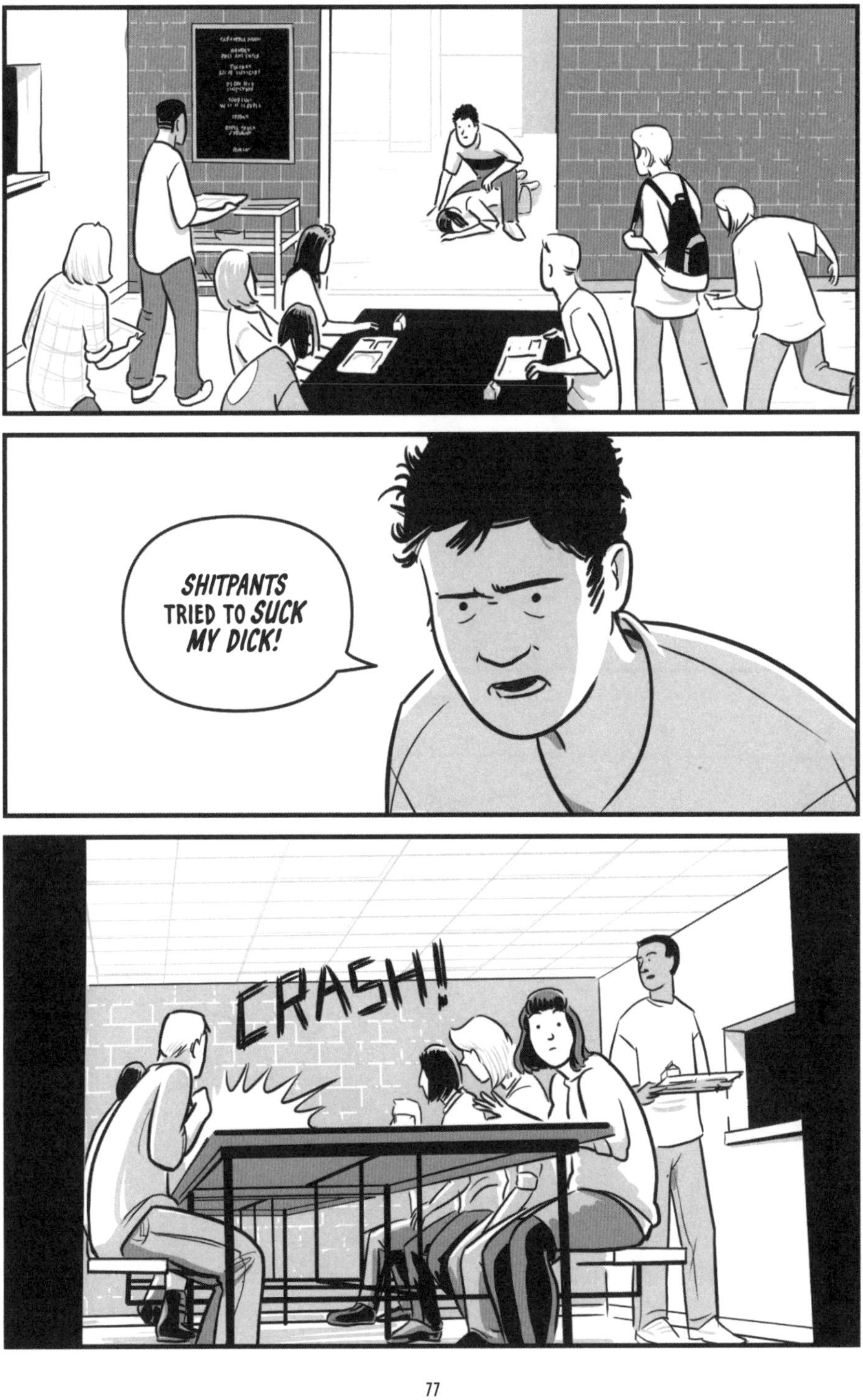
SHITPANTS TRIED TO SUCK MY DICK!
CRASH!

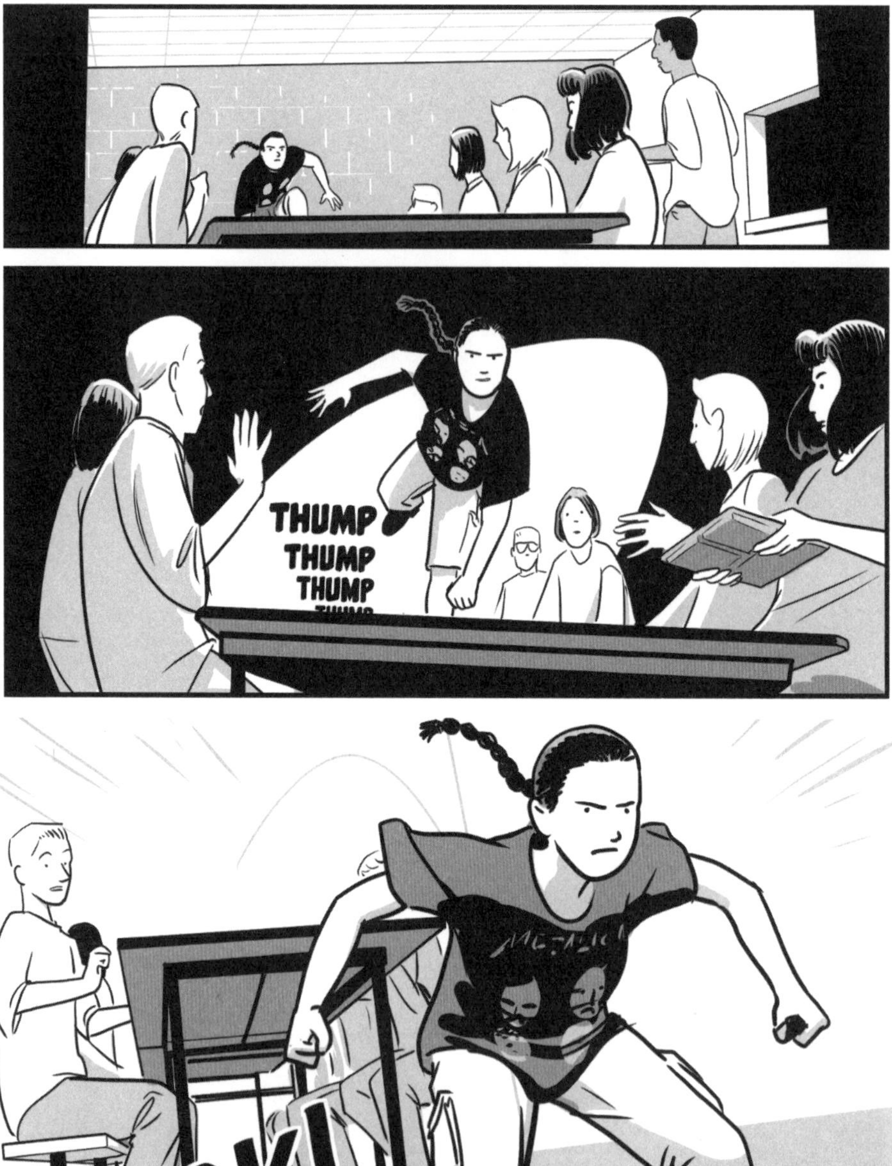
THUMP
THUMP
THUMP
KACK!

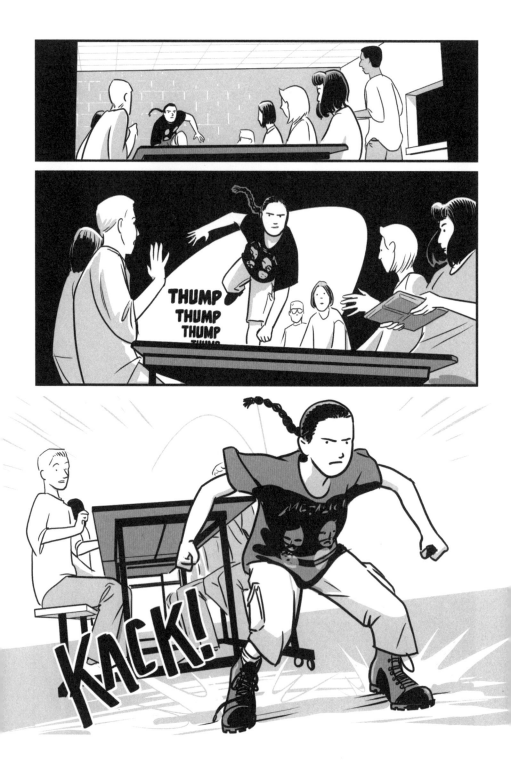

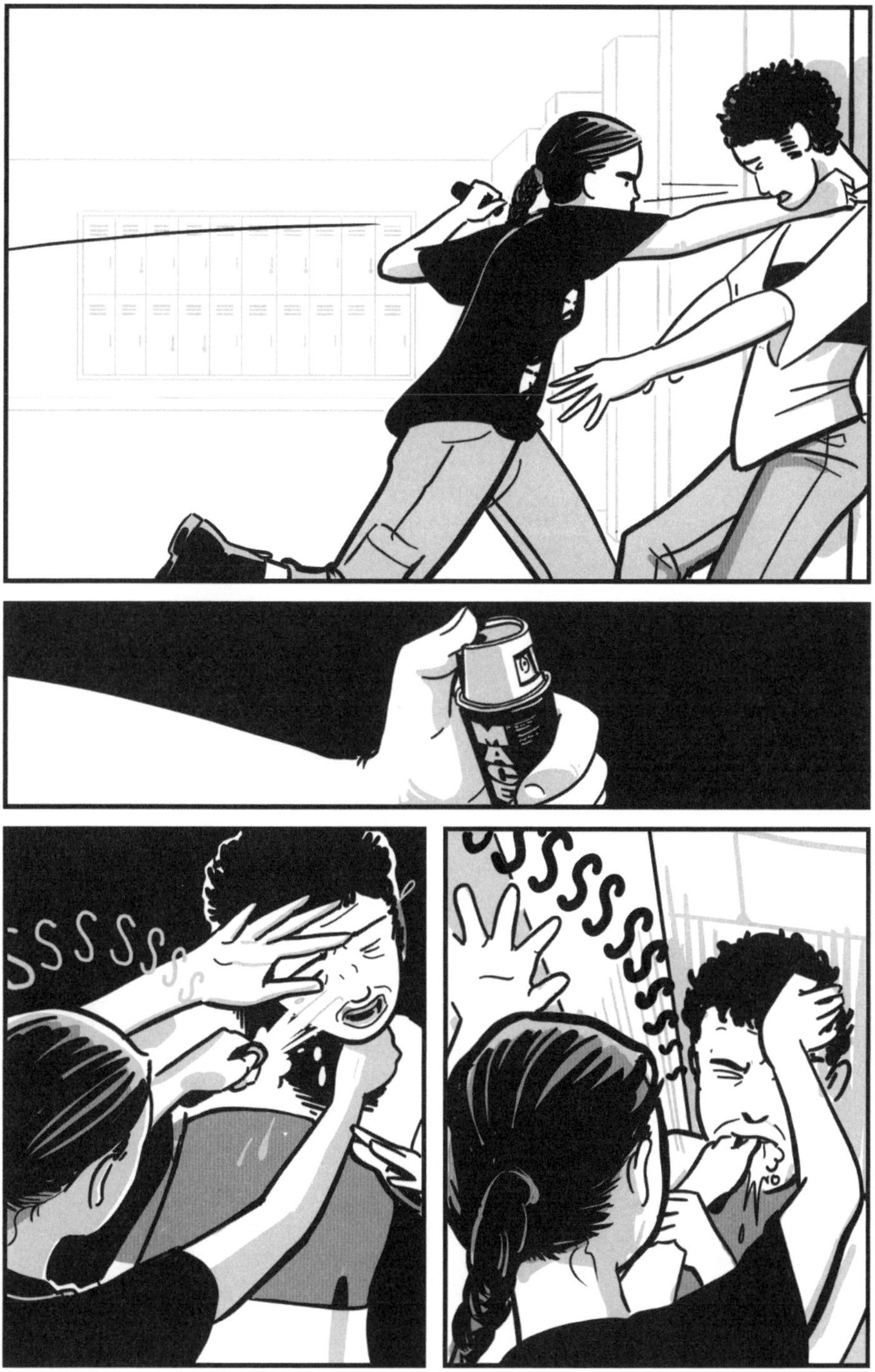
MACE
NO

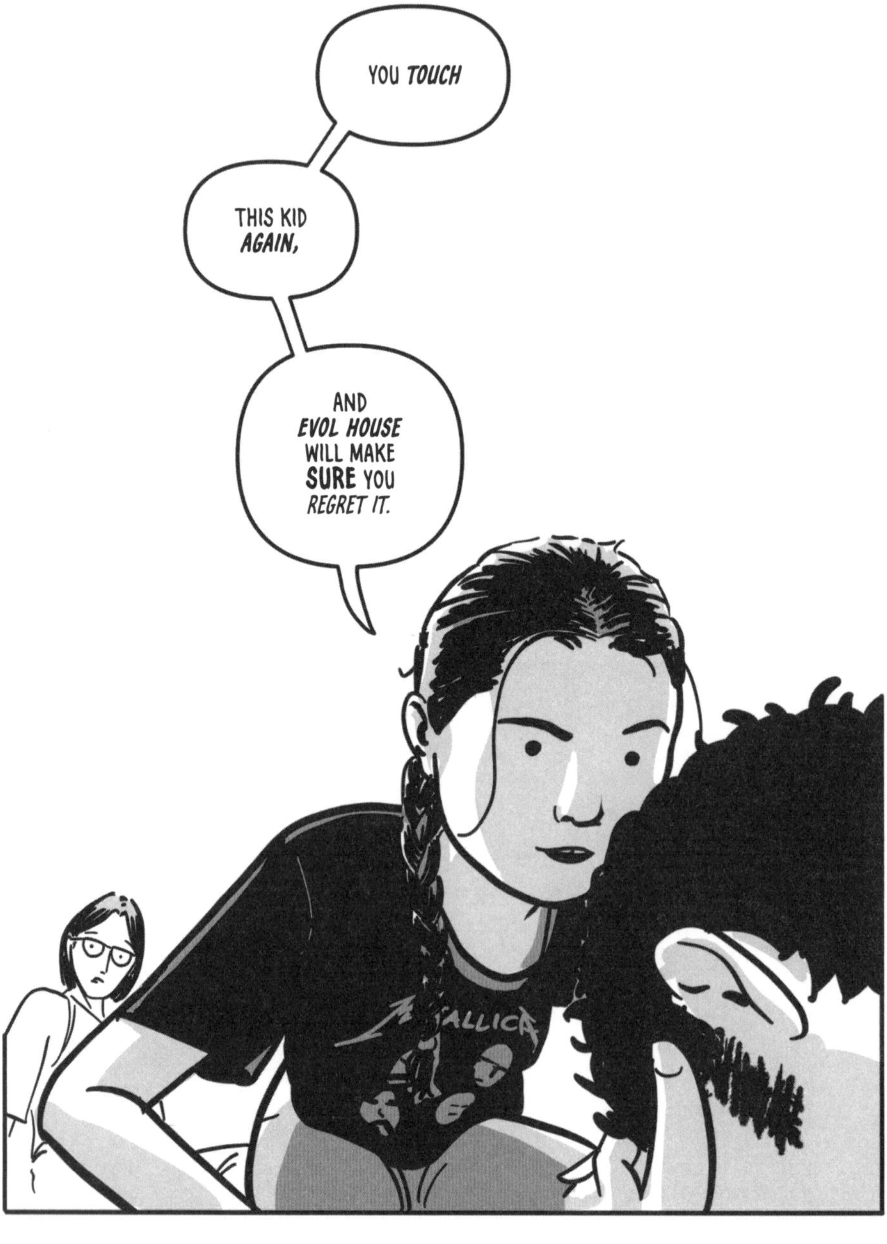
YOU *TOUCH*
THIS KID ***AGAIN,***
AND ***EVOL HOUSE*** WILL MAKE **SURE** YOU *REGRET IT.*
ALLICA

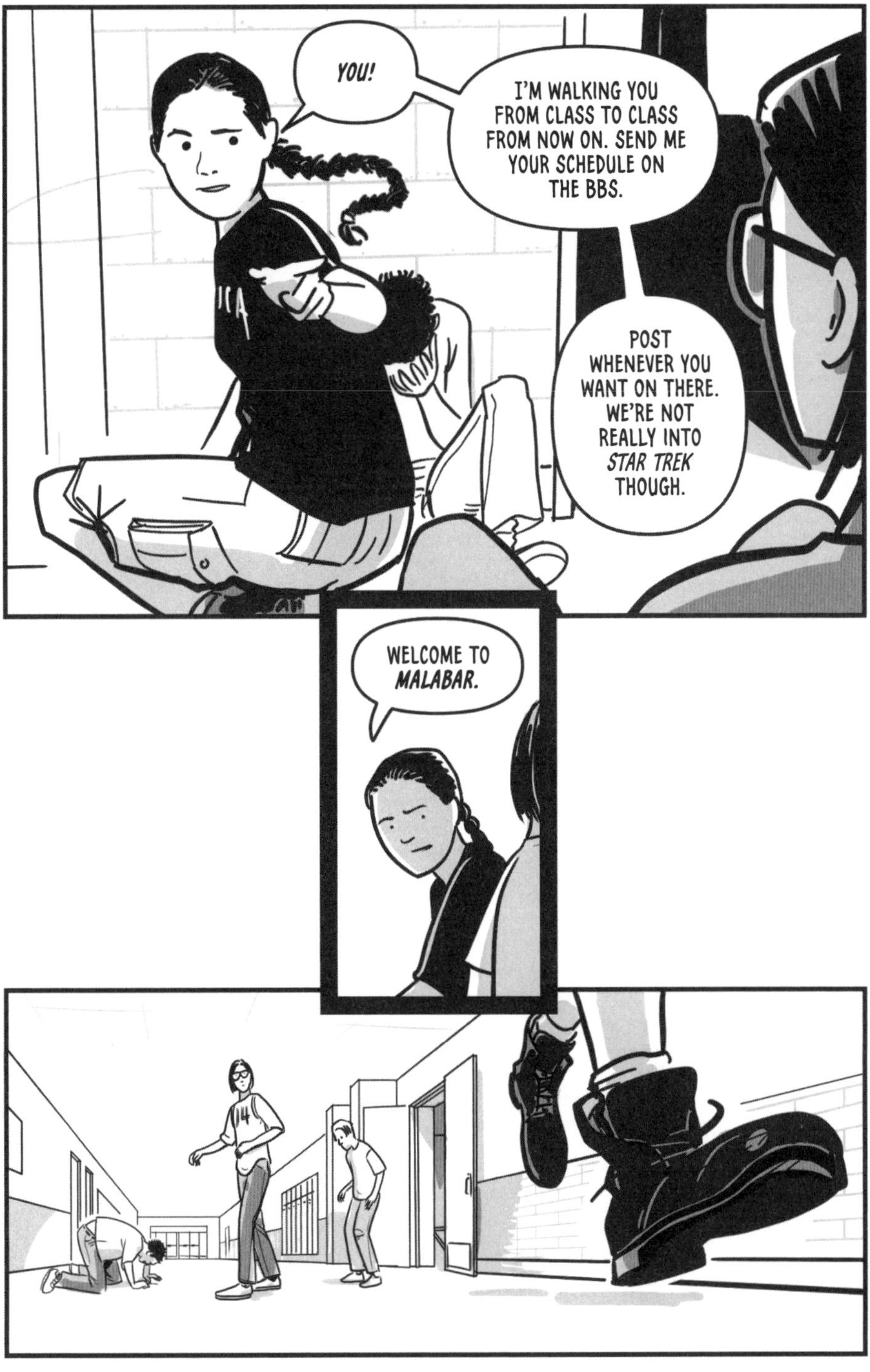
YOU!
I'M WALKING YOU FROM CLASS TO CLASS FROM NOW ON. SEND ME YOUR SCHEDULE ON THE BBS.
POST WHENEVER YOU WANT ON THERE. WE'RE NOT REALLY INTO *STAR TREK* THOUGH.
WELCOME TO *MALABAR.*

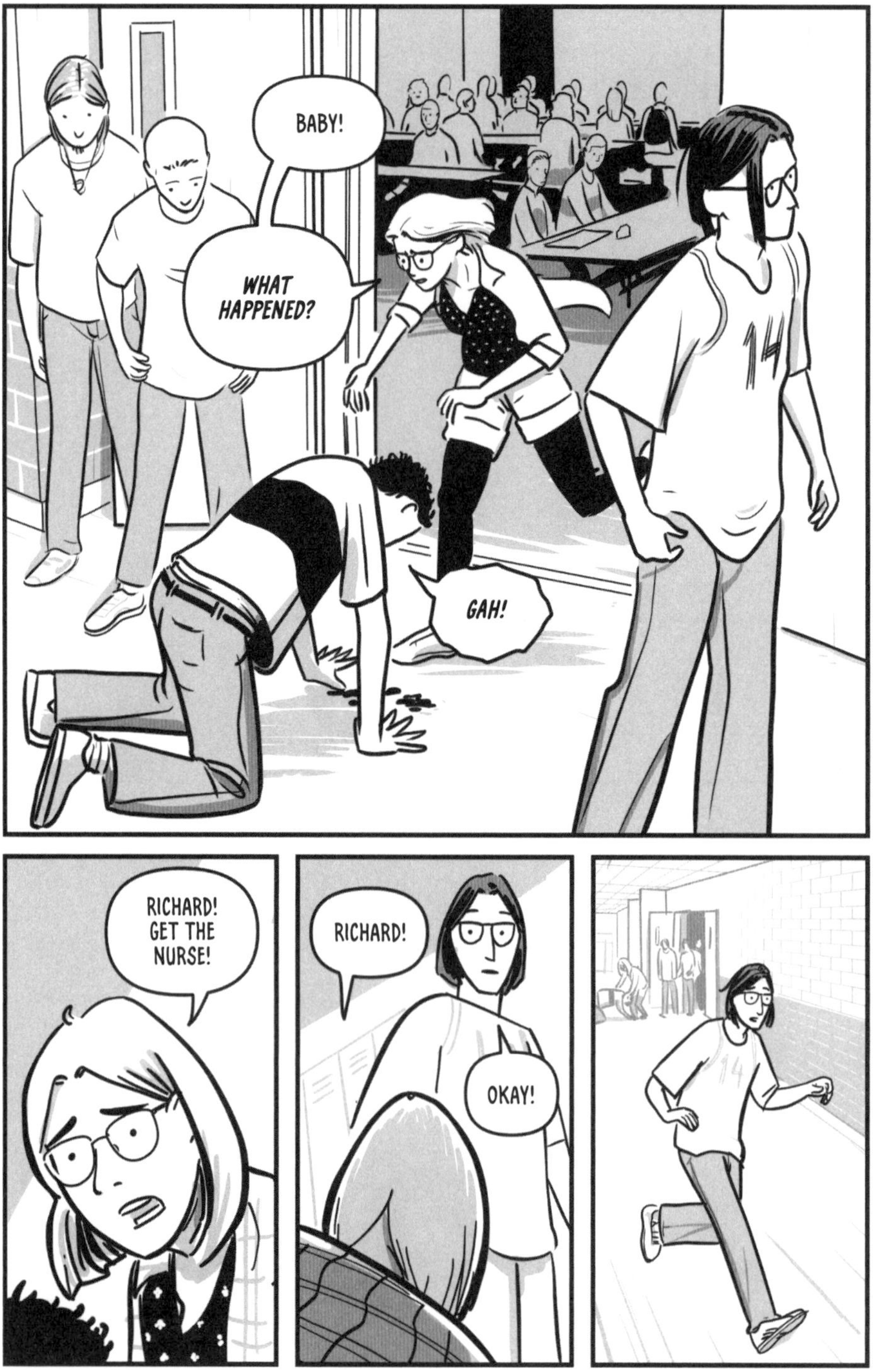
BABY!
WHAT HAPPENED?
GAH!
RICHARD! GET THE NURSE!
RICHARD!
OKAY!

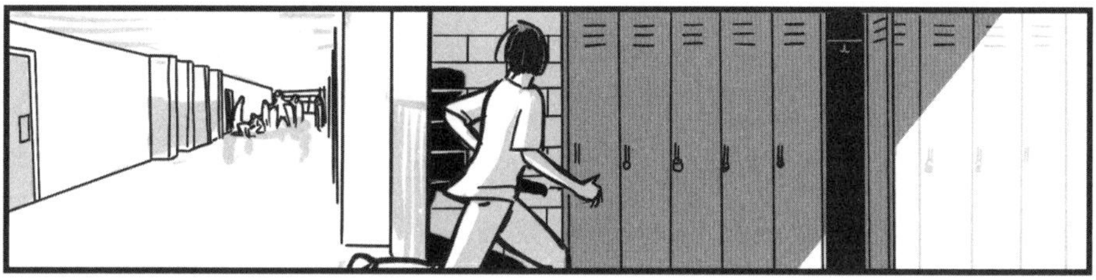

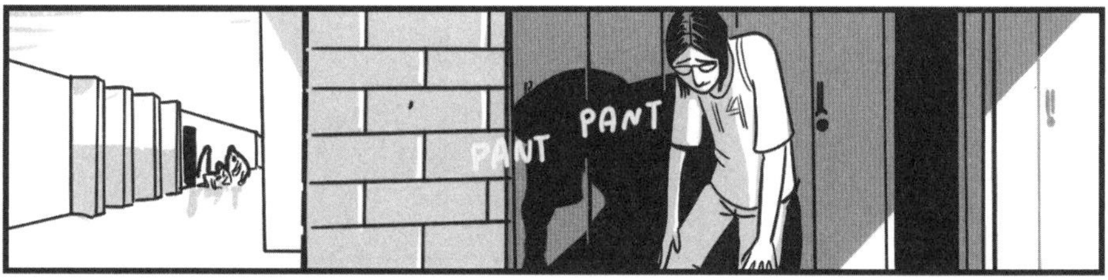
PANT PANT

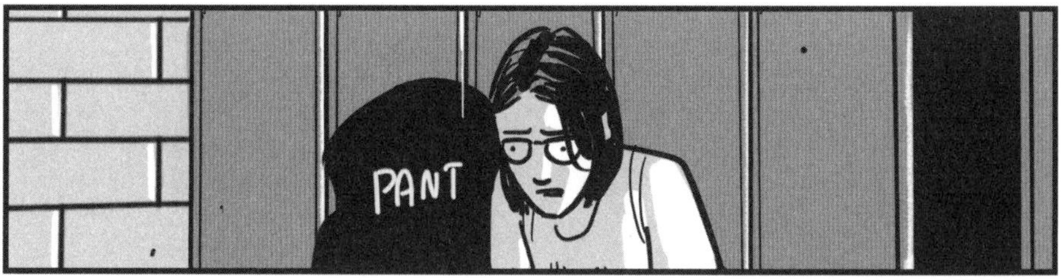
PANT

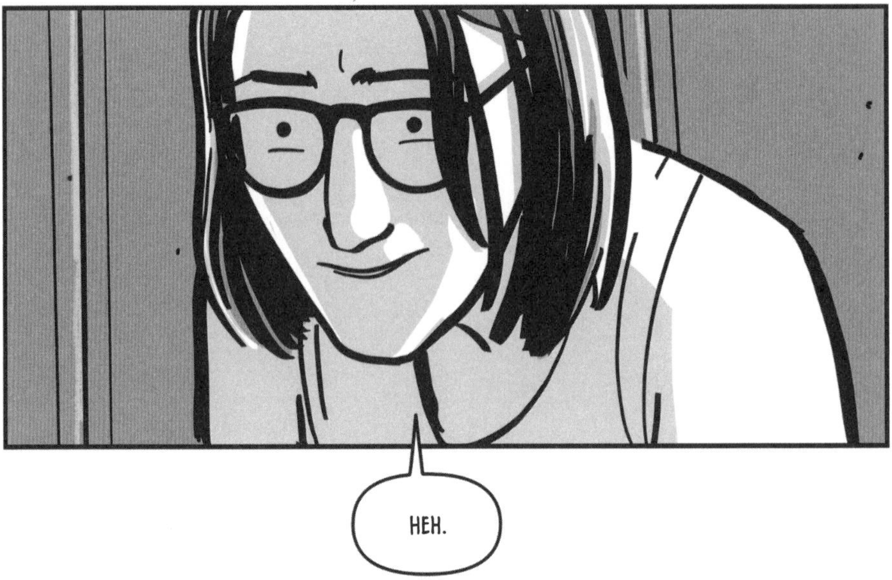
HEH.

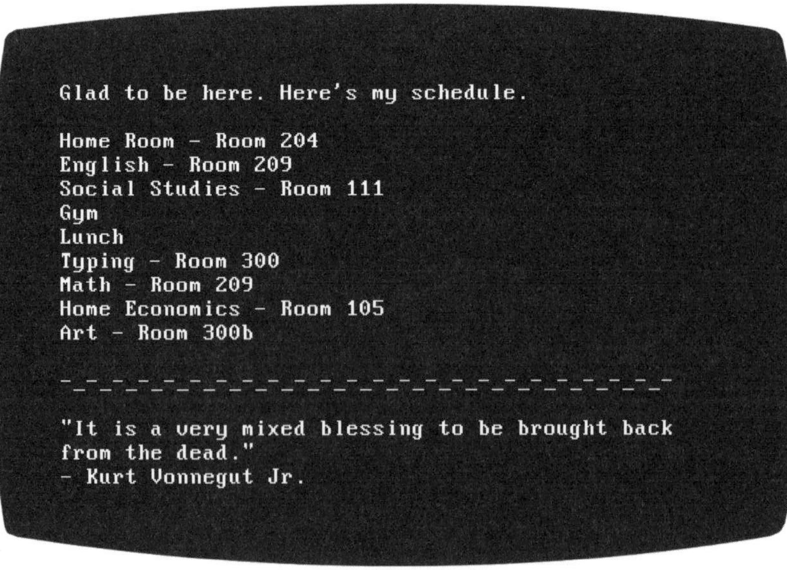
Glad to be here. Here's my schedule.
Home Room - Room 204
English - Room 209
Social Studies - Room 111
Gym
Lunch
Typing - Room 300
Math - Room 209
Home Economics - Room 105
Art - Room 300b
"It is a very mixed blessing to be brought back from the dead."
- Kurt Vonnegut Jr.

Chapter 3

EVERYTHING'S FINE

SAMURAI

GO d? p c++l u+ eˣ m+ s-/- n+ h fˣ !g w t+ r? !y

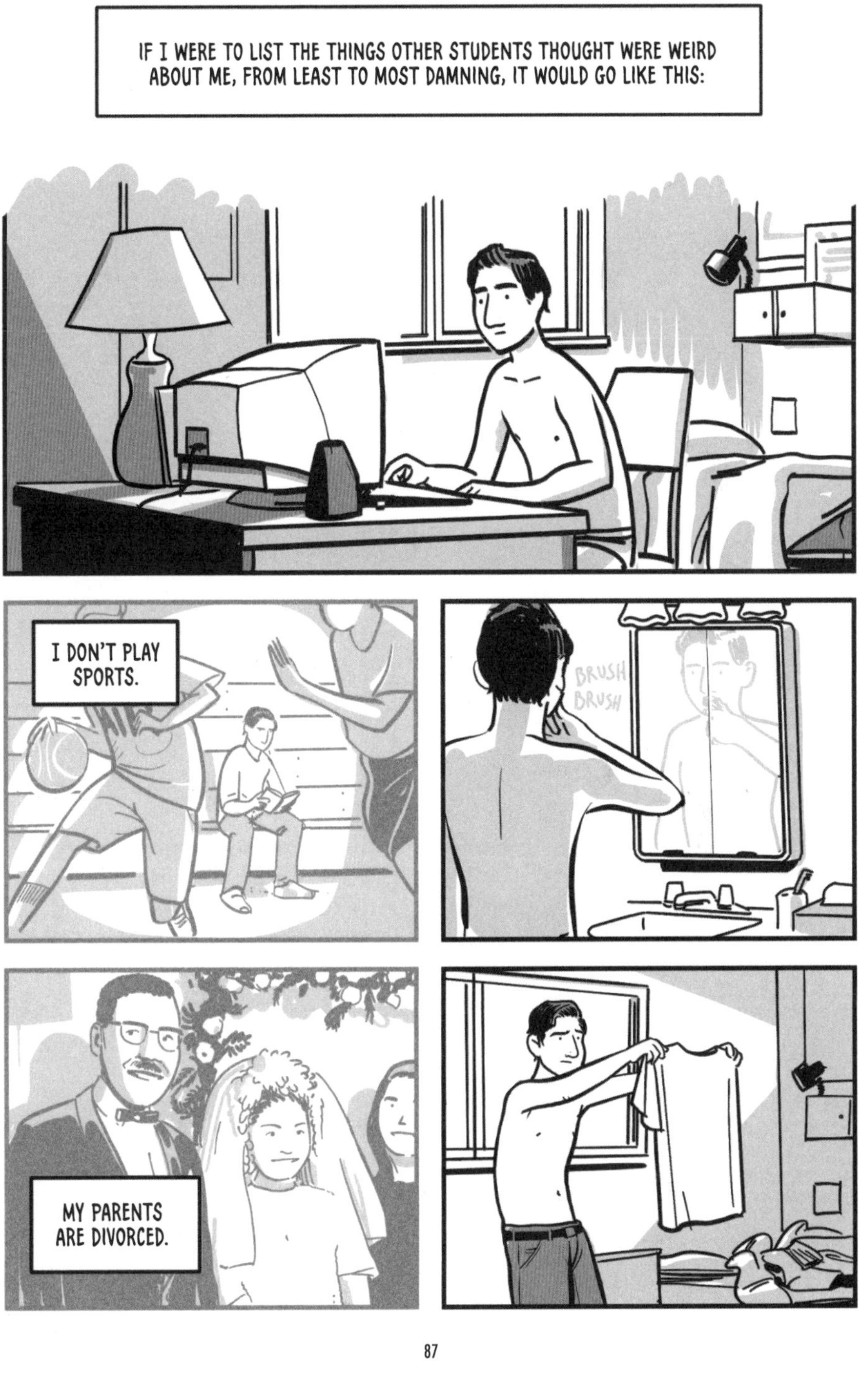
IF I WERE TO LIST THE THINGS OTHER STUDENTS THOUGHT WERE WEIRD ABOUT ME, FROM LEAST TO MOST DAMNING, IT WOULD GO LIKE THIS:
I DON'T PLAY SPORTS.
BRUSH
BRUSH
MY PARENTS ARE DIVORCED.

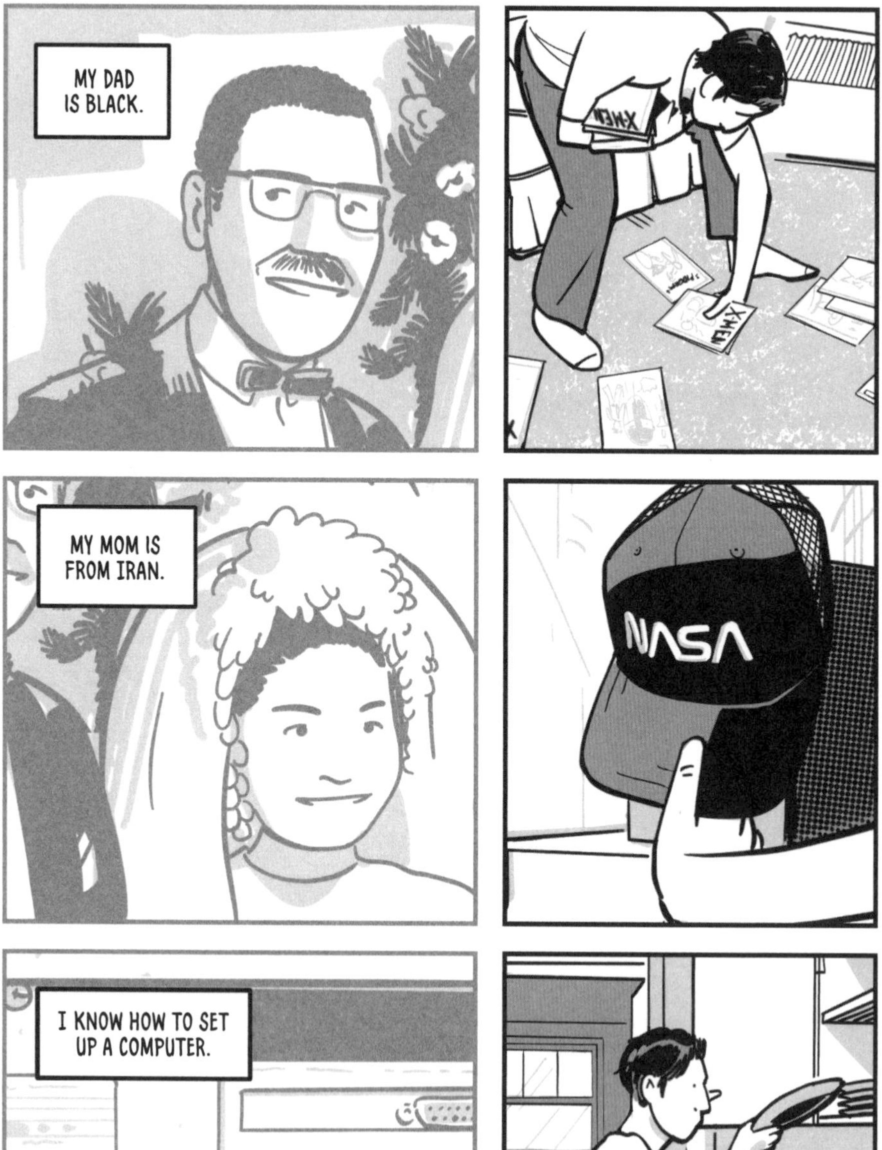
MY DAD IS BLACK.
X-MEN
X-MEN
MY MOM IS FROM IRAN.
NASA
I KNOW HOW TO SET UP A COMPUTER.

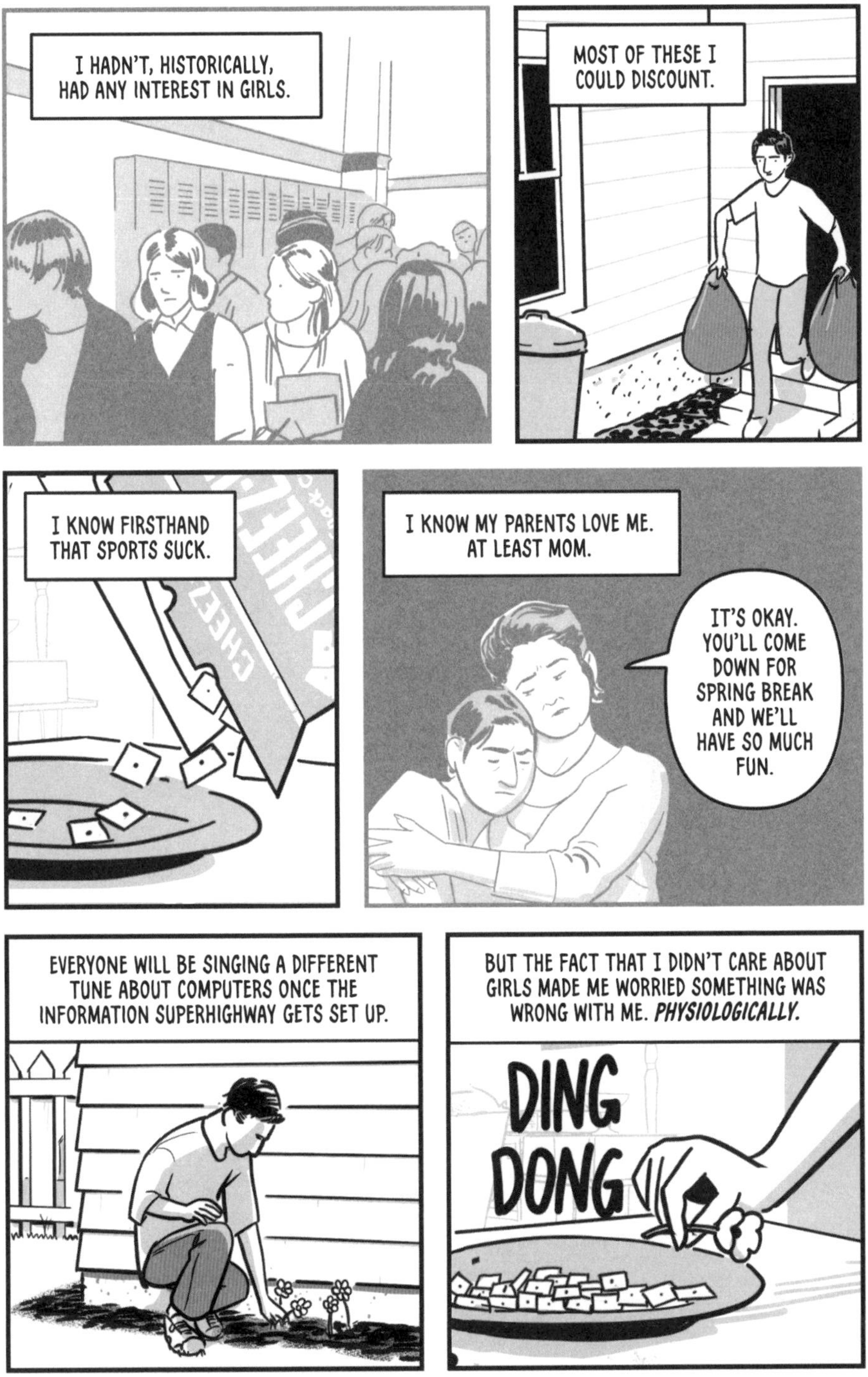
I HADN'T, HISTORICALLY, HAD ANY INTEREST IN GIRLS.
MOST OF THESE I COULD DISCOUNT.
I KNOW FIRSTHAND THAT SPORTS SUCK.
I KNOW MY PARENTS LOVE ME. AT LEAST MOM.
IT'S OKAY. YOU'LL COME DOWN FOR SPRING BREAK AND WE'LL HAVE SO MUCH FUN.
EVERYONE WILL BE SINGING A DIFFERENT TUNE ABOUT COMPUTERS ONCE THE INFORMATION SUPERHIGHWAY GETS SET UP.
BUT THE FACT THAT I DIDN'T CARE ABOUT GIRLS MADE ME WORRIED SOMETHING WAS WRONG WITH ME. *PHYSIOLOGICALLY.*
DING
DONG

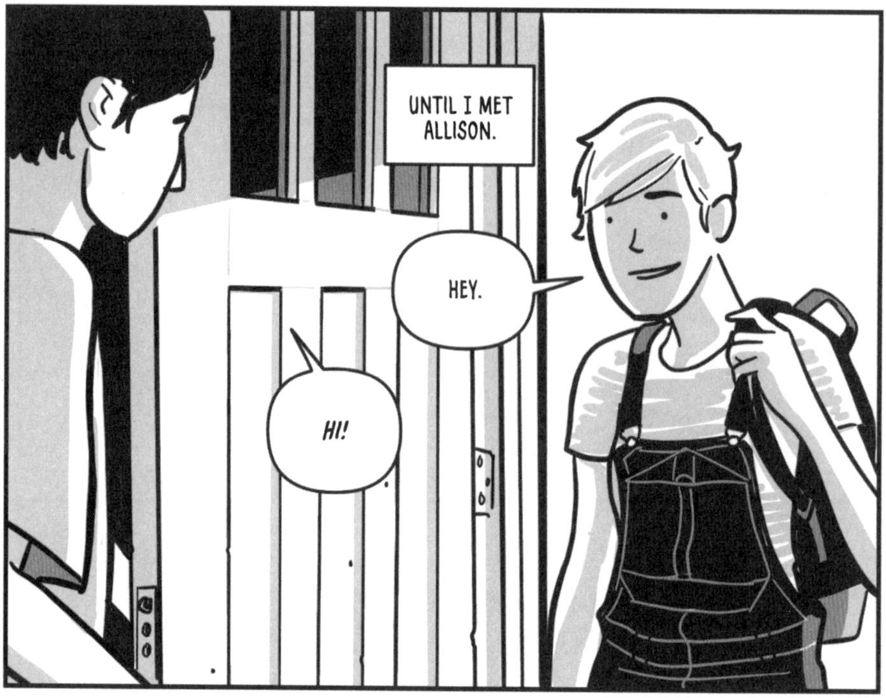
UNTIL I MET ALLISON.
HEY.
HI!

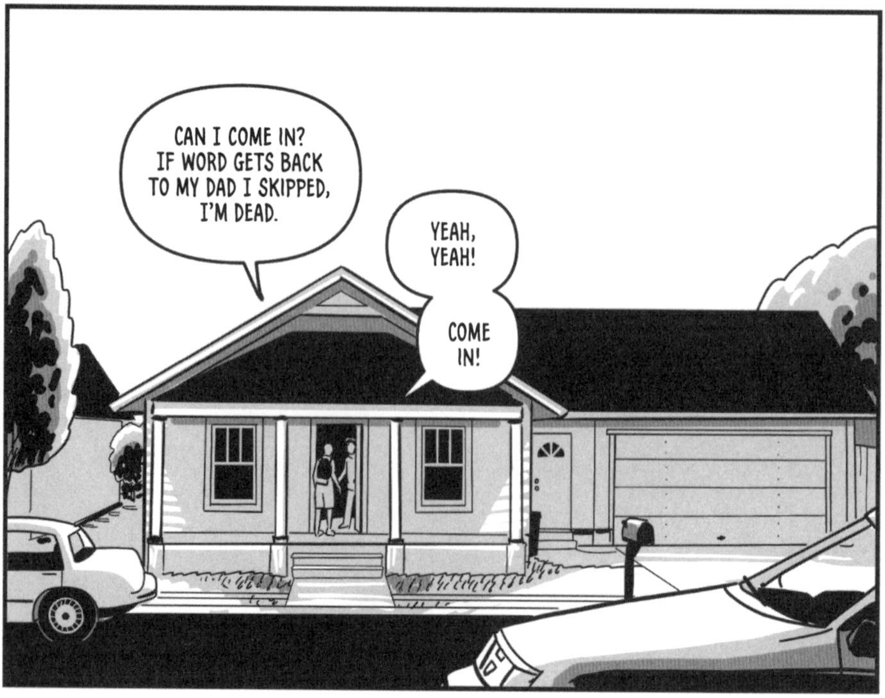
CAN I COME IN? IF WORD GETS BACK TO MY DAD I SKIPPED, I'M DEAD.
YEAH, YEAH!
COME IN!

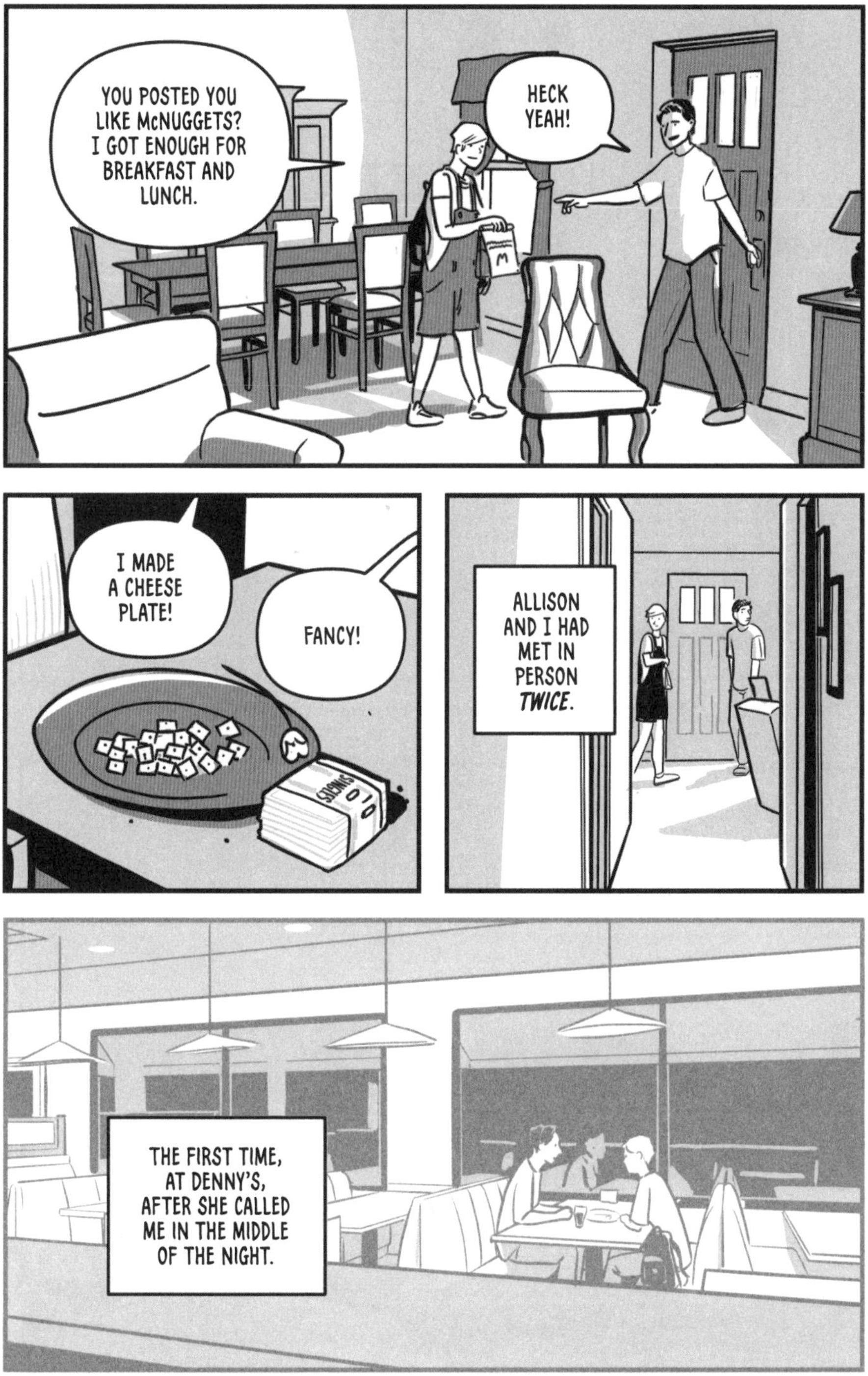
YOU POSTED YOU LIKE McNUGGETS? I GOT ENOUGH FOR BREAKFAST AND LUNCH.
HECK YEAH!
I MADE A CHEESE PLATE!
FANCY!
SINGLES
ALLISON AND I HAD MET IN PERSON *TWICE*.
THE FIRST TIME, AT DENNY'S, AFTER SHE CALLED ME IN THE MIDDLE OF THE NIGHT.

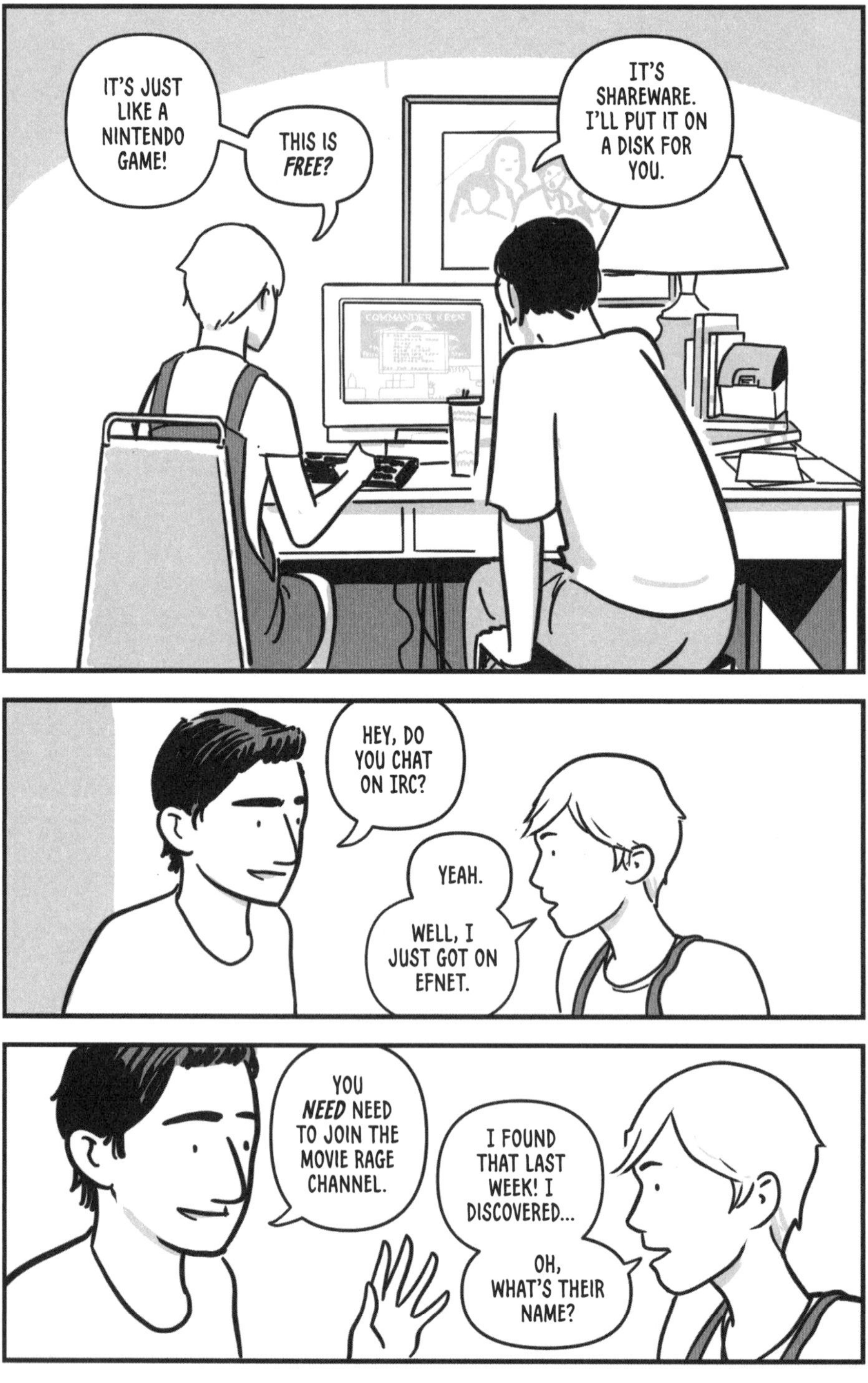
IT'S JUST LIKE A NINTENDO GAME!
THIS IS *FREE?*
IT'S SHAREWARE. I'LL PUT IT ON A DISK FOR YOU.
HEY, DO YOU CHAT ON IRC?
YEAH.
WELL, I JUST GOT ON EFNET.
YOU *NEED* NEED TO JOIN THE MOVIE RAGE CHANNEL.
I FOUND THAT LAST WEEK! I DISCOVERED...
OH, WHAT'S THEIR NAME?

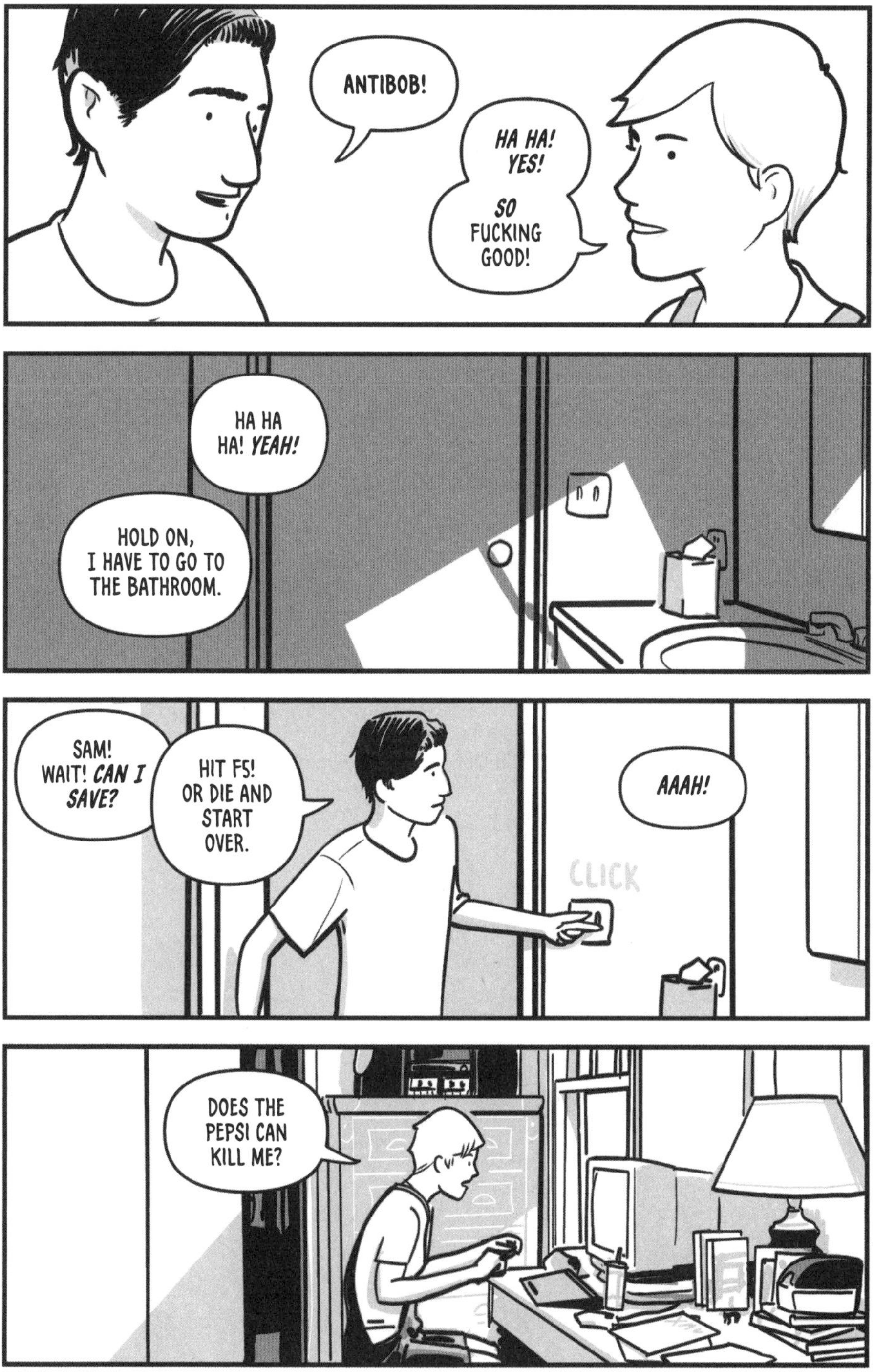
ANTIBOB!
HA HA! YES!
SO FUCKING GOOD!
HA HA HA! YEAH!
HOLD ON, I HAVE TO GO TO THE BATHROOM.
SAM! WAIT! CAN I SAVE?
HIT F5! OR DIE AND START OVER.
AAAH!
CLICK
DOES THE PEPSI CAN KILL ME?

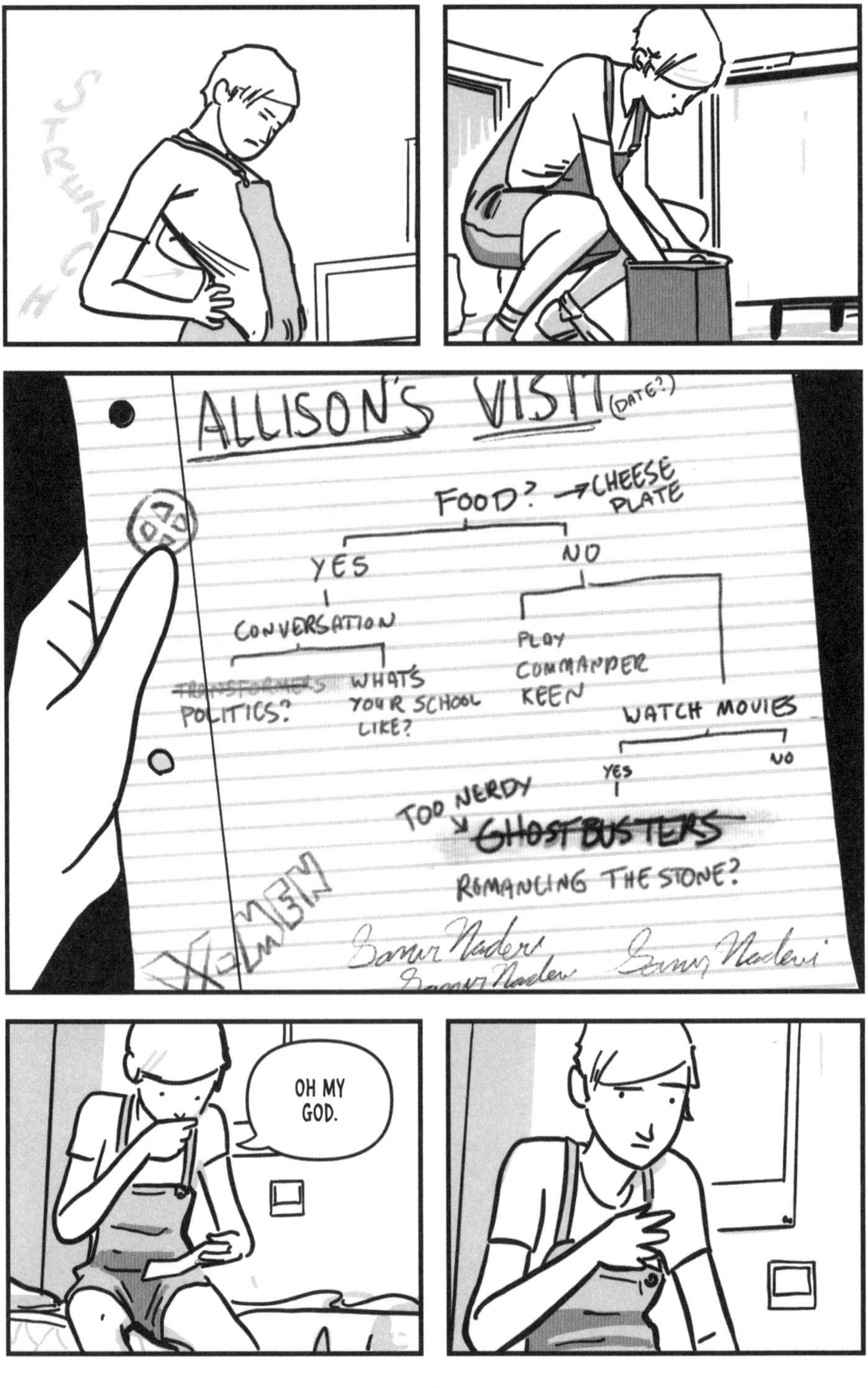
STRETCH
ALLISON'S VISIT (DATE?)
FOOD? → CHEESE PLATE
YES
NO
CONVERSATION
TRANSFORMERS
POLITICS?
WHAT'S YOUR SCHOOL LIKE?
PLAY COMMANDER KEEN
WATCH MOVIES
YES
NO
TOO NERDY
GHOSTBUSTERS
ROMANCING THE STONE?
X-MEN
Samir Naderi
Samir Naderi
Samir Naderi
OH MY GOD.

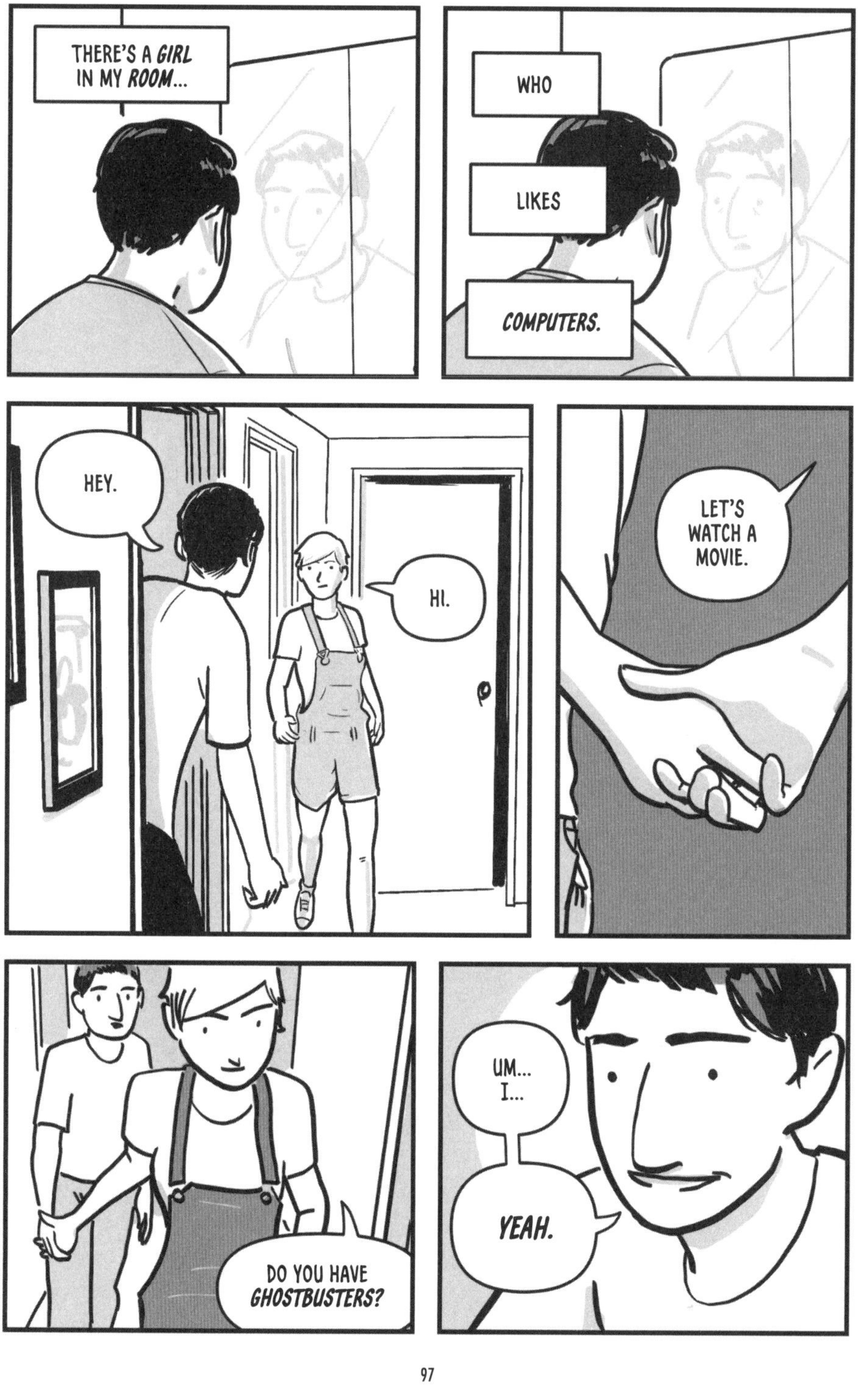
THERE'S A *GIRL* IN MY *ROOM*...
WHO
LIKES
COMPUTERS.
HEY.
HI.
LET'S WATCH A MOVIE.
DO YOU HAVE *GHOSTBUSTERS?*
UM... I...
YEAH.

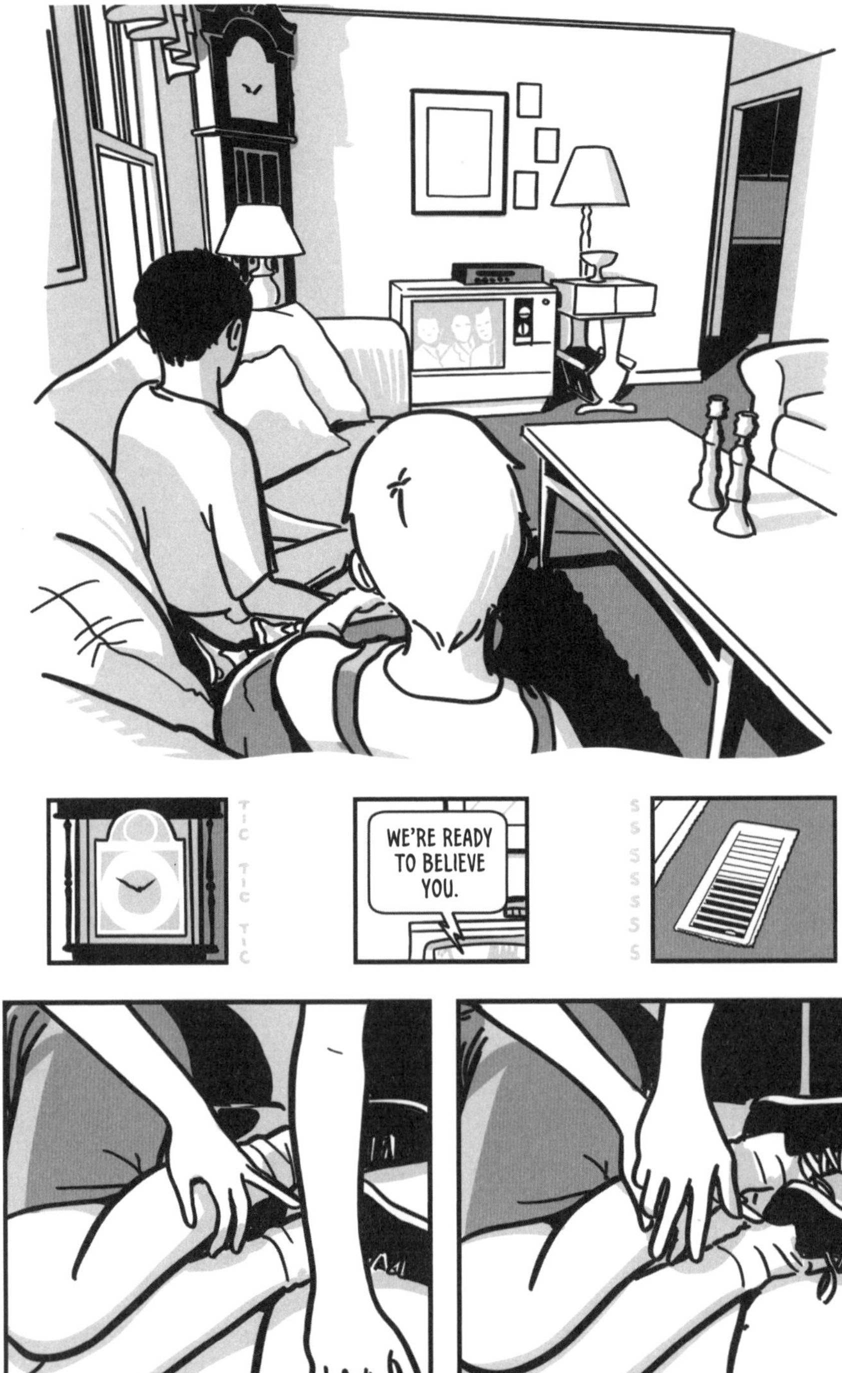
TIC TIC TIC
WE'RE READY TO BELIEVE YOU.
SSSSSS

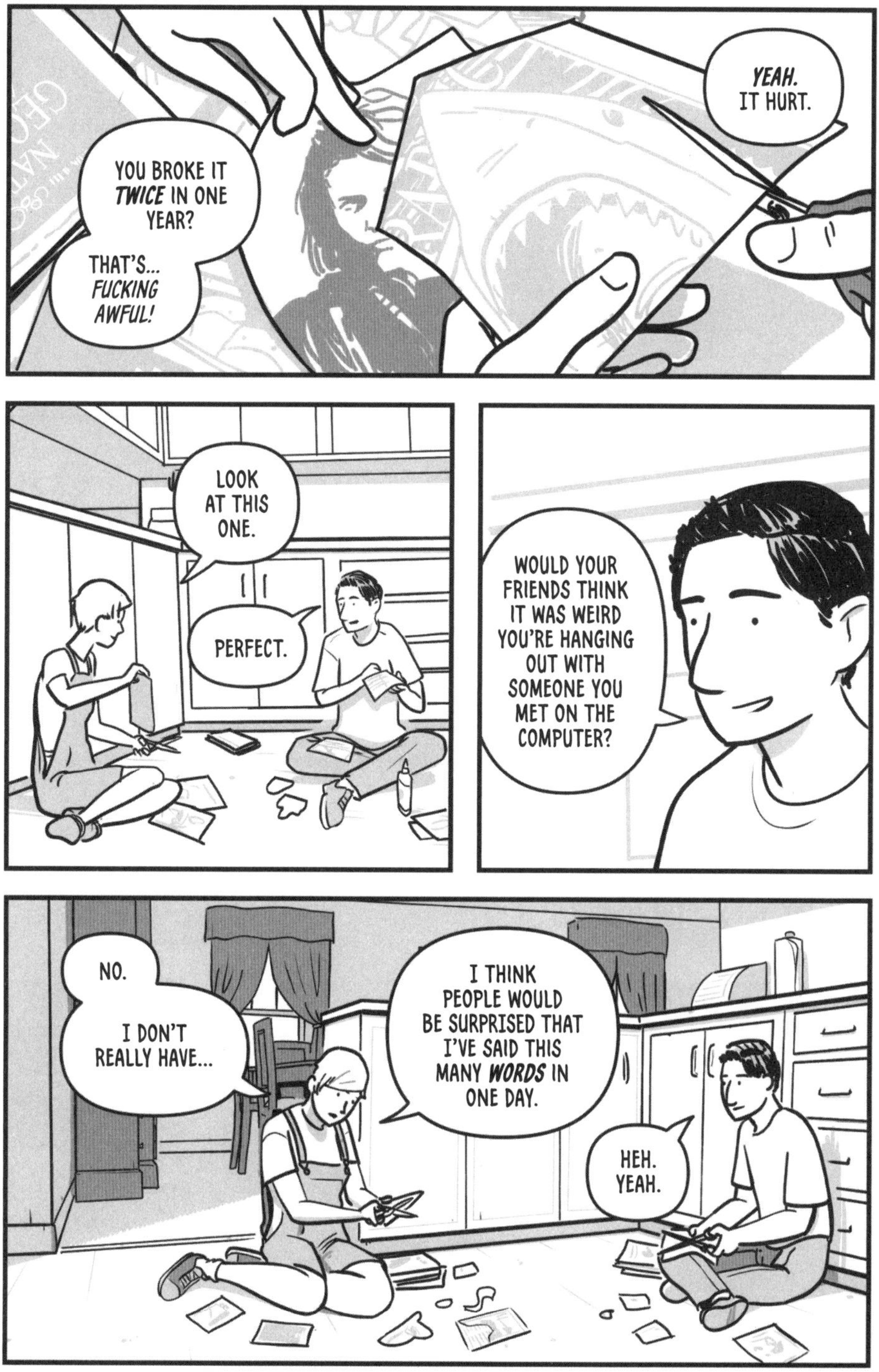
YOU BROKE IT *TWICE* IN ONE YEAR?
THAT'S... *FUCKING AWFUL!*
YEAH. IT HURT.
LOOK AT THIS ONE.
PERFECT.
WOULD YOUR FRIENDS THINK IT WAS WEIRD YOU'RE HANGING OUT WITH SOMEONE YOU MET ON THE COMPUTER?
NO.
I DON'T REALLY HAVE...
I THINK PEOPLE WOULD BE SURPRISED THAT I'VE SAID THIS MANY *WORDS* IN ONE DAY.
HEH. YEAH.

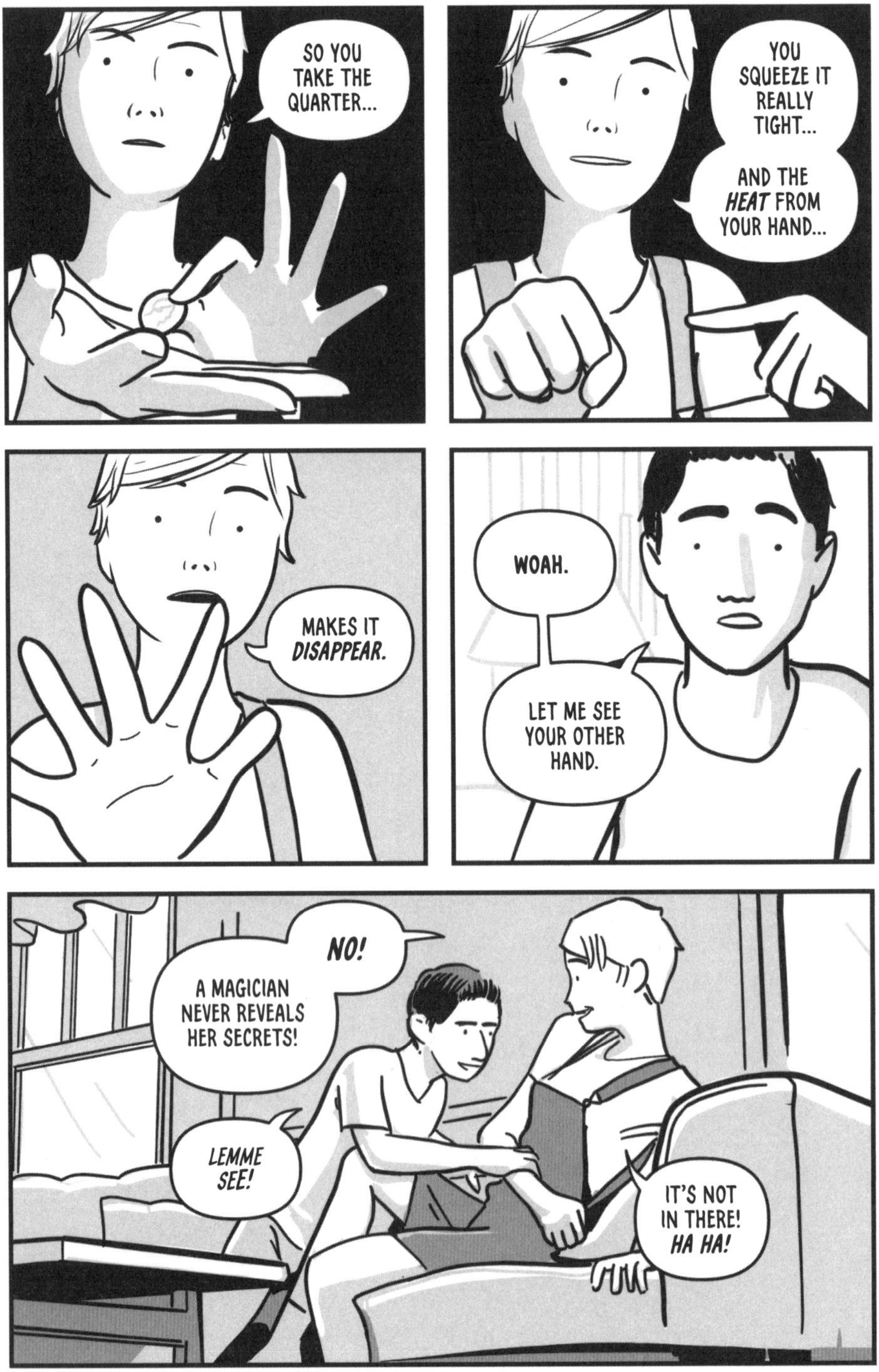
SO YOU TAKE THE QUARTER...
YOU SQUEEZE IT REALLY TIGHT...
AND THE *HEAT* FROM YOUR HAND...
MAKES IT *DISAPPEAR.*
WOAH.
LET ME SEE YOUR OTHER HAND.
NO!
A MAGICIAN NEVER REVEALS HER SECRETS!
LEMME SEE!
IT'S NOT IN THERE! *HA HA!*

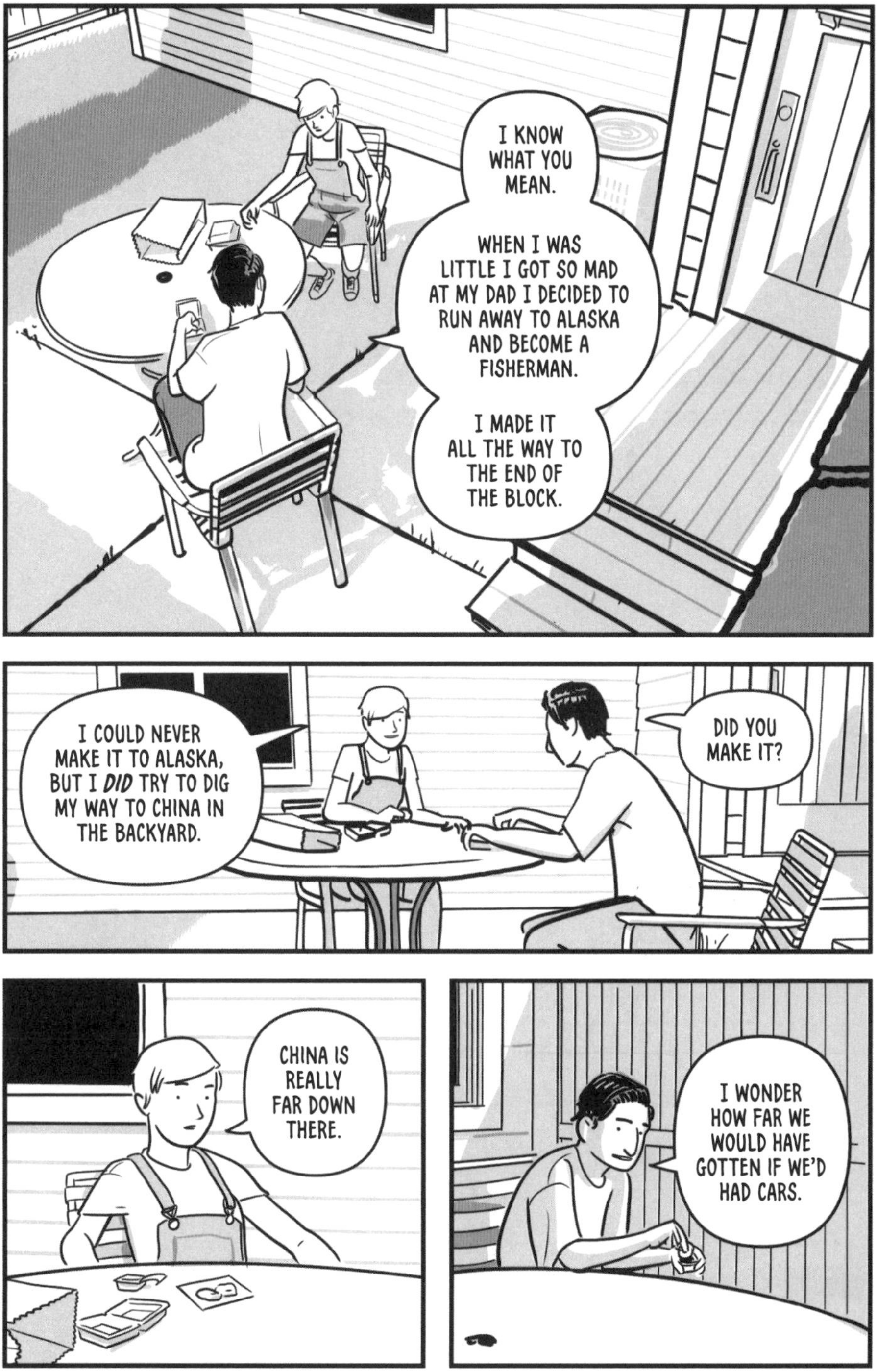
I KNOW WHAT YOU MEAN.
WHEN I WAS LITTLE I GOT SO MAD AT MY DAD I DECIDED TO RUN AWAY TO ALASKA AND BECOME A FISHERMAN.
I MADE IT ALL THE WAY TO THE END OF THE BLOCK.
I COULD NEVER MAKE IT TO ALASKA, BUT I *DID* TRY TO DIG MY WAY TO CHINA IN THE BACKYARD.
DID YOU MAKE IT?
CHINA IS REALLY FAR DOWN THERE.
I WONDER HOW FAR WE WOULD HAVE GOTTEN IF WE'D HAD CARS.

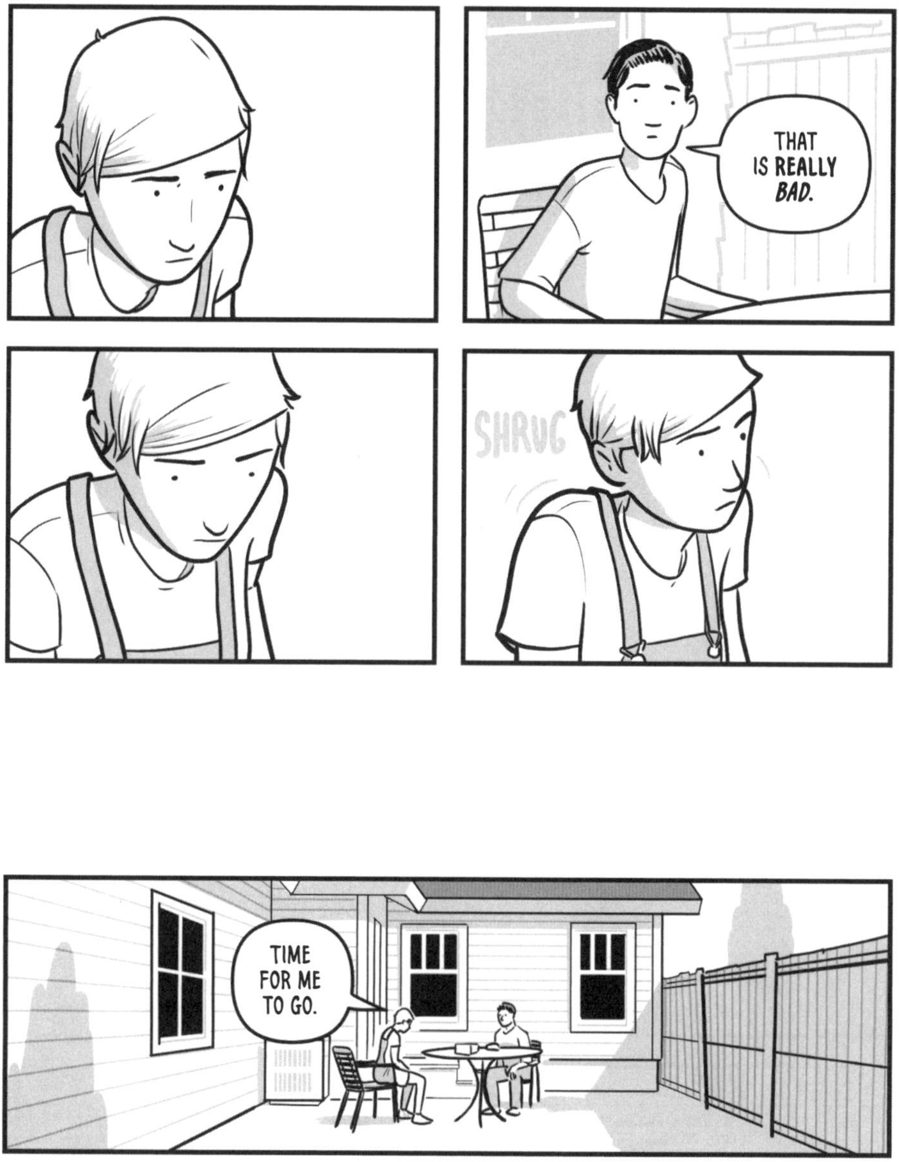
THAT IS REALLY BAD.
SHRUG
TIME FOR ME TO GO.

DOES SHE WANT ME TO KISS HER?

I DON'T KNOW WHEN THE NEXT TIME...

I DON'T KNOW IF I'LL EVER...

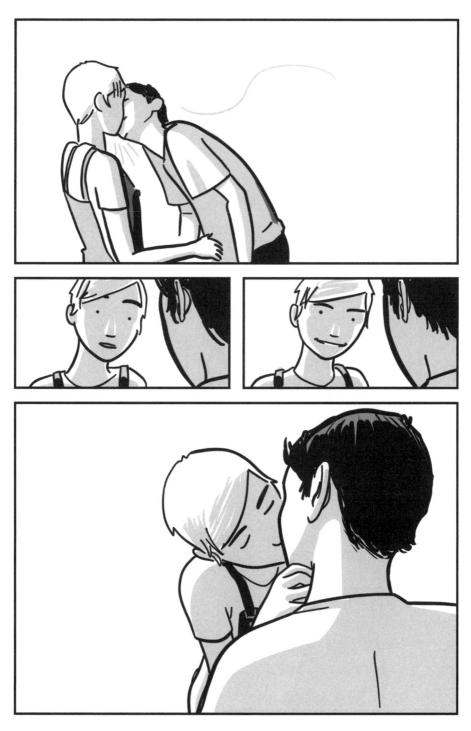

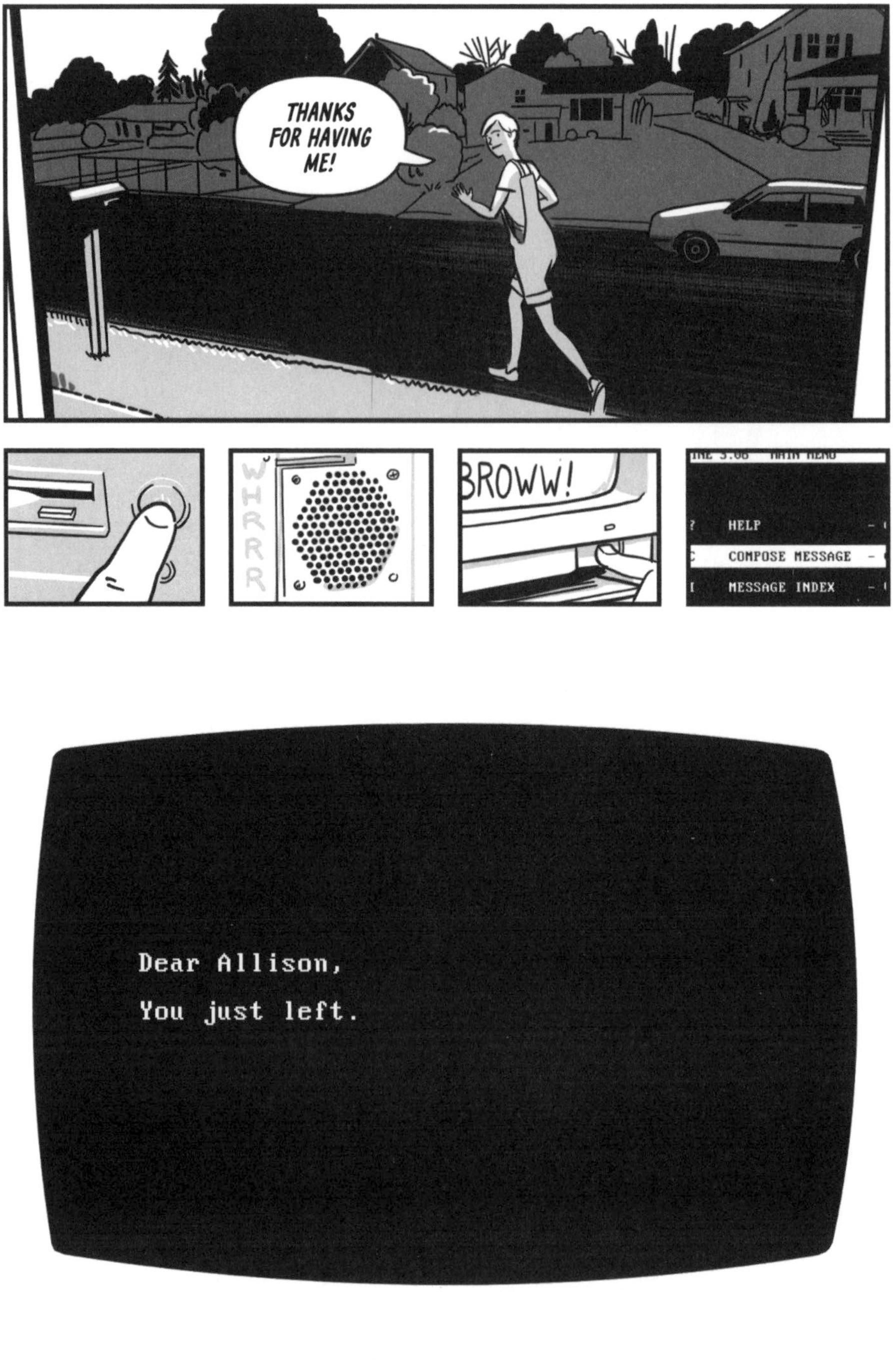
THANKS FOR HAVING ME!
WHRRR
BROWW!
HELP
COMPOSE MESSAGE
MESSAGE INDEX
Dear Allison,
You just left.

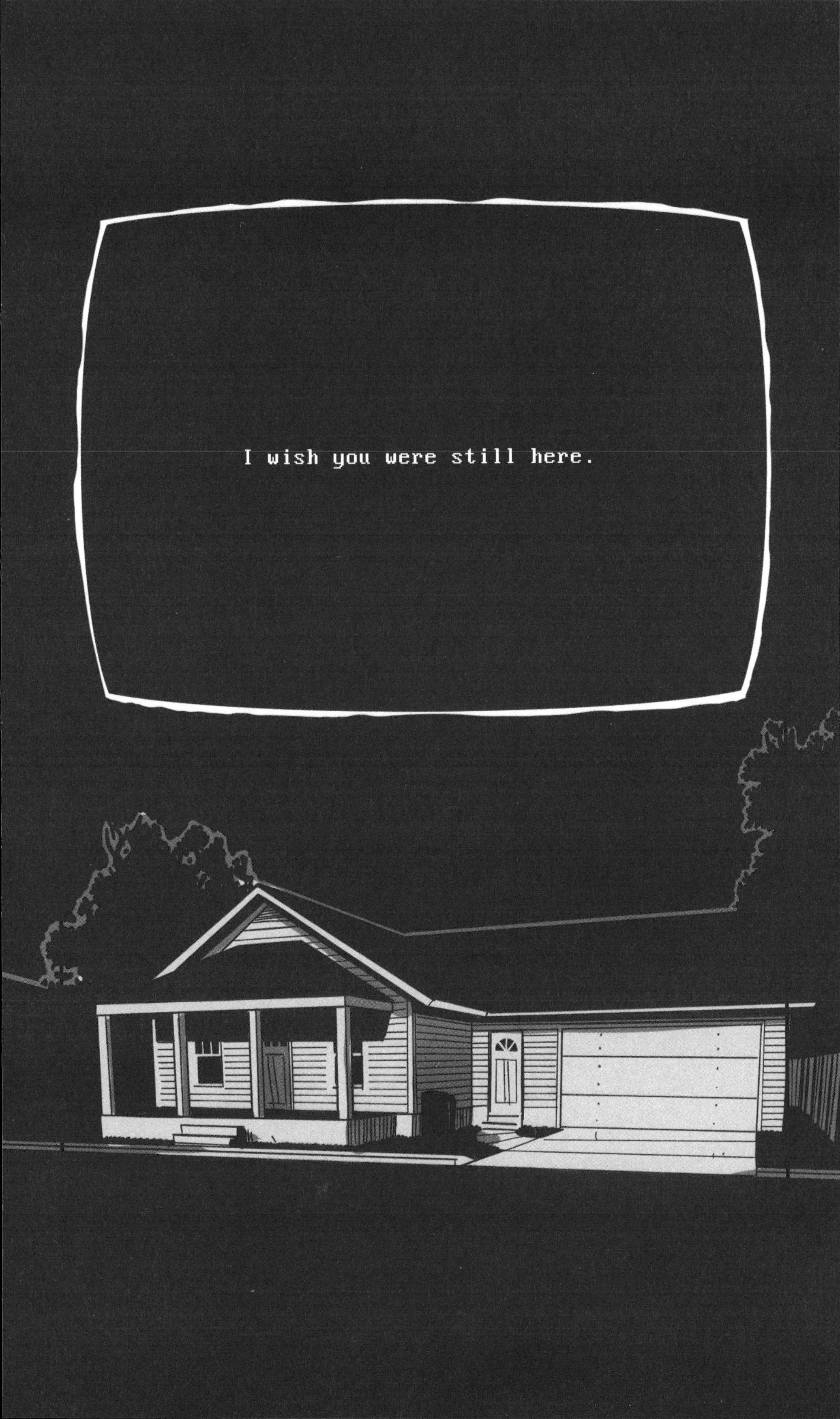
I wish you were still here.

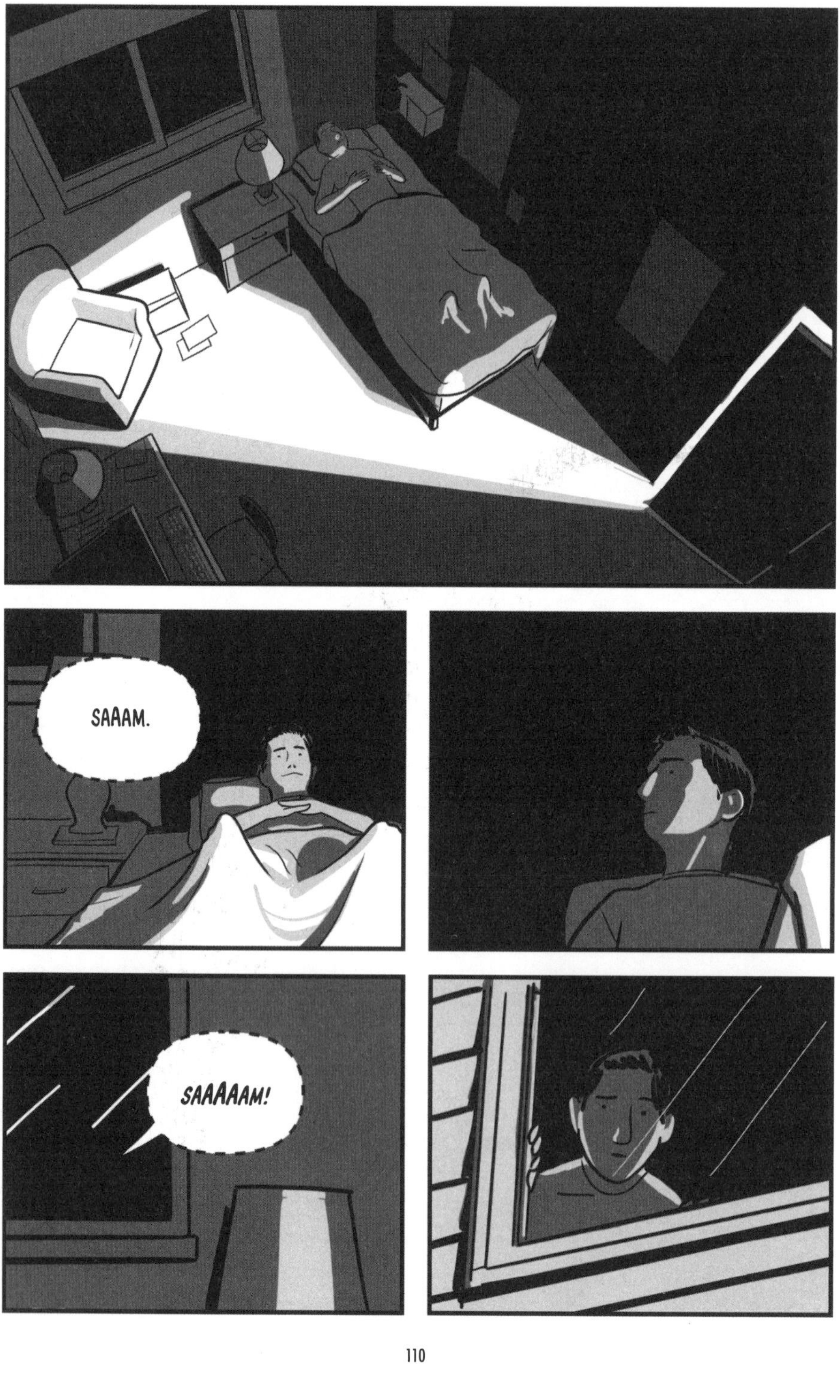
SAAAM.
SAAAAAM!

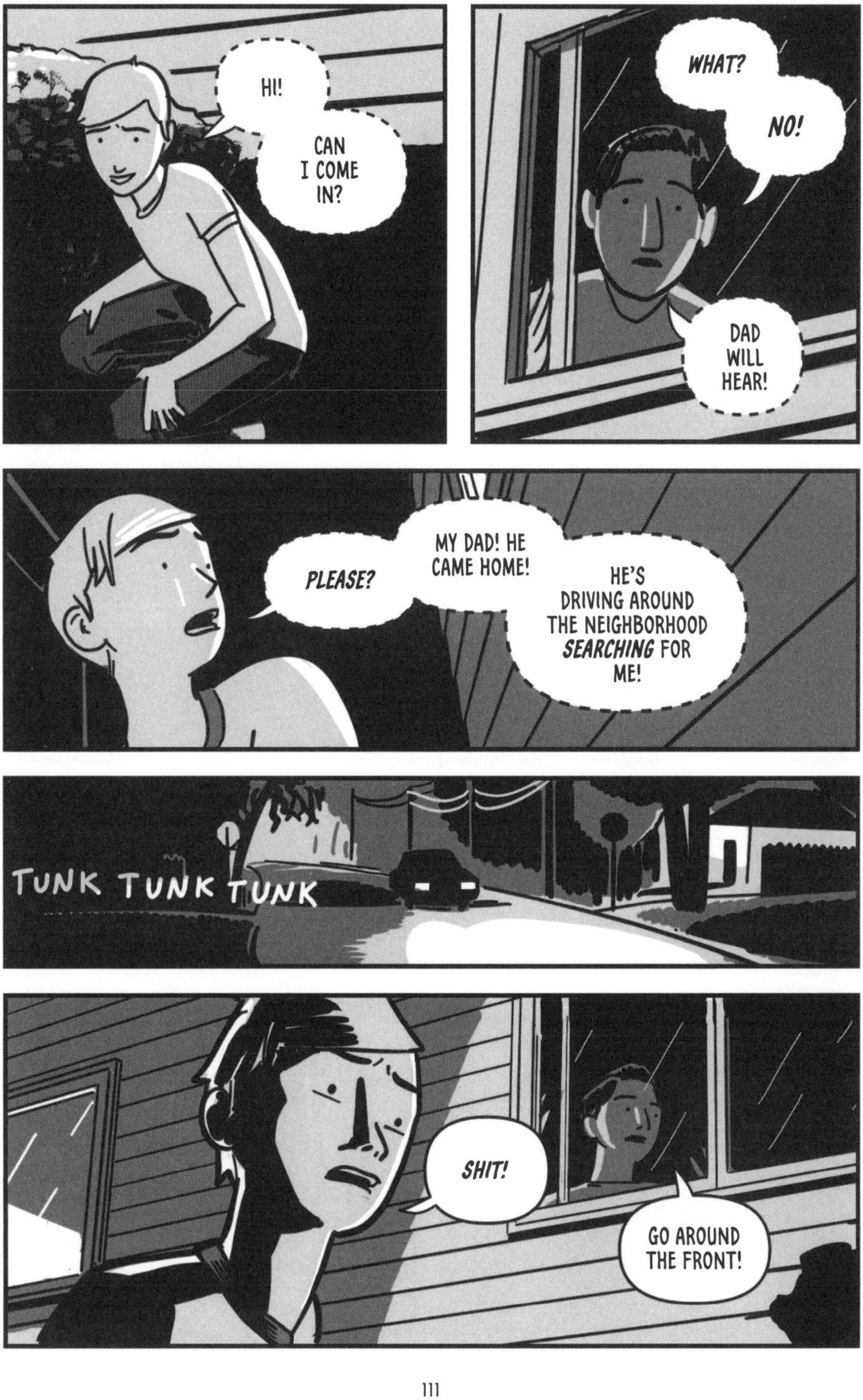
HI!
CAN I COME IN?
WHAT?
NO!
DAD WILL HEAR!
PLEASE?
MY DAD! HE CAME HOME!
HE'S DRIVING AROUND THE NEIGHBORHOOD *SEARCHING* FOR ME!
TUNK TUNK TUNK
SHIT!
GO AROUND THE FRONT!

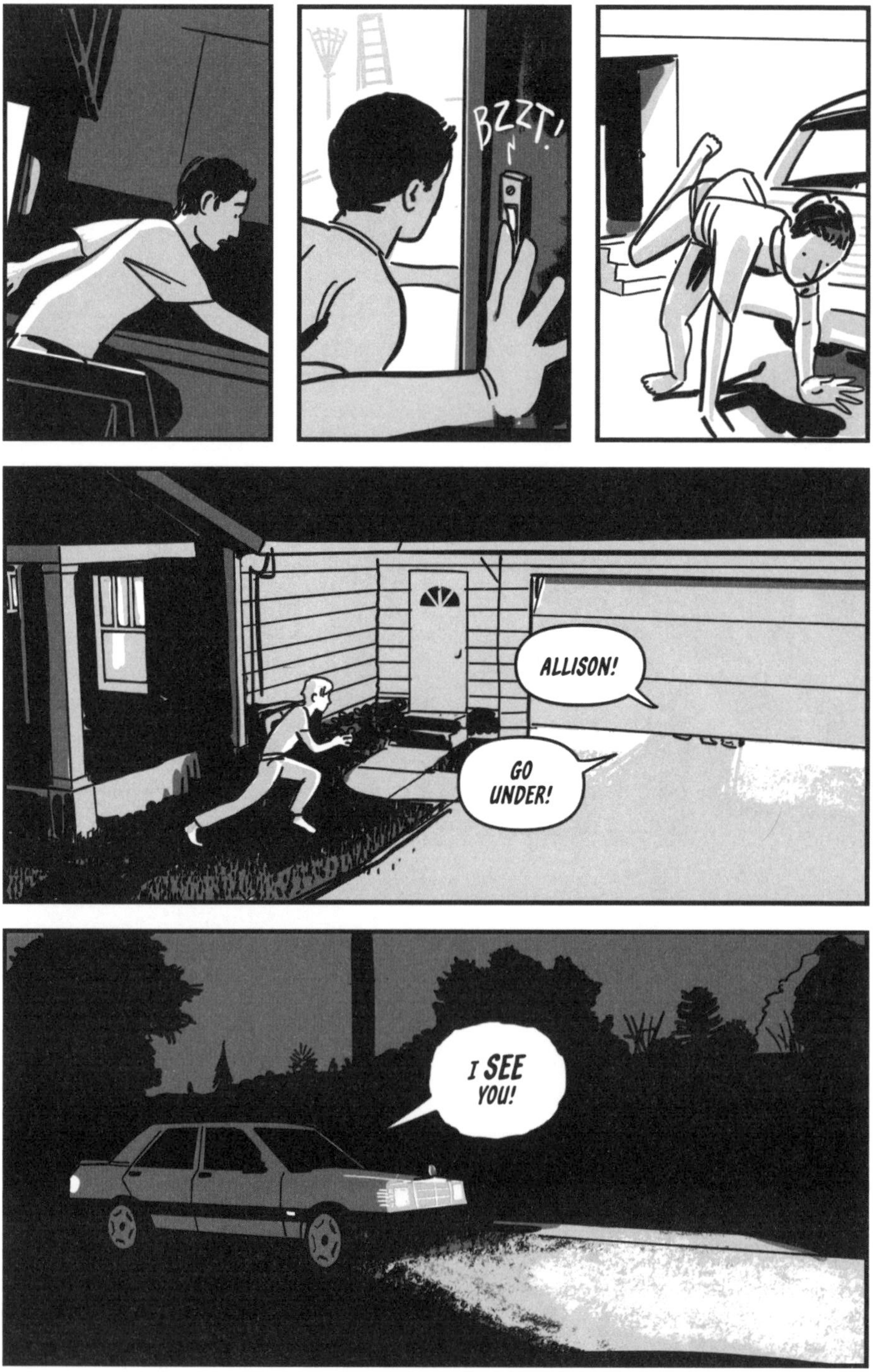
BZZT!
ALLISON!
GO UNDER!
I SEE YOU!

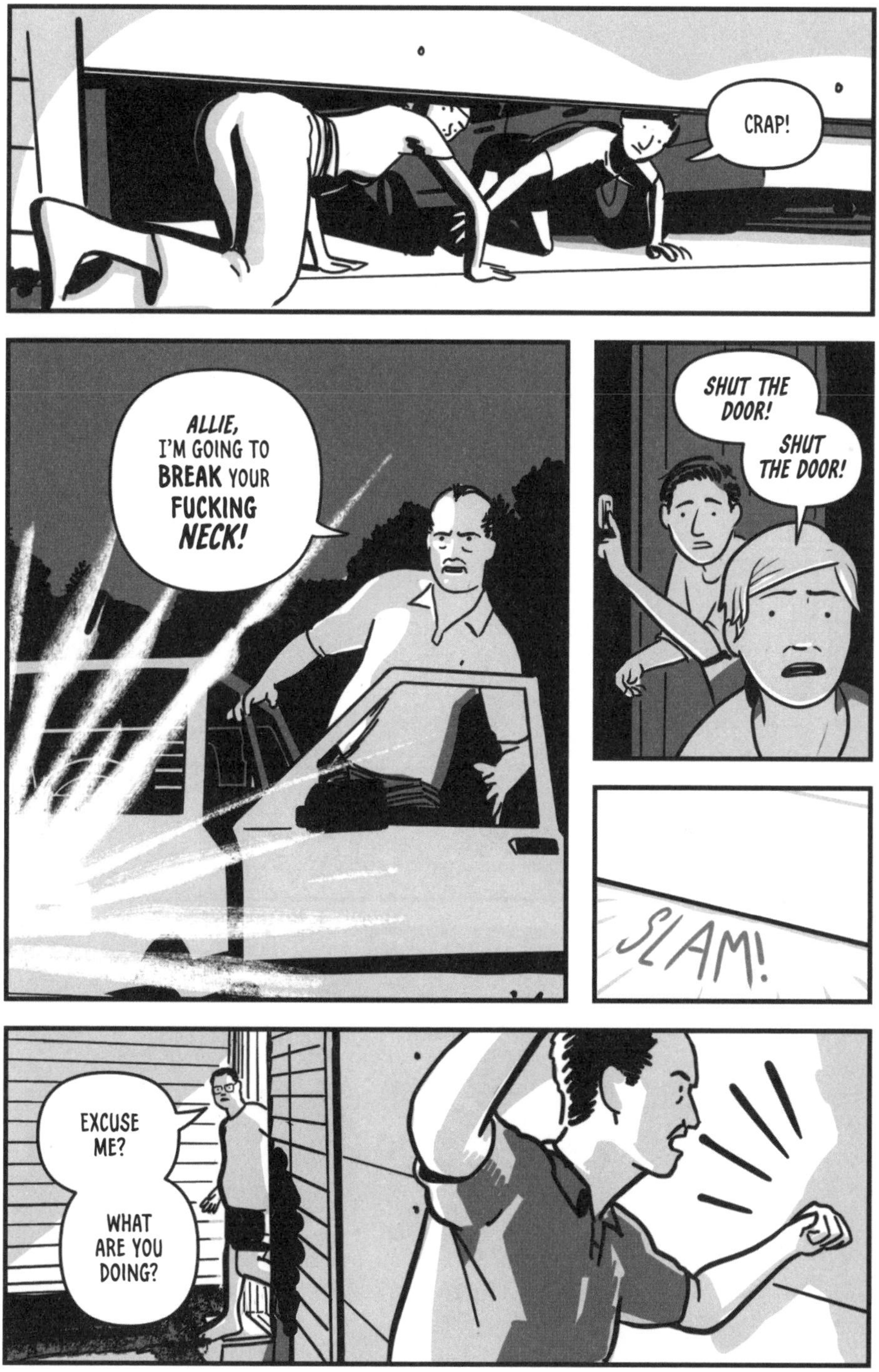
CRAP!
ALLIE, I'M GOING TO BREAK YOUR FUCKING NECK!
SHUT THE DOOR!
SHUT THE DOOR!
SLAM!
EXCUSE ME?
WHAT ARE YOU DOING?

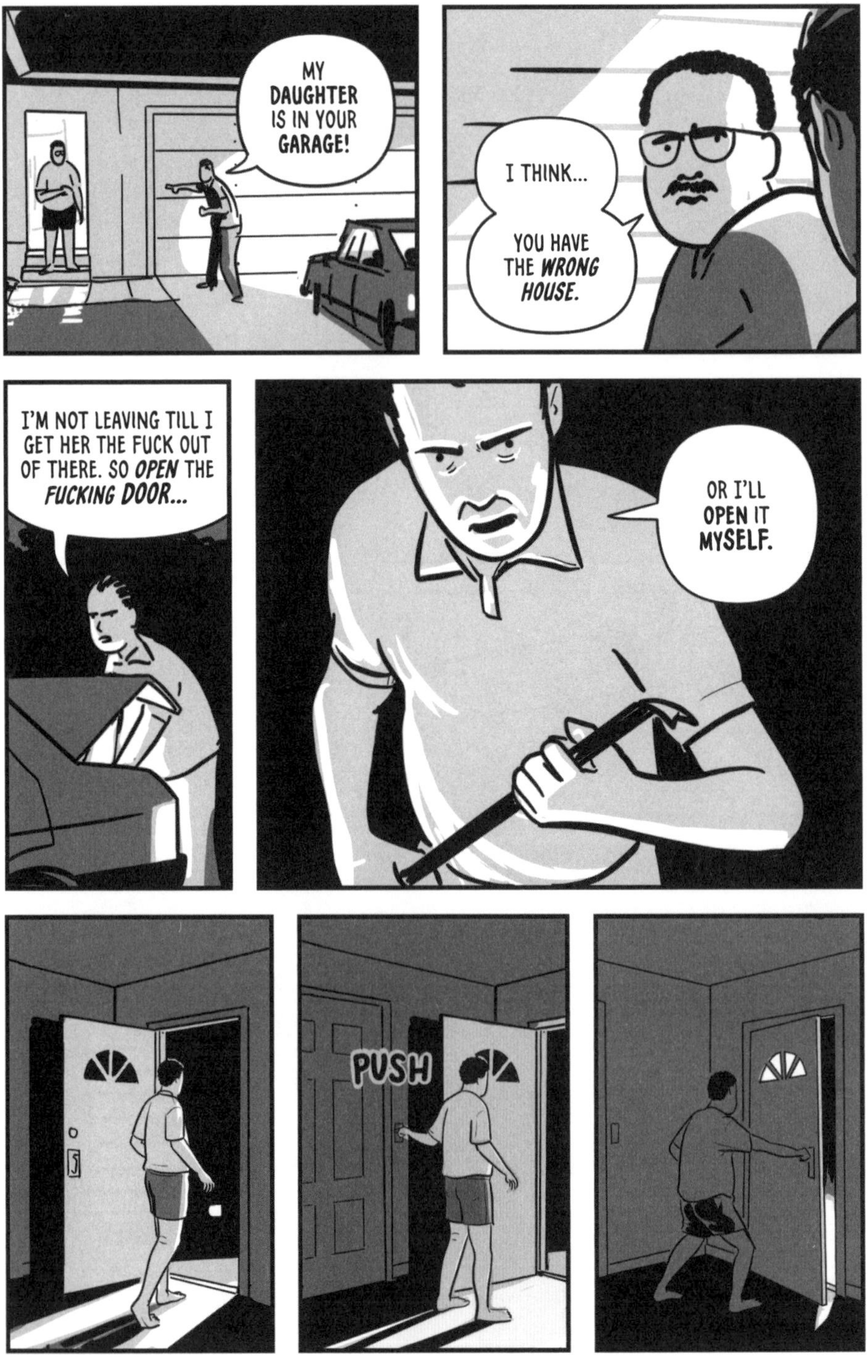
MY DAUGHTER IS IN YOUR GARAGE!
I THINK...
YOU HAVE THE *WRONG HOUSE.*
I'M NOT LEAVING TILL I GET HER THE FUCK OUT OF THERE. SO *OPEN* THE *FUCKING DOOR...*
OR I'LL OPEN IT MYSELF.
PUSH

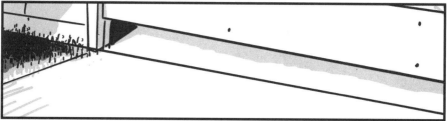

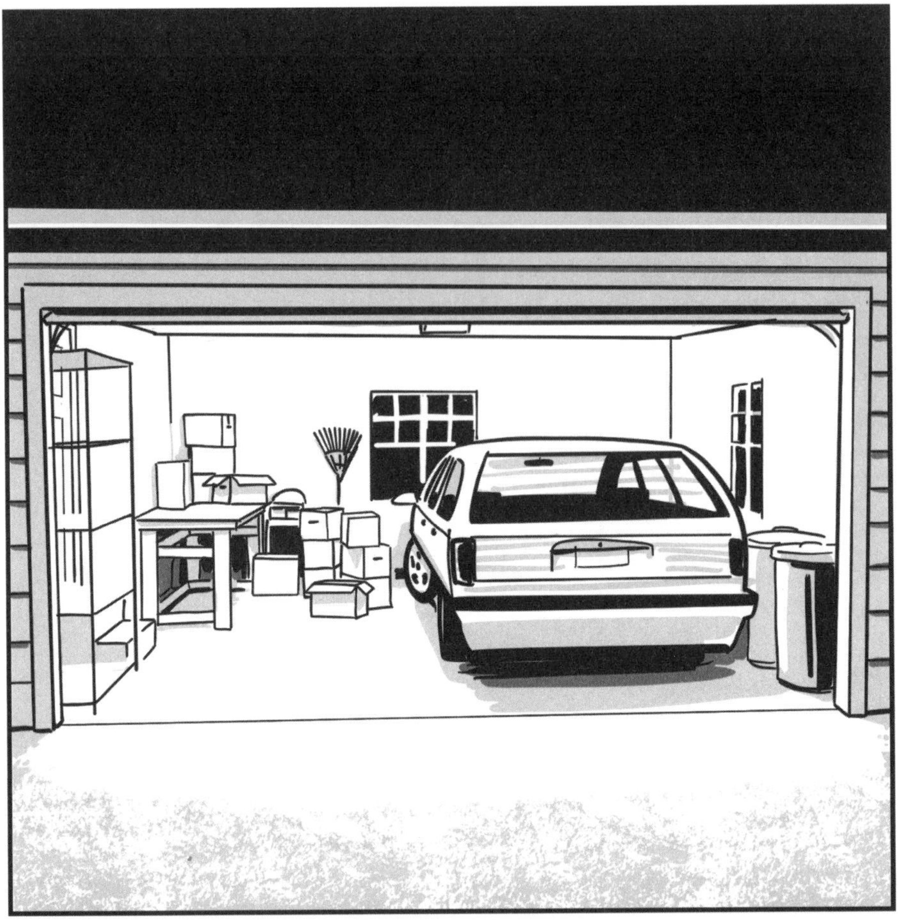

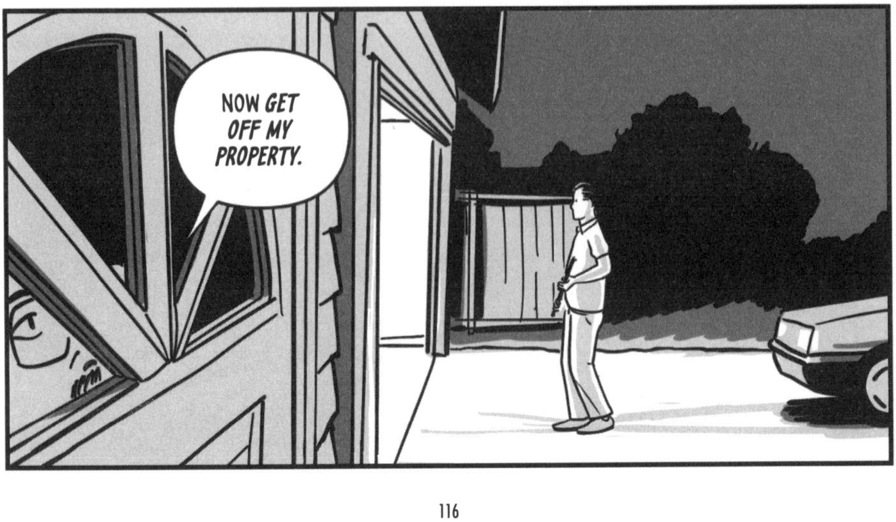
NOW GET OFF MY PROPERTY.

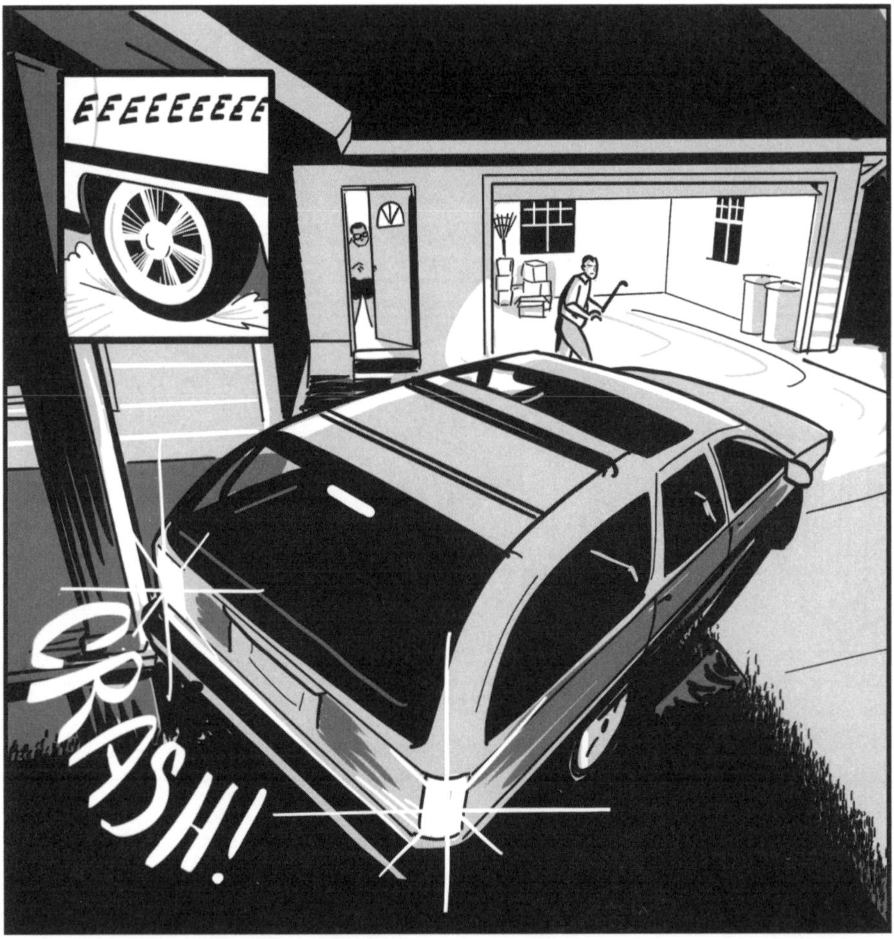
EEEEEEEEEE
CRASH!

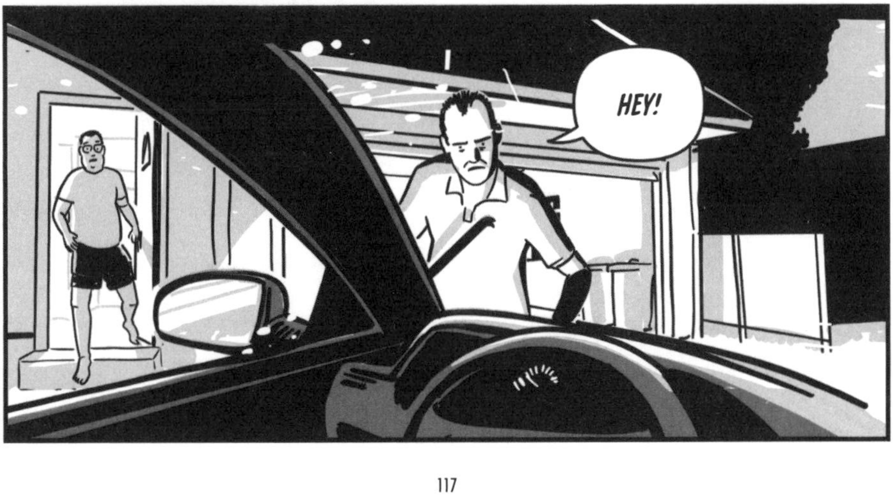
HEY!

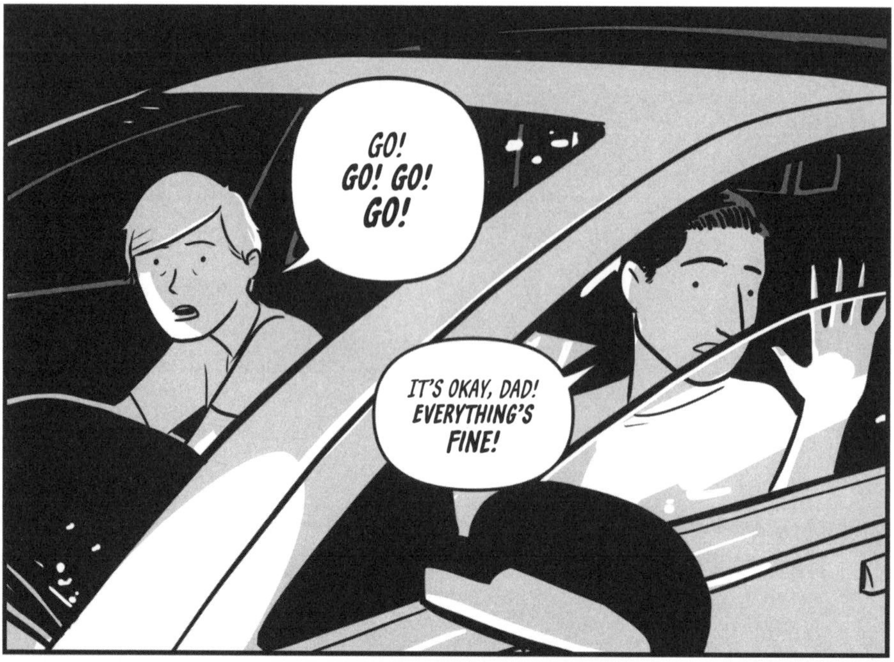
GO! GO! GO! GO!
IT'S OKAY, DAD! EVERYTHING'S FINE!
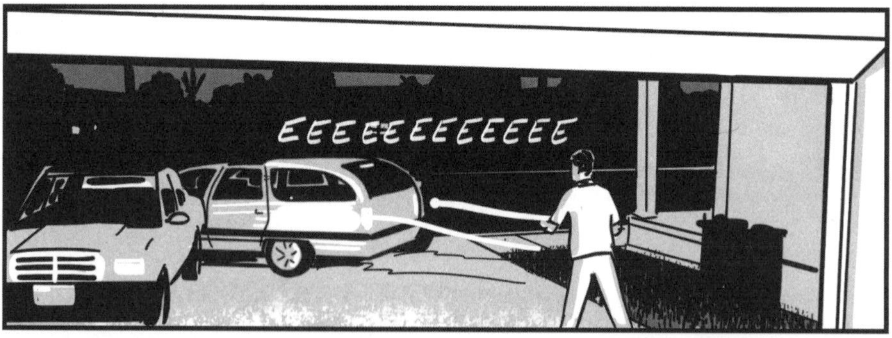
EEEEEEEEEEEEE
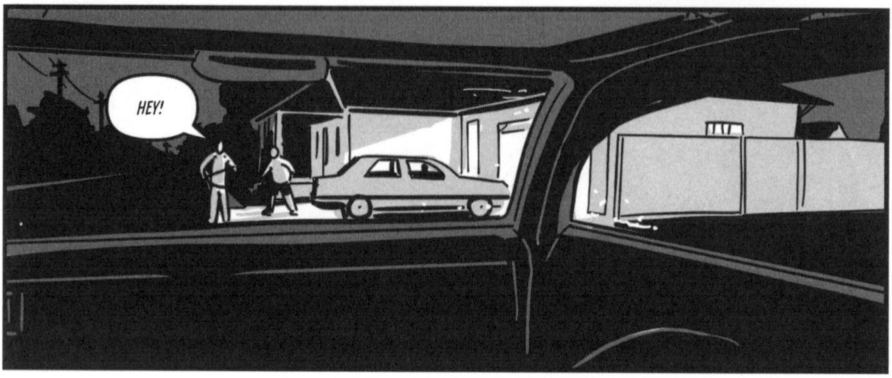
HEY!

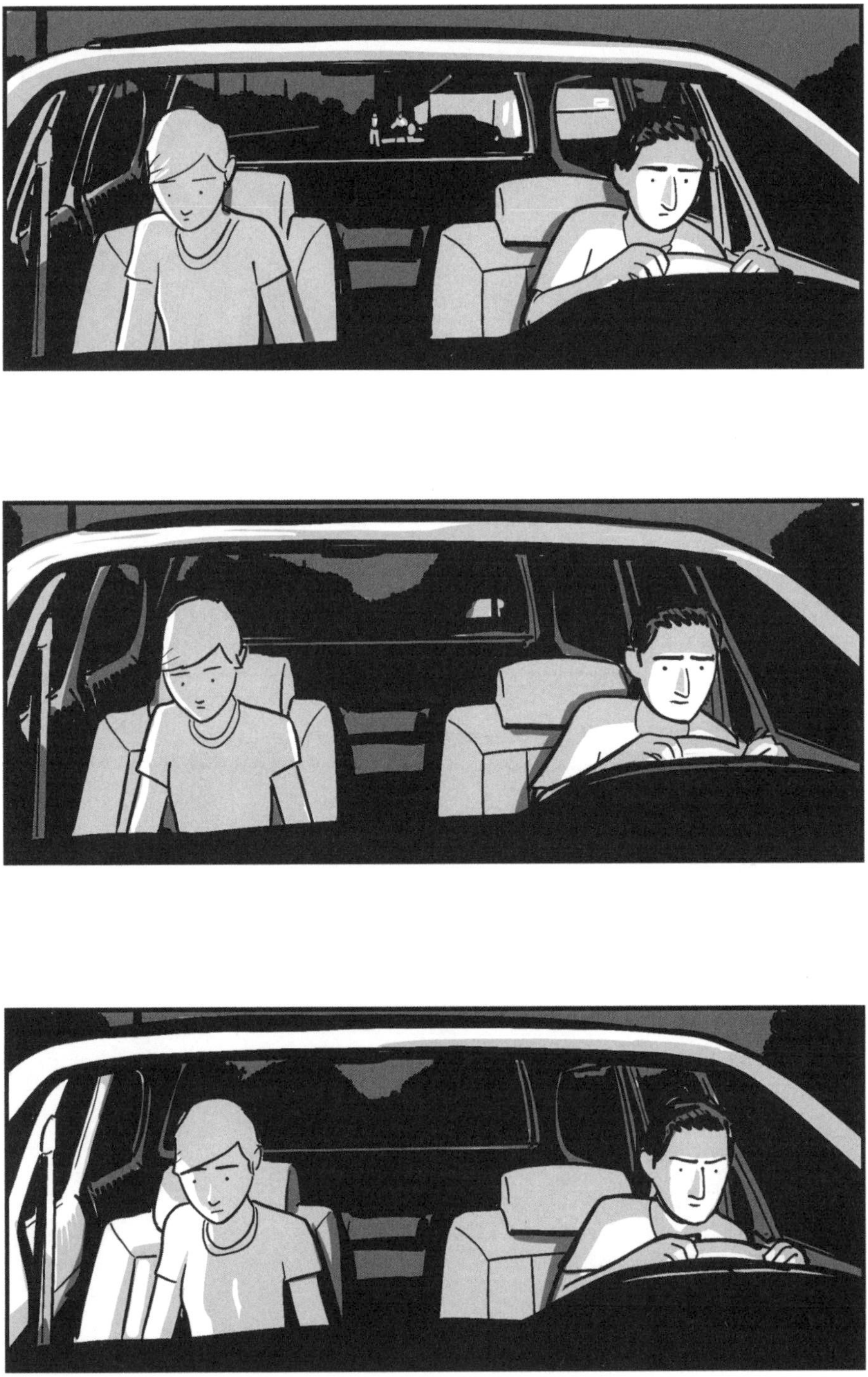

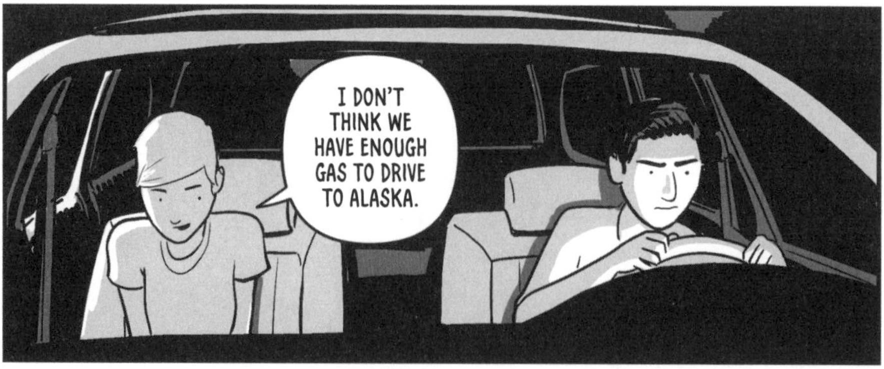
I DON'T THINK WE HAVE ENOUGH GAS TO DRIVE TO ALASKA.

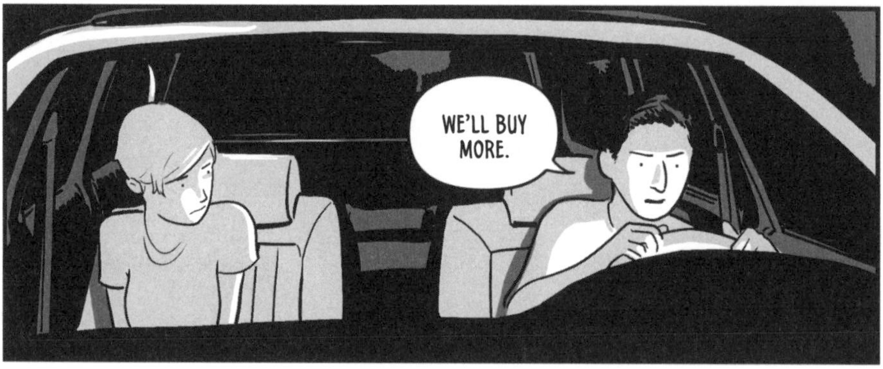
WE'LL BUY MORE.

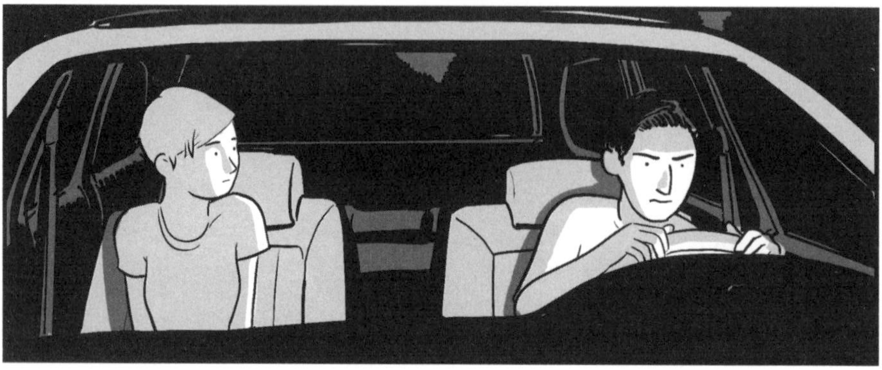

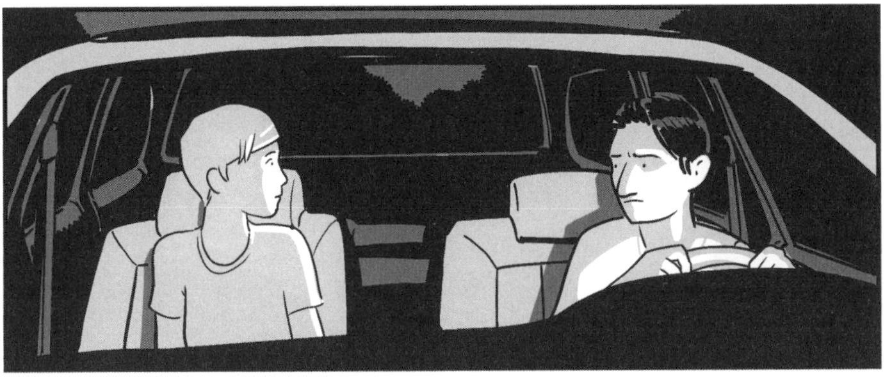

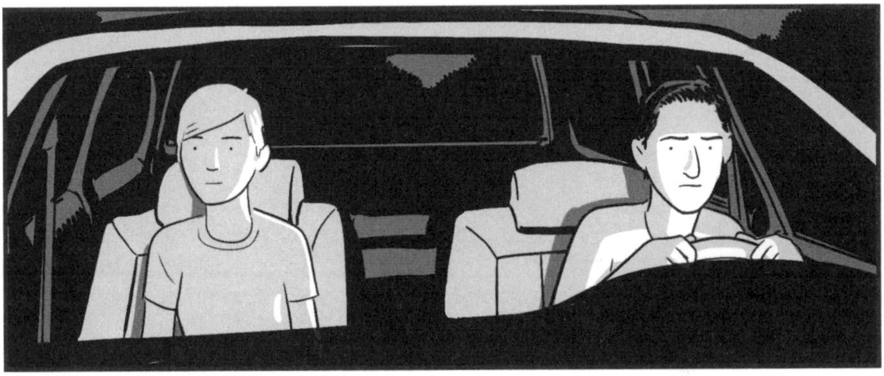

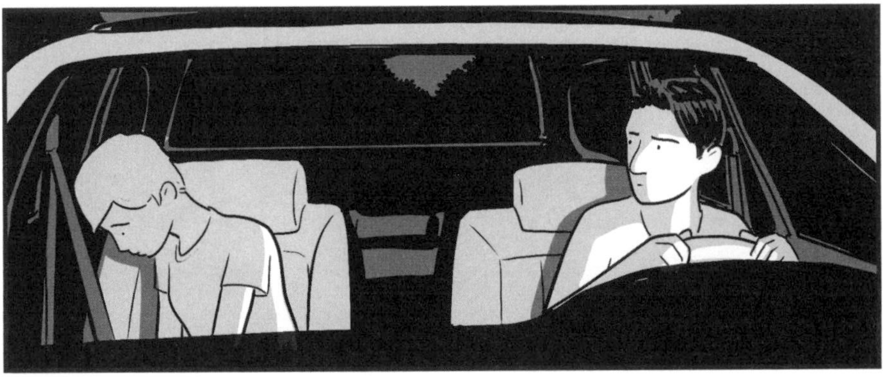

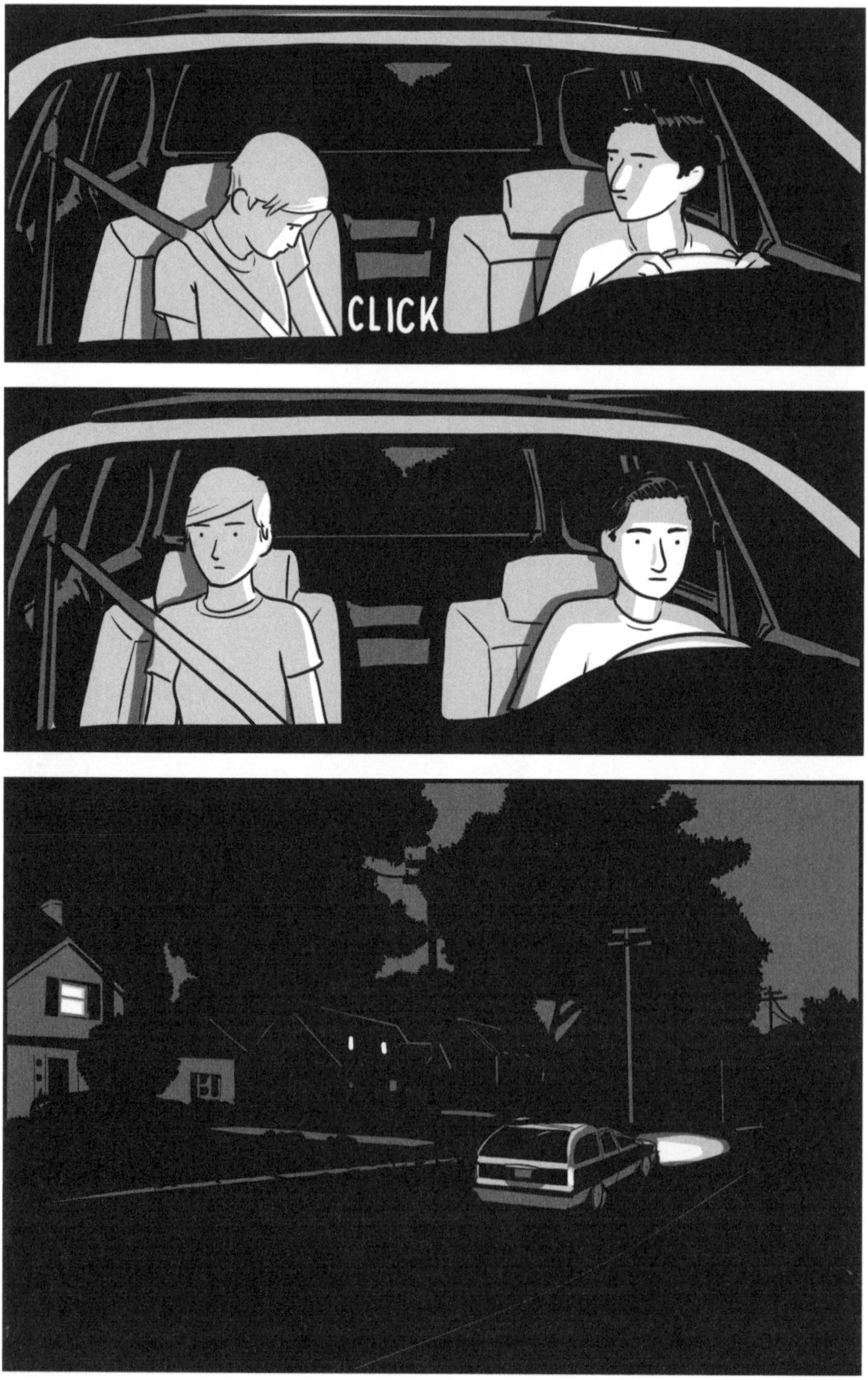
CLICK

Chapter 4

EVOL HOUSE

```
 _____
|  ____     _          _                            _       |
| |  _ \   (_)       | |                           | |      |
| | |_) |  _   ___  | |__    __ _  _ __   __| |     |
| |  _ <  | | / __| | '_ \  / _` || '__| / _` |     |
| | |_) | | || (__  | | | || (_| || |   | (_| |  _  |
| |____/  |_| \___| |_| |_| \__,_||_|    \__,_| (_) |
|_____|
```

GAT GCS GM GS d -p+ c+++(++++) l++(+++) u+@ eˣ
m(+) s+/- n--- hˣ !f(+) g+ w++ t++(+++) r? y?

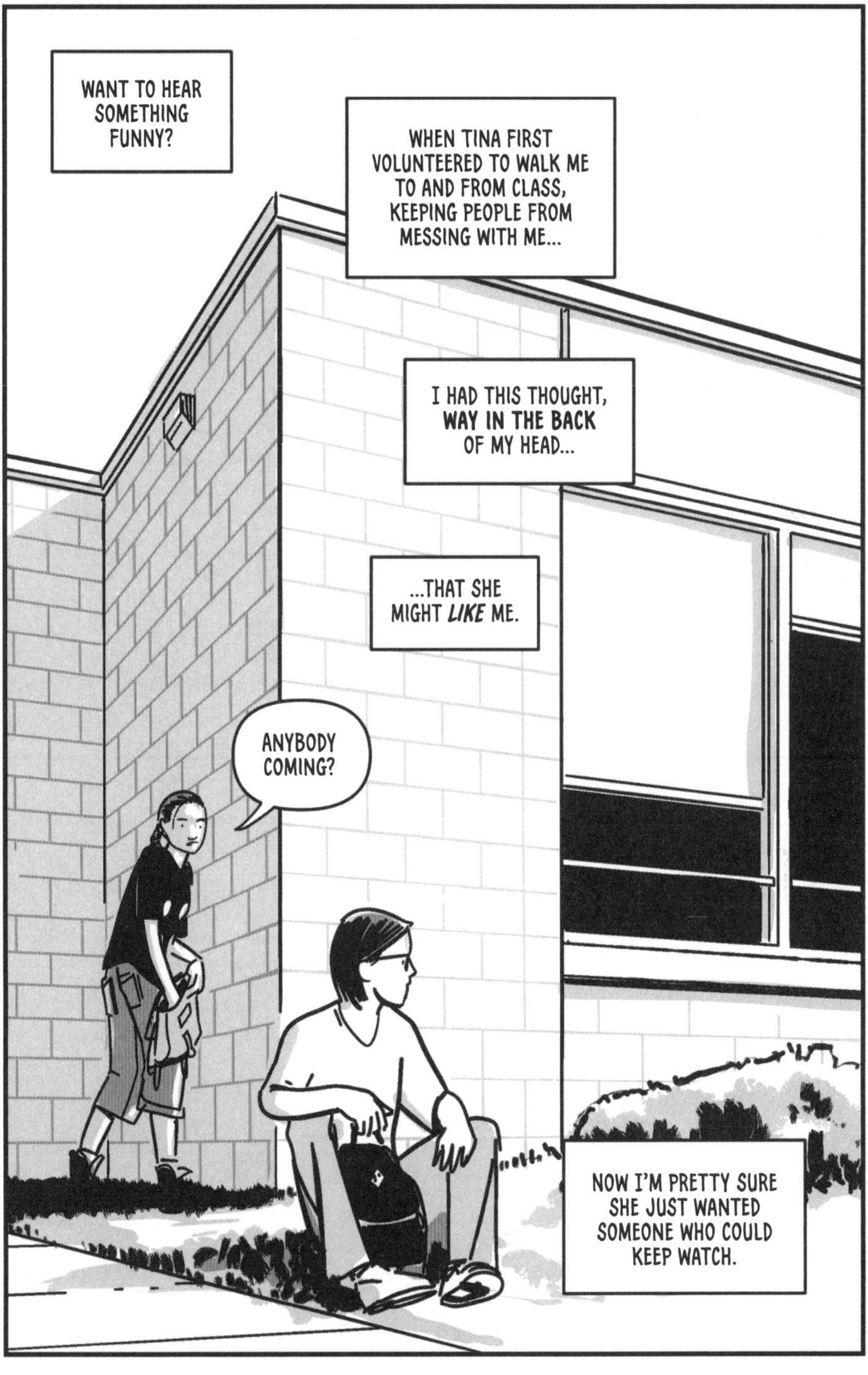
WANT TO HEAR SOMETHING FUNNY?
WHEN TINA FIRST VOLUNTEERED TO WALK ME TO AND FROM CLASS, KEEPING PEOPLE FROM MESSING WITH ME...
I HAD THIS THOUGHT, **WAY IN THE BACK** OF MY HEAD...
...THAT SHE MIGHT *LIKE* ME.
ANYBODY COMING?
NOW I'M PRETTY SURE SHE JUST WANTED SOMEONE WHO COULD KEEP WATCH.

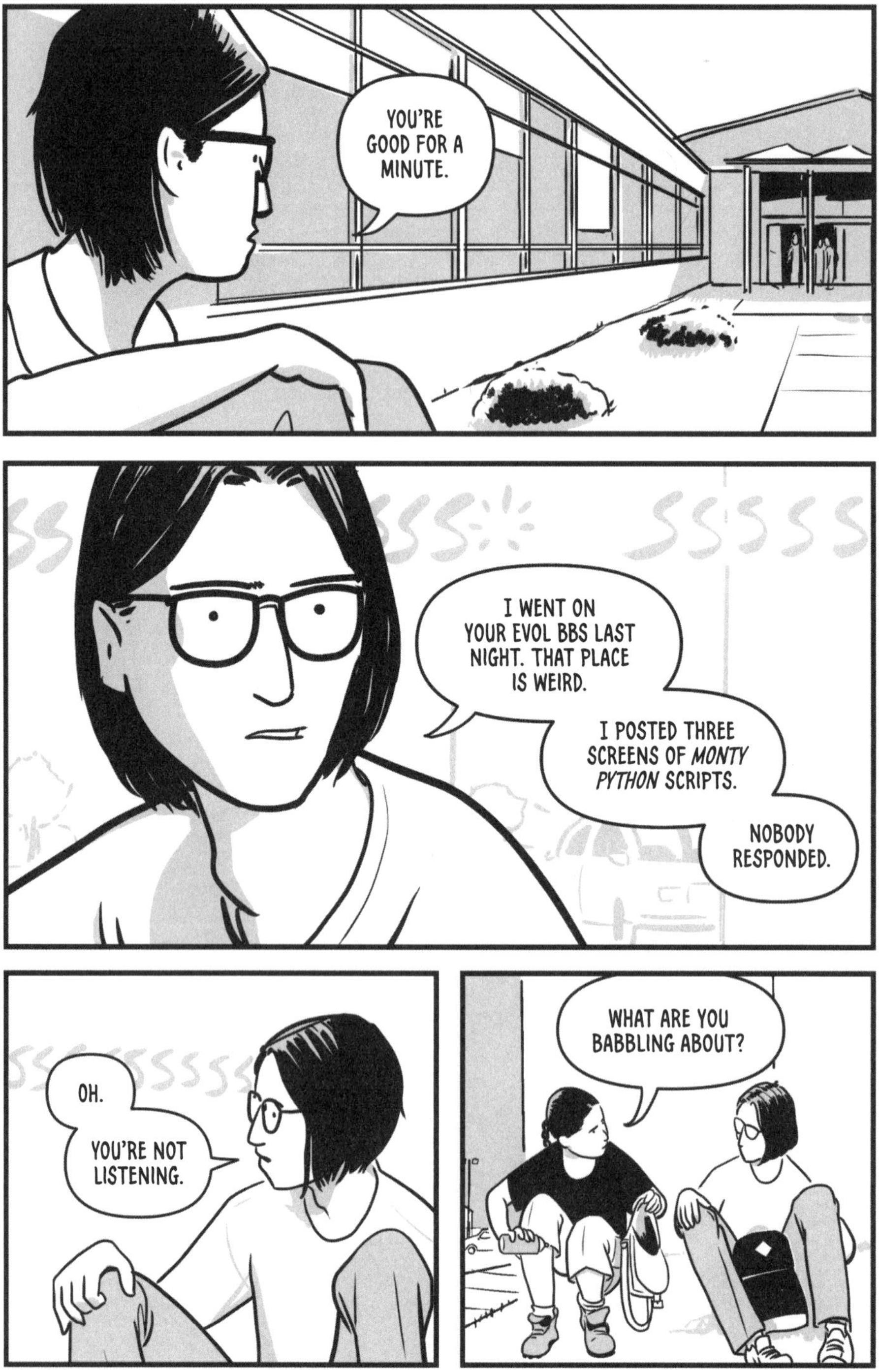
YOU'RE GOOD FOR A MINUTE.
I WENT ON YOUR EVOL BBS LAST NIGHT. THAT PLACE IS WEIRD.
I POSTED THREE SCREENS OF *MONTY PYTHON* SCRIPTS.
NOBODY RESPONDED.
OH.
YOU'RE NOT LISTENING.
WHAT ARE YOU BABBLING ABOUT?

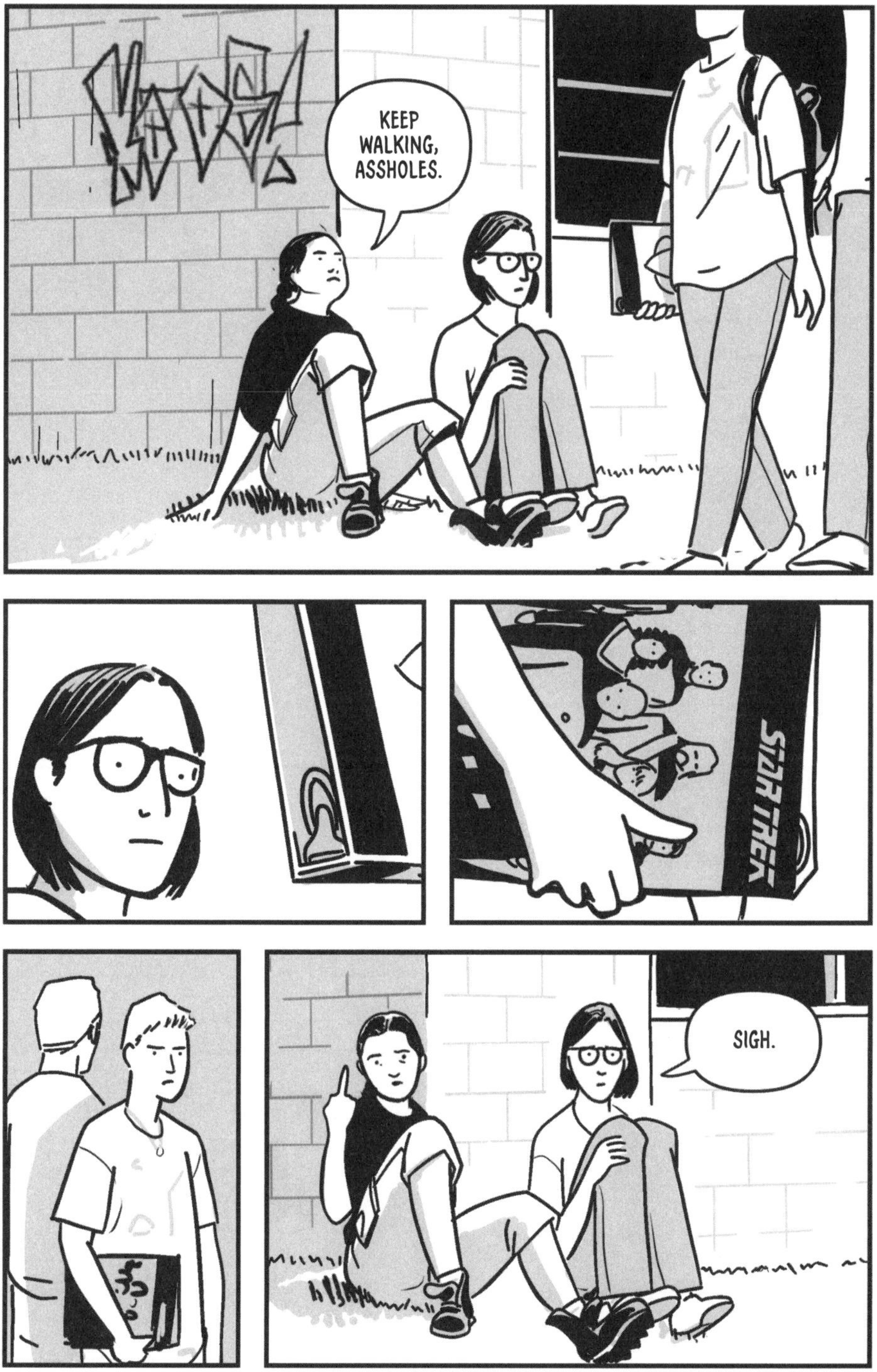
KEEP WALKING, ASSHOLES.
STAR TREK
SIGH.

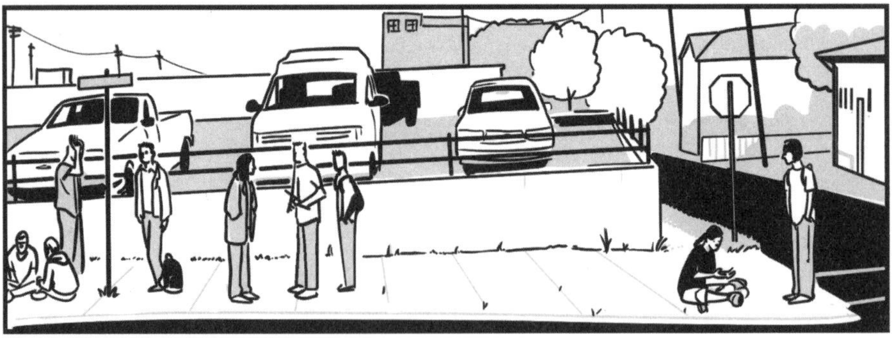

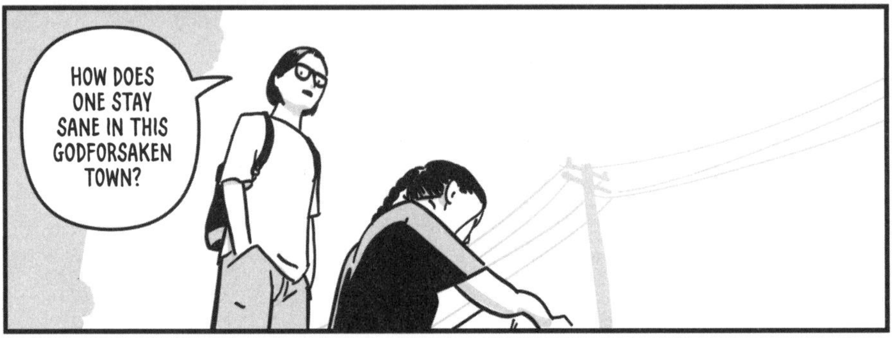
HOW DOES ONE STAY SANE IN THIS GODFORSAKEN TOWN?

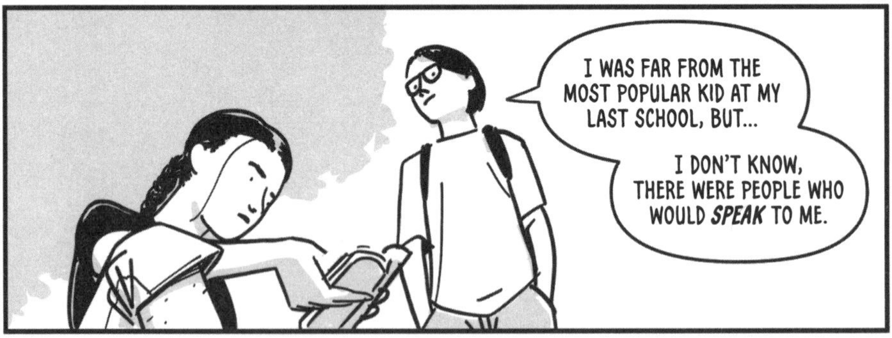
I WAS FAR FROM THE MOST POPULAR KID AT MY LAST SCHOOL, BUT...
I DON'T KNOW, THERE WERE PEOPLE WHO WOULD *SPEAK* TO ME.

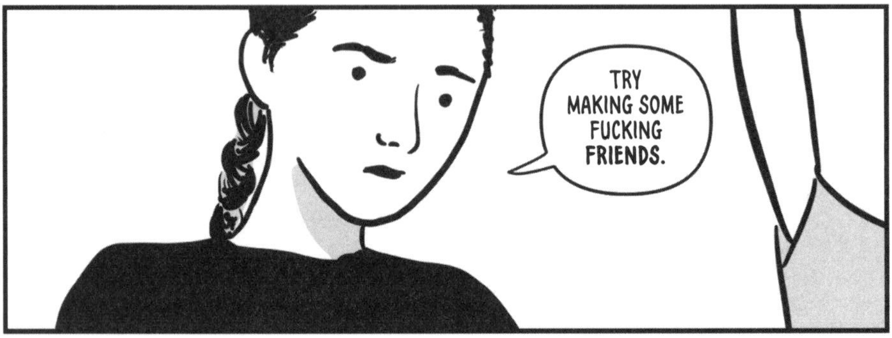
TRY MAKING SOME FUCKING **FRIENDS.**

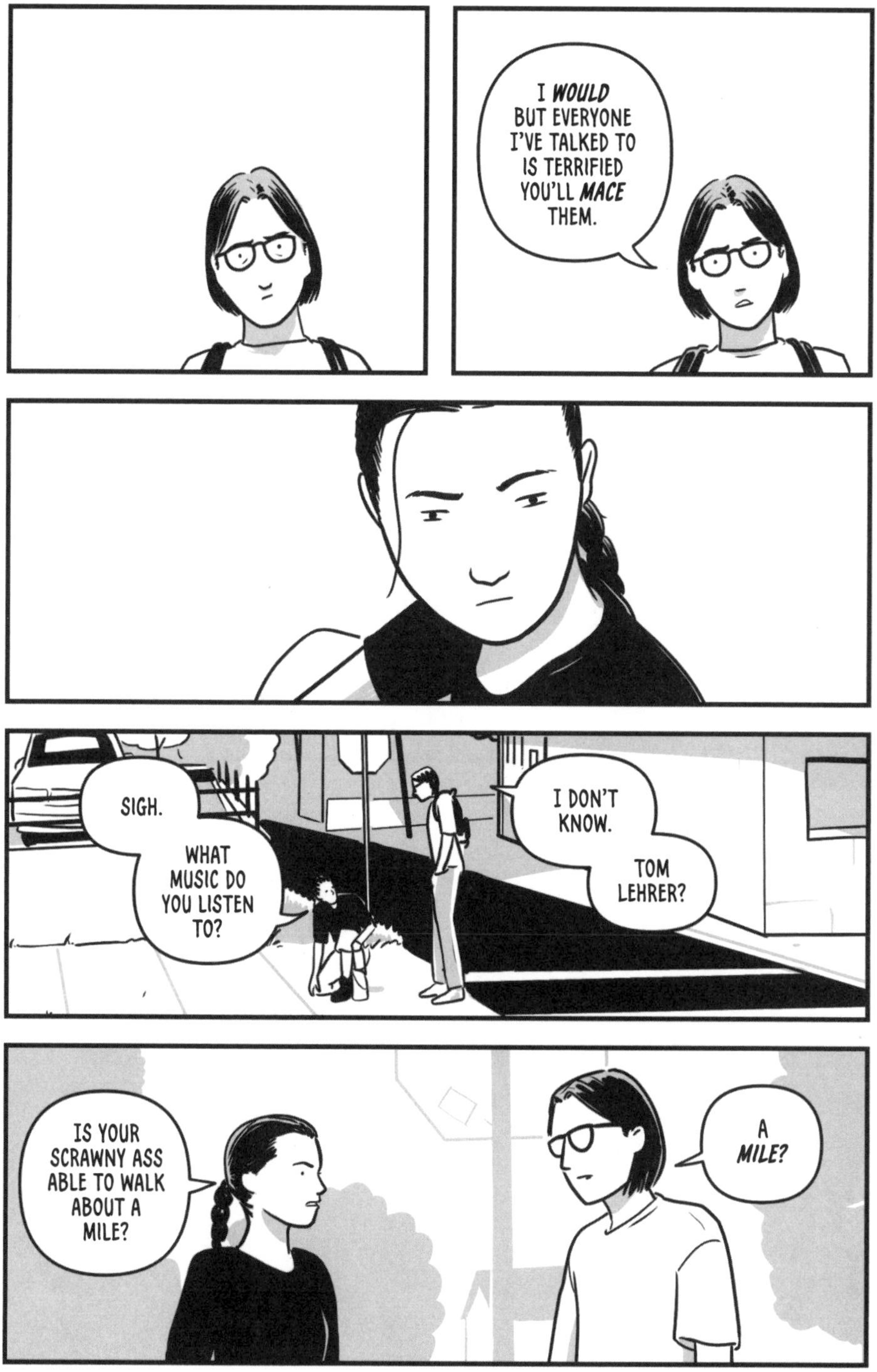
I *WOULD* BUT EVERYONE I'VE TALKED TO IS TERRIFIED YOU'LL *MACE* THEM.
SIGH.
WHAT MUSIC DO YOU LISTEN TO?
I DON'T KNOW.
TOM LEHRER?
IS YOUR SCRAWNY ASS ABLE TO WALK ABOUT A MILE?
A *MILE?*

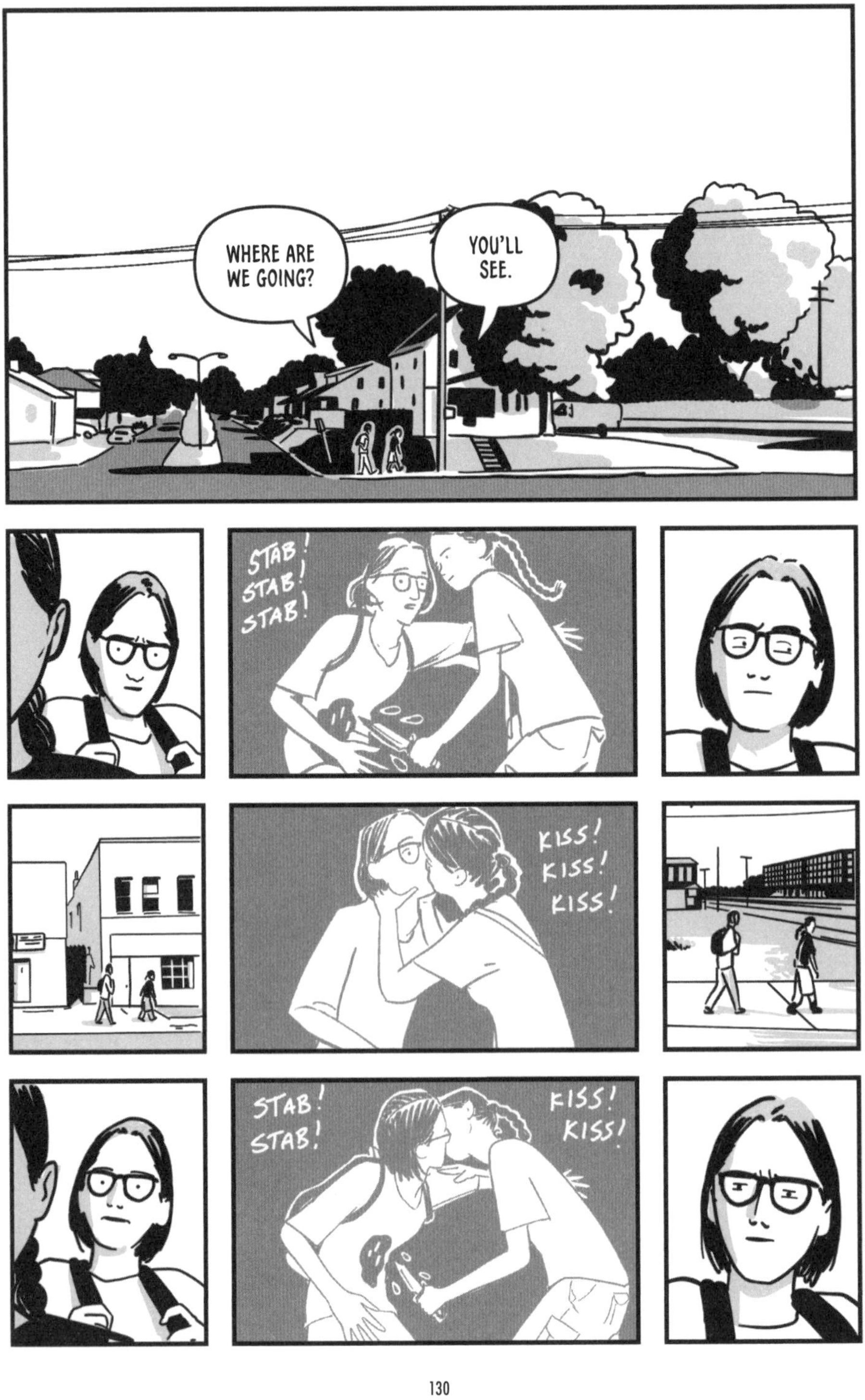
WHERE ARE WE GOING?
YOU'LL SEE.
STAB! STAB! STAB!
KISS! KISS! KISS!
STAB! STAB!
KISS! KISS!

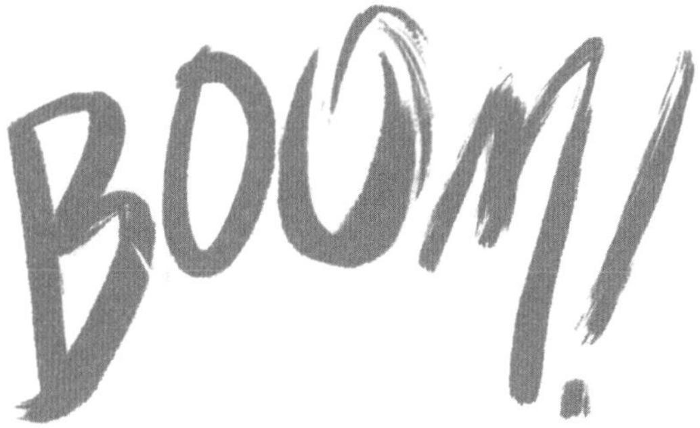
BOOM!

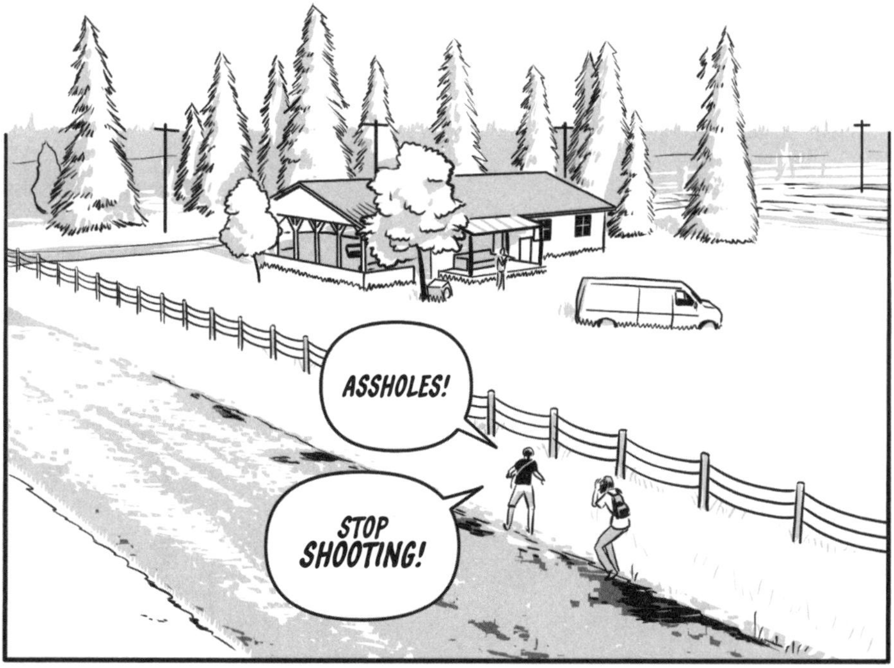
ASSHOLES!
STOP SHOOTING!

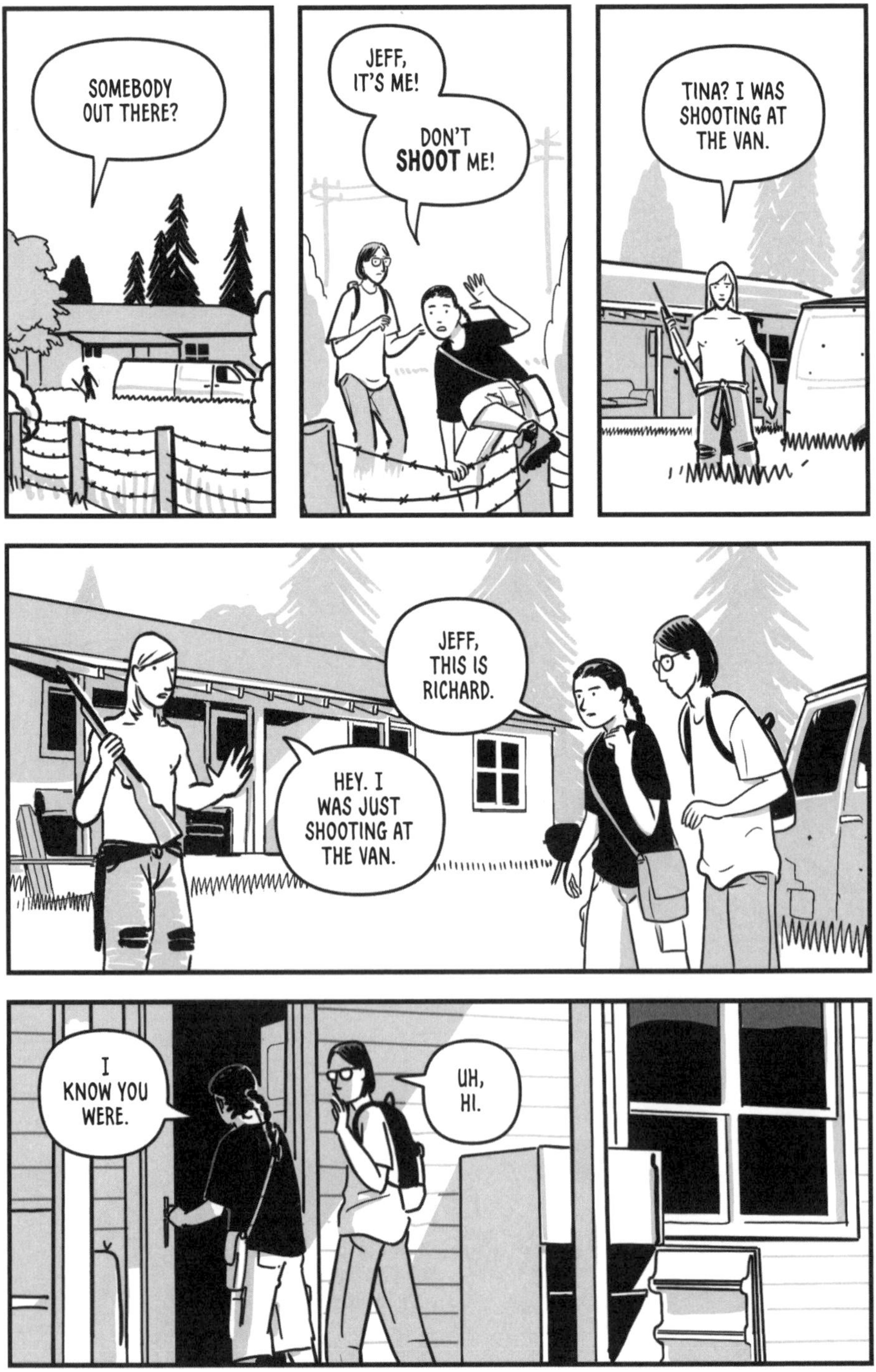
SOMEBODY OUT THERE?
JEFF, IT'S ME!
DON'T SHOOT ME!
TINA? I WAS SHOOTING AT THE VAN.
JEFF, THIS IS RICHARD.
HEY. I WAS JUST SHOOTING AT THE VAN.
I KNOW YOU WERE.
UH, HI.

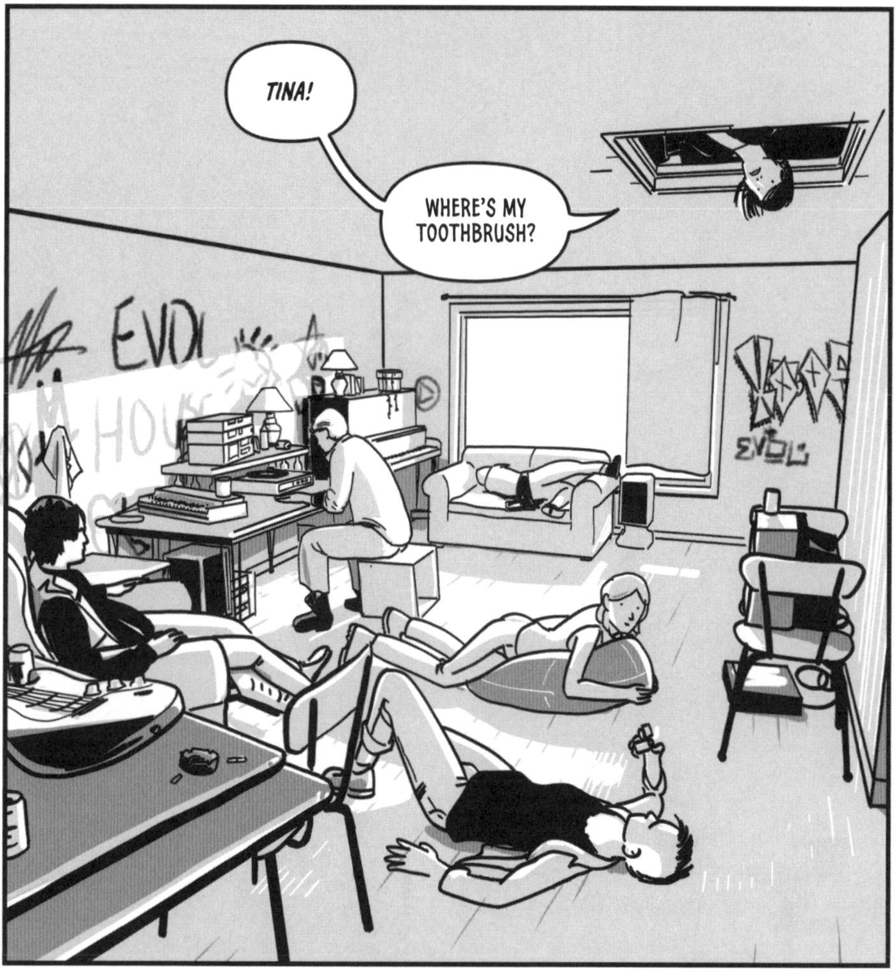
TINA!
WHERE'S MY TOOTHBRUSH?

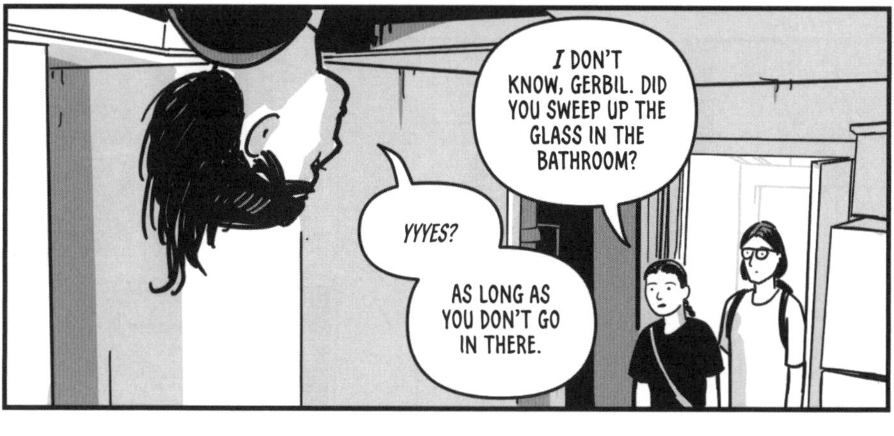
I DON'T KNOW, GERBIL. DID YOU SWEEP UP THE GLASS IN THE BATHROOM?
YYYES?
AS LONG AS YOU DON'T GO IN THERE.

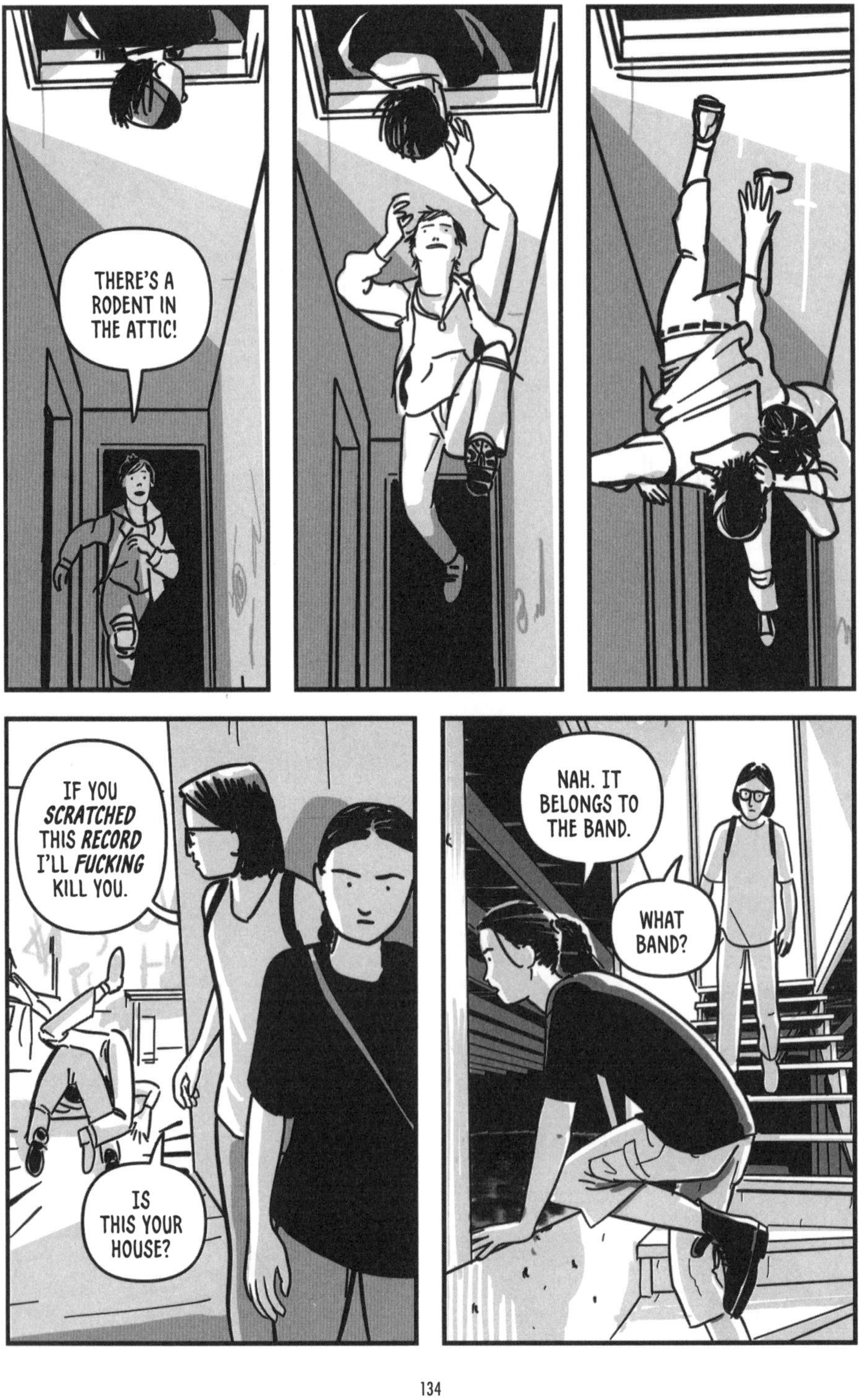
THERE'S A RODENT IN THE ATTIC!
IF YOU *SCRATCHED* THIS *RECORD* I'LL *FUCKING* KILL YOU.
IS THIS YOUR HOUSE?
NAH. IT BELONGS TO THE BAND.
WHAT BAND?

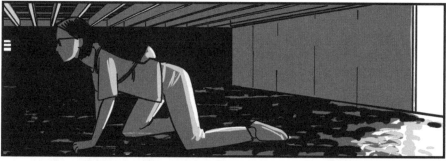

HERE.

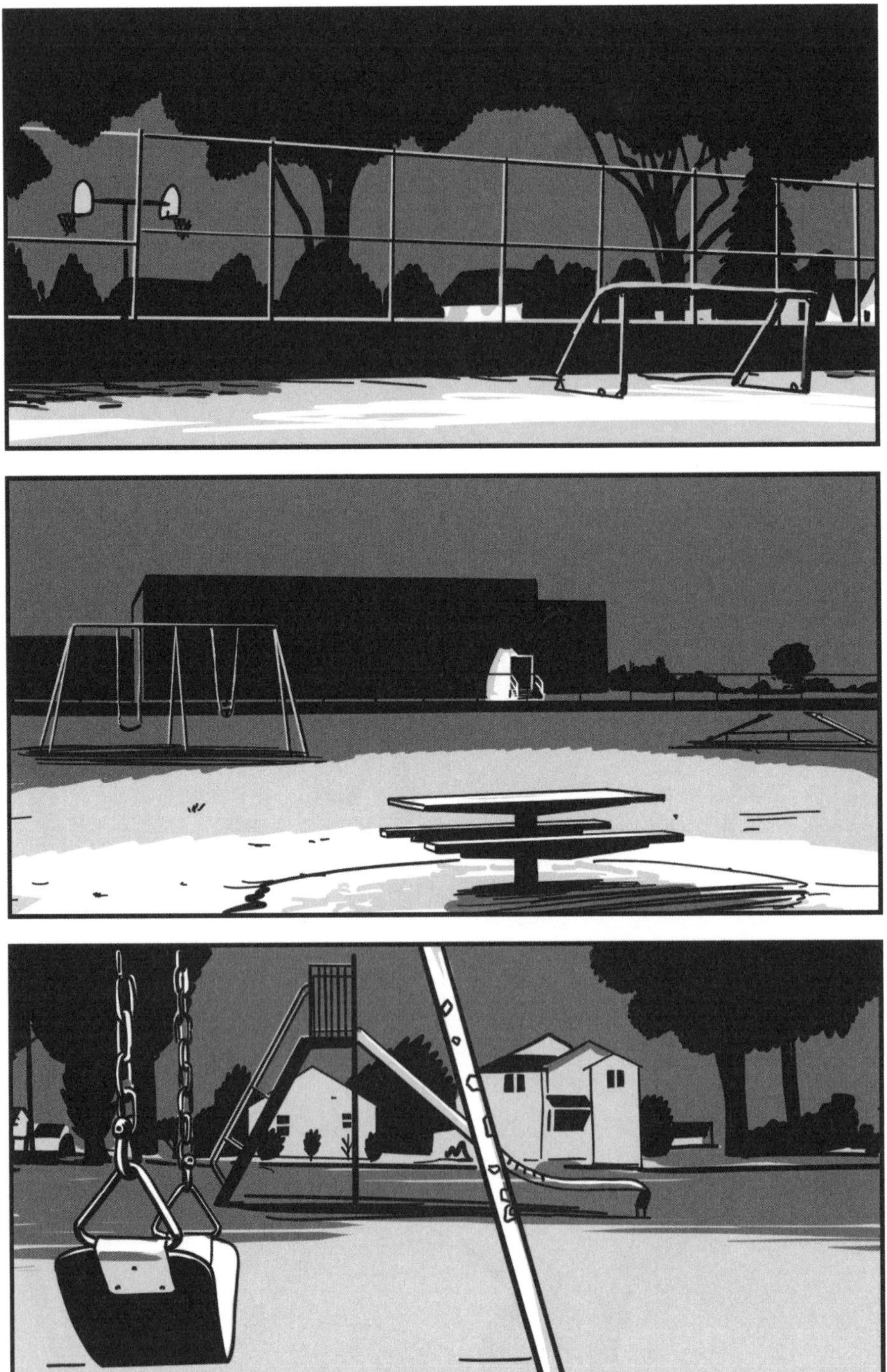

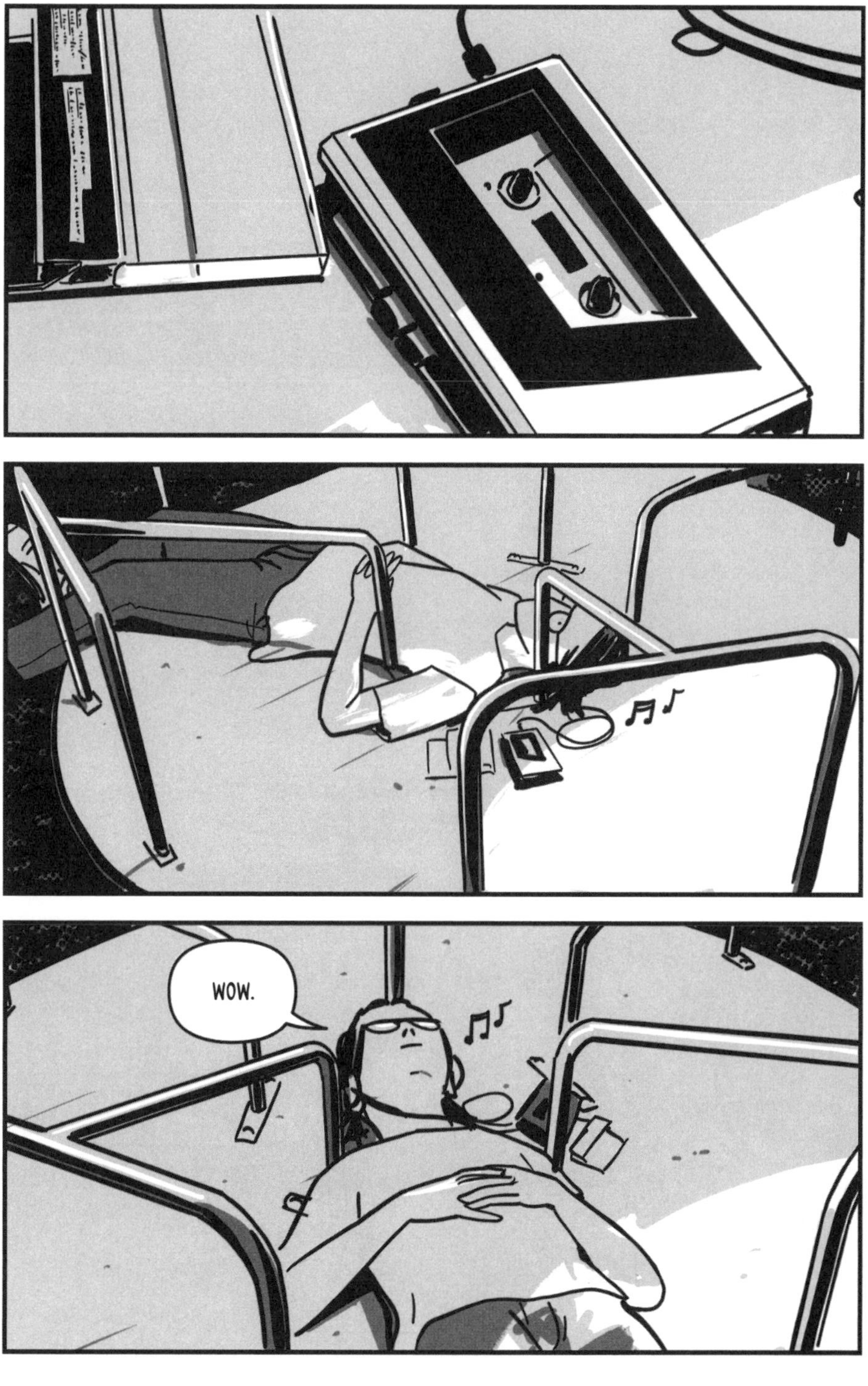
WOW.

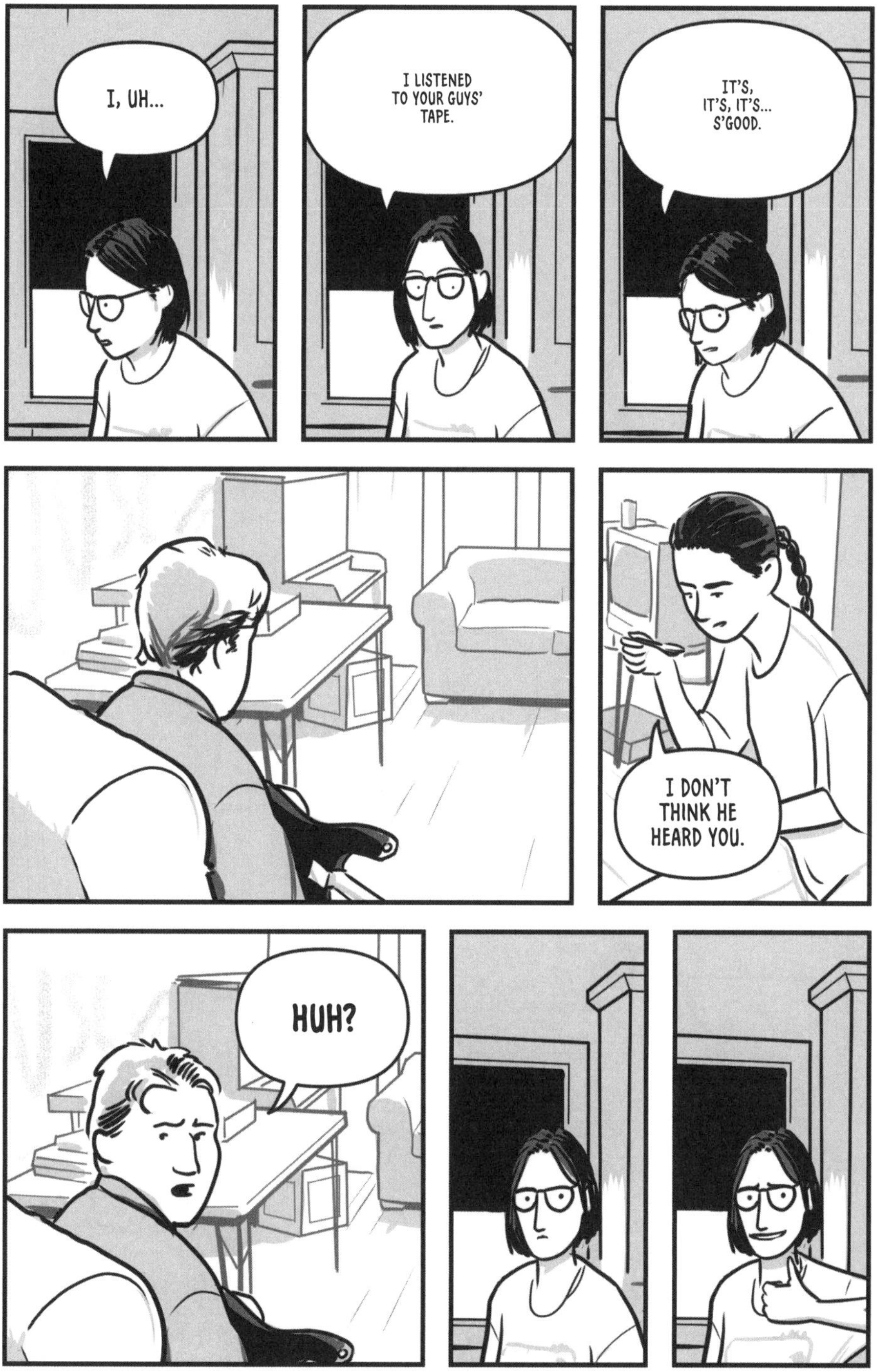
I, UH...
I LISTENED TO YOUR GUYS' TAPE.
IT'S, IT'S, IT'S... S'GOOD.
I DON'T THINK HE HEARD YOU.
HUH?

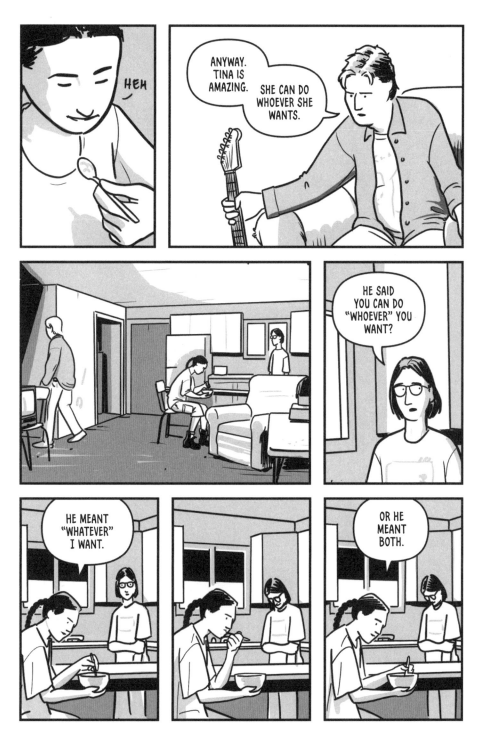

143

BOOM!

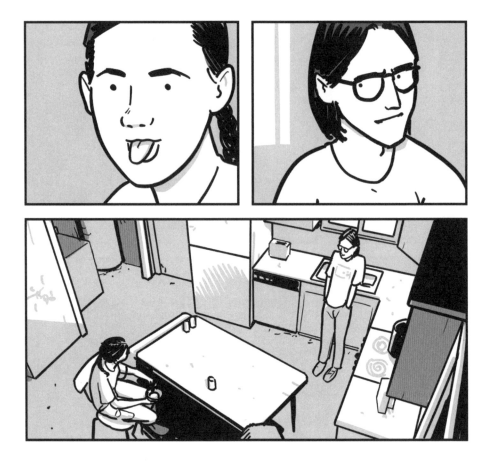

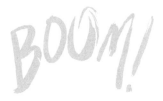

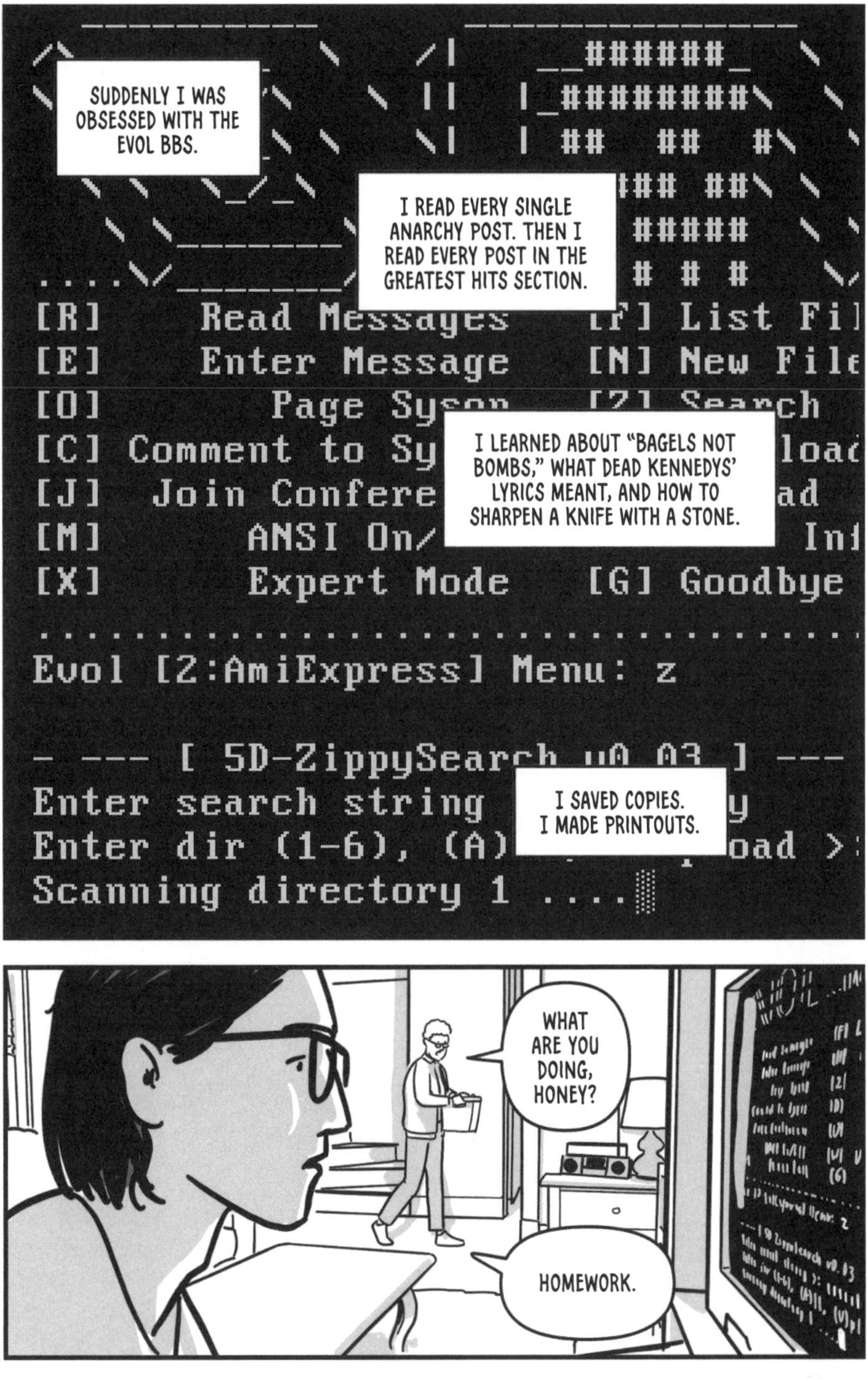
SUDDENLY I WAS OBSESSED WITH THE EVOL BBS.
I READ EVERY SINGLE ANARCHY POST. THEN I READ EVERY POST IN THE GREATEST HITS SECTION.
[R] Read Messages
[E] Enter Message
[N] New File
[O] Page Sysop
[C] Comment to Sy
[J] Join Confere
[M] ANSI On/
[X] Expert Mode
[G] Goodbye
I LEARNED ABOUT "BAGELS NOT BOMBS," WHAT DEAD KENNEDYS' LYRICS MEANT, AND HOW TO SHARPEN A KNIFE WITH A STONE.
Evol [2:AmiExpress] Menu: z
Enter search string
Enter dir (1-6), (A)
Scanning directory 1 ....
I SAVED COPIES. I MADE PRINTOUTS.
WHAT ARE YOU DOING, HONEY?
HOMEWORK.

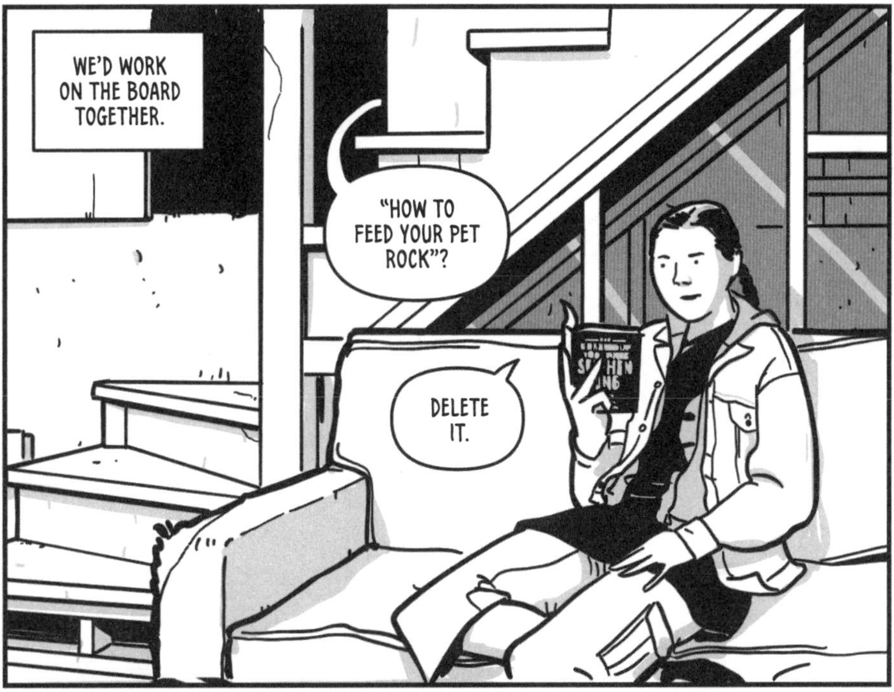
WE'D WORK ON THE BOARD TOGETHER.
"HOW TO FEED YOUR PET ROCK"?
DELETE IT.

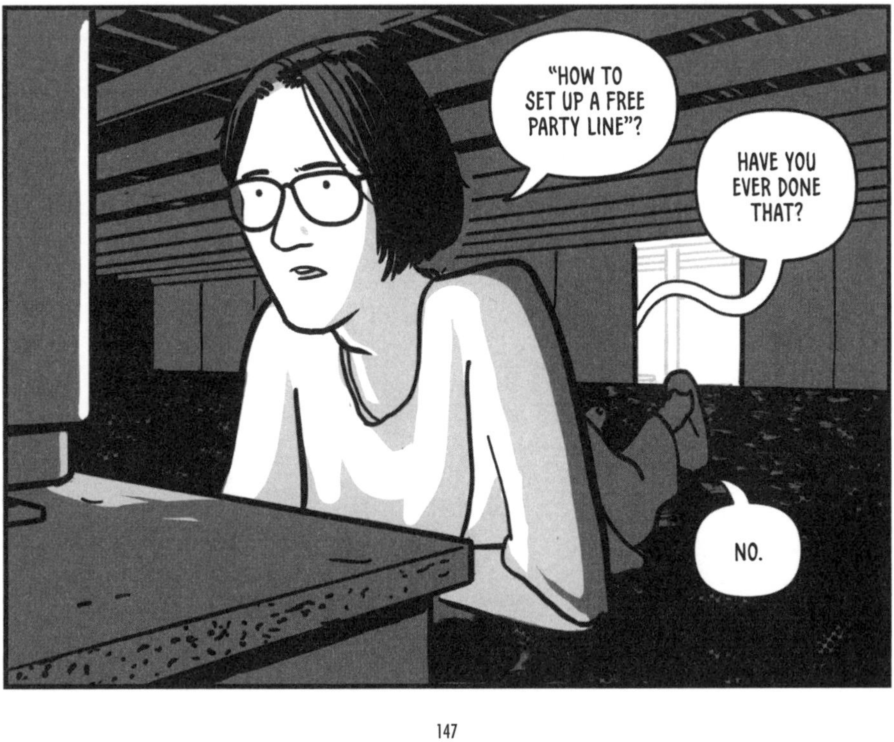
"HOW TO SET UP A FREE PARTY LINE"?
HAVE YOU EVER DONE THAT?
NO.

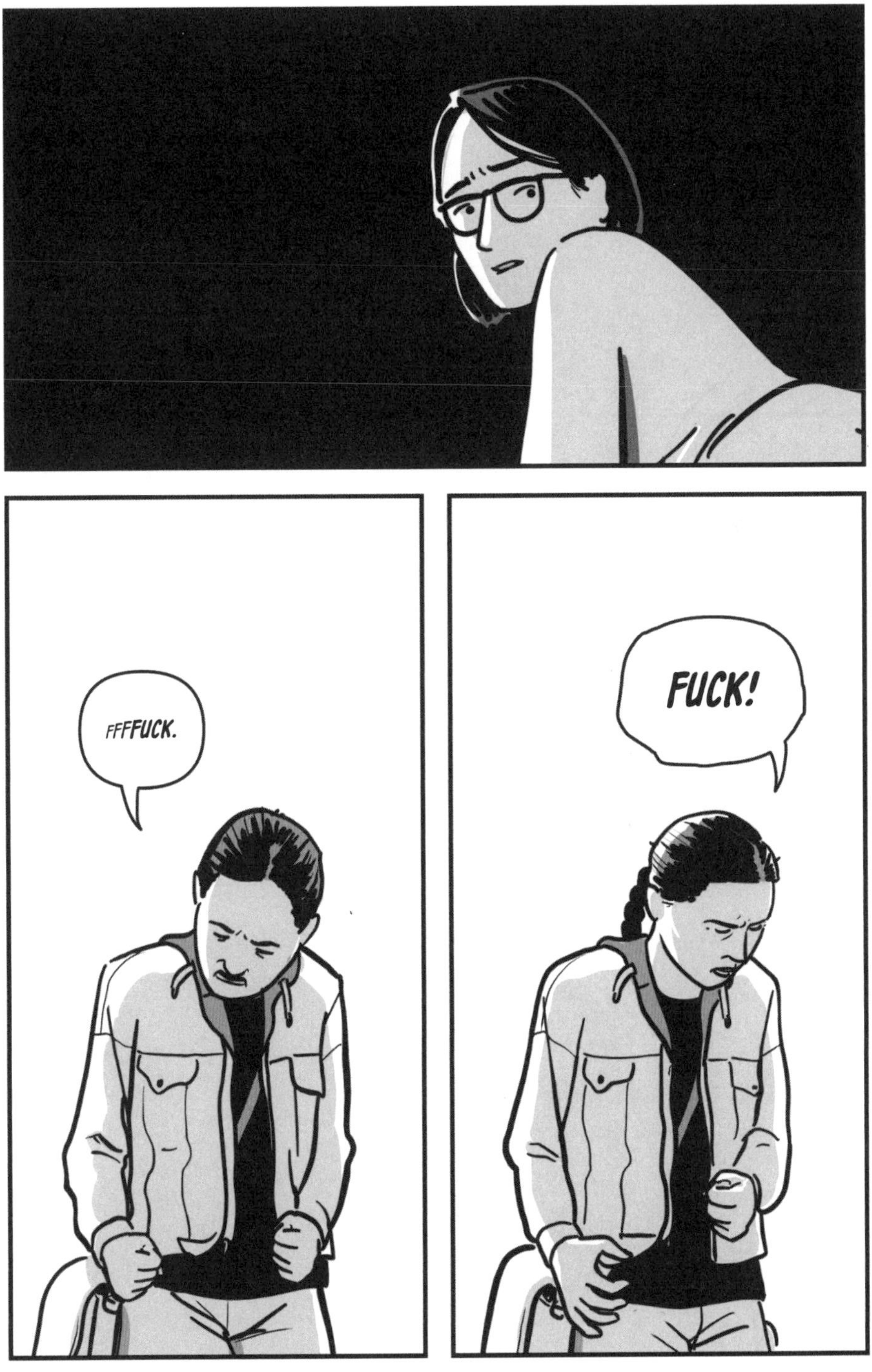
FFFFUCK.
FUCK!

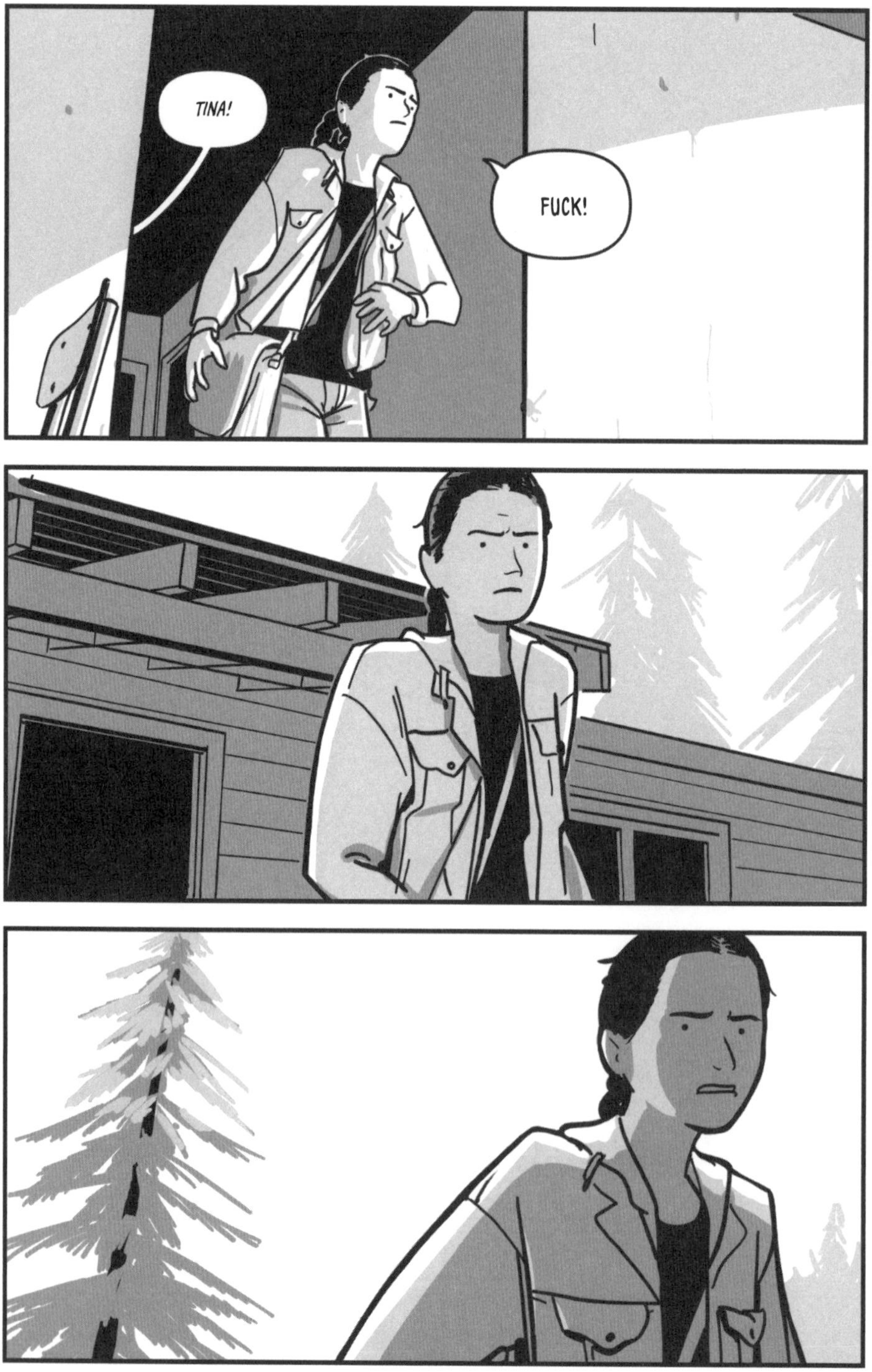
TINA!
FUCK!

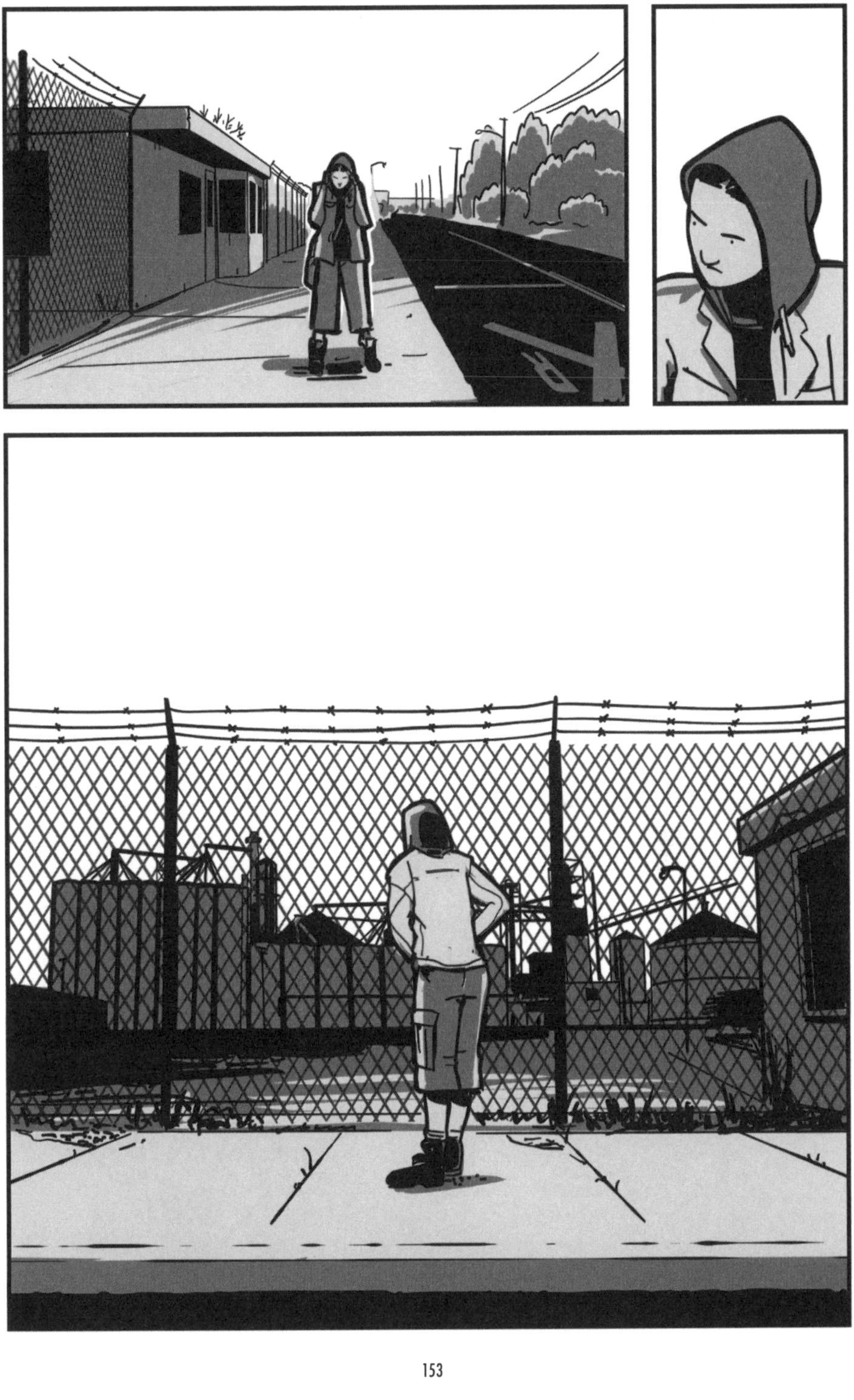

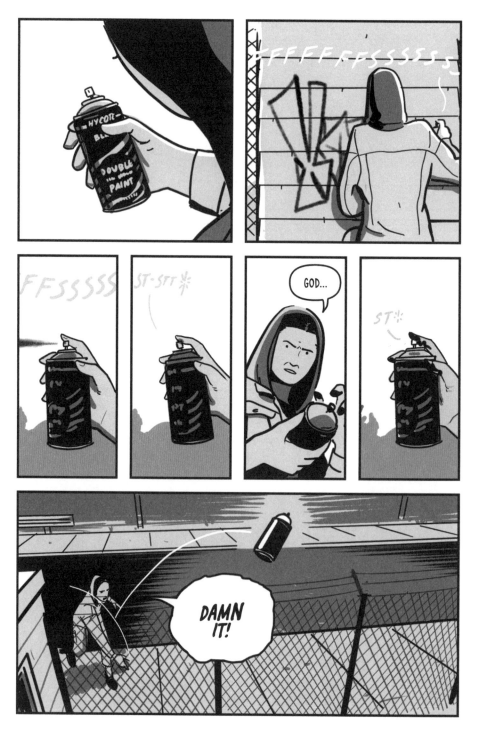

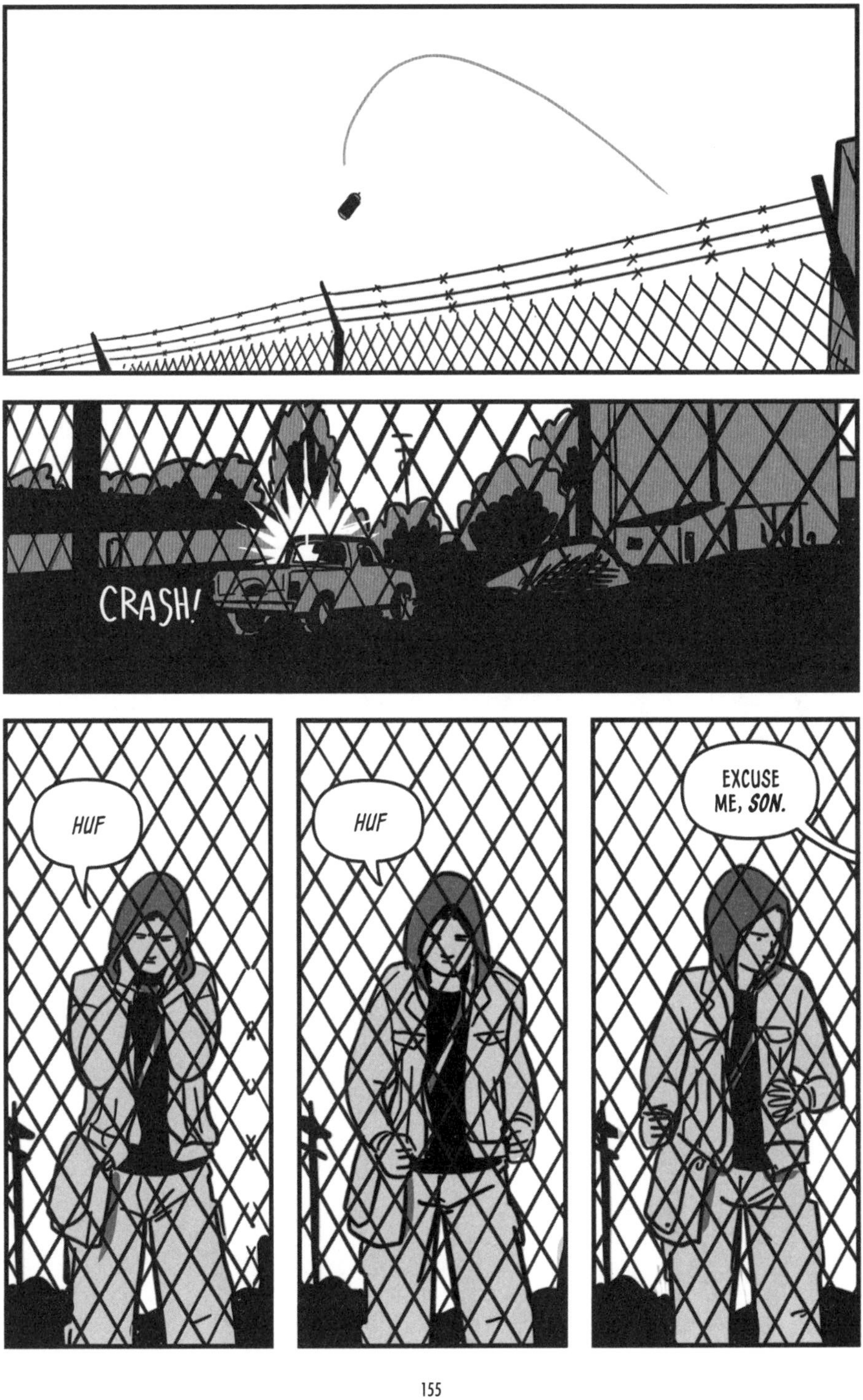
CRASH!
HUF
HUF
EXCUSE ME, SON.

156

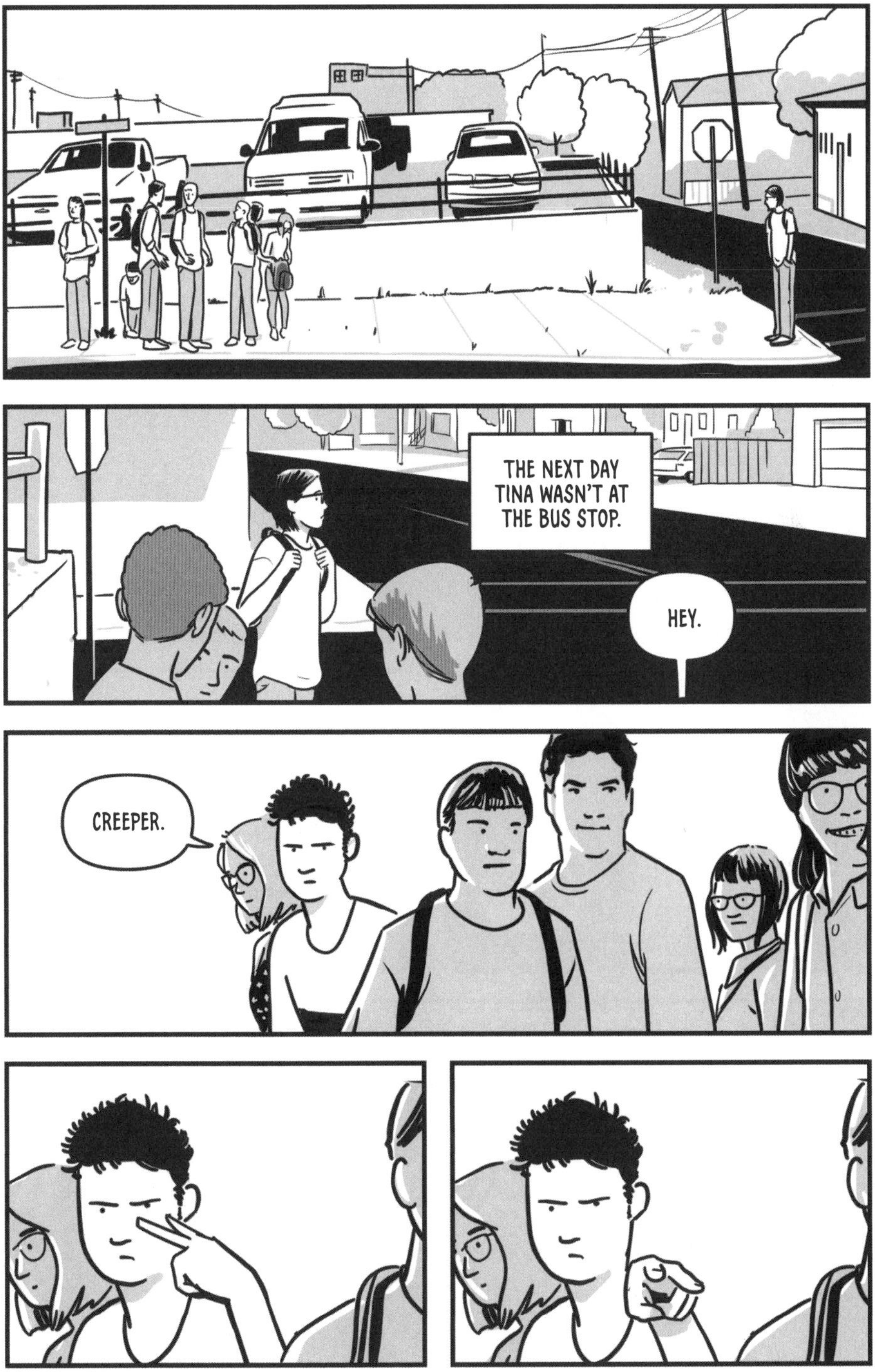
THE NEXT DAY TINA WASN'T AT THE BUS STOP.
HEY.
CREEPER.

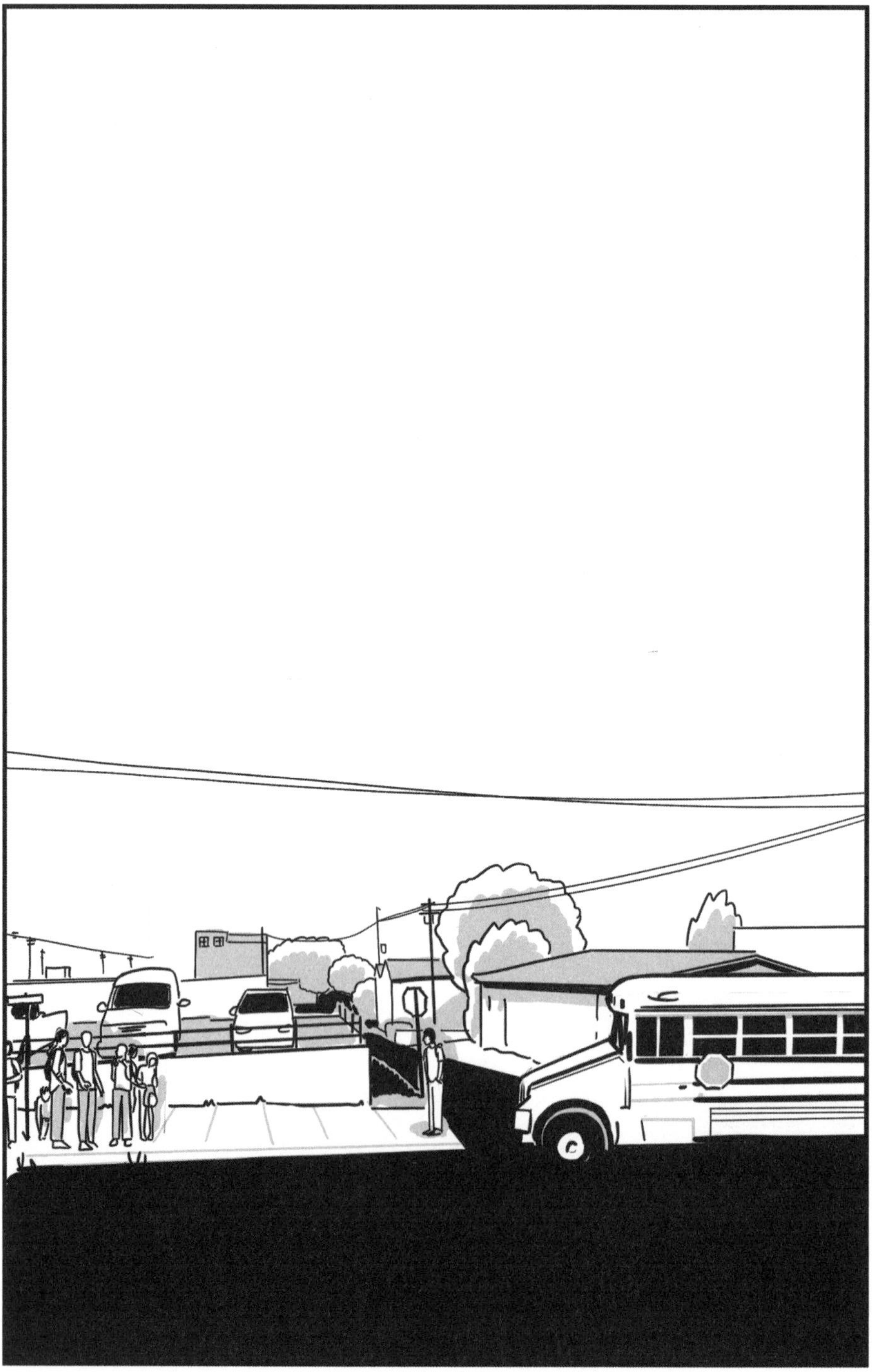

Chapter 5

KAOS

Richard

GAT GCS GM GS d -p+ c+++(++++) l++(+++) u+@ e×
m(+) s+/- n--- h× !f(+) g+ w++ t++(+++) r? y?

161

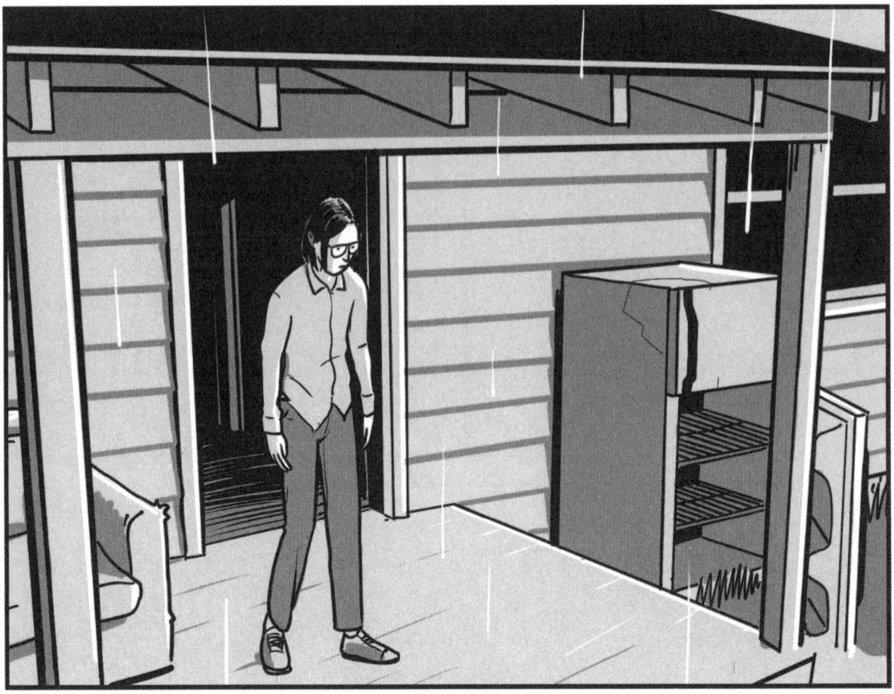

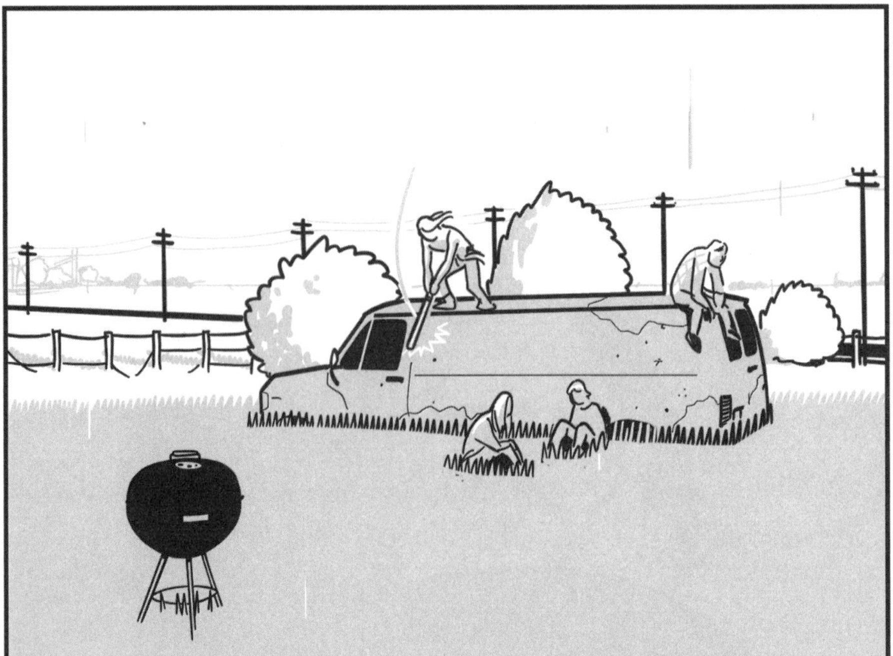

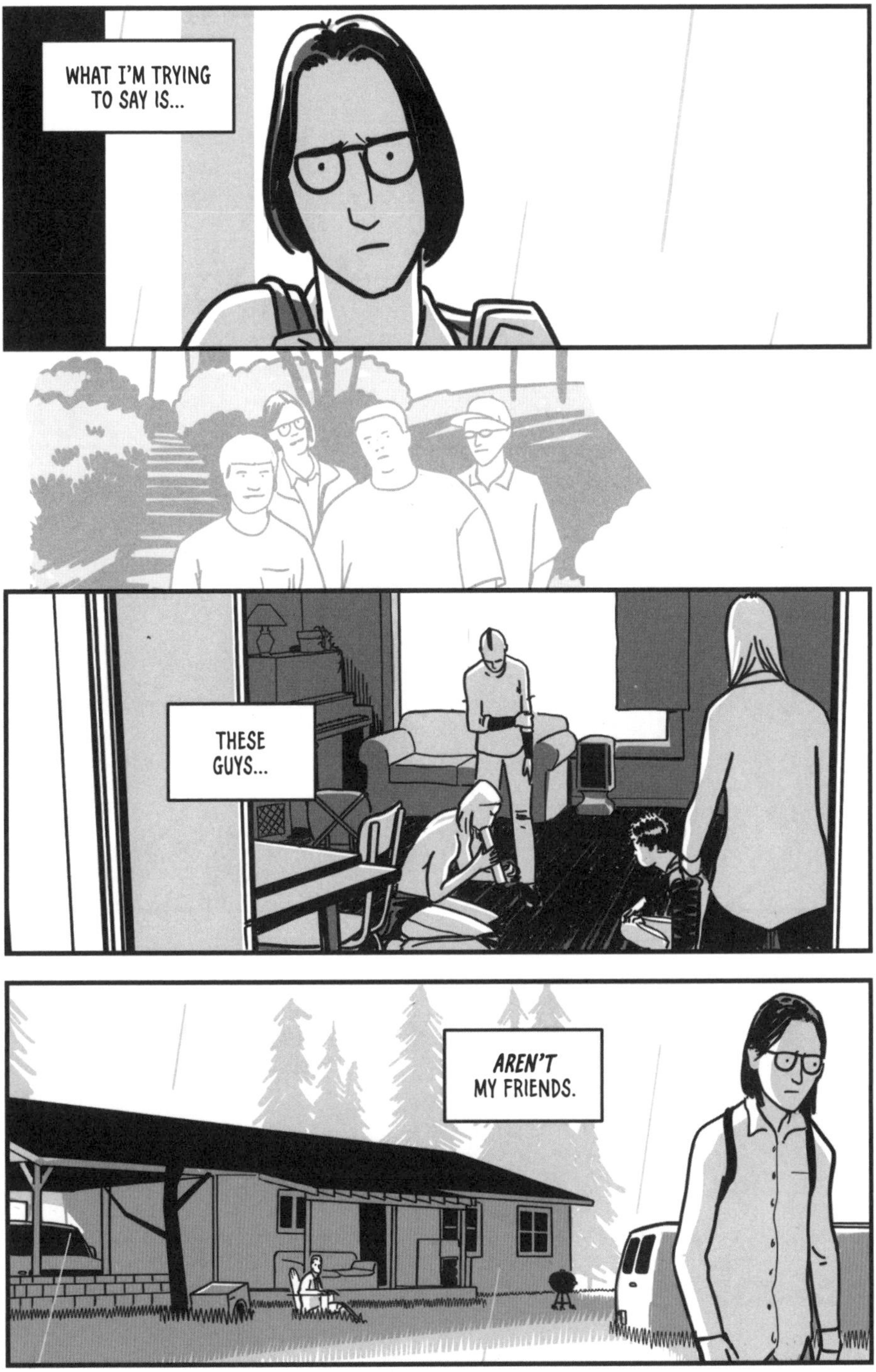
WHAT I'M TRYING TO SAY IS...
THESE GUYS...
AREN'T MY FRIENDS.

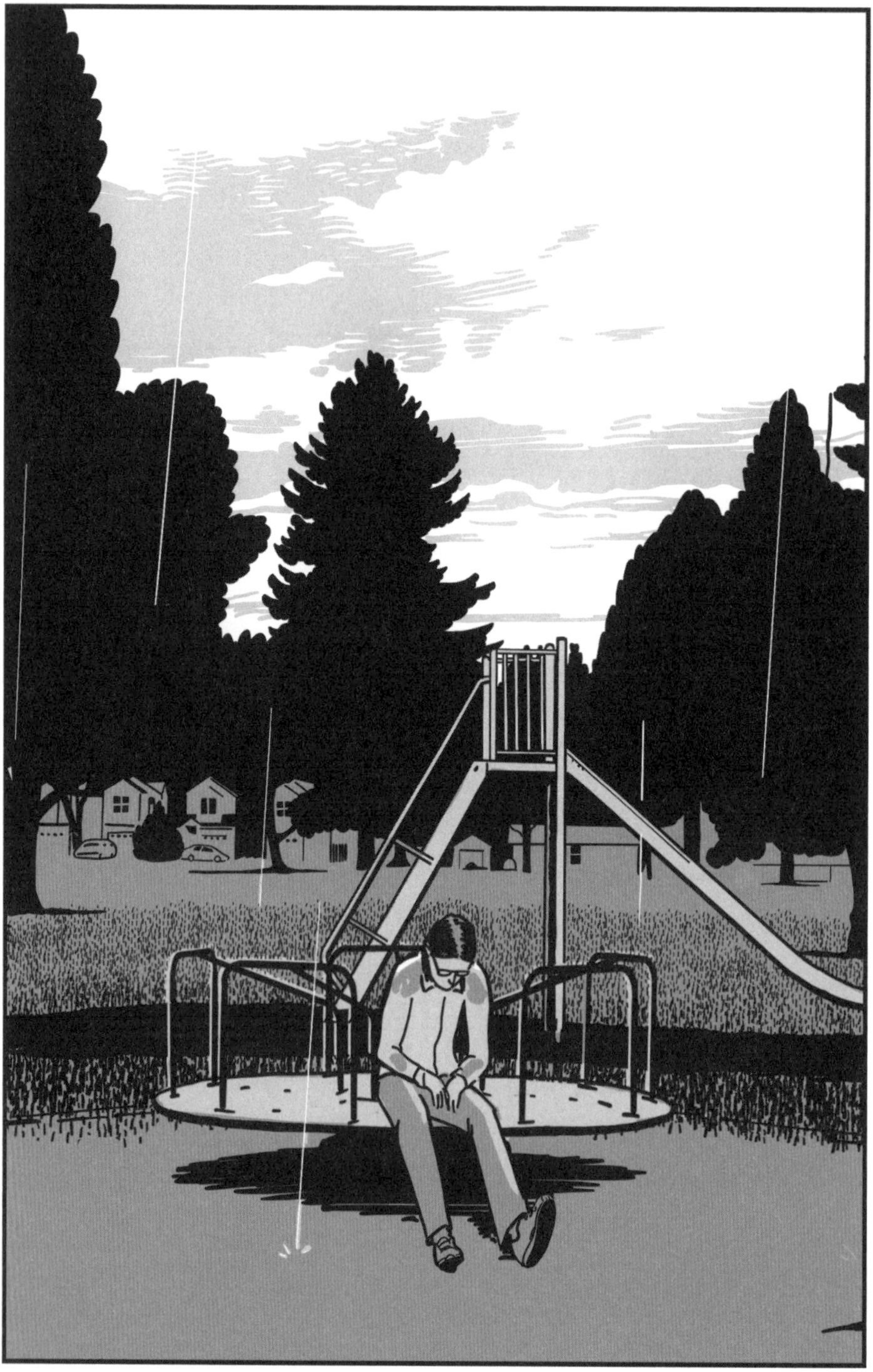

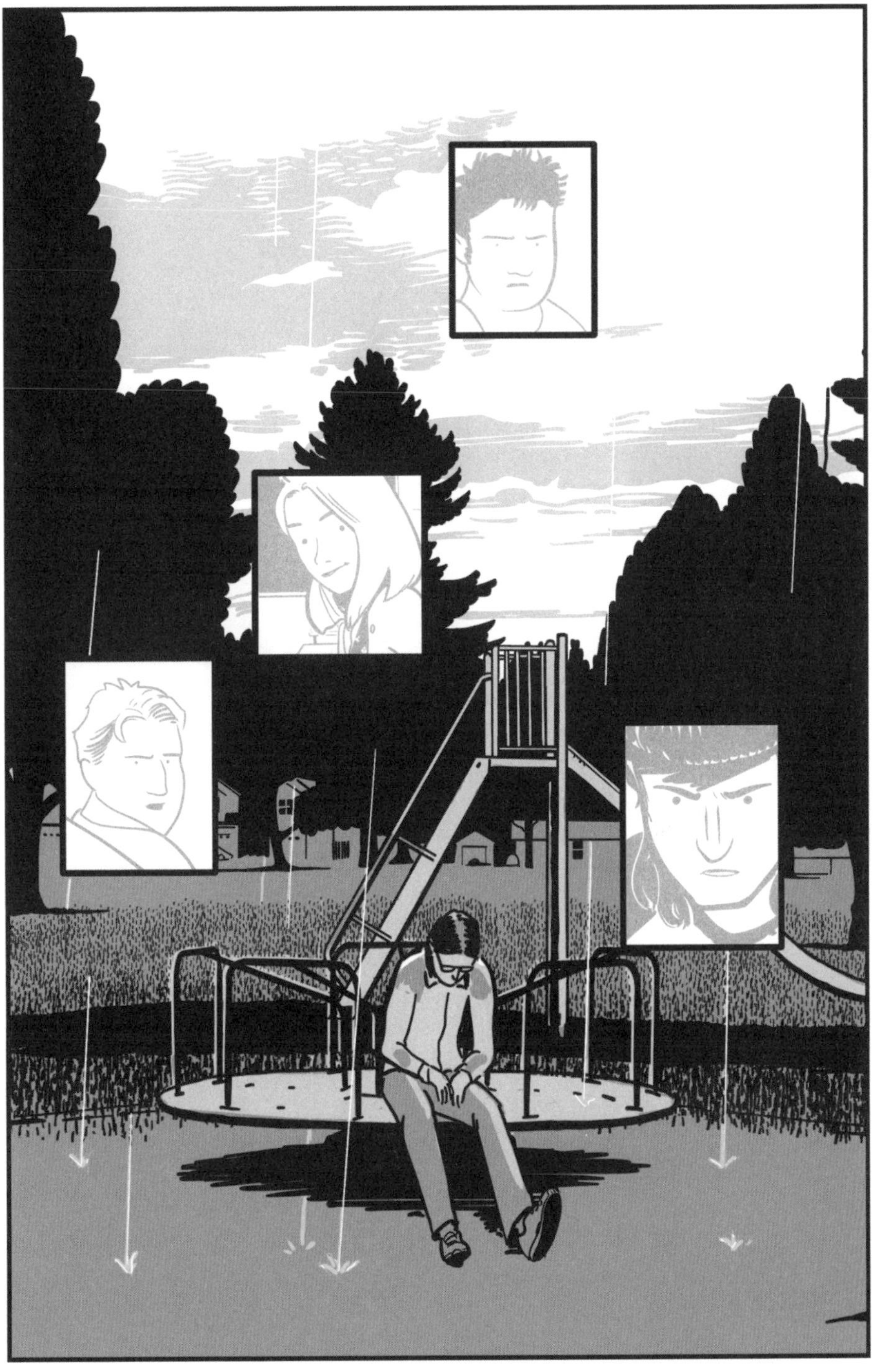

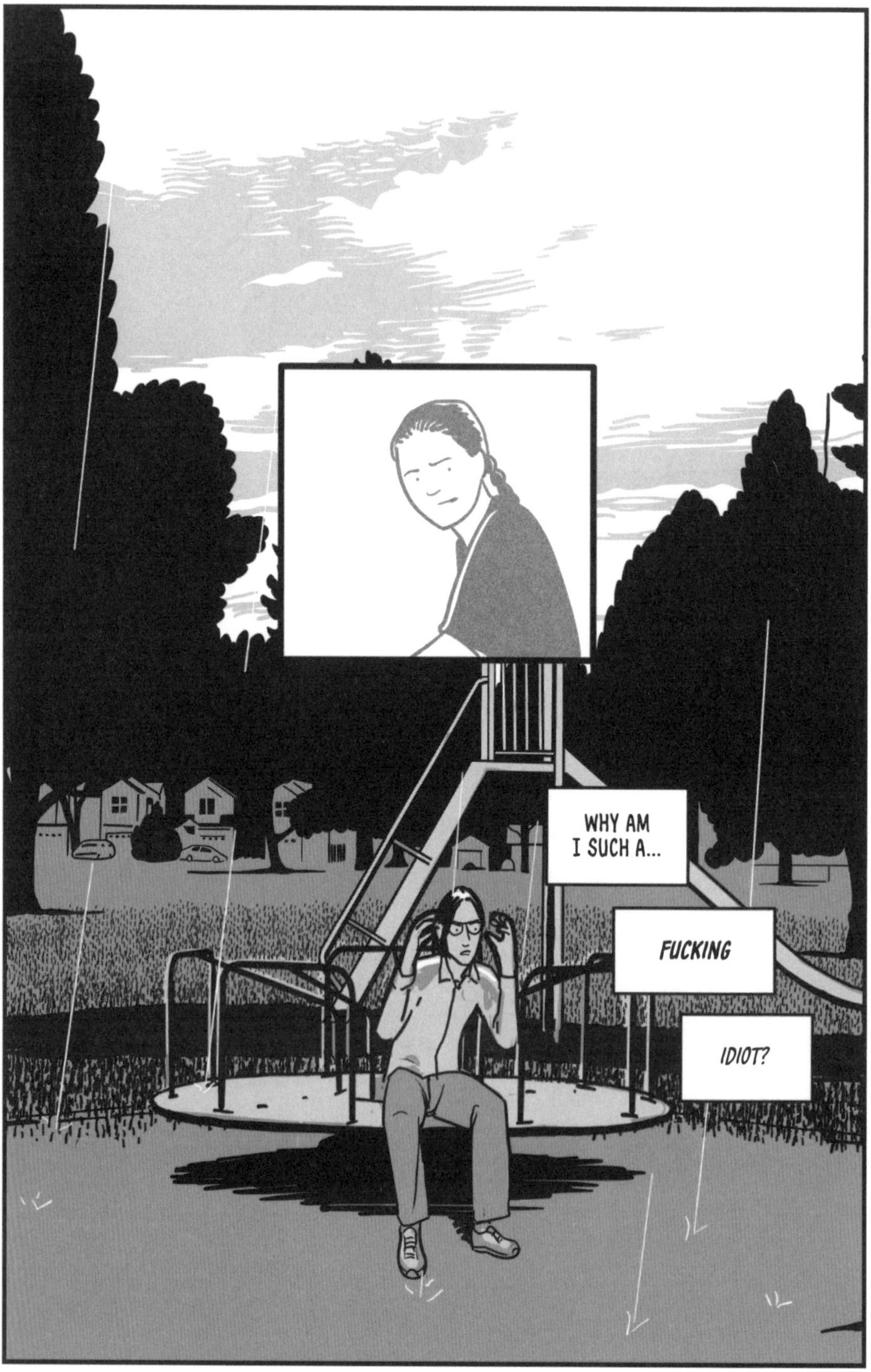
WHY AM I SUCH A...
FUCKING
IDIOT?

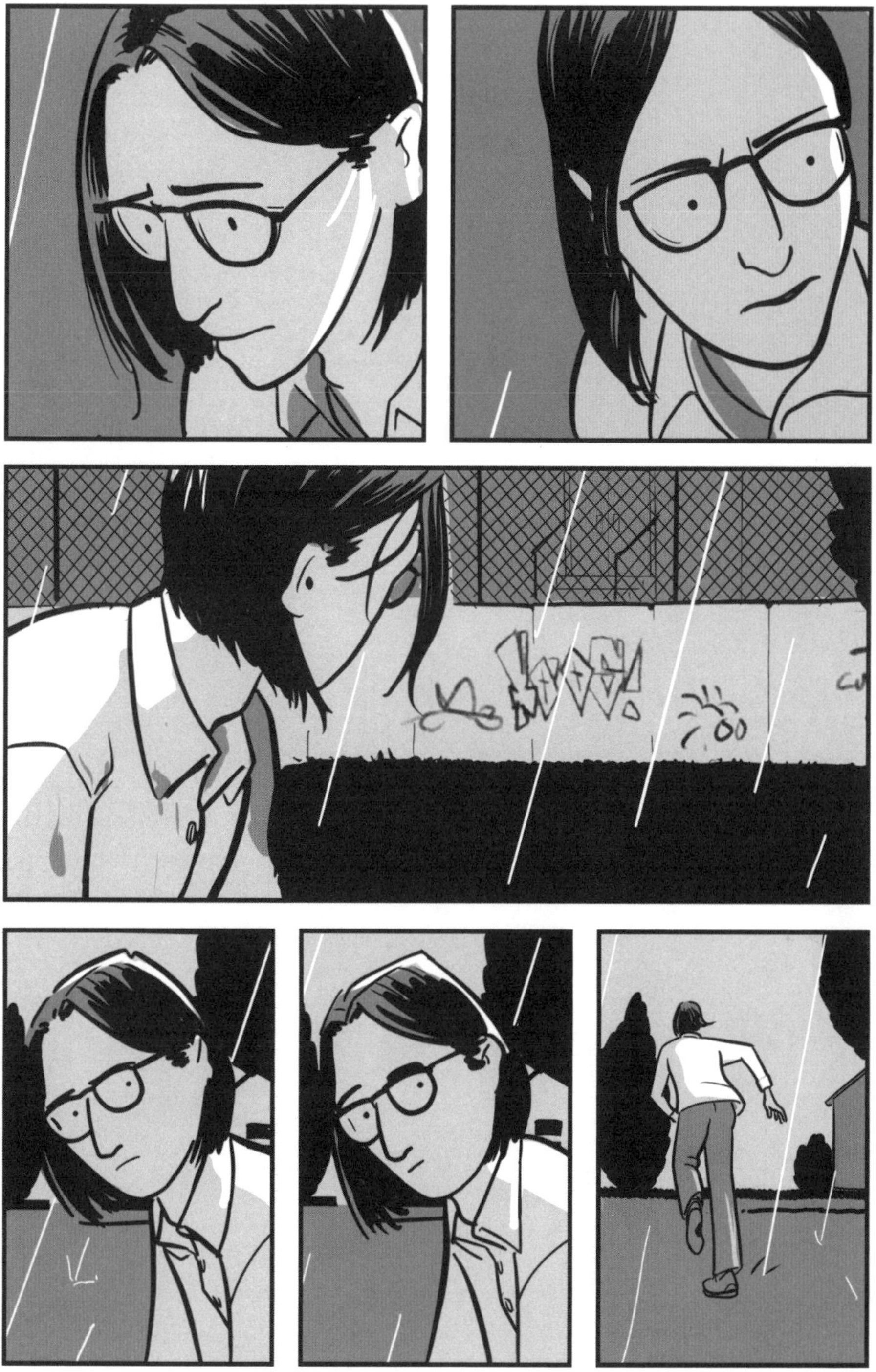

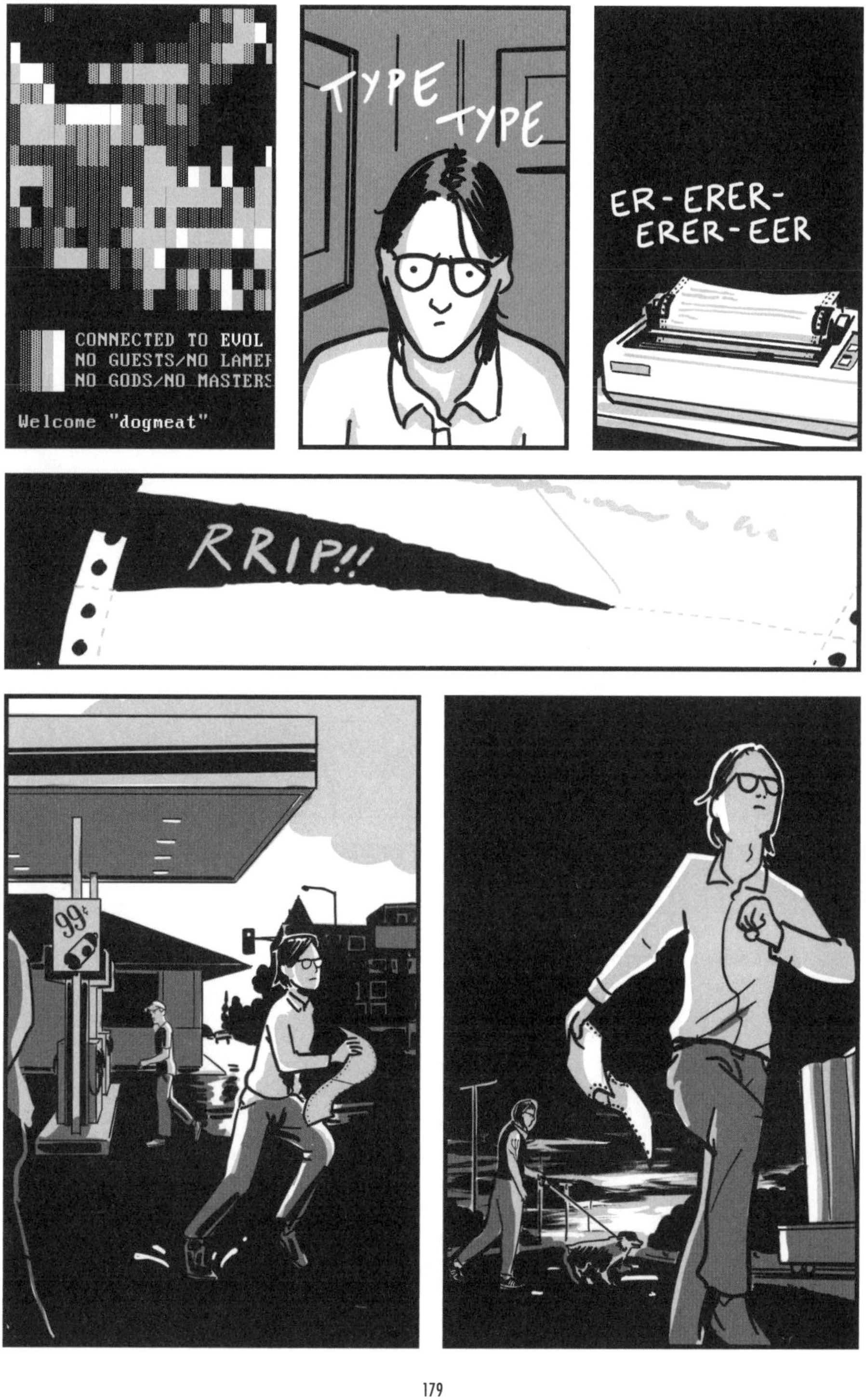
CONNECTED TO EVOL
NO GUESTS/NO LAMEF
NO GODS/NO MASTERS
Welcome "dogmeat"
TYPE TYPE
ER-ERER-ERER-EER
RRIP!!
99¢

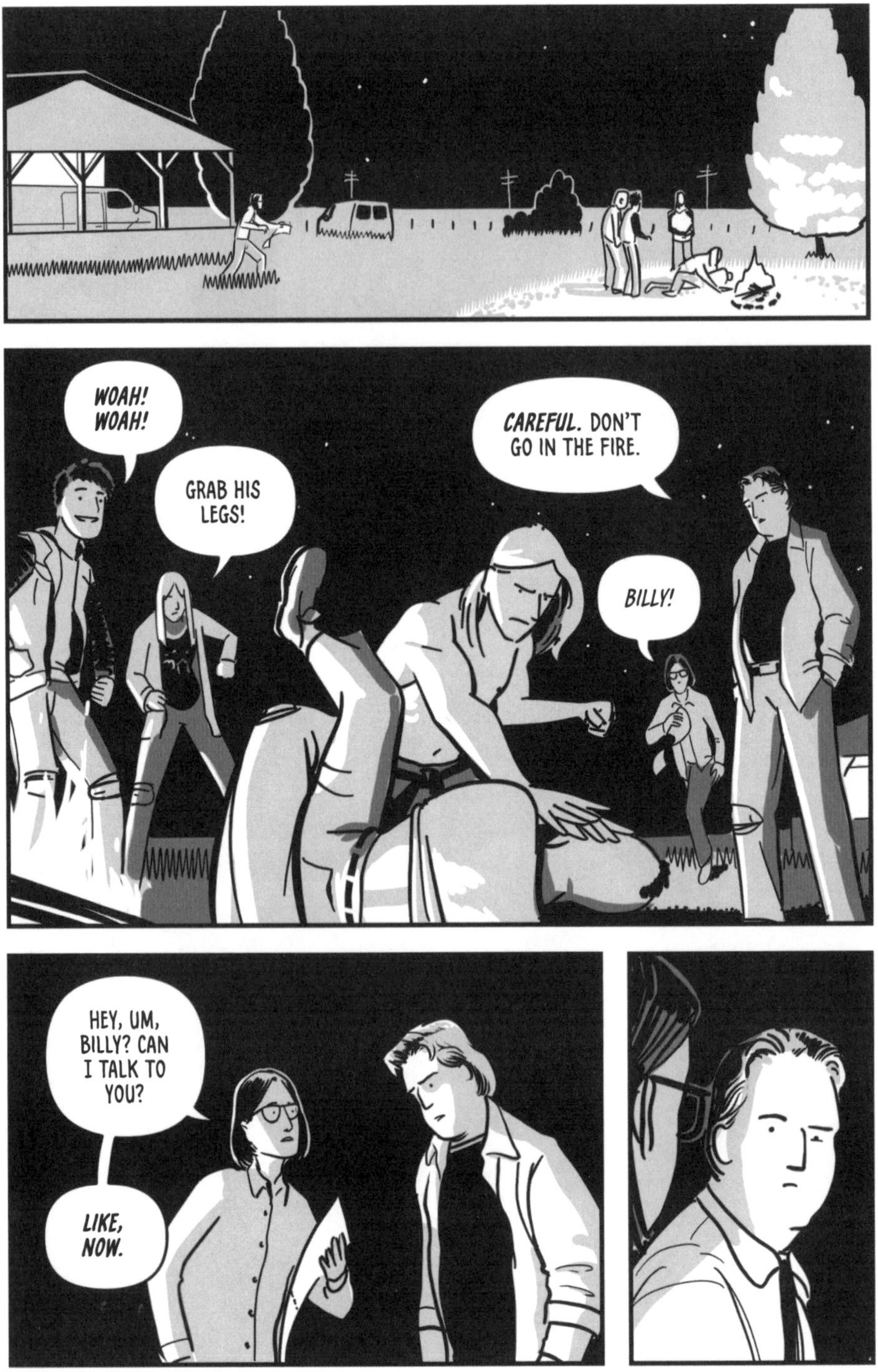
WOAH! WOAH!
GRAB HIS LEGS!
CAREFUL. DON'T GO IN THE FIRE.
BILLY!
HEY, UM, BILLY? CAN I TALK TO YOU?
LIKE, NOW.

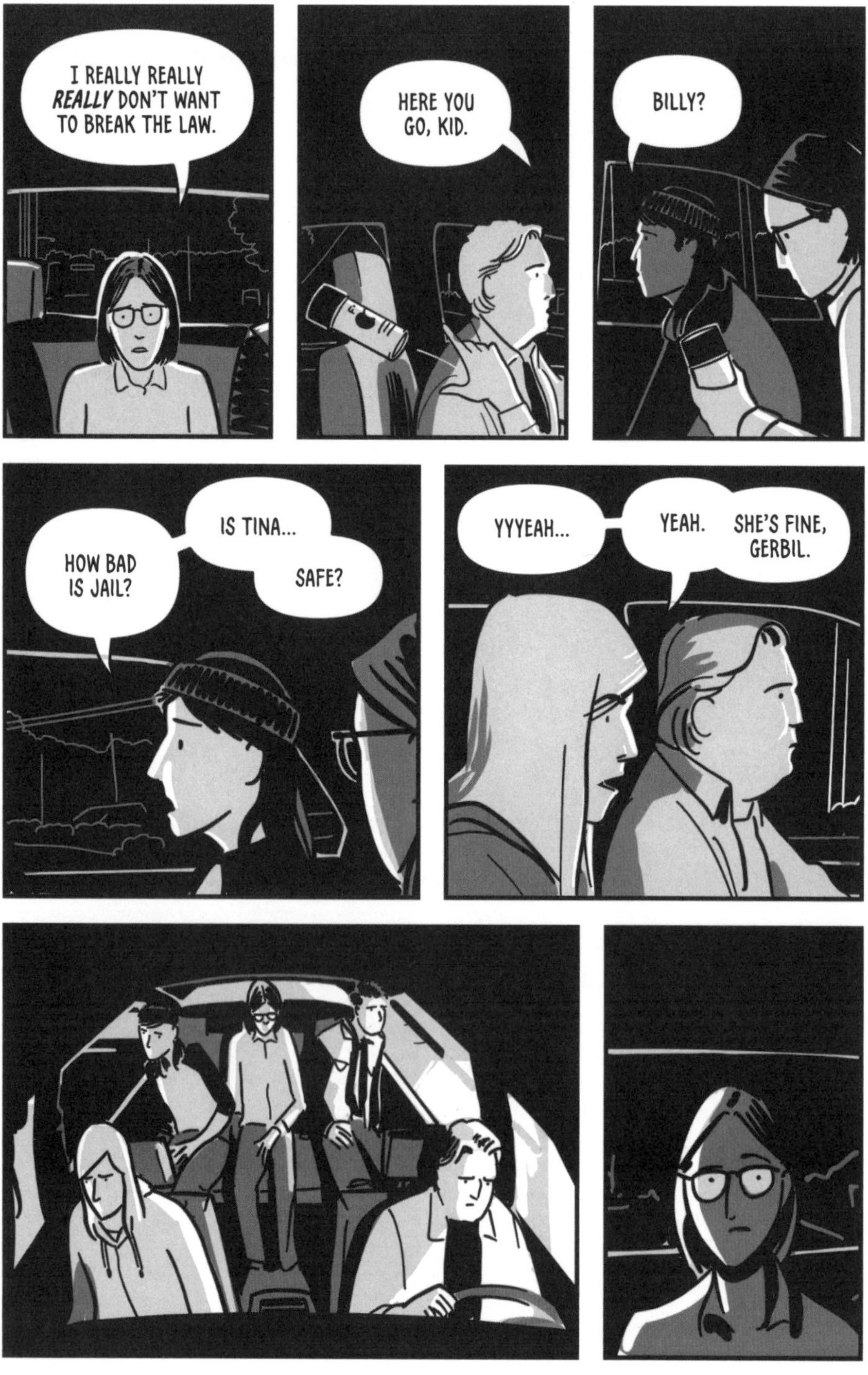
I REALLY REALLY *REALLY* DON'T WANT TO BREAK THE LAW.
HERE YOU GO, KID.
BILLY?
HOW BAD IS JAIL?
IS TINA...
SAFE?
YYYEAH...
YEAH.
SHE'S FINE, GERBIL.

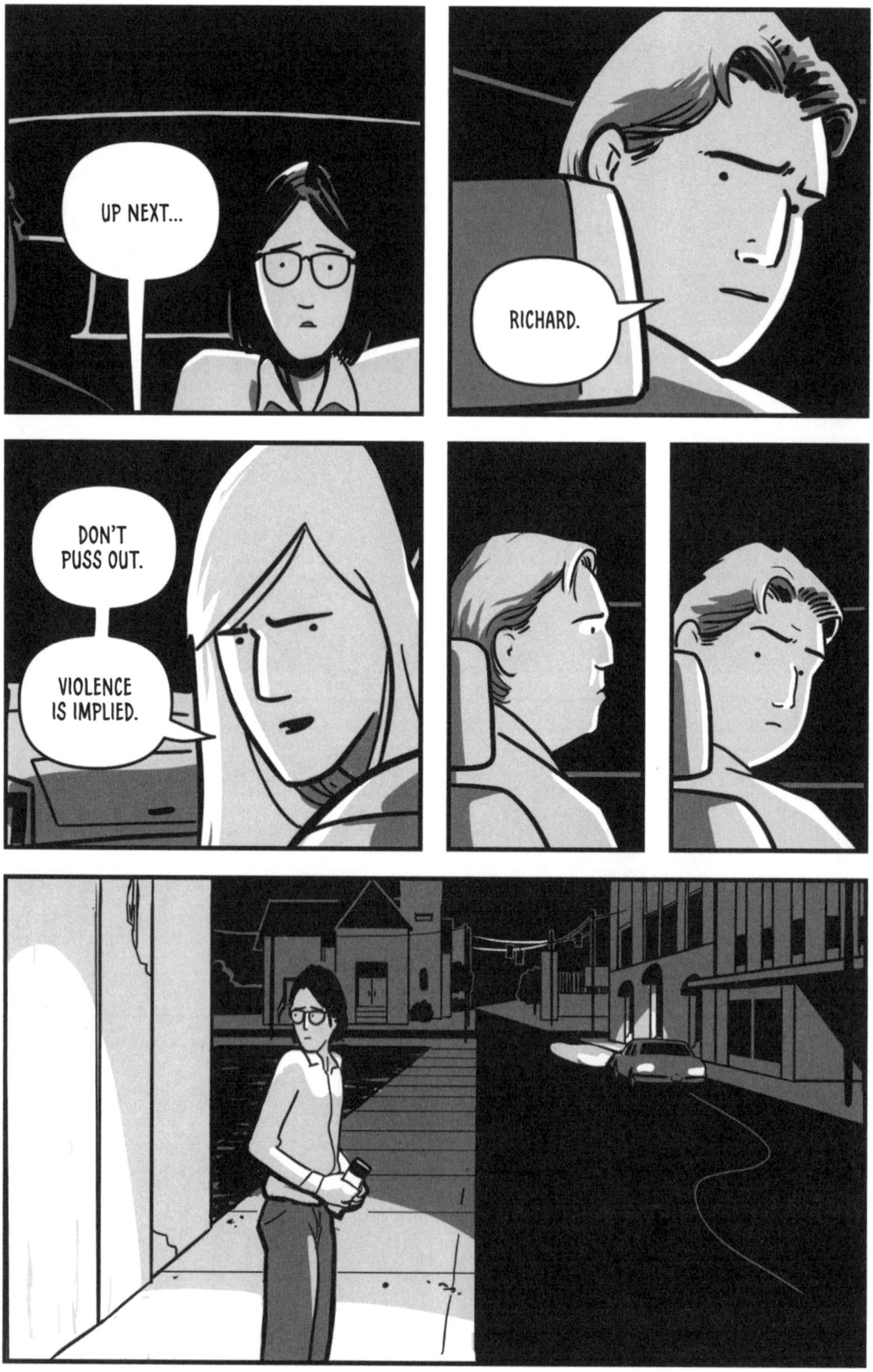
UP NEXT...
RICHARD.
DON'T PUSS OUT.
VIOLENCE IS IMPLIED.

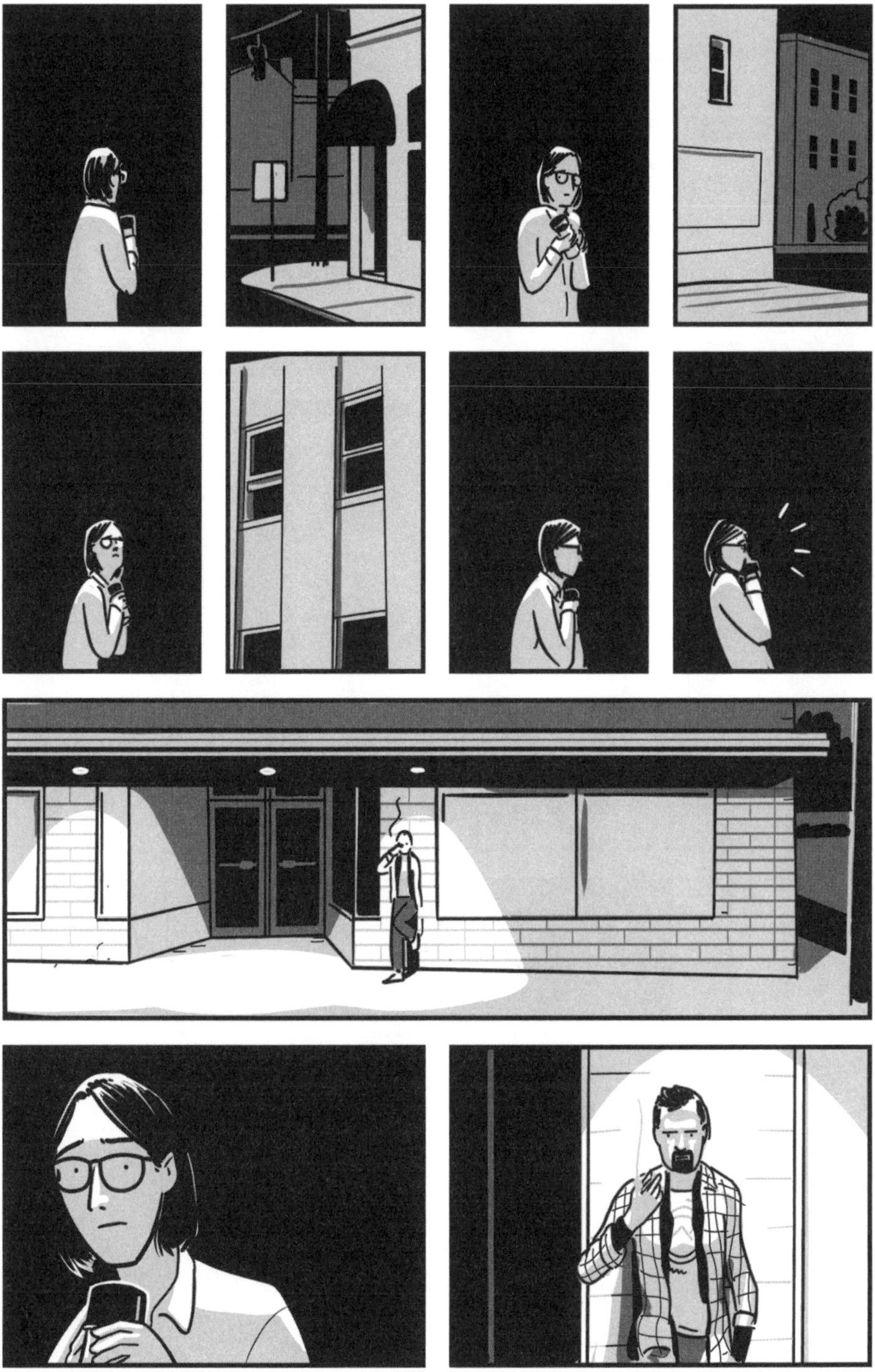

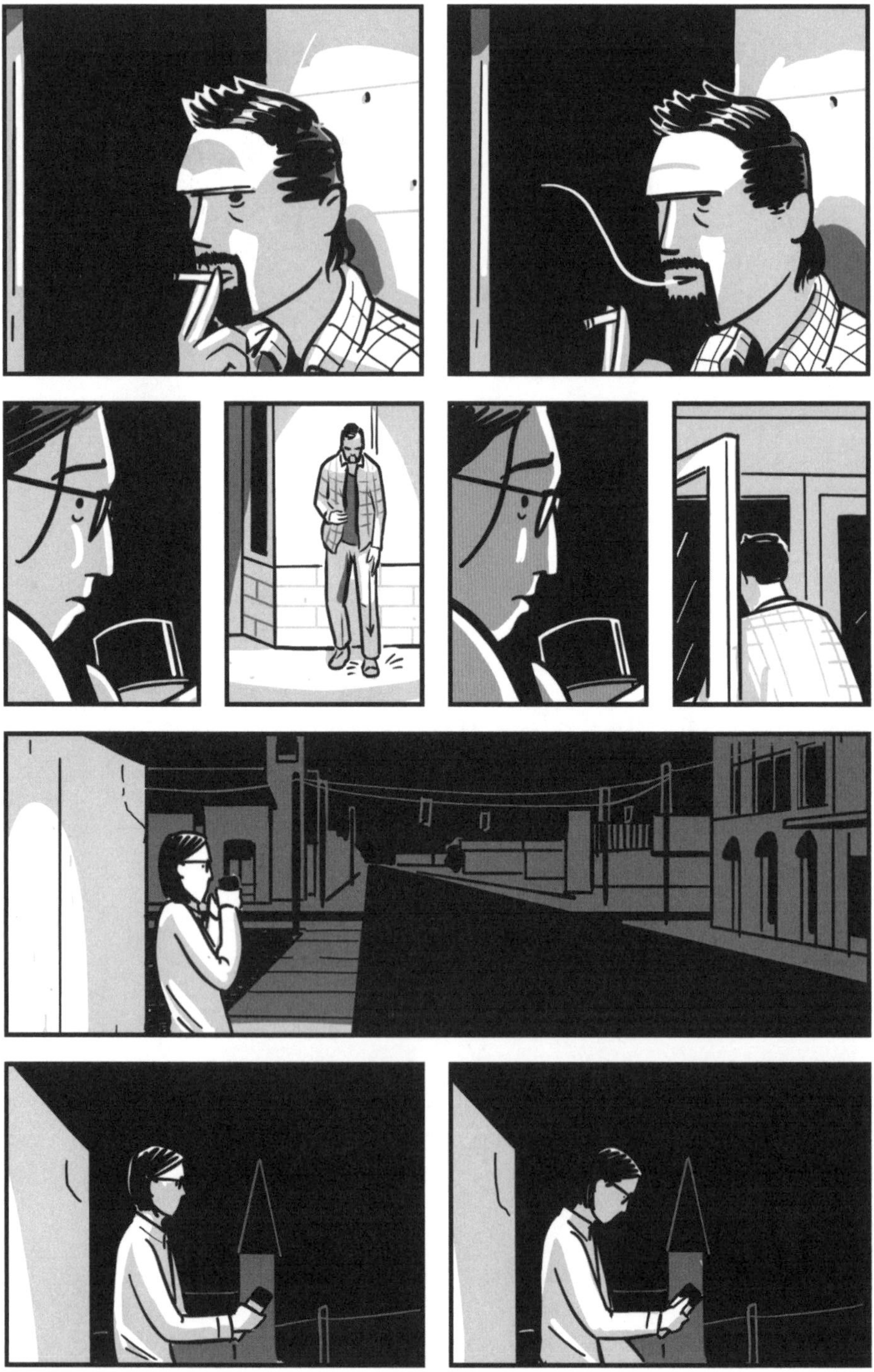

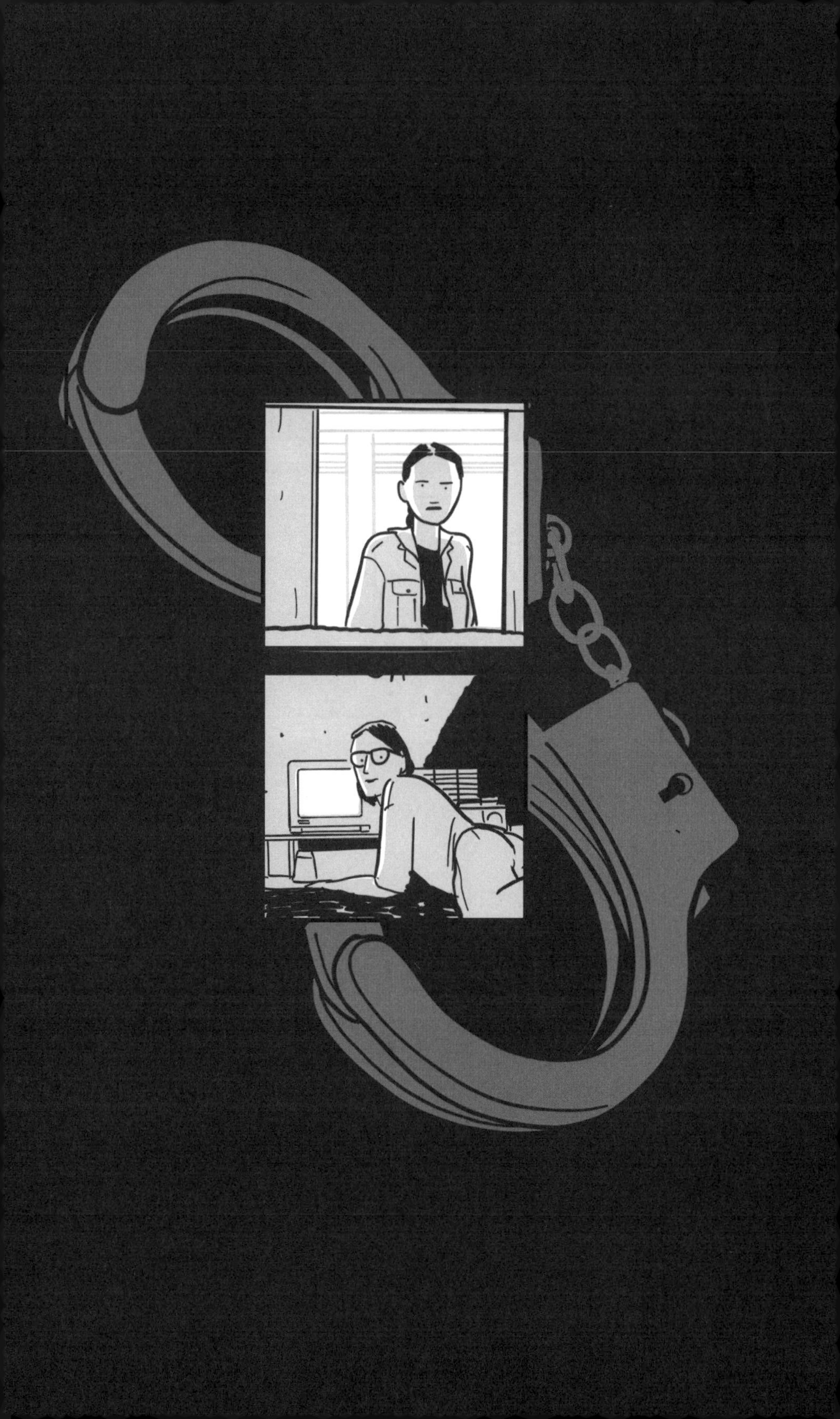

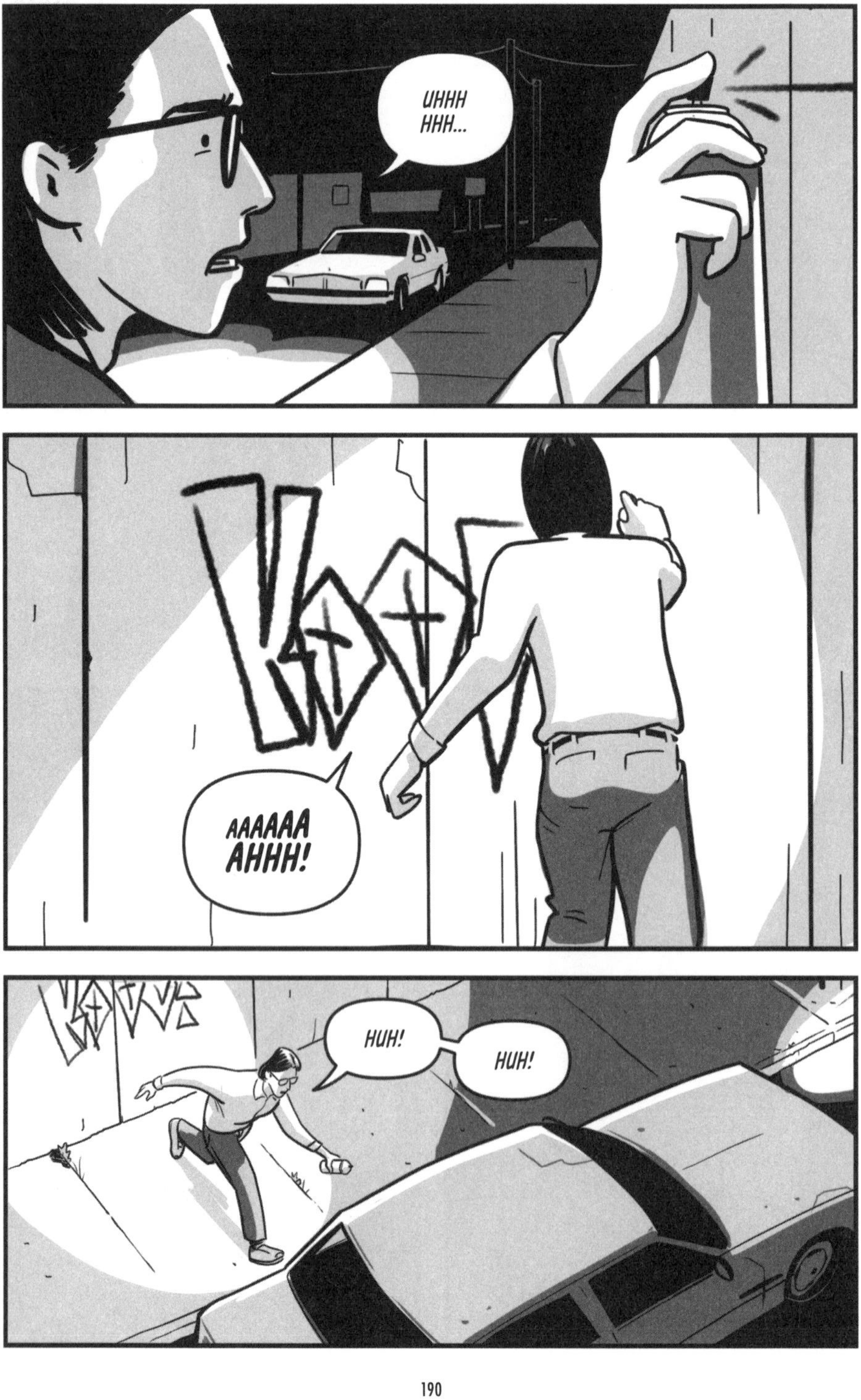
UHHH HHH...
AAAAAA AHHH!
HUH!
HUH!

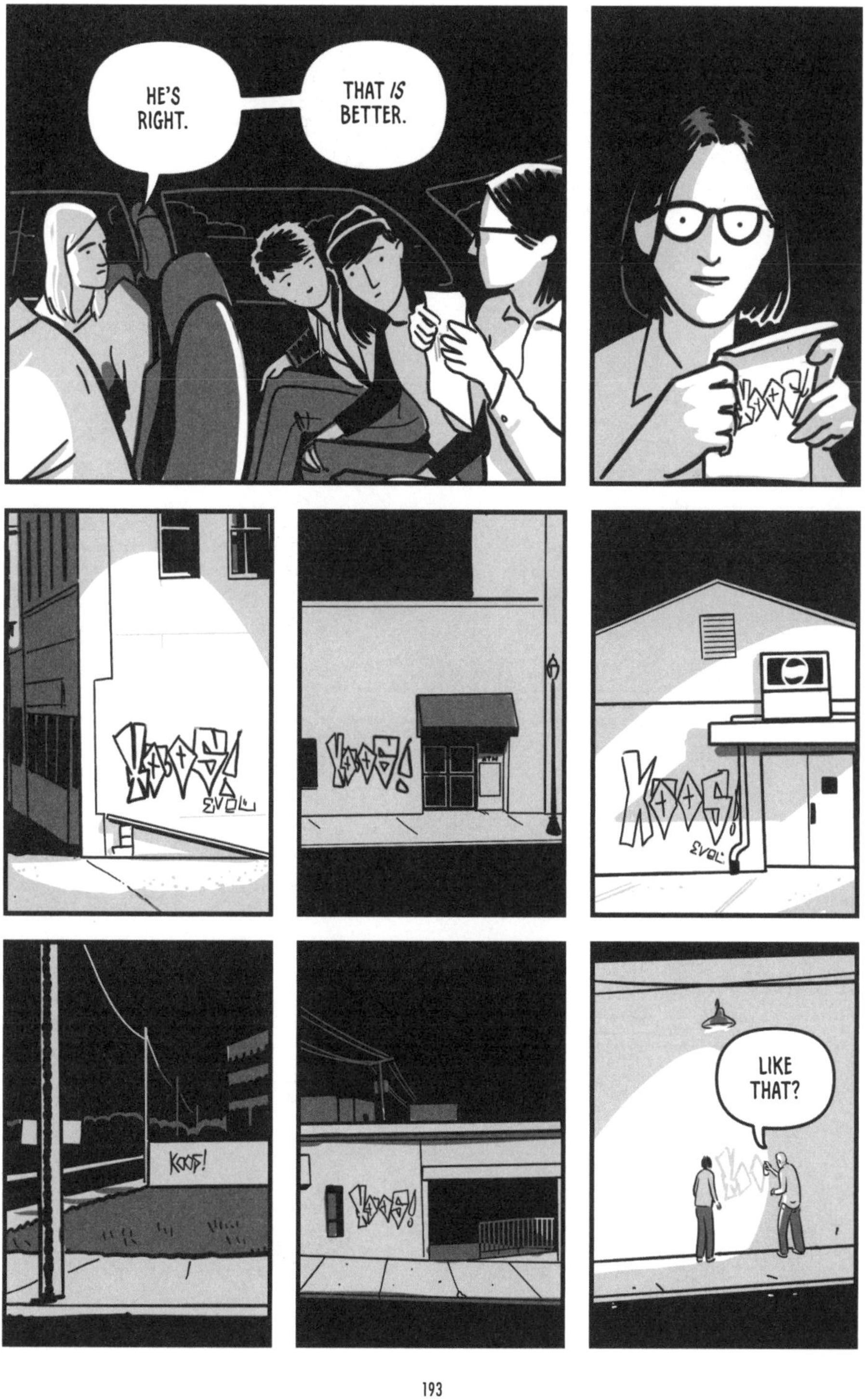
HE'S RIGHT.
THAT *IS* BETTER.
KOOS!
KOOS!
KOOS!
KOOF!
KOOS!
LIKE THAT?

194

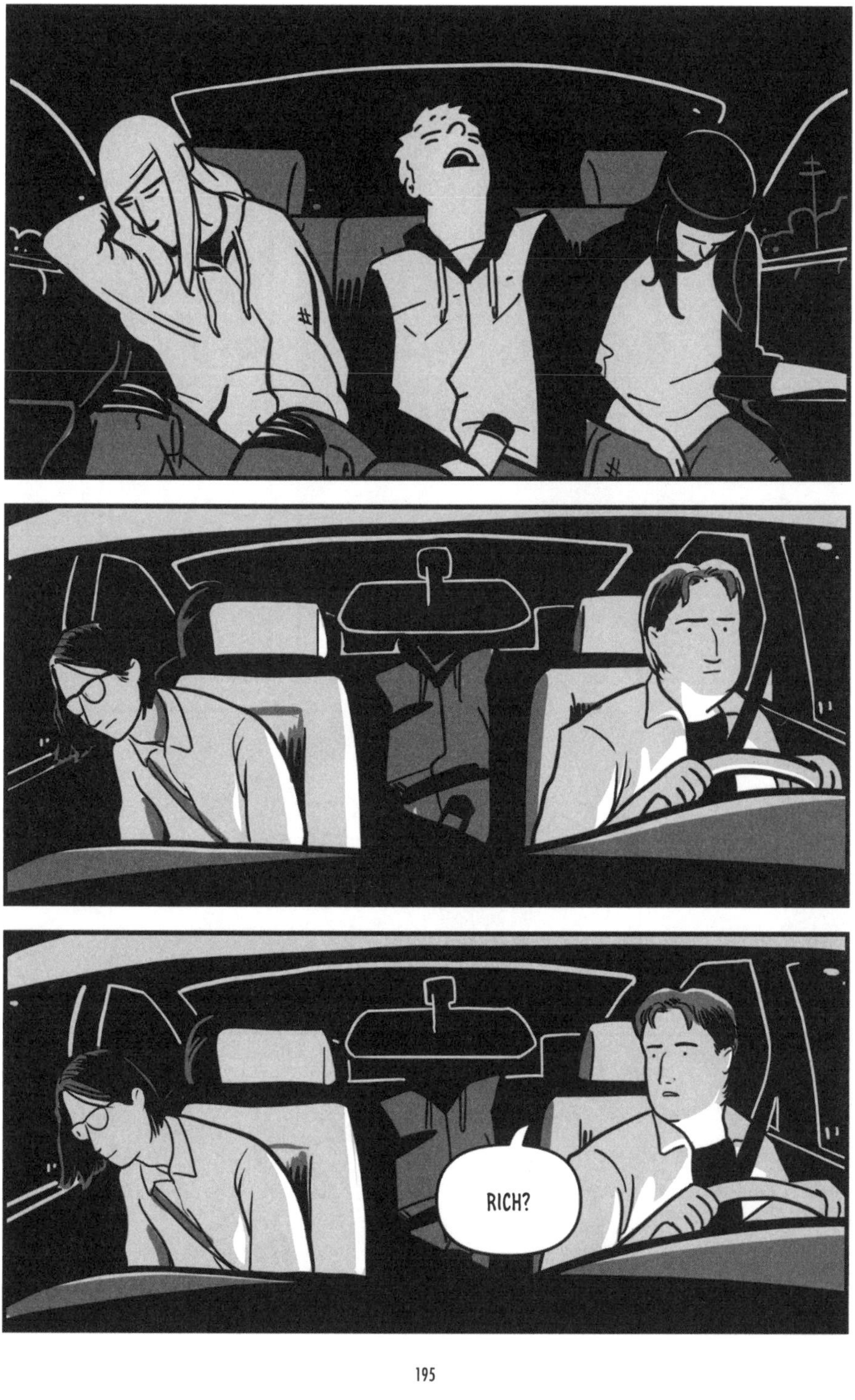
RICH?

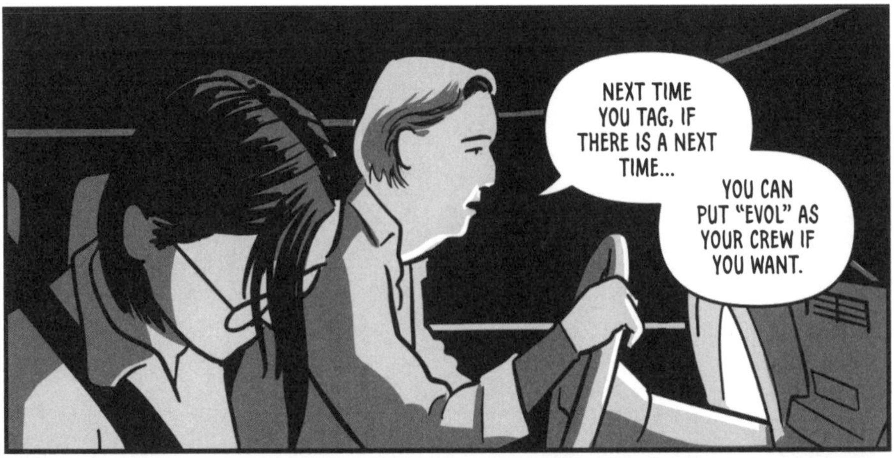
NEXT TIME YOU TAG, IF THERE IS A NEXT TIME...
YOU CAN PUT "EVOL" AS YOUR CREW IF YOU WANT.

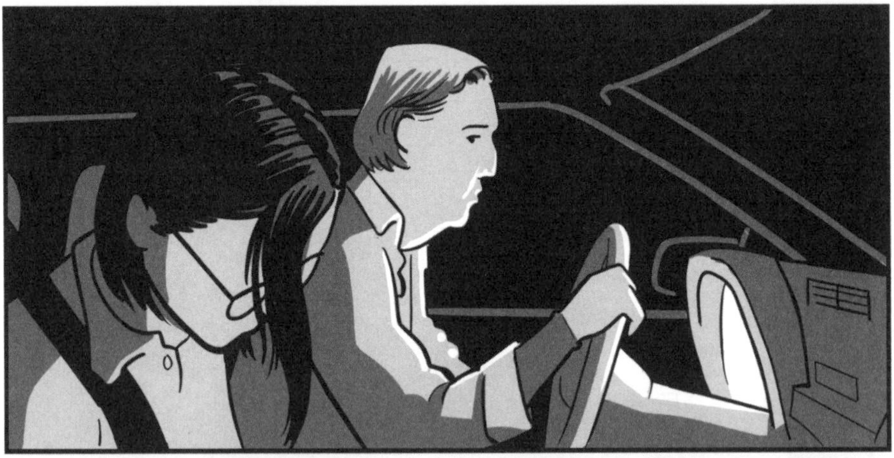

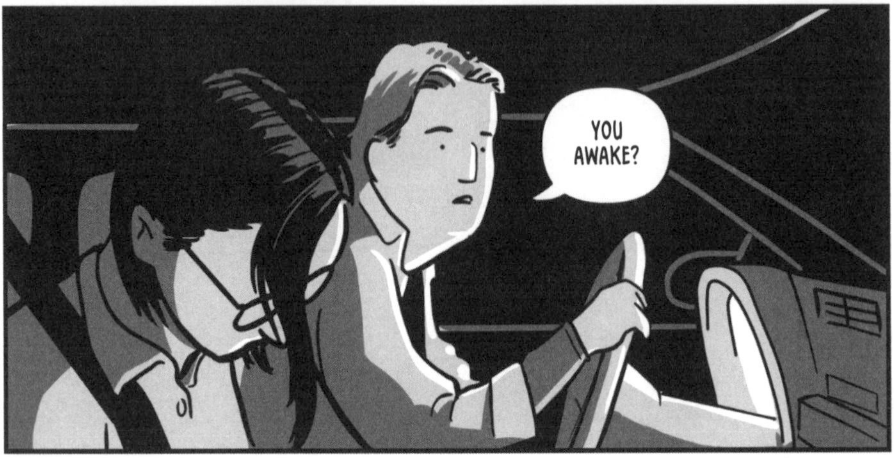
YOU AWAKE?

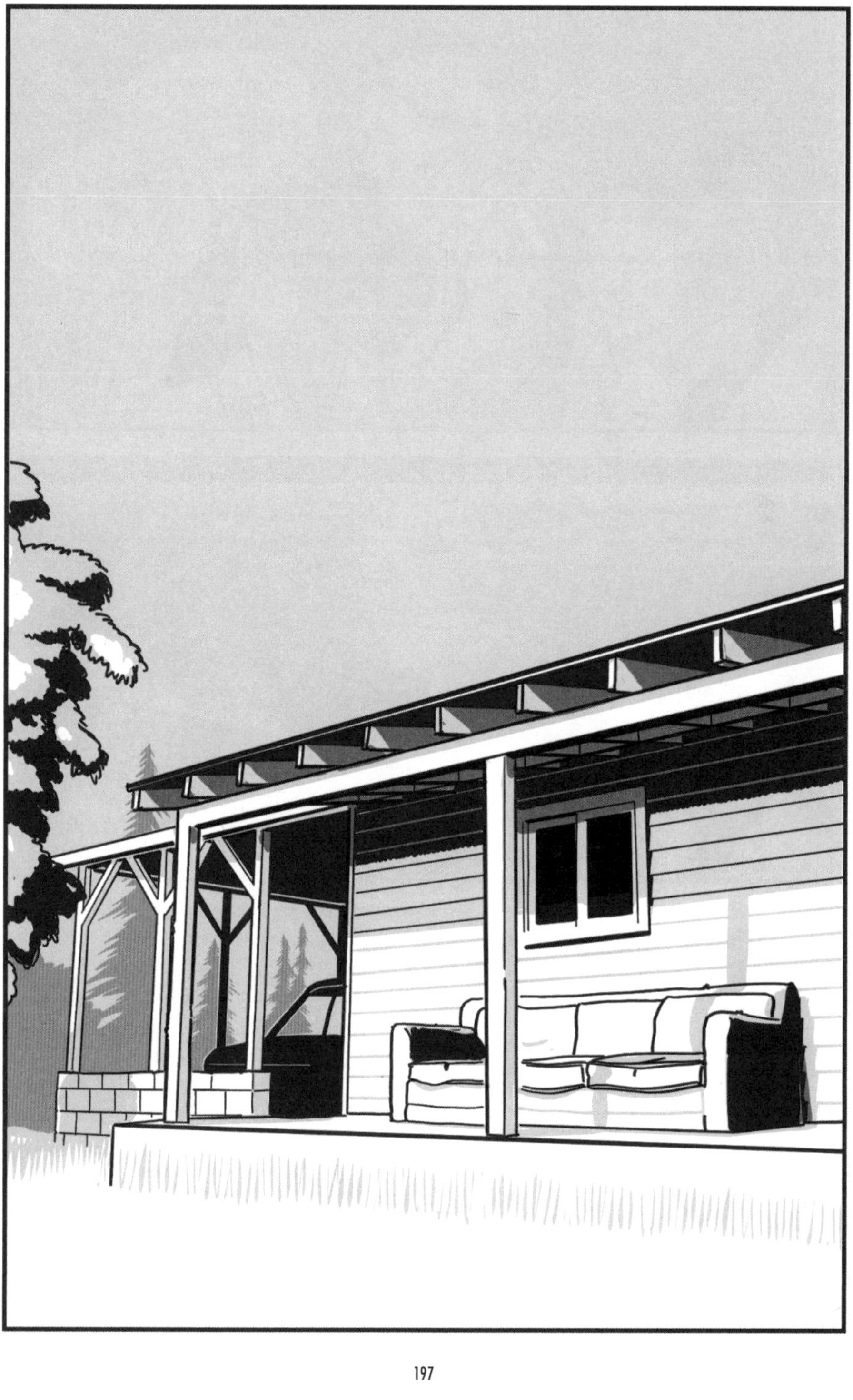

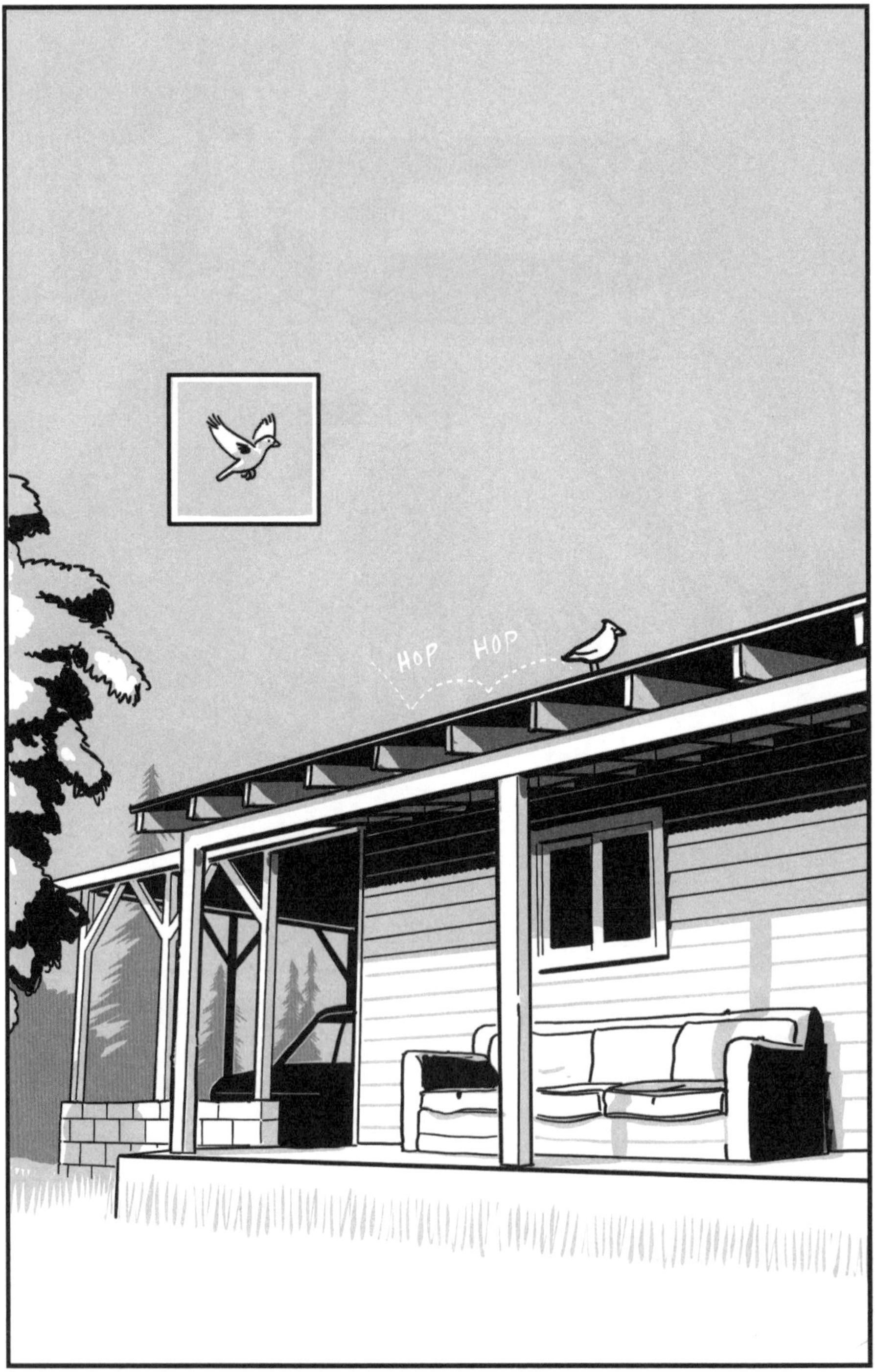
HOP HOP

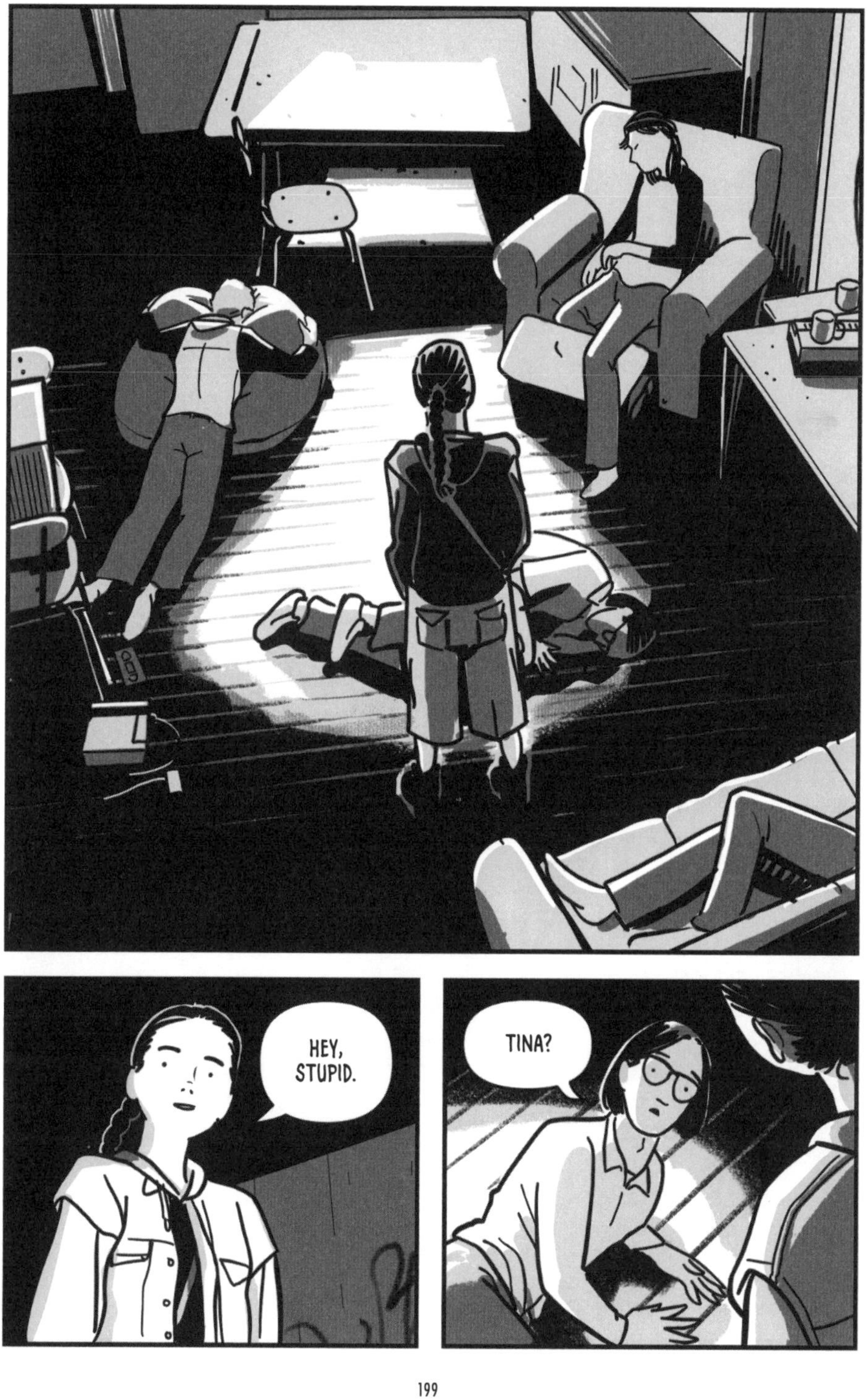
HEY, STUPID.
TINA?

201

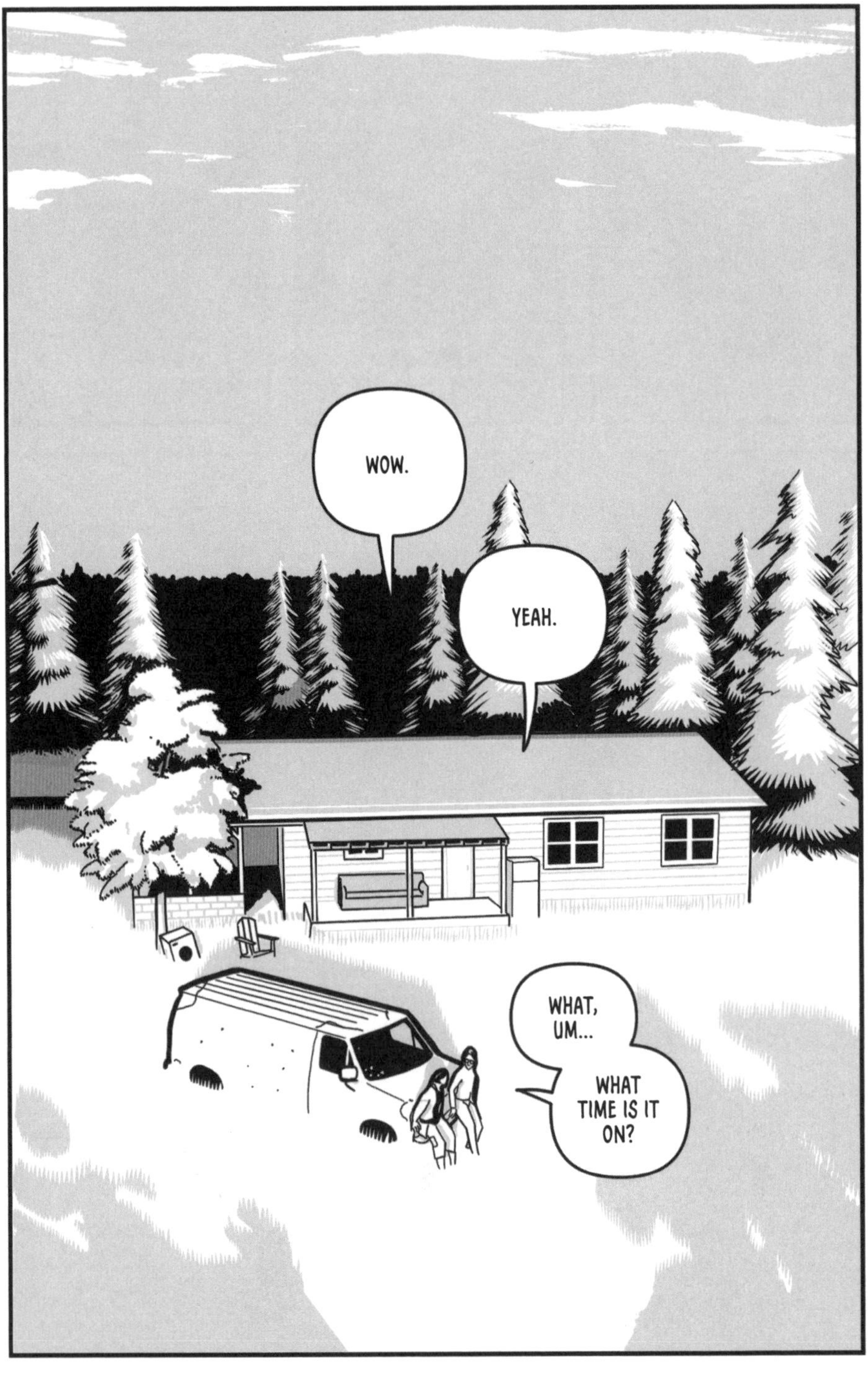
WOW.
YEAH.
WHAT, UM...
WHAT TIME IS IT ON?

Chapter 6

RETENTION OF VISION VANISH

/\ /\ /\ /\ /\ /\ /\ /\ /\ /\
\/ \/ \/ \/ \/ \/ \/ \/ \/ \/

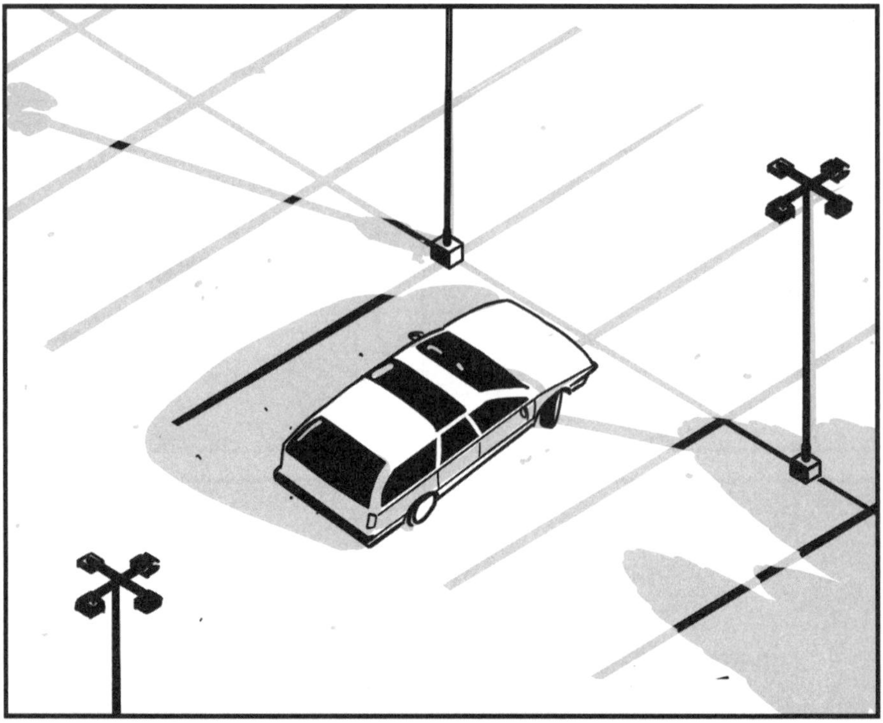

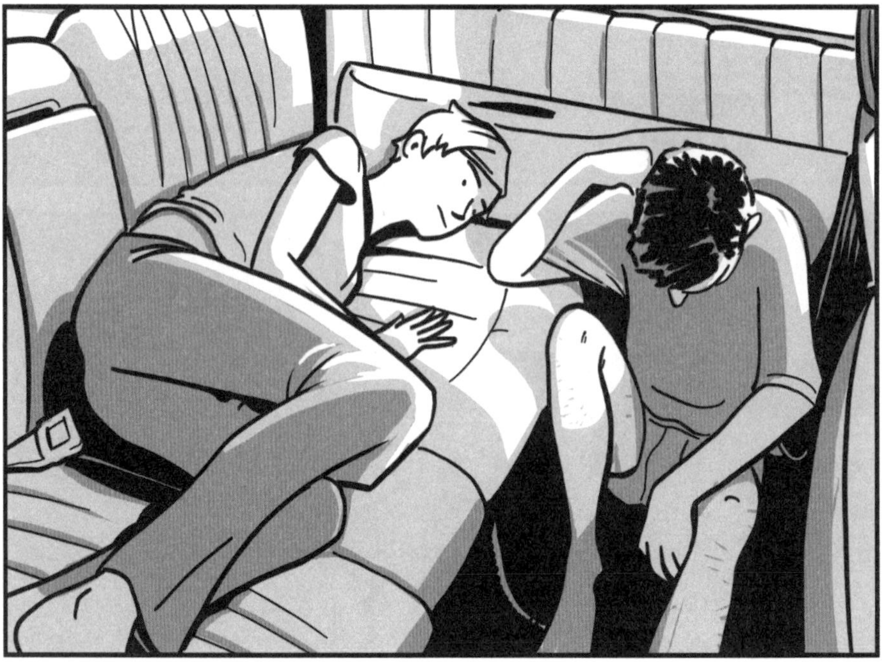

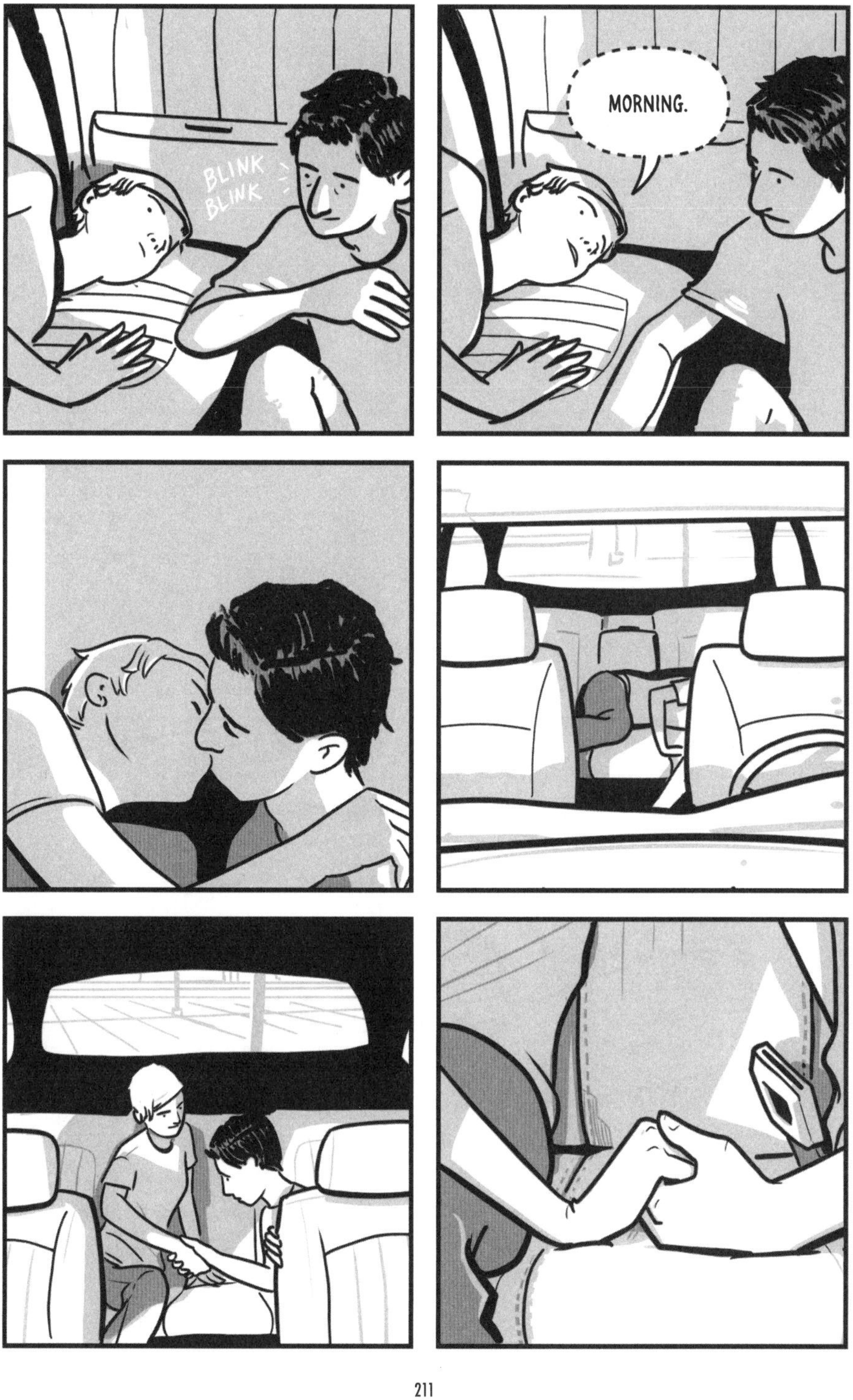
BLINK
BLINK
MORNING.

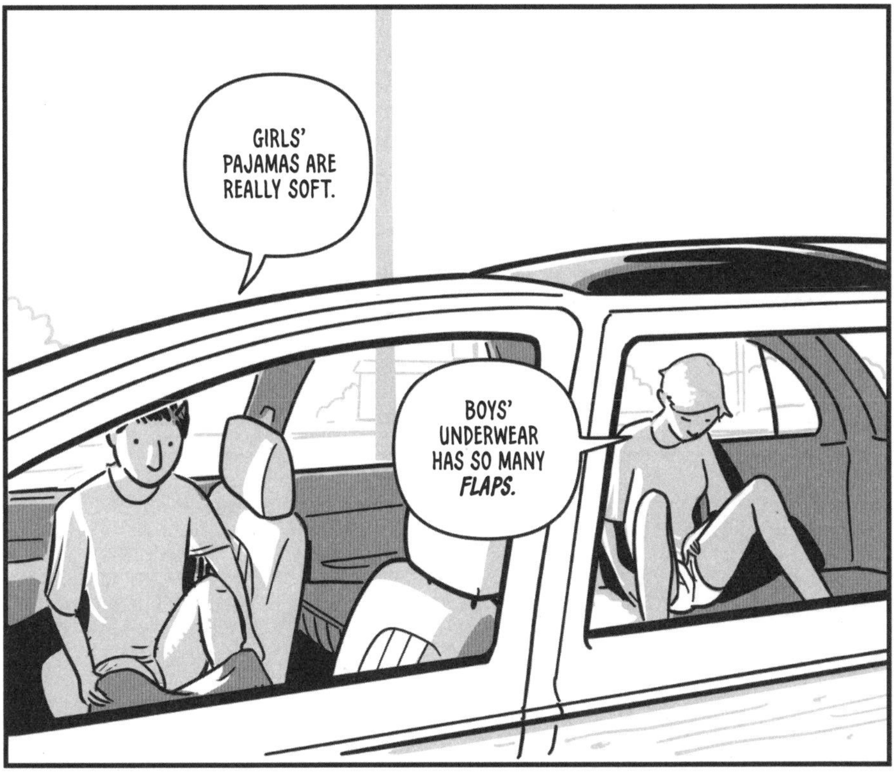
GIRLS' PAJAMAS ARE REALLY SOFT.
BOYS' UNDERWEAR HAS SO MANY *FLAPS.*

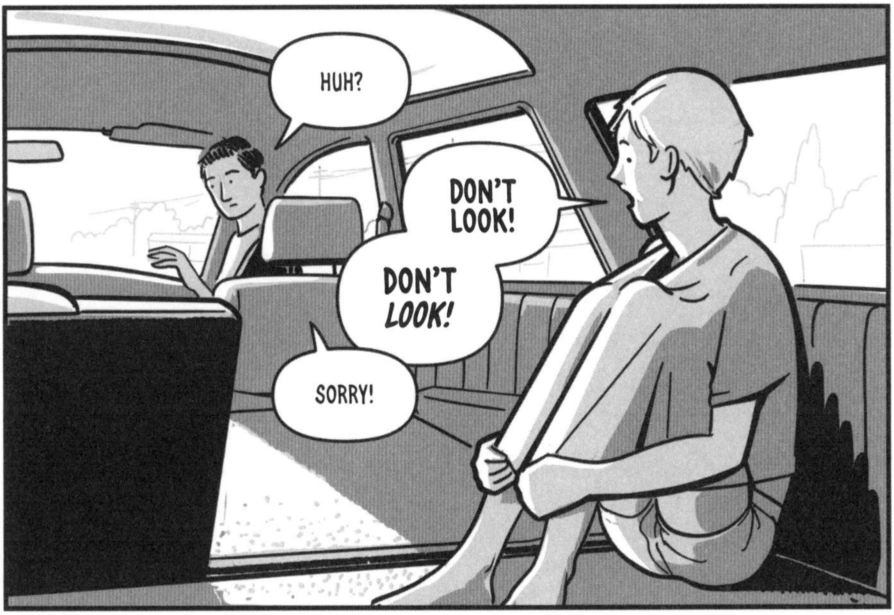
HUH?
DON'T LOOK!
DON'T *LOOK!*
SORRY!

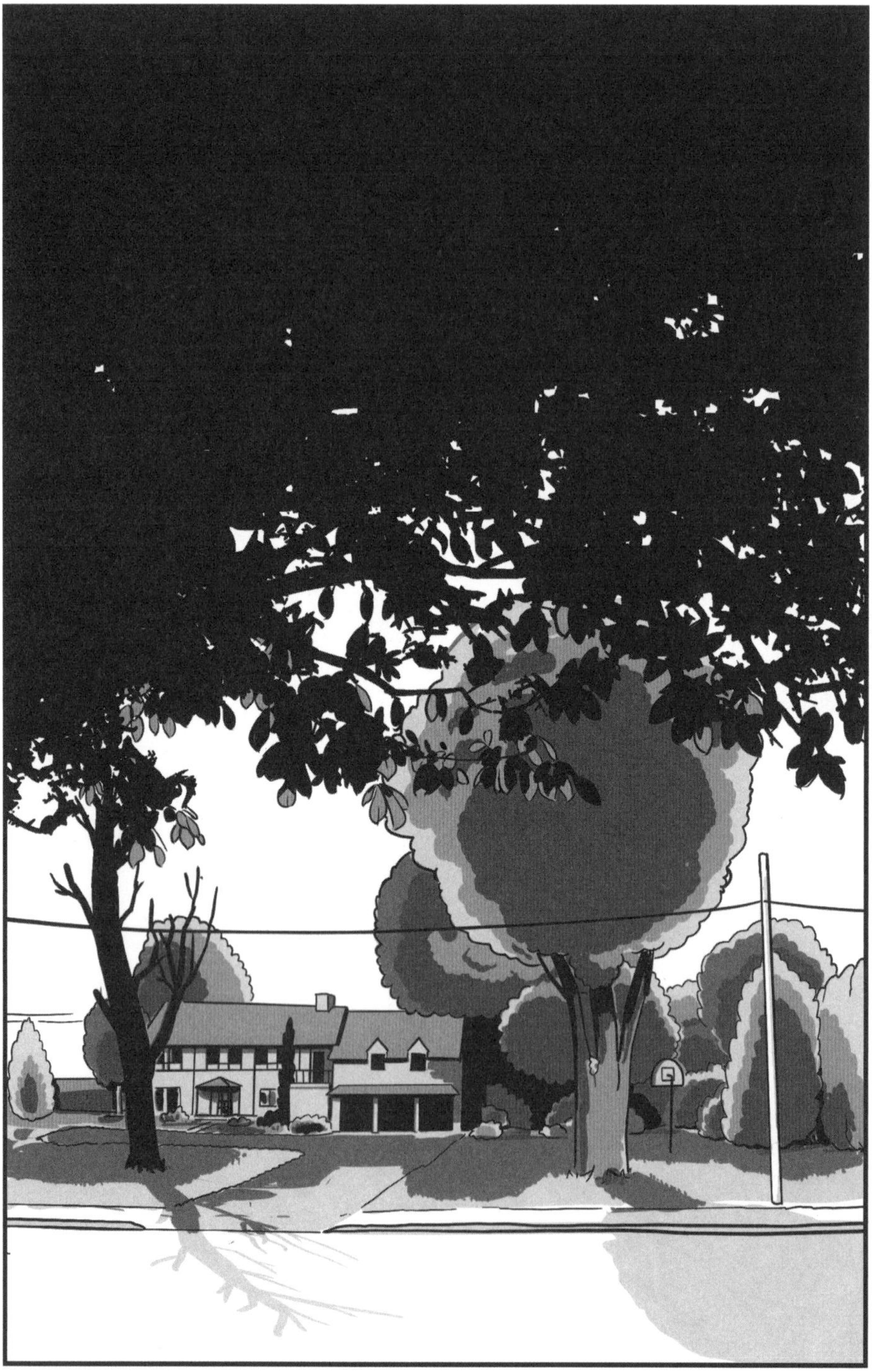

217

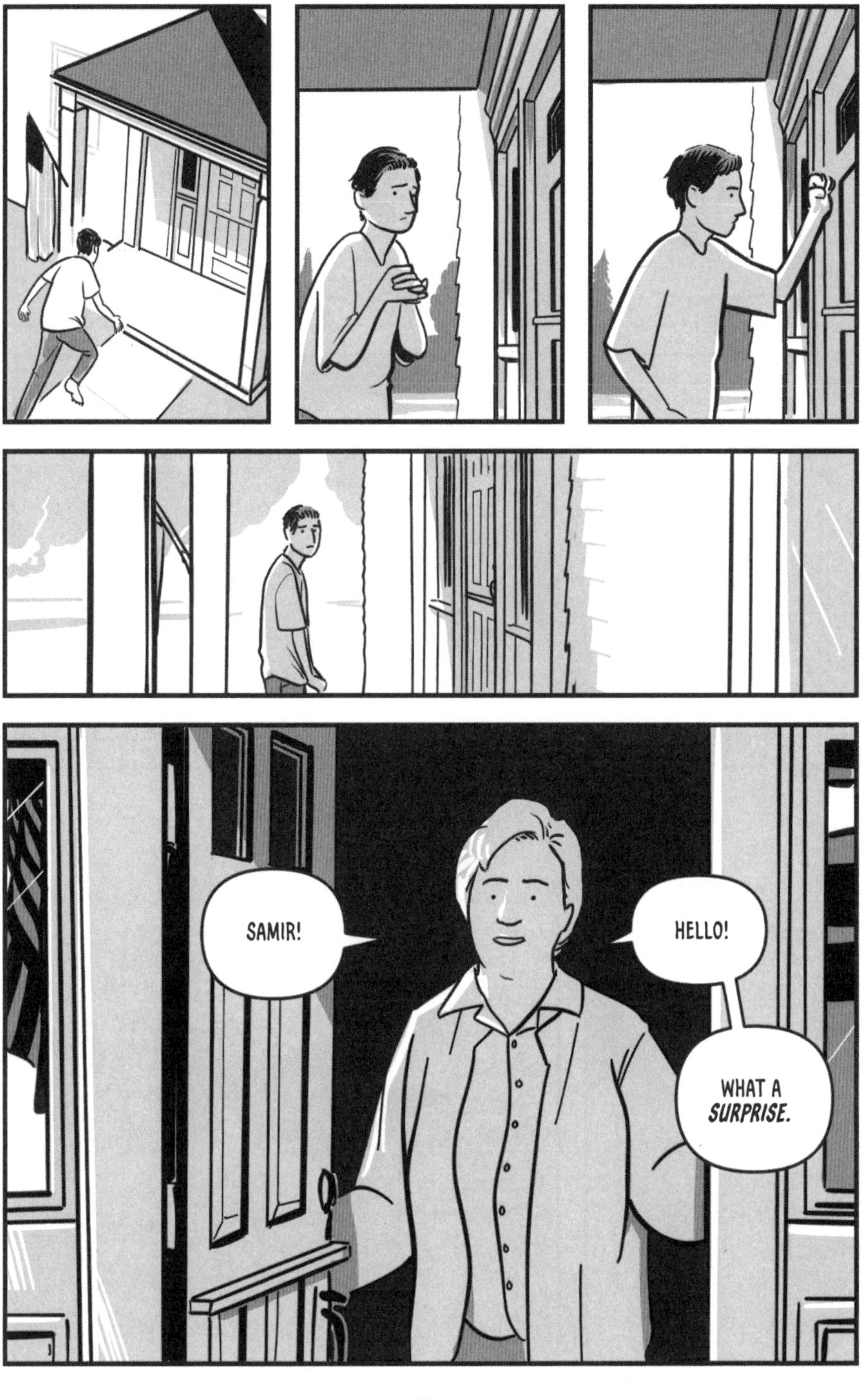
SAMIR!
HELLO!
WHAT A SURPRISE.

221

BUT HERE I AM.

FREE.

225

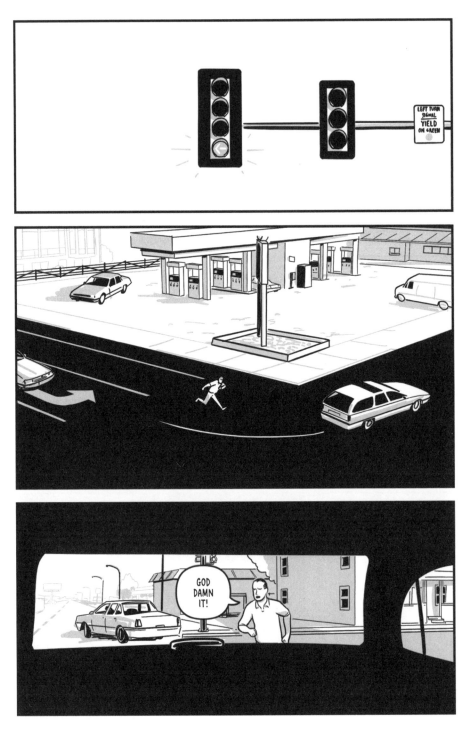

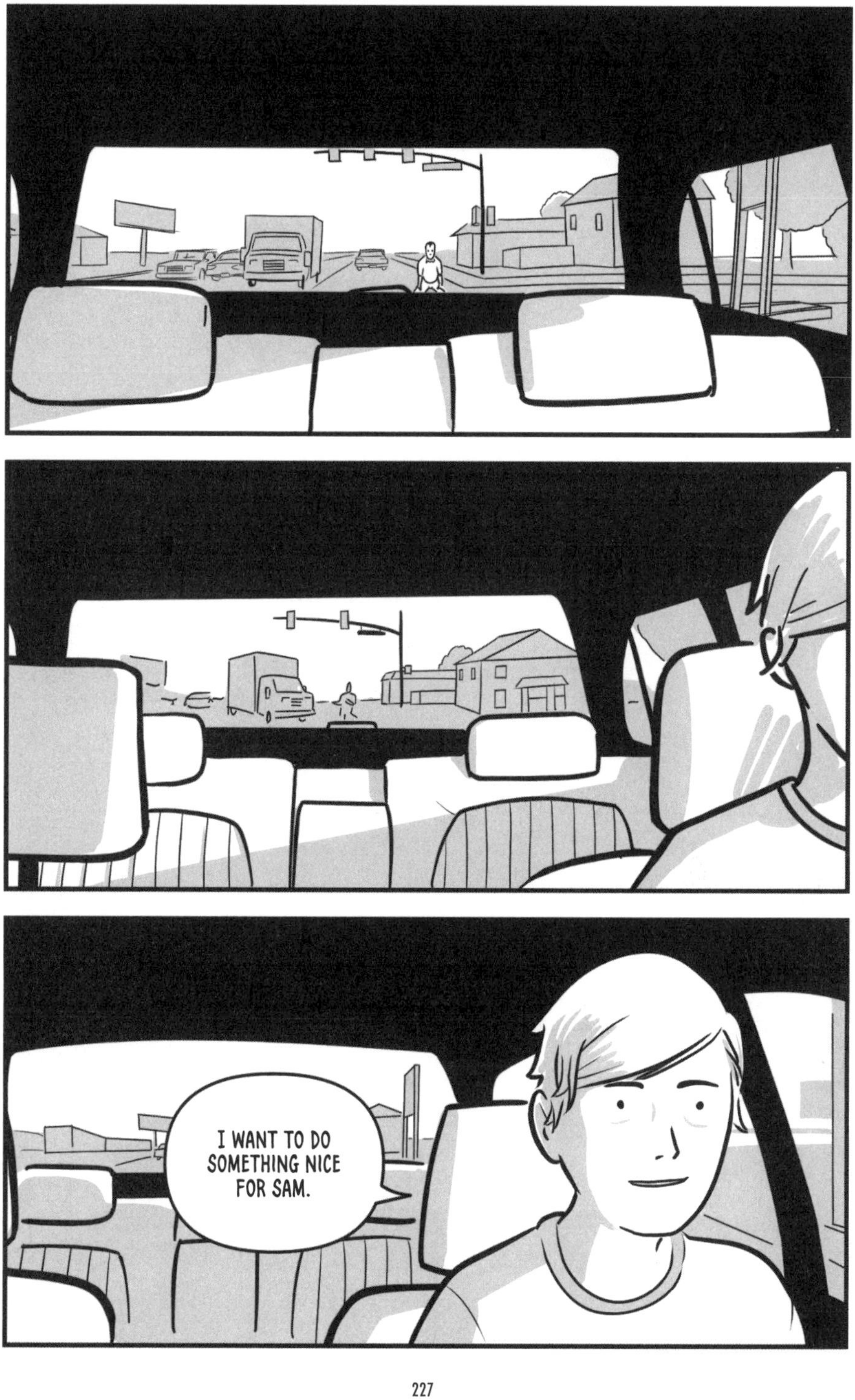
I WANT TO DO SOMETHING NICE FOR SAM.

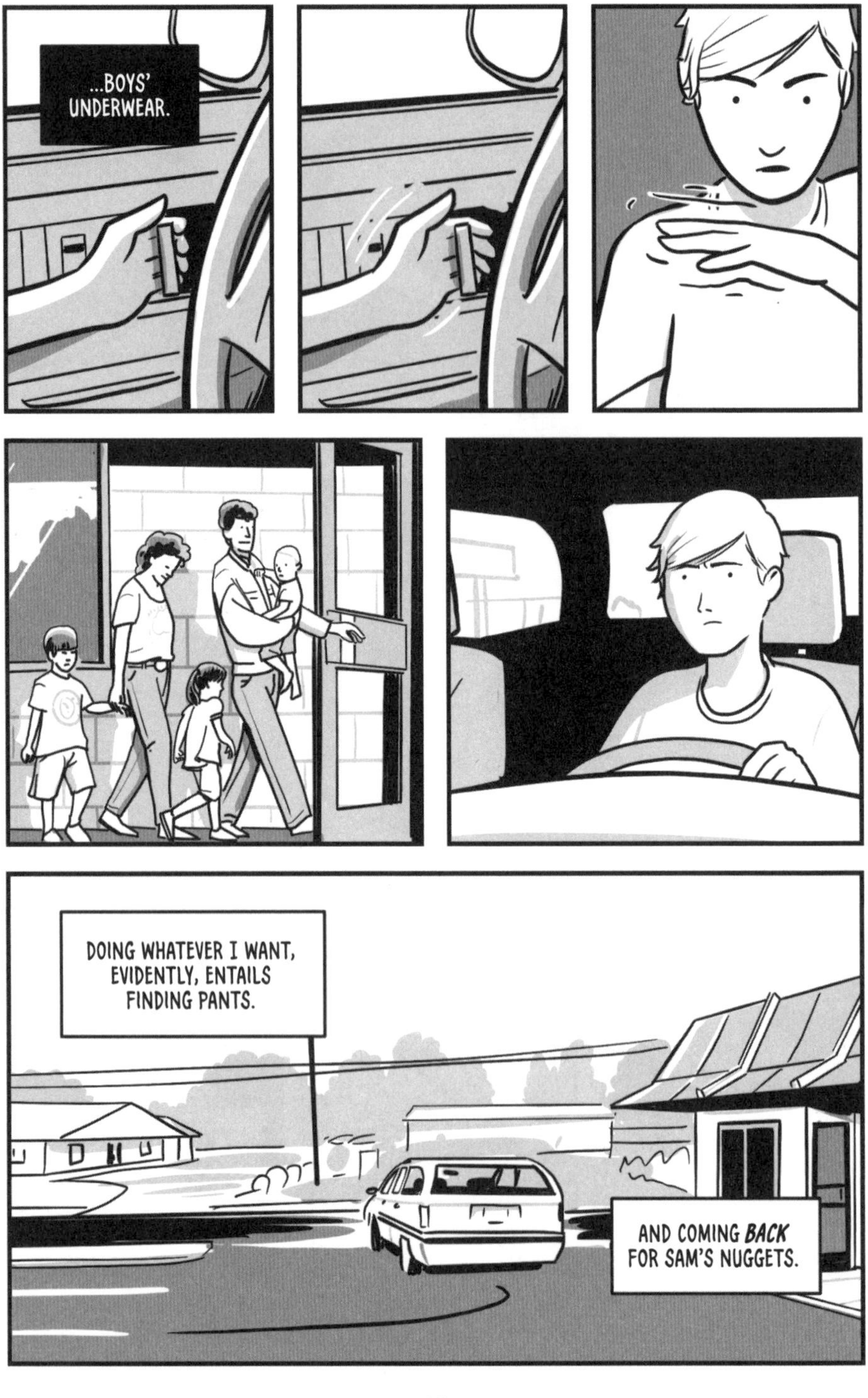
...BOYS' UNDERWEAR.
DOING WHATEVER I WANT, EVIDENTLY, ENTAILS FINDING PANTS.
AND COMING *BACK* FOR SAM'S NUGGETS.

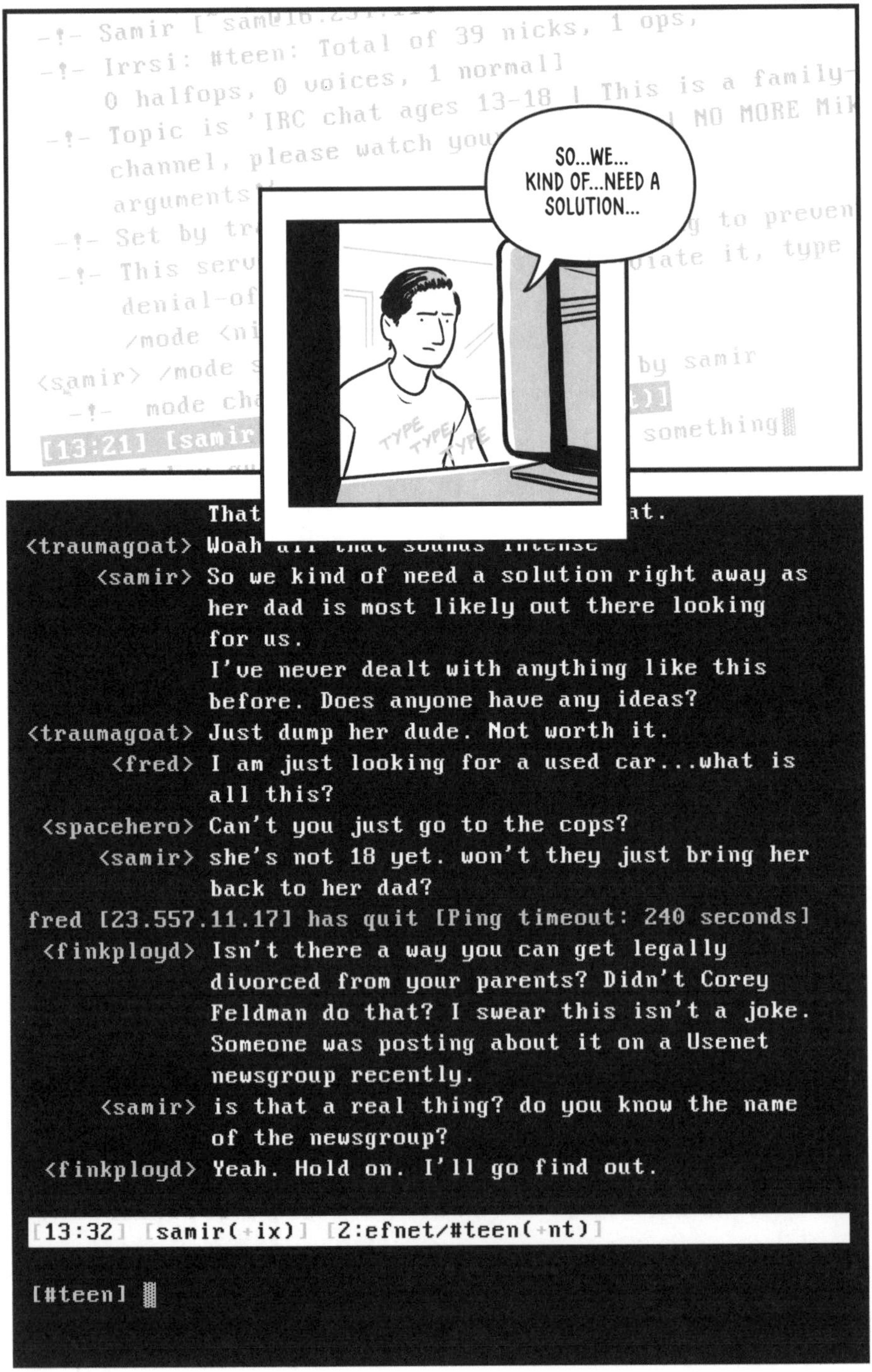

-!- Samir [sam@16.23.1...
-!- Irrsi: #teen: Total of 39 nicks, 1 ops,
    0 halfops, 0 voices, 1 normal]
-!- Topic is 'IRC chat ages 13-18 | This is a family-
    channel, please watch you... | NO MORE Mi...
    arguments...
-!- Set by tr...   ...g to preven...
-!- This serv...   ...late it, type
    denial-of...
    /mode <ni...
<samir> /mode s...   by samir
    -!- mode ch...   ...)]
[13:21] [samir...   something▊

SO...WE...
KIND OF...NEED A
SOLUTION...

That ...   ...at.
<traumagoat> Woah all that sounds intense
     <samir> So we kind of need a solution right away as
             her dad is most likely out there looking
             for us.
             I've never dealt with anything like this
             before. Does anyone have any ideas?
<traumagoat> Just dump her dude. Not worth it.
      <fred> I am just looking for a used car...what is
             all this?
 <spacehero> Can't you just go to the cops?
     <samir> she's not 18 yet. won't they just bring her
             back to her dad?
fred [23.557.11.17] has quit [Ping timeout: 240 seconds]
 <finkployd> Isn't there a way you can get legally
             divorced from your parents? Didn't Corey
             Feldman do that? I swear this isn't a joke.
             Someone was posting about it on a Usenet
             newsgroup recently.
     <samir> is that a real thing? do you know the name
             of the newsgroup?
 <finkployd> Yeah. Hold on. I'll go find out.

[13:32] [samir(+ix)] [2:efnet/#teen(+nt)]

[#teen] ▊

232

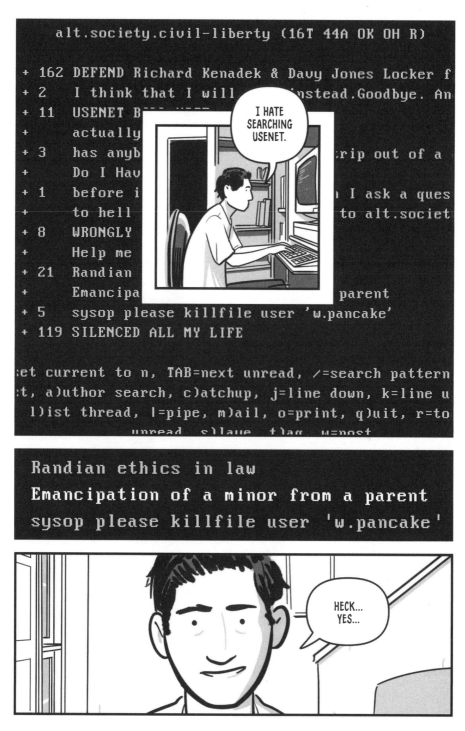

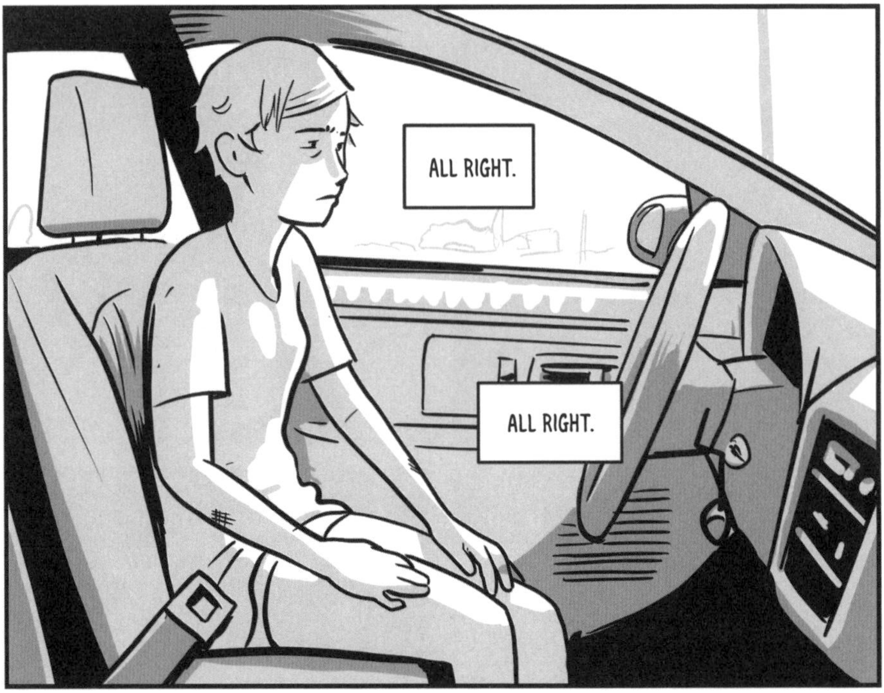
ALL RIGHT.
ALL RIGHT.

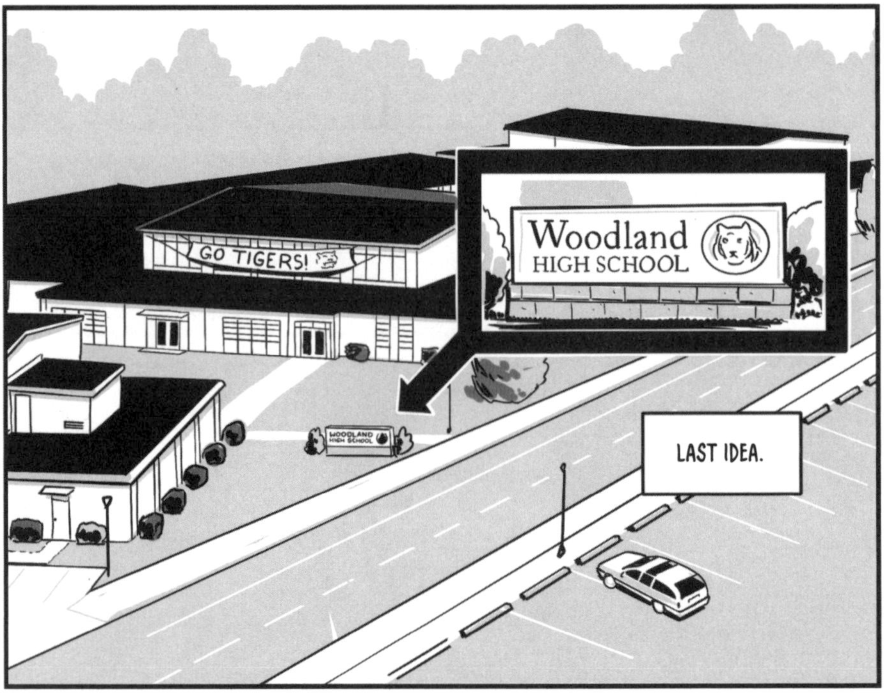
GO TIGERS!
Woodland
HIGH SCHOOL
LAST IDEA.

From: kaos@info.coolhouse.net
Newsgroups: alt.society.civil-liberty
In-Reply-To: <u31.111$UI2.11089@news.bellsouth.net>
Subject: Re: Emancipation of a Minor from a Parent

In response to cwpitts earlier, it's totally
possible for a court to decide to separate you from
your parents if it's in your or their best interest.
You mentioned a family friend who's a lawyer? I'd
contact them. Or drop me a line. There are other
options.

-=X=- -=X=- -=X=-

"With the first link, the chain is forged. The first
speech censured... the first thought forbidden...
the first freedom denied, chains us all, irrevocably."
419-958-4143

FRICKING...

PERFECT!

the first fre

419-958-4143

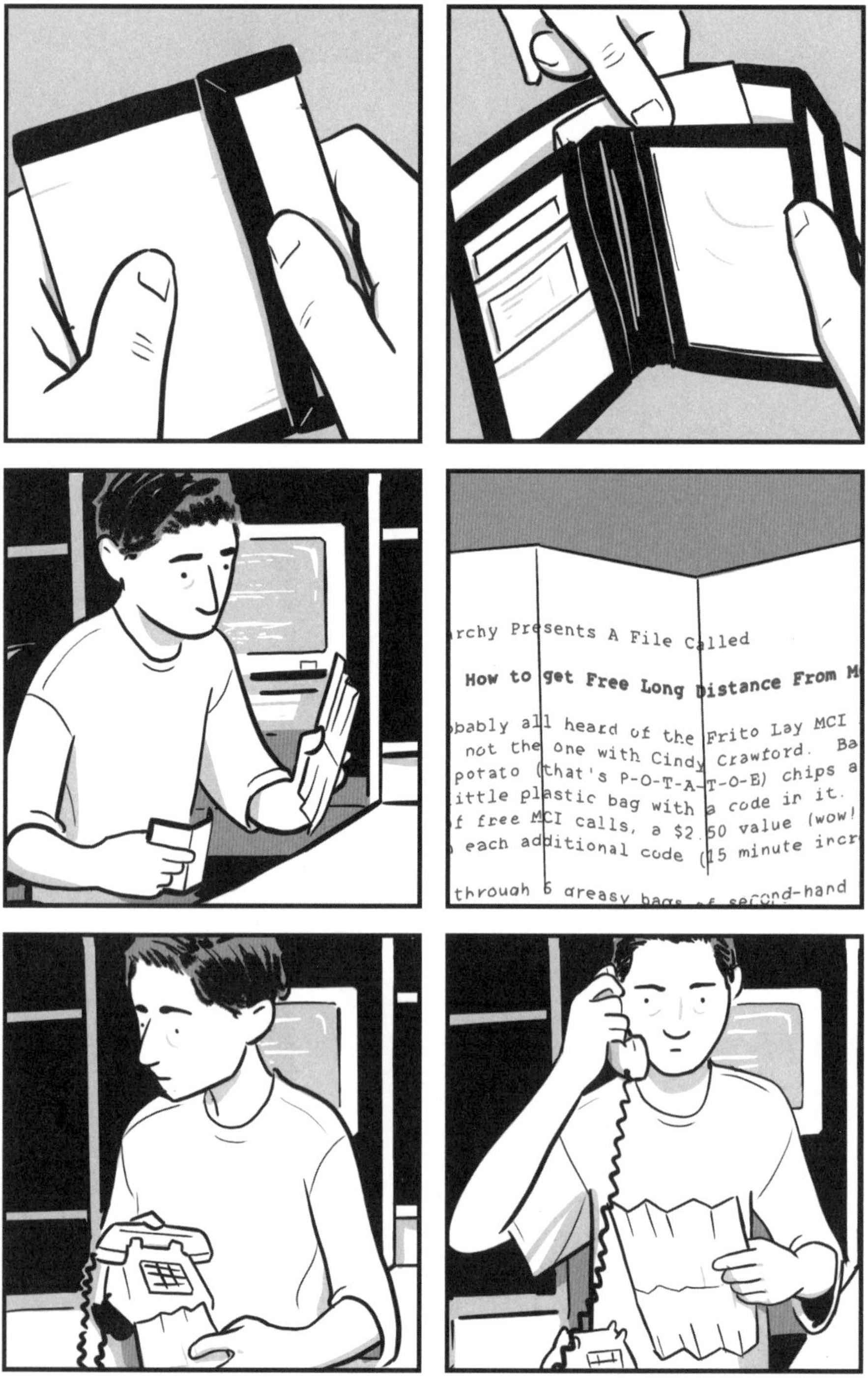
rchy Presents A File Called
How to get Free Long Distance From M
bably all heard of the Frito Lay MCI
not the one with Cindy Crawford. Ba
potato (that's P-O-T-A-T-O-E) chips a
ittle plastic bag with a code in it.
f free MCI calls, a $2.50 value (wow!
each additional code (15 minute incr
through 6 greasy

239

241

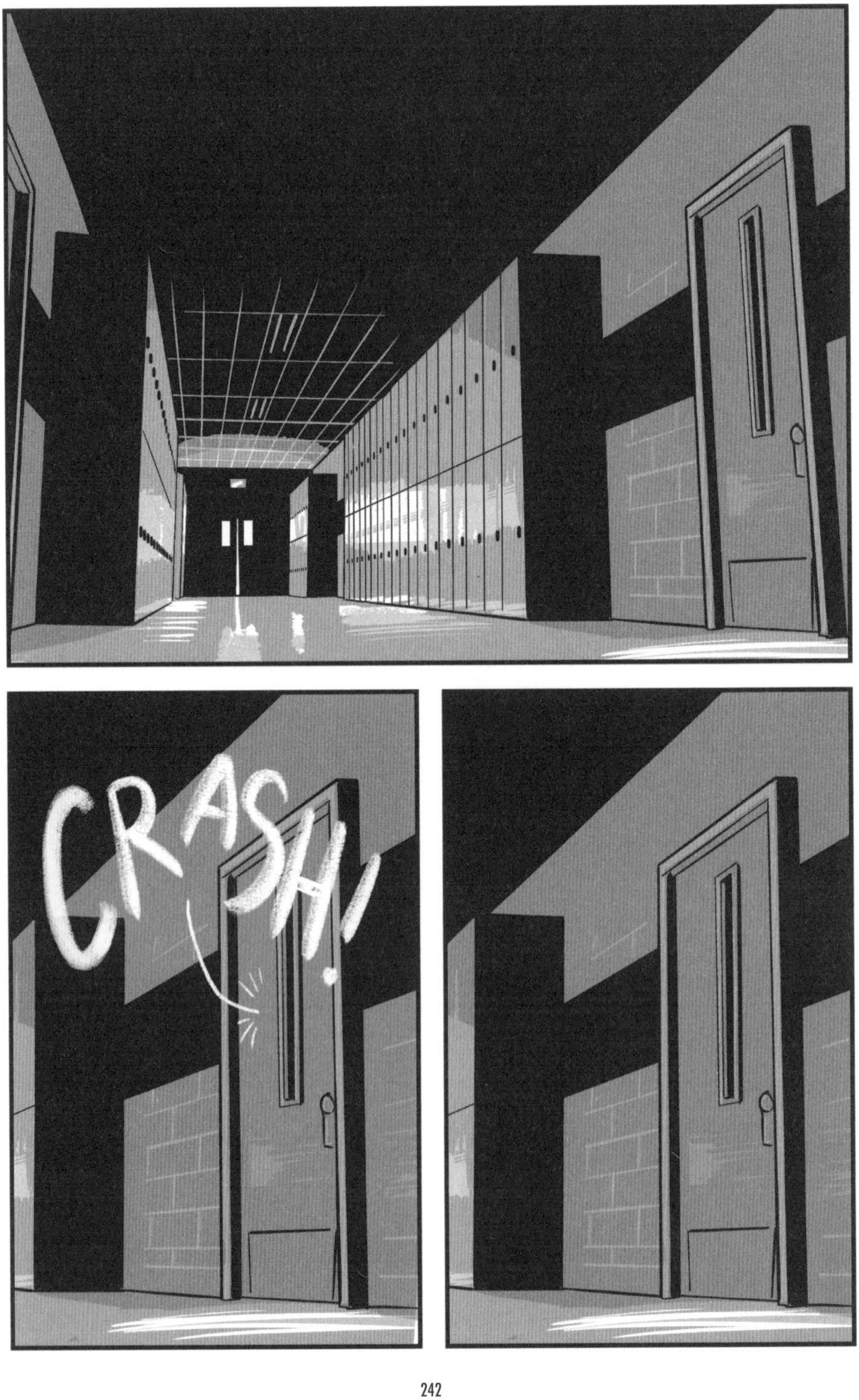
CRASH!

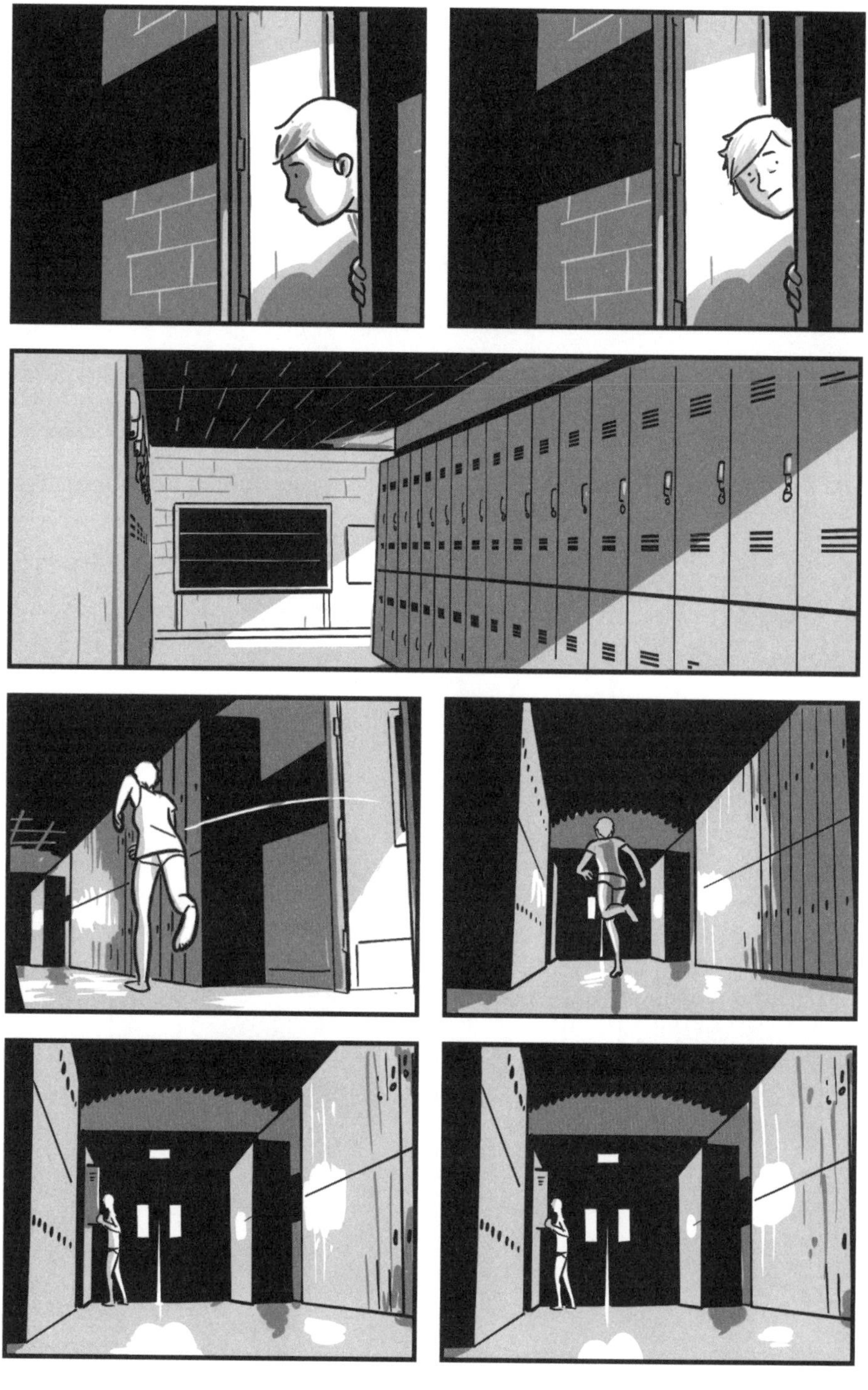

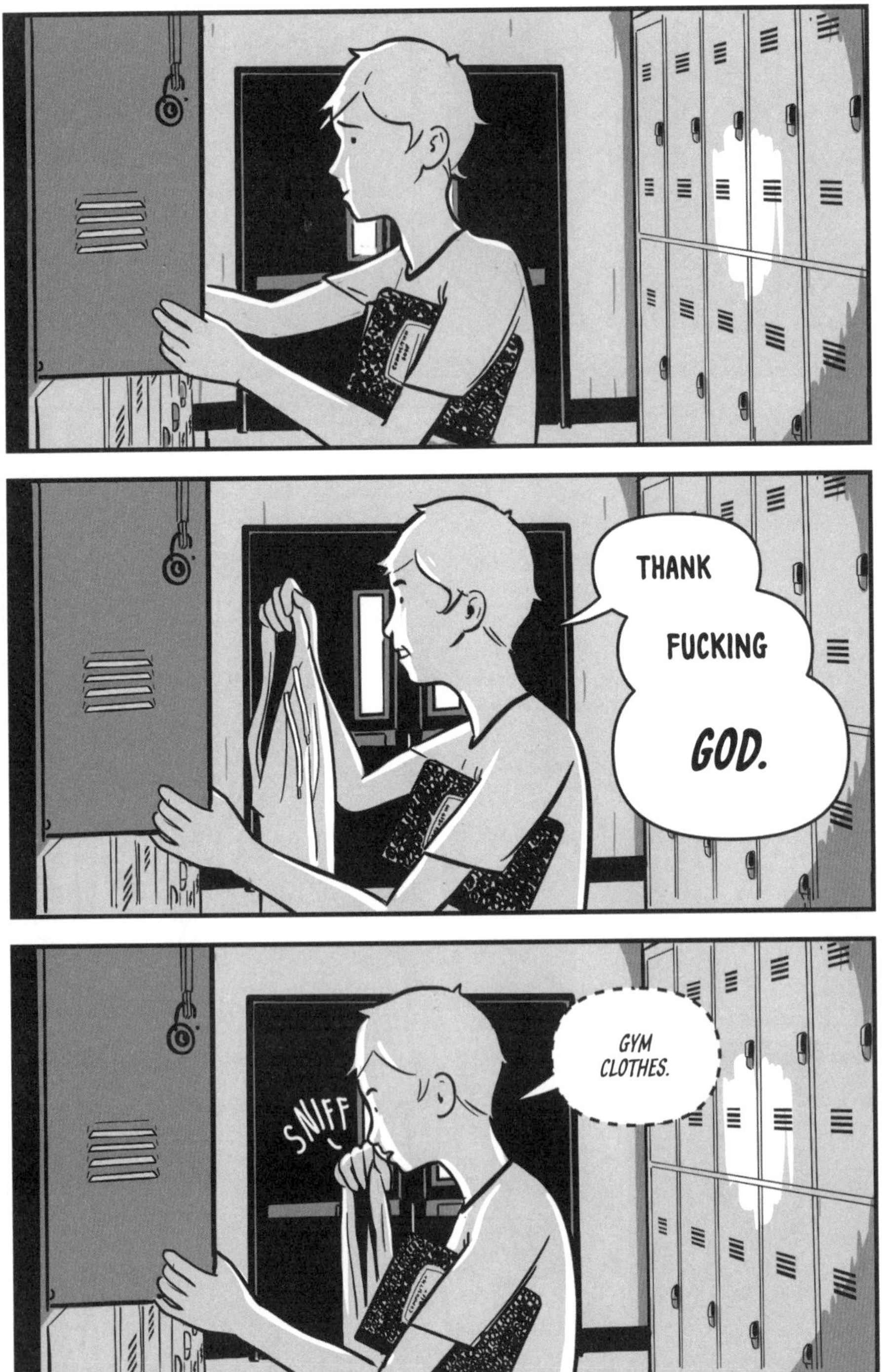
THANK FUCKING GOD.
SNIFF
GYM CLOTHES.

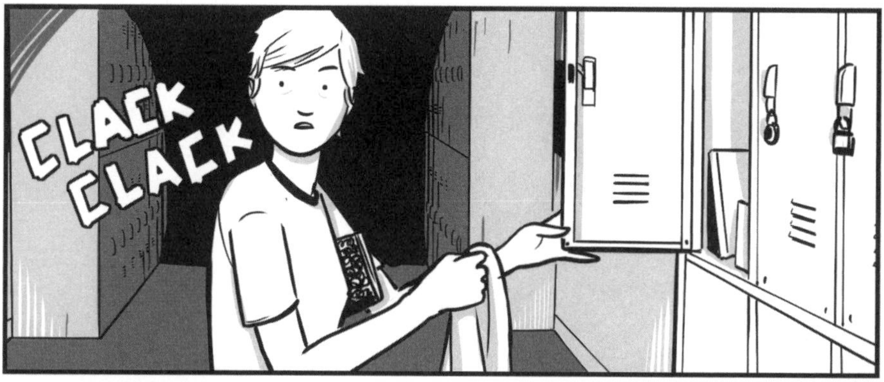
CLACK
CLACK

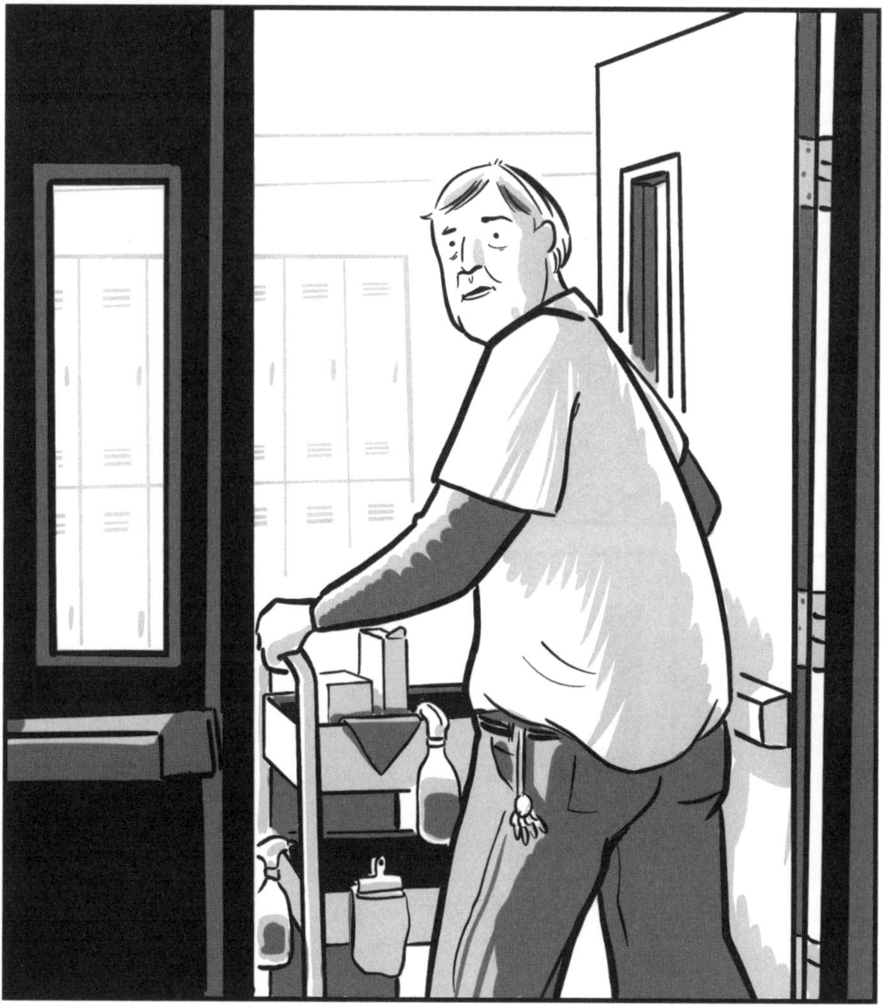

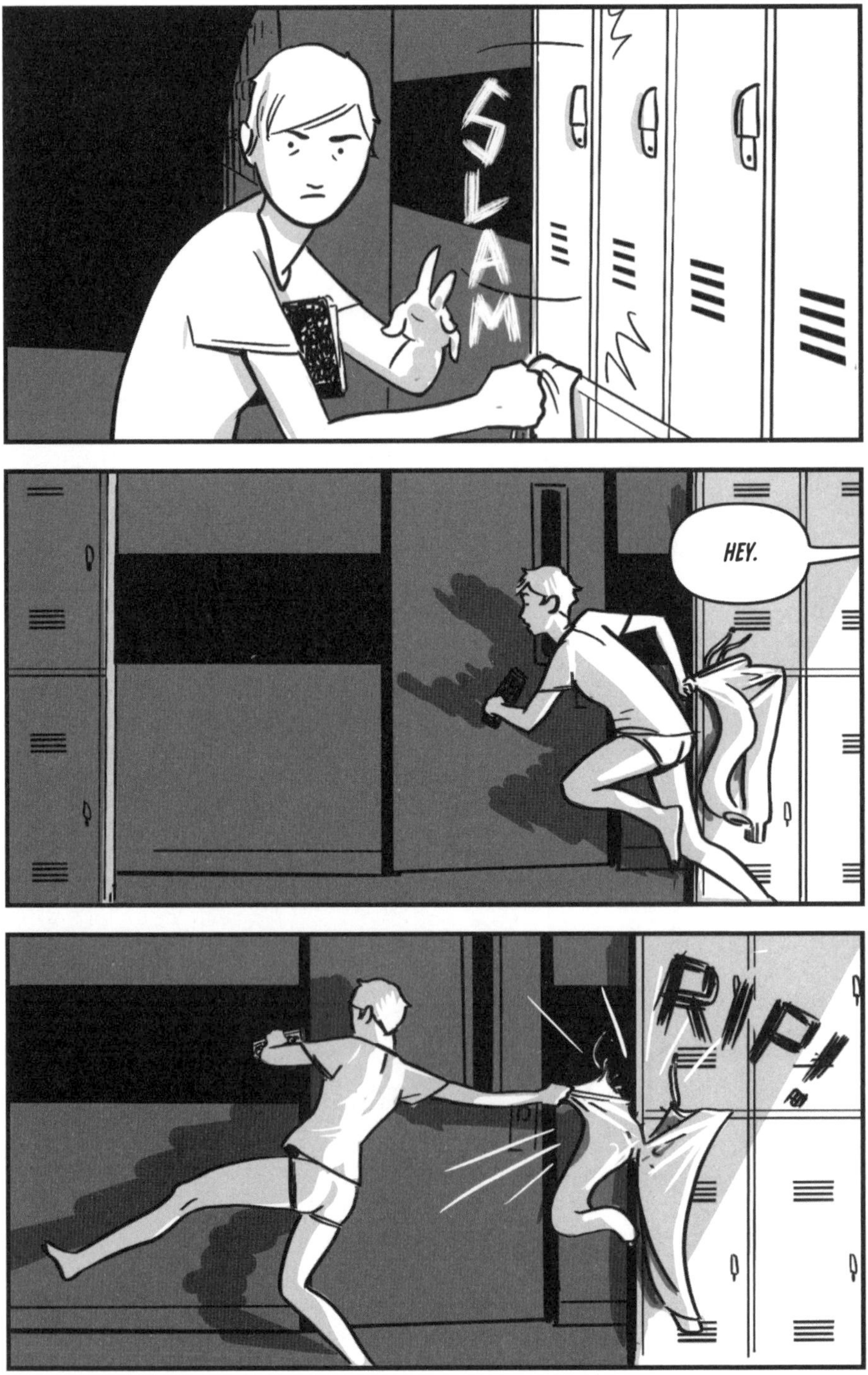
SLAM
HEY.
RIP!

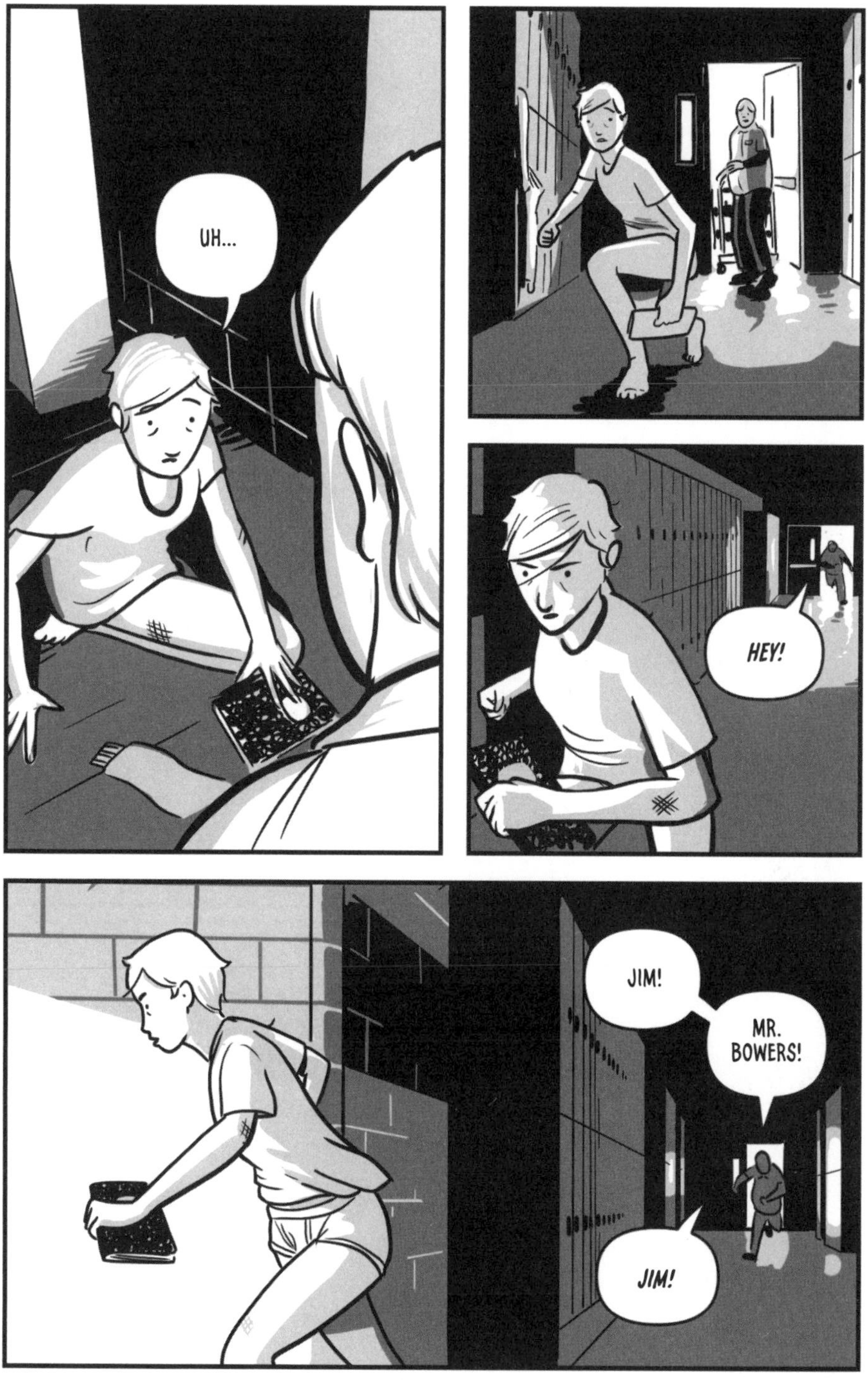
UH...
HEY!
JIM!
MR. BOWERS!
JIM!

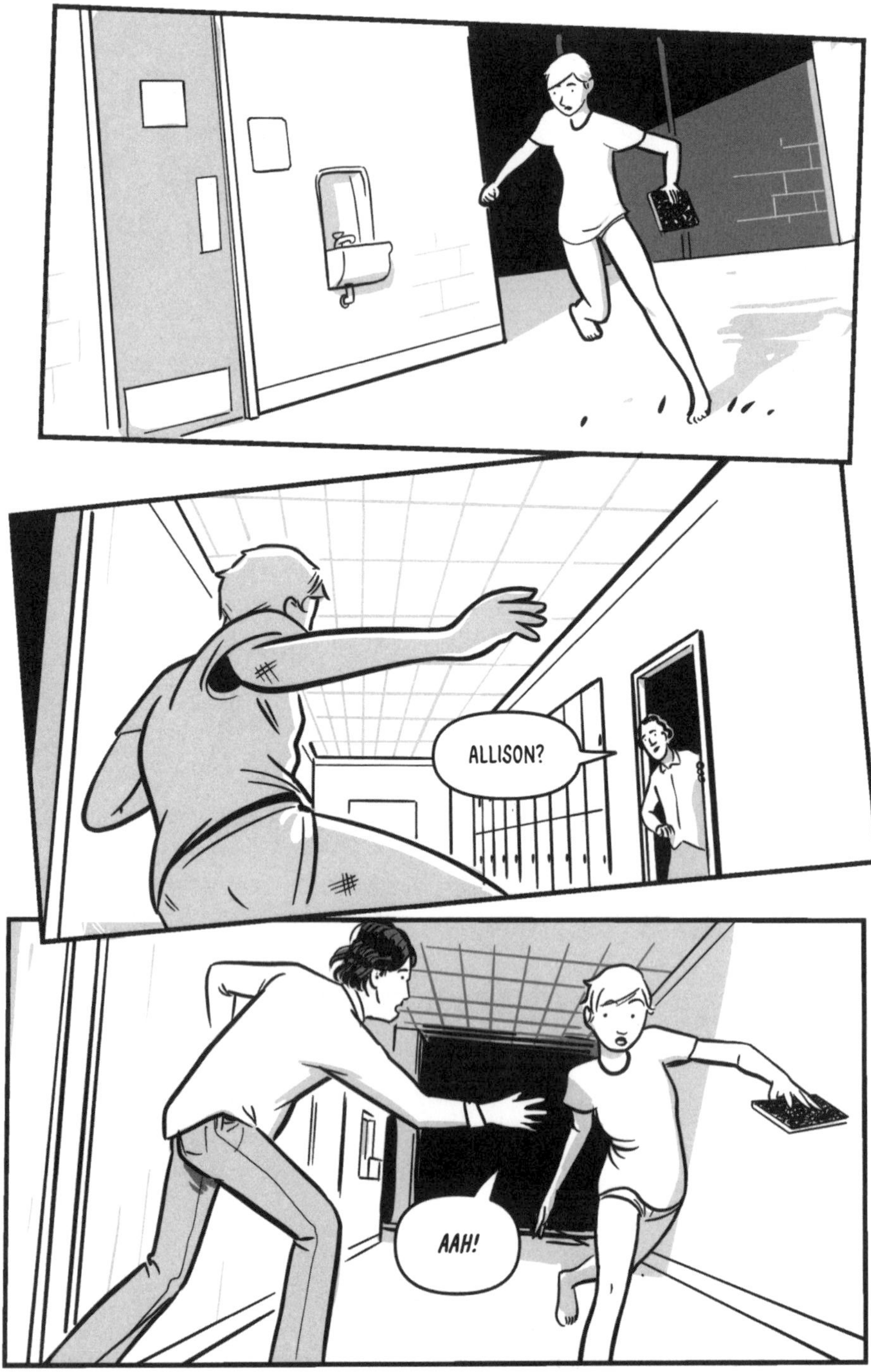
ALLISON?
AAH!

249

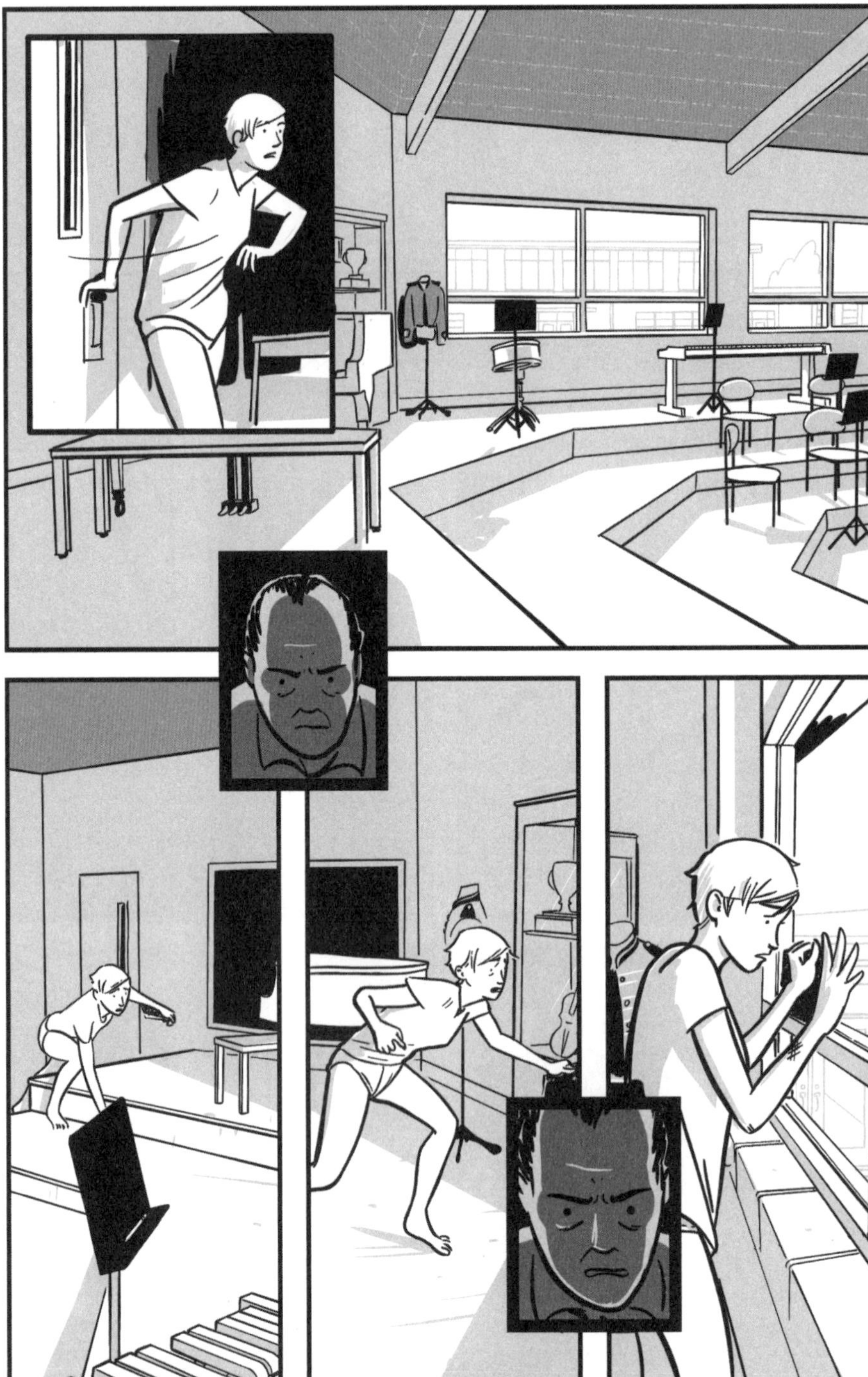

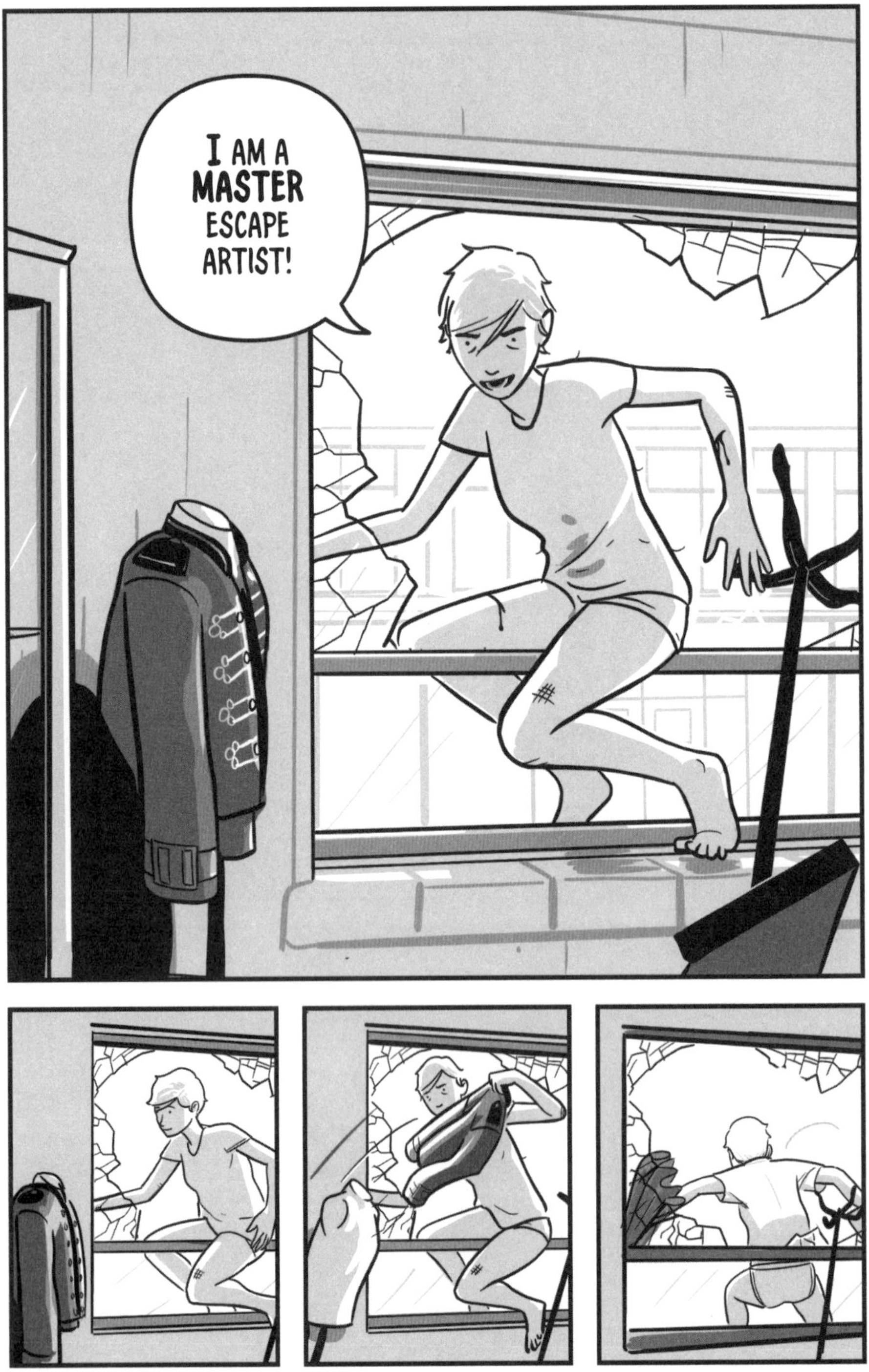
I AM A MASTER ESCAPE ARTIST!

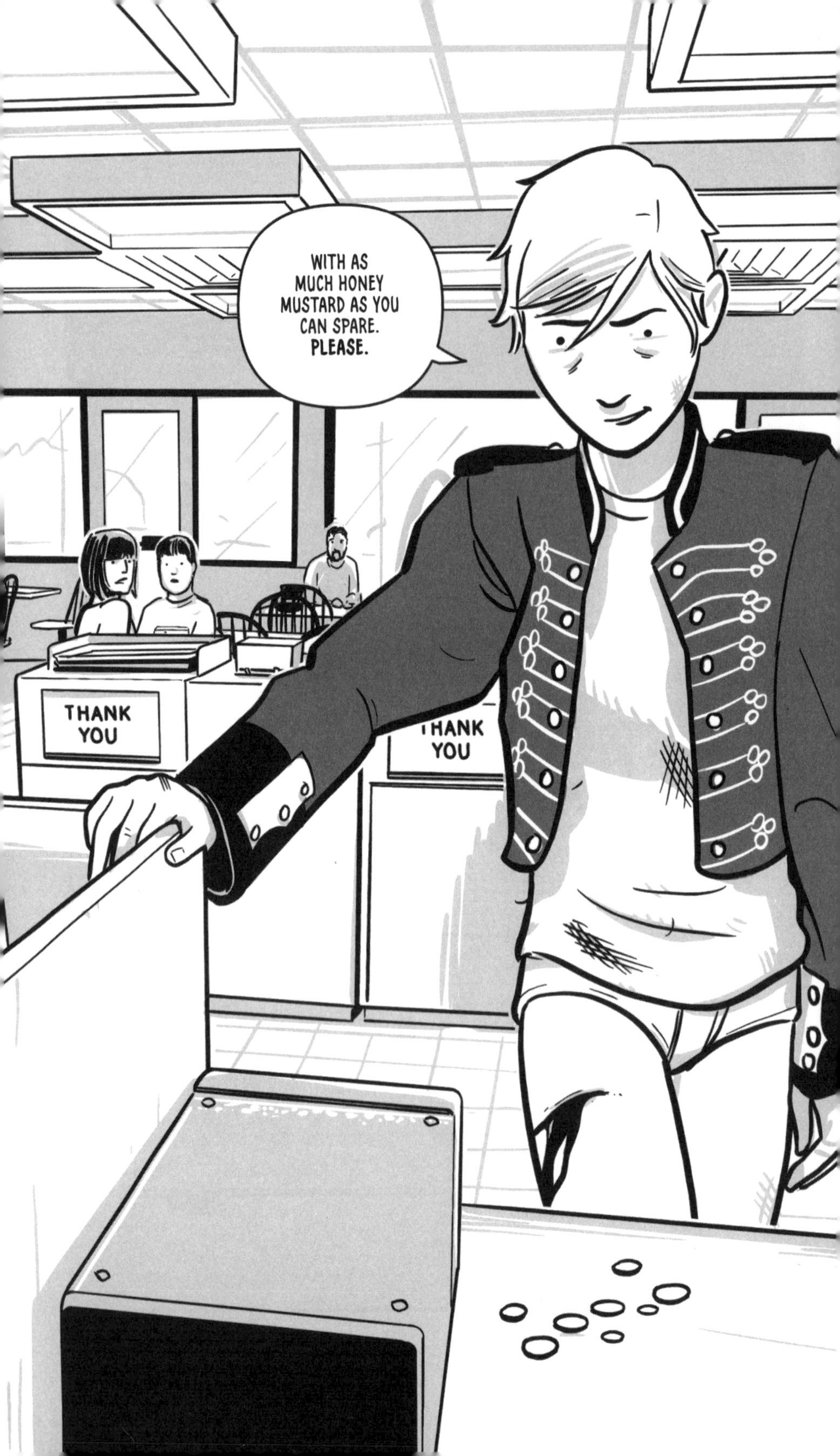
WITH AS MUCH HONEY MUSTARD AS YOU CAN SPARE. **PLEASE.**
THANK YOU
THANK YOU

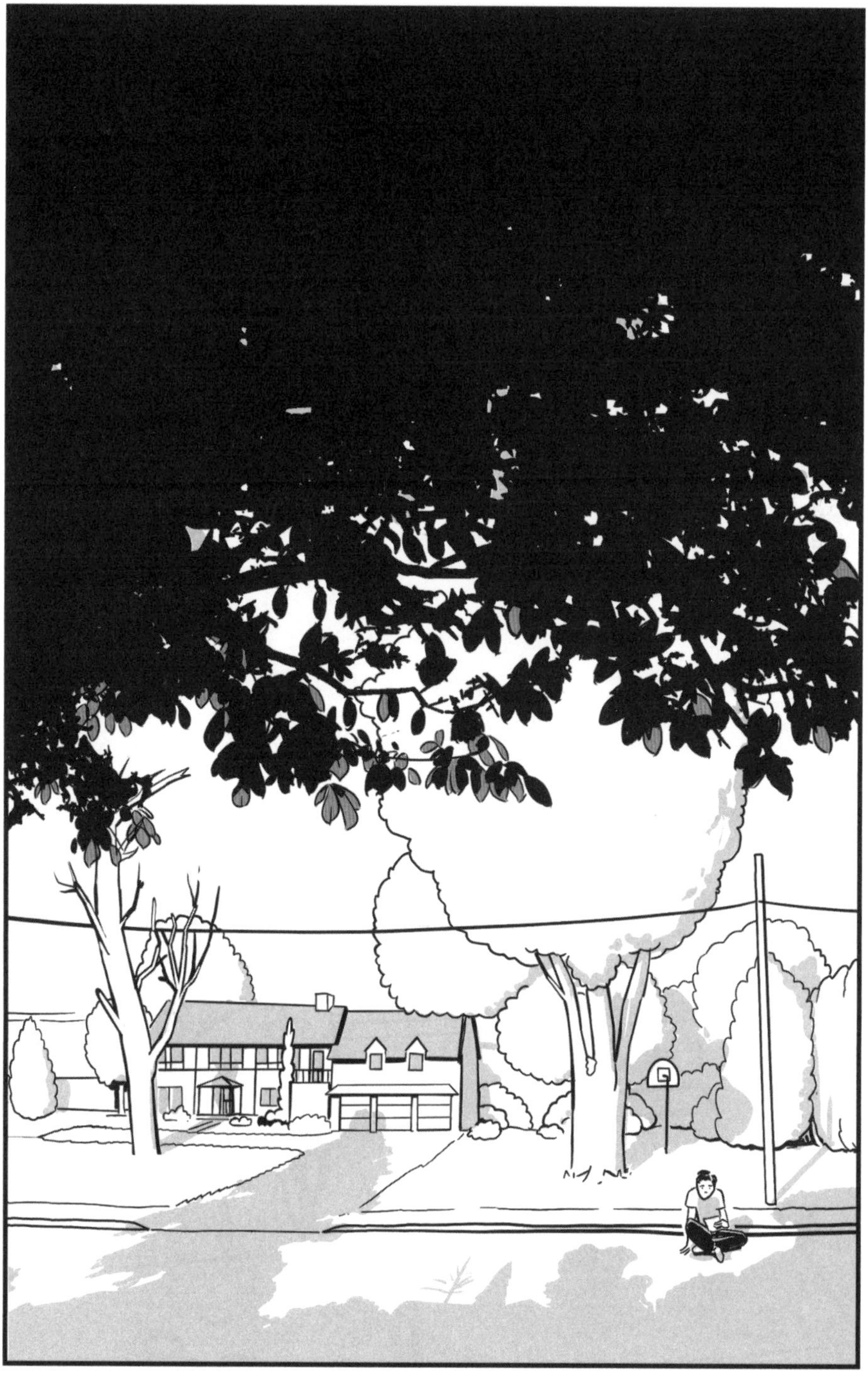

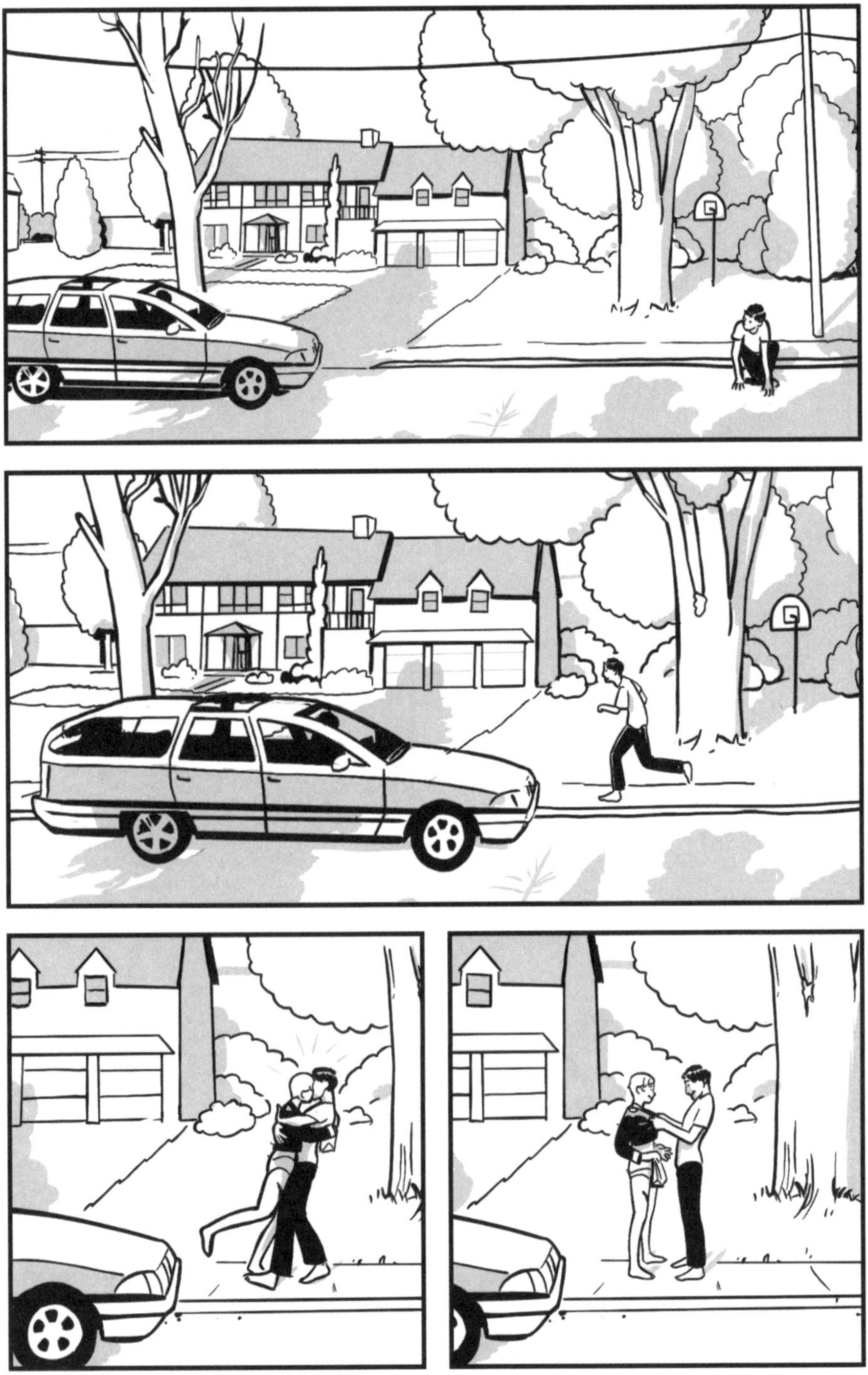

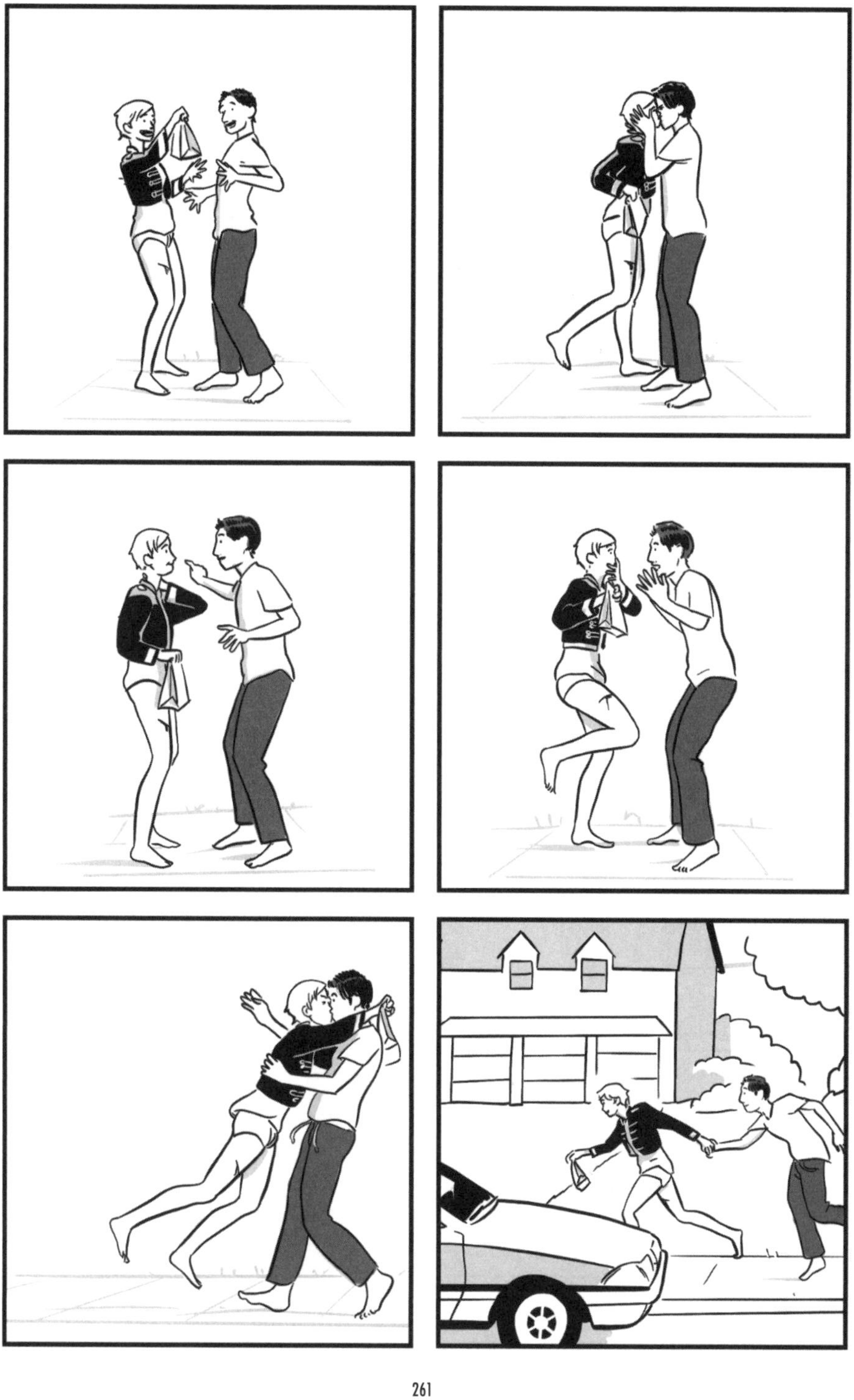

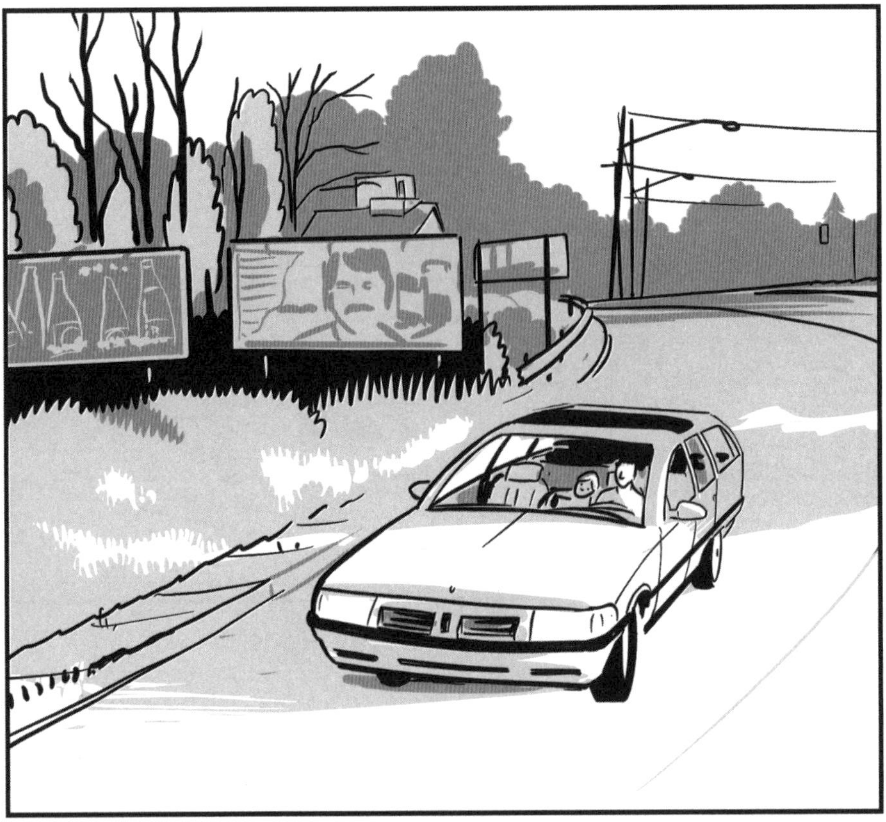

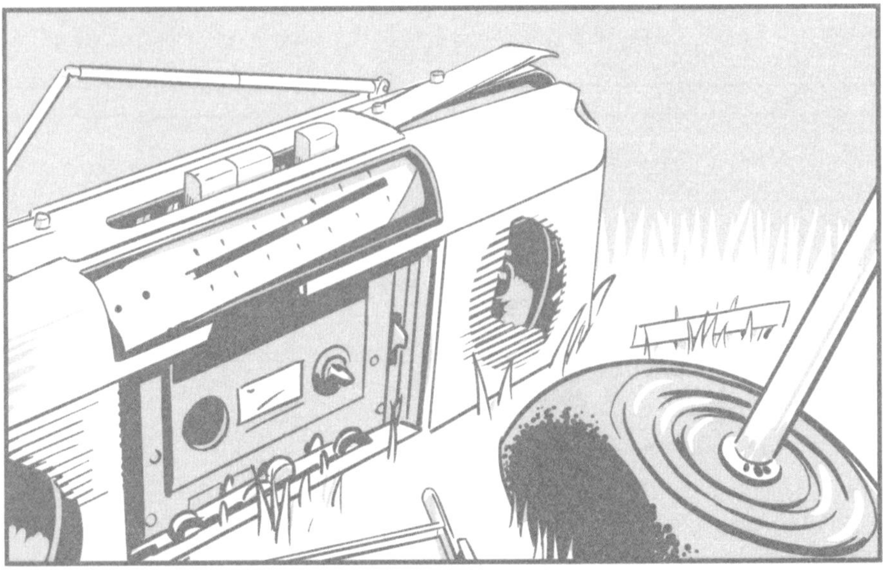

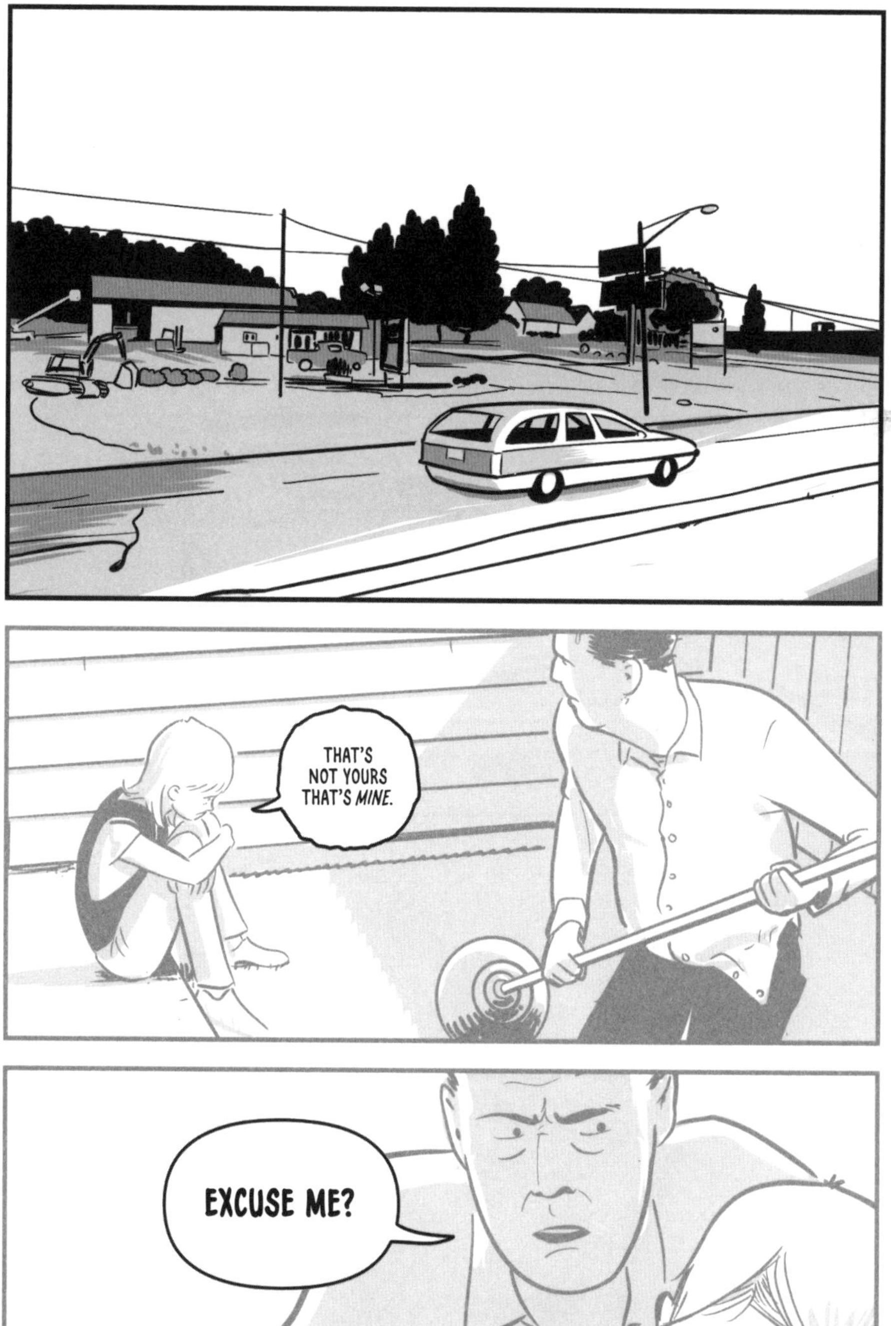
THAT'S NOT YOURS THAT'S *MINE*.
EXCUSE ME?

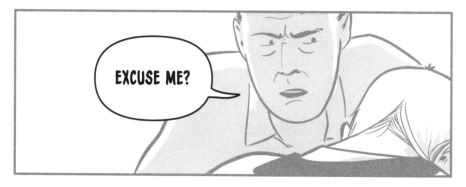

266

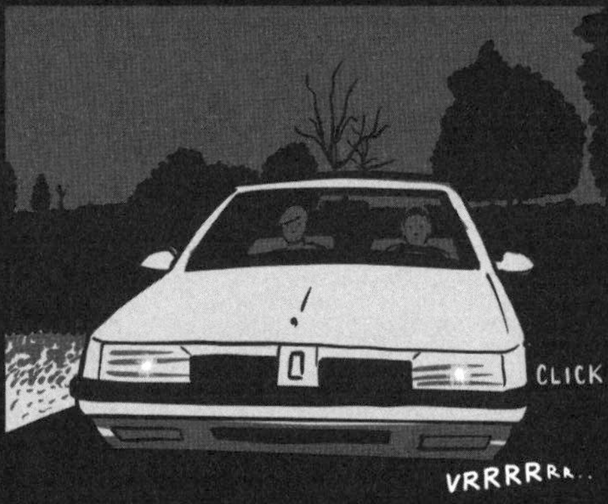
CLICK
VRRRRrr..

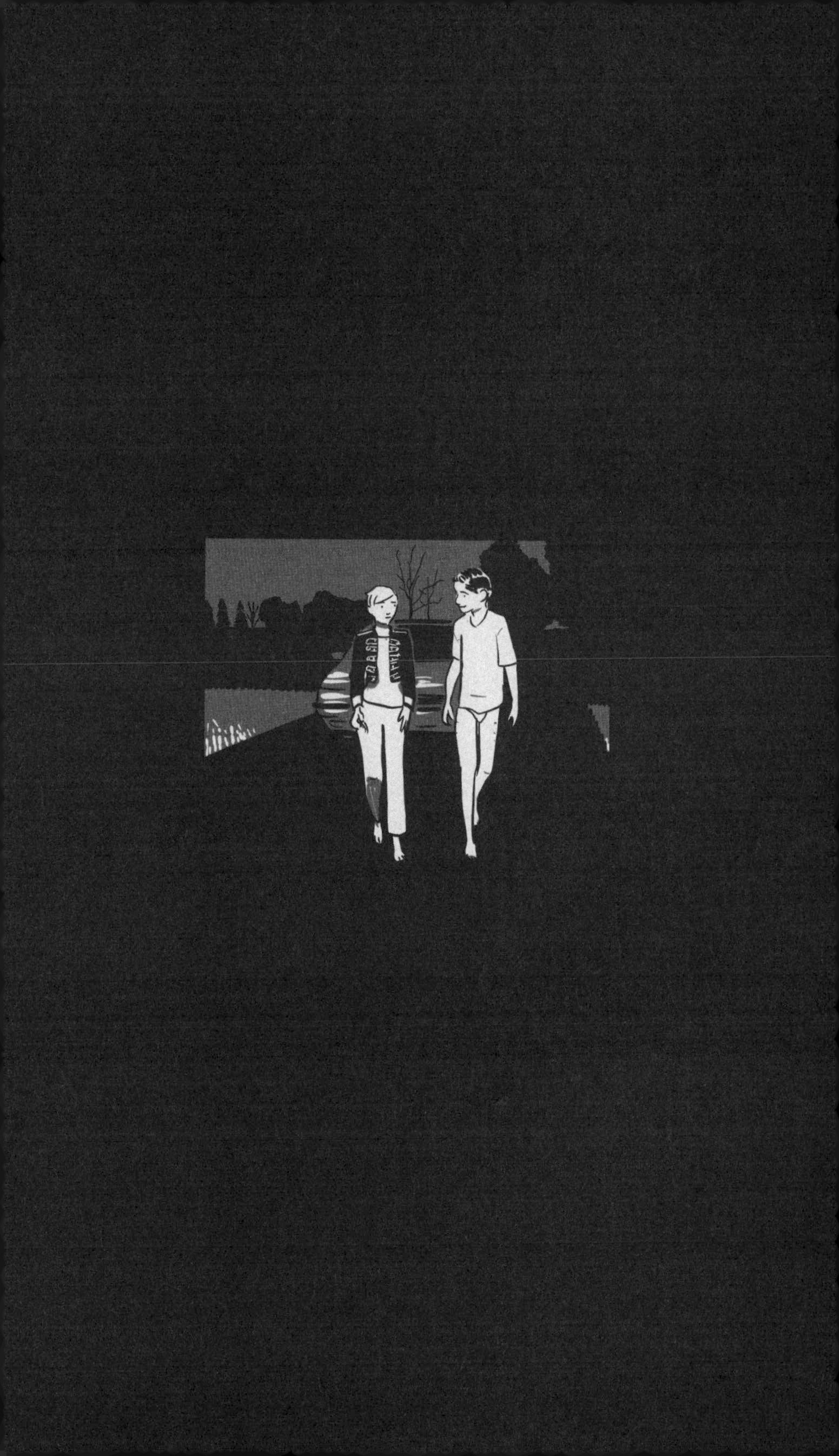

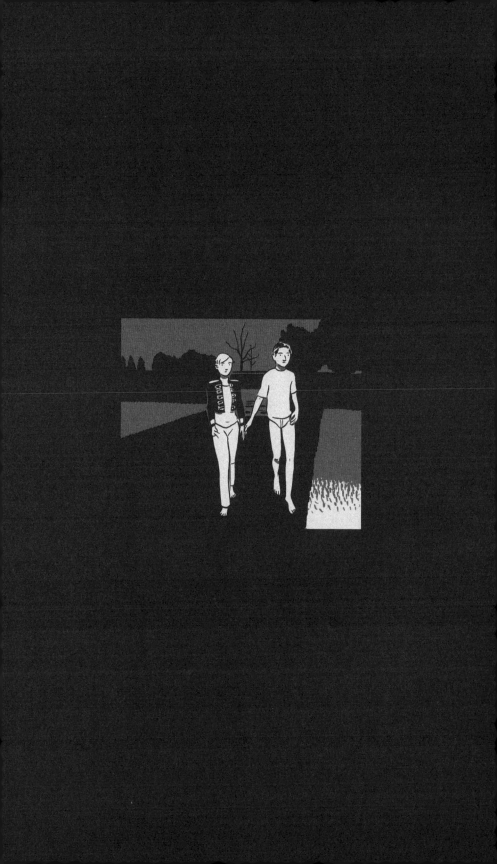

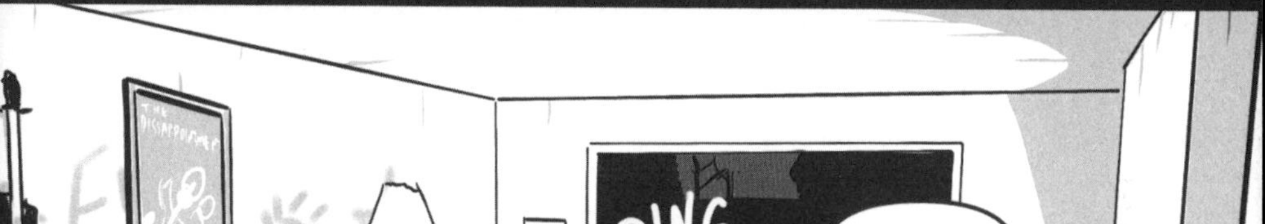
DING DONG!
I GOT IT!

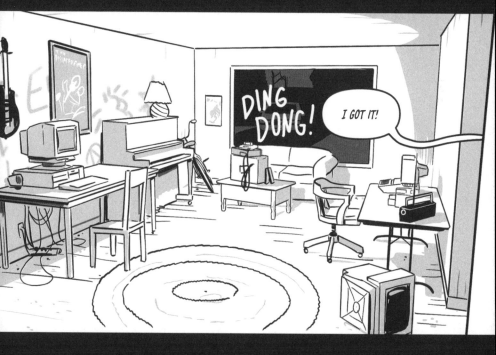

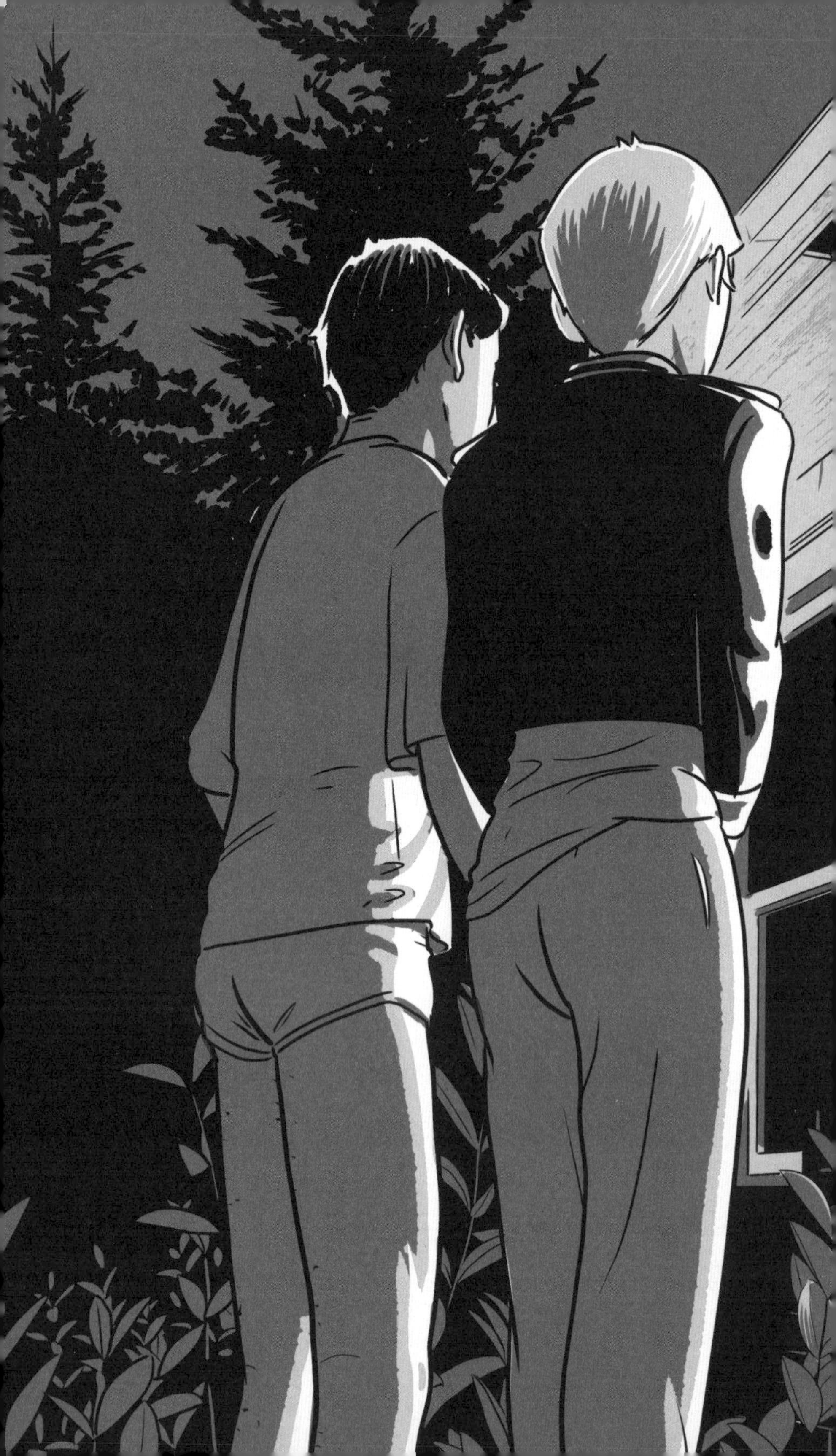

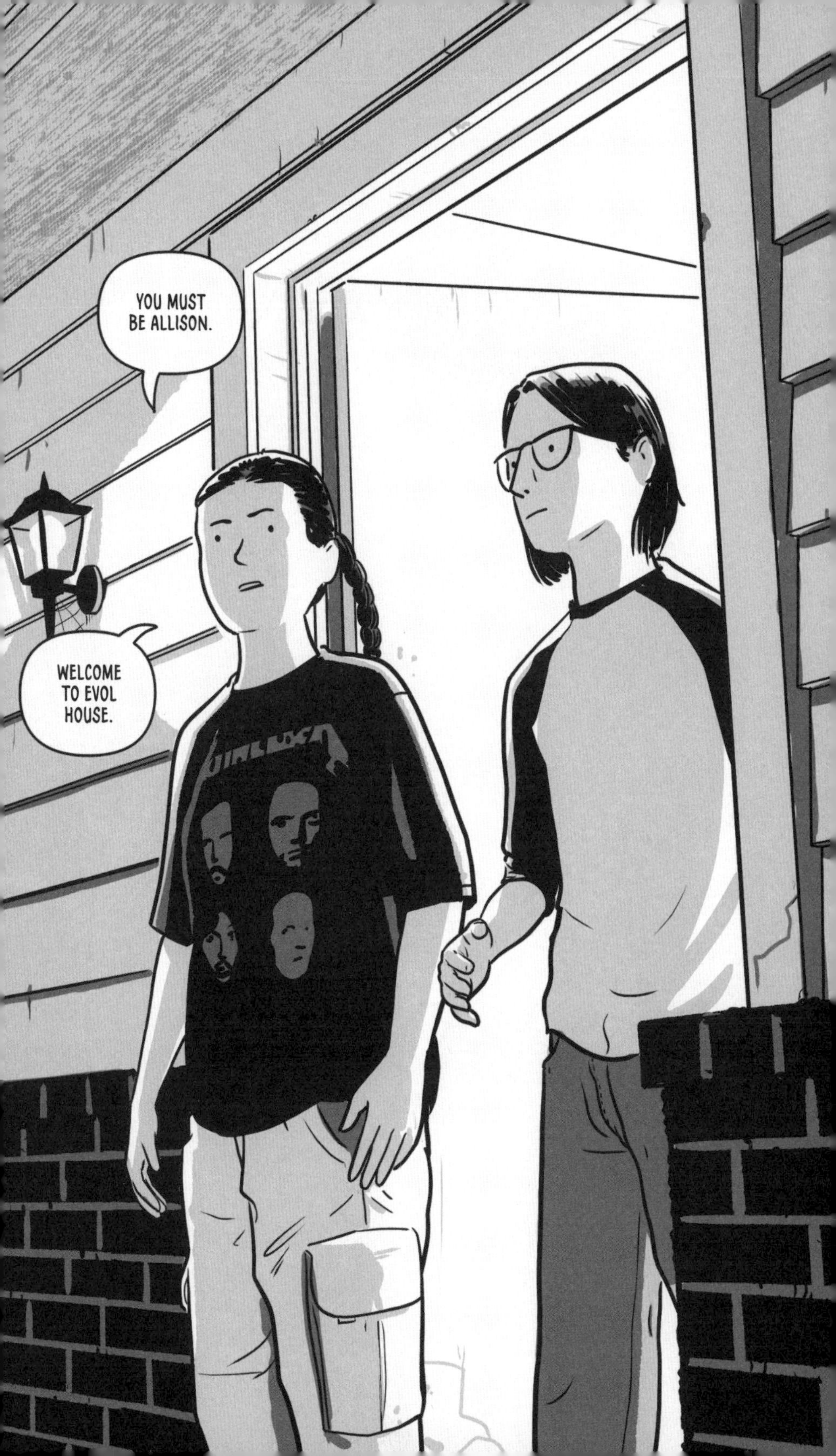
YOU MUST BE ALLISON.
WELCOME TO EVOL HOUSE.

THANK YOU

Andrew Arnold
Andy Baio
Andy McMillan
Angela Piller
Anis Mojgani
Barb Fitzsimmons
Barry Deutsch
Brooke Shelly
Bryan Williams
Carson Mischel
Charlie Douma
Charlie Olsen
Cheri Kessner
Chris A'Lurede
Chris Higgins
Cory Doctorow
Dan Wineman
David Gordon Green
David Pedroni
Debbie Deuble Hill
Dylan Meconis
Eberhardt Press
Fergus
Fozzy
Helioscope Studio
J. Holden
Jack Lee
Jason Scott
Jello Biafra
Joe Besch
Josh Millard
Julian Lawitschka
Katie Lane
Kelly Thompson
Kevin Simmons

Kirby Ferguson
Lucy Bellwood
Martha Maynard
Michael Kurt
Nora Ryan
Pat Castaldo
Pete Kyrou
Rich Thomas
Rose Pleuler
Sarah Mirk
Ted Dahmke
The Enthusiasm Collective
The Independent Publishing
    Resource Center
Wesley Mueller
Will Nevin
XOXO Outpost
Yori Kvitchko

System:~ id$ who -HTu
USER   S   COMMENT
Andrew Arnold   -   Editorial Director
Barb Fitzsimmons   -   Creative Director
Martha Maynard   -   Design Assistant
Rose Pleuler   -   Associate Editor
Rich Thomas   -   Publishing Director

HarperAlley is an imprint of HarperCollins Publishers.

www.harperalley.com
www.incredibledoom.com
www.matthewbogart.net
www.jesseholden.com

System:~ id$ stat -cf ~/incredible_doom.*

ISBN 978-0-06-306494-2 (trade bdg.)
ISBN 978-0-06-306493-5 (pbk.)

Typography by Matthew Bogart
21 22 23 24 25 EP   10 9 8 7 6 5 4 3 2 1
❖
First Edition

System:~ id$ more ~/.plan
Incredible Doom vol 2 coming 2022
.plan (END)